Kinahan Cornwallis

The Conquest of Mexico and Peru

prefaced by The discovery of the Pacific - an historical narrative poem

Kinahan Cornwallis

The Conquest of Mexico and Peru
prefaced by The discovery of the Pacific - an historical narrative poem

ISBN/EAN: 9783337383190

Printed in Europe, USA, Canada, Australia, Japan

Cover: Foto ©Andreas Hilbeck / pixelio.de

More available books at **www.hansebooks.com**

THE CONQUEST OF

MEXICO AND PERU

PREFACED BY

THE DISCOVERY OF THE PACIFIC:

An Historical Narrative Poem

KINAHAN CORNWALLIS,

AUTHOR OF "THE SONG OF AMERICA AND COLUMBUS; OR, THE STORY OF
THE NEW WORLD," &c.

NEW YORK:
PUBLISHED AT THE OFFICE OF THE DAILY INVESTIGATOR,'
52 BROADWAY.
1893.

THE CONQUEST OF MEXICO AND PERU:

(*Prefaced by The Discovery of the Pacific.*)

AN HISTORICAL NARRATIVE IN VERSE.

PREFACE.

While each of the following stories in verse of the Discovery of the Pacific and the Conquest of Mexico and Peru, is separate, and complete in itself as far as it goes, it is really a continuation of the history of America during the period of discovery and exploration, from the time embraced in my previous poem, —"The Song of America and Columbus, or the Story of the New World,"—to the discovery of the Mississippi, to say nothing of the bird's-eye view of the United States of America.

That first volume of the history of America seemed much too colossal for this busy age, but the present one is—like Pelion on Ossa—more colossal still, inasmuch as—to come down from poetical to arithmetical figures—it contains 165 pages more of verse and about 5940 additional lines. This, if not staggering, is anything but a recommendation to a man in a hurry, and every one is more or less in a hurry nowadays. Yet "what is writ is writ," and—unlike the man bent on talking us to death—it is always easy to shut up a book.

I have nothing to recall, and I can conscientiously claim for the volume the same historical accuracy, in every respect, that marks its predecessor, and while the strict observance of this *sine qua non* hampered my muse in the composition of the work, it obviously enhances its value as an historical study. Excepting Irving and Prescott, probably no prose historian of the age of discovery and exploration in the New World ever studied and collated more authorities, original and modern, on the subject, or tried harder, or with a more unbiased mind, to discover and tell the true story of the career and voyages of Columbus and his followers, as well as that of the discovery of the Pacific and the conquest of Mexico and Peru, than I have done. For these extensive and laborious researches I have little to show, except to close students of the period, but I feel amply repaid by the consciousness that there is not an error of fact, in verse or foot-note, in the whole of the two volumes. This, of course, is a poor claim for a writer of verse to make, for historical accuracy is entirely secondary to its poetical merit, but had I written in prose instead of verse, it would doubtless be appreciated as a cardinal virtue, or, at least, for all it is worth.

I may also lay the flattering unction to my soul that probably no other man has worked so hard or so long in studying historical material relating to the progress of discovery and colonization in the

New World without hope of fee or reward, as I have done in the composition of this history in verse of the European conquests in America. But it has been a source of intellectual pleasure to me from first to last, and I do not regret one moment of the time spent in the task, while I am as indifferent and unexpectant as to its pecuniary results as if we lived in a paradise where money and property were things unknown. Epic poems are, I know, very unfashionable. The popular taste is for fragments and *fricassees*, but the mere example of non-conformity is often salutary in its effects. At any rate, I have written *con amore*, and am not in the least afraid of being out of the fashion; while, as to money, I would hardly take the trouble to cross the street to make a million of dollars if I had enough without it, for, " Enough is as good as a feast," and, by a merciful dispensation of Providence, we cannot take our ducats away with us to that bourne whence no traveller returns.

But I advocate thrift none the less, for no man appreciates the importance of having enough more than I do, and literature—especially verse and all that is embraced in the higher literature—is still, as it was in Dr. Johnson's time, a very poor crutch, although it may be a good walking cane. Hence I make my daily bread in a bakery not devoted to poesy, and far removed from Parnassus.

Yet, busy as I have been in Wall Street every day, I have always found enjoyment in turning my thoughts and labor, during leisure hours, in other directions, and, in this case, I have been impelled by my enthusiastic devotion to the study of the early history of the New World. For only one thing have I to ask the reader's forgiveness, and that is for telling so long a story, although so alluring and picturesque is the theme, that, for my own part, I should never tire of it if it went on like Tennyson's brook—forever.

As it is, the pictures, or panoramas, I have here painted in words of the Discovery of the Pacific, the Conquest of Mexico and the Conquest of Peru, commemorate the grandest events in the history of America after its Discovery, and these stand out like great landmarks in the history of the World— the stepping-stones to an expanding civilization, while the Discovery of America by Columbus was— in the light of its mighty train of splendid consequences—the greatest and the most momentous event in the World's history since the birth of the Redeemer of mankind.

KINAHAN CORNWALLIS.

BOOK THE FIRST.—PRELUDE.

THE DISCOVERY OF THE PACIFIC
AND THE PROGRESS OF DISCOVERY IN THE NEW
WORLD
AFTER THE FIRST VOYAGE OF COLUMBUS,
EMBRACING A COMPLETE CHRONICLE OF VOYAGES
AND EVENTS PRIOR TO THE CONQUEST
OF MEXICO.

BOOK THE FIRST.

THE DISCOVERY OF THE PACIFIC.

PART I.

COLUMBUS AND HIS FOLLOWERS.

WHEN first Columbus found this Western World,
And at San Salvador his canvas furled—
While gladly bidding that fair island hail,—
He drew aside, magician-like, the veil
That erst had hid the Old World from the New,
And one he made for evermore the two.
Four hundred years since then have passed away,
And mark the splendid New World of to-day!
What grander prize could mortal man have won?
What greater deed could mortal man have done?
Columbia in her grandeur tells the tale,
And from her throne now bids Columbus hail—
The deathless hero of the hemisphere—
The Western Sea's immortal pioneer.
Queen of the Western World he lives in thee,
Thou Sovereign of a nation vast and free!

Columbus sailed through darkness into light,
Yet lived and died in nigh Cimmerian night,
For though he gave the New World to the Old,
He never heard its wondrous story told.
To him 't was Asia—not a country new—
That burst, where'er he voyaged, on his view.
He sought a western passage to Cathay,
But found a prize far grander on his way—
The richest prize that e'er the sea revealed.
'T was strange the truth to eyes like his was sealed.
But none the less the boon to man has been—
Save the doomed Indian—and the world has seen
No grander growth than this our New World
    shows.
How great the debt the world Columbus owes!
He paved the way to empire in the West,
And now behold him by the world caressed!
America illuminates his name.
Columbia consecrates anew his fame,
And glorifies the hero of the Sea,
Who sowed the seed of harvests yet to be.
Quadro-Centennial songs to him be sung,
And joyous peals of belfry bells be rung,
For ne'er again will deed like his be done—
The deed by which immortal fame was won ;
For now no continent remains unknown
To add fresh wealth and glory to a throne.
What inspiration led him thus to steer
And open to the world a hemisphere?
What happy chance, combined with skilled design,
As if the guide had been a hand divine?

Columbus greater, grander, nobler seems
As Time upon his mem'ry brightly beams,
And more and more, colossal and unique,
He through the ages seems to us to speak.

His figure through the deep perspective looms,
And Fame his name with glowing light illumes.
Intrepid searcher of the Western Sea
He—in his glory—lives eternally,
And all the nations glorify his deed
And harvests gather where he planted seed.
Momentous deed !   The birth of Christ alone
Surpasses that which made this New World known.

II.

America ! the Western World's domain,
Which, magnet-like, allures across the main,
Give fire, and inspiration, to my strain.
Let me recall the enterprise of yore,
Which led exploring vessels to thy shore,
Since first Columbus found San Salvador,
And each event, in order, bring to view—
The Old World's ancient commerce with the New.
The annals of this New World let me tell,
And on the deeds of brave explorers dwell.
The story of Columbus I have told,
But mark the train of navigators bold,
Who followed in the great explorer's wake
And saw the dawn, through night, barbaric, break.
First came the dauntless Cabots—sire, and son—
Who glory as the fruit of daring won,
And ere Columbus—lo !—" Eureka ! "—cried,
As they the sleeping Continent espied—*

---

* Although the Western Hemisphere was discovered by
Columbus in 1492, it was not until his third voyage—in
August, 1498—that he first sighted the Continent of America,
where it is intersected by the numerous branches of the Orinoco, fourteen months previous to which, namely in June, 1497,
it had been discovered—in the latitude, it is supposed, of about

The rich reward of noble enterprise,
Which kindled gladness in their searching eyes.
From Albion's cliffs, across the stormy main,
They sailed, intent on honor more than gain,
And ran along the bluff New England shore,
And south to where Floridian breakers roar,
When Famine o'er their course its shadow threw,
And mutineers arose among the crew.
Then homeward bound, they left the coast behind—
The Western mainland they were first to find.
These—after great Columbus—foremost stood
In bold adventure o'er Atlantic's flood,
And gave the British banner to the breeze
Where ne'er before 't was seen upon the seas,
And so, by brave example, led the way
For Britain's commerce at a later day,
And those intrepid toilers it has bred—
A race of sailors to the waters wed.
Then, German, and Italian, ships were made
The vehicles of England's scanty trade,
And maritime adventure scarce was known
Where proud Britannia sat her island throne.
Thus with this mighty Continent in view,
The pilgrims from her sea-beat shores were few,

---

fifty-six degrees, far to the north of the straits of Belle Isle—
by John Cabot and his son Sebastian, who had sailed with
two vessels in the previous month from Bristol, England,
under the auspices of Henry VII., but at their own expense,
on a voyage of exploration ; and following this discovery they
coasted the mainland as far as the southern end of Florida,
when a mutiny breaking out among the crew they returned to
England. John Cabot was a Venetian merchant who had
long resided in Bristol, and Sebastian was born there. In the
following year Sebastian Cabot made a second voyage to the
American Continent, his main object, as in the previous instance, being the discovery of a northwest passage to India.

And eighty years or more, from Cabot's day
Had o'er the New World slowly passed away
Ere Britain's flag o'er Britons waved on high
Beneath the dome of its expansive sky,*
While with each other, other nations vied,
The spoils of savage conquest to divide :
But ah! what woes they carried in their train—
France, Portugal, and sanguinary Spain,
Whose paths with blood where'er they went were
   dyed.
Oft o'er the tragic story I have sighed.
There, erst, the Red Man lived in wild delight,—
His Past, and Future, like his Present, bright,—
Ne'er dreaming of Invasion's cruel blight.

Behold, how Cortez ravaged Mexico,
And laid the Empire, and its ruler low—
Impelled by av'rice, and religious zeal,
And fortified with armor's glitt'ring steel.
See how Pizarro, with his cruel horde,
Laid waste Peru, and put it to the sword,—
Its peaceful people slew in wanton hate,—
And with them one who'd earned a better fate—
Atahualpa, its last Inca, proud,—
Its temples ravaged, and an awful shroud

---

* England put forward a claim to vast regions of North
America some years after their discovery by the Cabots, a
portion of which she ultimately colonized, but more than
eighty years elapsed before she took any very decided step
toward the permanent occupation of any part of America, and
meanwhile the coast was explored by other nations. To the
frugal maxims of Henry VII. and unpropitious events of the
reign of Henry VIII., Edward VI. and the bigoted Mary, this
neglect of the colonization of the country may be attributed.
The first real attempt at its settlement was made by Queen
Elizabeth in 1576, when Frobisher's expedition sailed.

Of deep despair, threw o'er the hapless land,
Accurst by that marauding Spanish band.
Alas! for them, the Children of the Sun,
Their glory o'er—their race forever run.

III.

While still Columbus sailed the Western seas,
And envied Man his indolence, and ease,
Beneath the lustre of a summer sun—
His third eventful voyage just begun—
Spain made the New World—saving Hayti—free
To all her sons, of high and low degree—
A royalty exacting on their gains,
No cost, but only profit, to be Spain's.
'T was then Alonzo de Ojeda cried—
"With Christ, and the Madonna, for my guide,
I'll sail again the New World waters, wide,
And gather in abundance golden ore,
And spread the gospel on each savage shore ;—
I, who with great Columbus served of yore.
But mark me, mine will yet eclipse his fame,
For I'm resolved to win a grander name!"
Four caravels gave Seville to her son,
Who dreamed of triumphs certain to be won,
And with Amerigo Vespucci sailed,
His mind ambitious, and his body mailed.*

---

* Ojeda, who had sailed with Columbus on his second voyage,
aided by Bishop Fonseca, at the head of the Department of
the Indies, obtained the royal license for the expedition, and
also the charts, and journals of Columbus, and left Spain with
four ships equipped by the merchants of Seville, on the 20th
of May, 1499, to make discoveries in the New World. Amerigo Vespucci, a Florentine gentleman, accompanied Ojeda,
and owing to the chart and descriptions of the New World,
that he published on his return, it acquired his name, and by
universal consent this was retained, notwithstanding its ob-
vious injustice to Columbus.

He longed to spread discov'ry in the West,
And gather laurels on the ocean's breast,
And find a realm of beauty in the South.
Ere long he reached the Orinoco's mouth,
And far along the continent explored,
While pearls, and gold, he added to his hoard.
Enchanting prospects met his wond'ring eyes,
Which sparkled oft with pleasure, and surprise.
And native throngs regaled him with their songs,
Unconscious, then, of their impending wrongs:
And there he found a wand'ring English fleet,
And marvelled much the rovers, thus, to meet;
But England's records fail to tell the tale
That from her shores such e'er were known to sail.
Anon he touched at Hayti's island shore,
By stealth to glean where he had gleaned before ;
But he was forced by Roldan thence to flee,
And—homeward bound—again he sailed the sea,
And fanned the flame of enterprise in Spain,
Though scanty, save in glory, was his gain :
But greater glory, far, Vespucius gained,
Though to the sea, and arms, but little trained.
Fame at a bound Americus attained.
He told the New World's story with his pen,
And brought it thus within the common ken,
And drew a chart of all the coasts he'd seen,
And all of those where Spaniards e'er had been,
And left Columbus coldly in the shade,
By selfish ends, and low ambition swayed.
Spain quickly with the New World linked his name,
And all the world has since prolonged his fame—
The fame that by an accident was won,
And everlasting wrong was swiftly done.
By this caprice Columbus lost his due,
The Muse, historic, only, holding true.
But in Columbia—mark !—he lives, anew.

Alonzo Nino, to adventure prone,
And basking in the favor of the Throne,
Was next to leave the Spanish shore behind,
Expecting in the New World wealth to find,
And reap a splendid harvest of renown,
And win both praise, and titles from the Crown.
His comrade, Guerra, joined him in the deed,
And mingled Christian zeal with boundless greed.
Companions of Columbus they had been,
And where they'd wandered once they longed to
    glean.
They chose Ojeda's course—the beaten track—
And bore, in rich abundance, treasure back,
But to the store of knowledge added naught:
Yet with incitement their return was fraught,
For all who saw the wealth the wand'rers brought
Were eager in their track, themselves, to sail—
In calm to glide, or face the whistling gale.
Then Pinzon followed with his caravels.*
"Farewell!" he cried, and wept the Palos belles.
He steered his squadron south, and crossed the
    line,
And felt the sun with tropic fervor shine,
And saw it set with grandeur in the west,
With all the sky in gorgeous colors dressed,
And ocean bathed in their refulgent glow,
While winds to his amazement ceased to blow.
None the Equator e'er had crossed before,
And all on board a look of wonder wore.
He landed with the Amazon in view,
And saw its waters join the ocean blue.

---

* Vincent Yanez Pinzon having built four caravels, sailed
from Palos, in Spain, in December, 1499, and after touching
at the Cape de Verde Islands, steered boldly south and was
the first person known to have crossed the Equator.

He raised the Cross, and solemnized the Mass,
But there the natives he enslaved, alas!
He lured them, by a stratagem, from shore,
And after that, it met their gaze no more:
But Retribution followed at his heels,
And tempests thundered grandly o'er his keels,
While ocean, in commotion, wildly tossed,
And of the four, three caravels were lost.
He well deserved his loss, the wretch so base,
Who thus could traffic in the human race.
From Lisbon sailed ere he returned to Spain—
To add renown to King Emanuel's reign—
Don Pedro Cabral, bound for Hindostan,
And—later on—the realm of Kubla Khan.
With thirteen ships, and castled caravels.*
As these—so History the story tells—
To shun the calms along the Guinea shore
Due westward—an imposing squadron—bore,
Don Pedro sighted unexpected land—
A rugged coast, but picturesque, and grand,
Where bloom, and verdure, beautified the view,
And royal palms, like sentient beings, grew,
And rainbow-tinted birds among them flew,
While monkeys climbed the trees to see the fleet,
And parrots gave the signal to retreat.
Like amethystine drops, and ruby showers,
The paroquets emerged from leafy bowers,
And flashed in constellations through the air.
Don Pedro cried—" The clime is wondrous fair ! "
And, landing, claimed it for the Portuguese;
Then bending in devotion, on his knees,
He placed a cross beneath the spreading trees,

---

* The caravels had "castles," or high cabins, built at the bow and stern.

And murmured—"Country of the Holy Cross!
The Christian's triumph is the Heathen's loss!"
And so 't was called by Cabral and the Throne,
Long ere its modern name—Brazil—was known.
Along the coast the vessels held their way,
And reached, at length, a broad, majestic bay,
Where mighty mountains looked, in splendor, down,
And on the shining waters seemed to frown,
Their rugged sides, colossal, clear, and bold,
Touched by the ardent sun with rays of gold,
While further inland, lofty peaks arose,
Their pointed summits lightly capped with snows;
And near them, yet apart—alone, and grand—
A naked rock o'erlooked the smiling land—
A massive peak, but strangely bleak, and bare—
A sentinel forever stationed there—
And with the mountains round it for a frame—
"The Sugar Loaf," its celebrated name.
That bay was Rio's, then unknown to fame.

IV.

Whoe'er has wandered where, now, Rio lies,
Has gazed on beauty with admiring eyes,
And seen the voiceless Organ Mountains rise,
With peaks aspiring to the flashing skies,
And felt the charm of grandeur o'er him steal,
For there to see the prospect, is to feel.
The city's broad, white wilderness of streets,
The roving and delighted vision meets,
With green hill-sides, and gardens full of bloom,
All redolent of exquisite perfume,
And girdled by a purple mountain-ring,
In whose deep shadows birds of beauty sing,
While high above, Bonito's peak is seen—
A lance-like mountain, with a point as keen—

And Corcovado's stark, and mighty ridge
That spans the sky like some celestial bridge.
Far to the right and left the bay extends,
And, as it glitters, picturesquely bends.
Along its shores the feath'ry palms appear,
And orange-groves are clustered far and near,
While over all the Sugar Loaf presides,
And to the sunlight bares its sweeping sides.
Whoe'er has from the city wandered wide,
And to the mighty, lonely forest hied,
In silent awe its majesty has felt,
And on the scene his mind has, later, dwelt;
For.Nature there is lovely, and profound,
And man seems but a pigmy on the ground
By those colossal trunks that soar so high
They seem to reach the over-hanging sky:
Yet there embraced by parasites they die.
Black tomb-like gorges open to his view—
With mountain torrents leaping wildly through,
And roaring as they rush to reach the sea,
Impatient as a captive to be free—
As through the forest he his way pursues,
'Mid vegetation rich in countless hues.
Vast granite boulders tapestried with fern,
He through the tangled mazes can discern,
And over-arching leaves of mammoth size,
That strike each fresh beholder with surprise.
The dark and gloomy green of orange-trees—
Which murmur softly in the summer breeze—
Contrasts with the poncetta's crimson flame,
While mutely the liana's coils proclaim
The fate that waits on all they gather round—
Each tree a giant in their meshes bound.
The huge and spiky cactus, with its thorns,
The undergrowth, at intervals, adorns,
And when upon the scene Night's shadows fall,

The jaguar to his mate is heard to call,
The bat whirrs past with shrill and ghostly cry,
The wide-winged vulture swoops in search of prey,
And fire-flies dance, like spirits blithe, and gay,
Or stars descended from the Milky Way.

V.

His eastern course Don Pedro still pursued
Across the ocean's trackless solitude,
But swiftly to the King the tidings sent
That he had found—perchance—a continent.
The King thereon was eager to explore,
And bade Vespucci sail, and seek its shore,
Which done, he found the land was known before,
By Cabot, and Columbus, brought to view.
He hesitated what 't was best to do.
The Pope's partition this decreed to Spain—
The hemisphere dividing 'tween the twain—
But was Don Pedro's deed to be in vain?
No! not while he—Emanuel—lived to reign!
The rival kings contended for the soil,
Each claiming that to him belonged the spoil;
But Spain, at length, relinquished all her claim,
And so 't was left to swell her rival's fame.

VI.

Still great in prowess were the Portuguese,
Who aimed to rule the empire of the seas;
And saw with hatred, and a jealous eye,
Spain's rival flag o'er distant regions fly,
And longed to spread discov'ry o'er the main,
And dim the glory of that rival's reign.
Cortereal espoused his nation's cause,
And coveted his countrymen's applause,

And from his purse the needed means supplied
To search the western ocean, far and wide,
And, through it, find a passage to the East,
Whose pictured riches were his mental feast :
But all in vain he sought for famed Cathay,
And, disappointed, northward turned away,
To sight, at length, the isle of Newfoundland,
And then—exploring—pass from strand to strand,
And—later—through the broad St. Lawrence glide,
And safe in Labrador at anchor ride,
And trade with Esquimaux along the shore,
Where none—save Norsemen—e'er had been before.
There icebergs rose like islands from the sea—
A scene the painter's eye delights to see—
While on them shone the sun's refulgent rays,
And made their sides with dazzling colors blaze—
Green, purple, yellow, blue, and orange-red.
Rich lights, and shadows, on them grandly played,
And all alike in splendid hues arrayed,
While Arctic birds, in flights, around them flew,
And lent the charm of motion to the view.
To Labrador he quickly bade adieu,
And Lisbon gave the wand'rer welcome home ;
But he was prone, where'er he could, to roam,
And sailed, ere long, again, for Labrador,
And, after that, was heard of nevermore.

VII.

Spain toward the New World cast an eager eye,
And—"To the Indies!" was the nation's cry.
De Lepe from Palos westward ploughed the main,
Though little was his own, or country's gain.
By St. Augustine's cape 't was his to sail,
But Time has o'er his record thrown a veil.
Bastides shared his country's deep unrest,

And sailed from Cadiz for the glowing west,
With golden visions, born of boundless hope,
And fancies wild, unbridled in their scope.
He coasted Terra Firma's wooded shore—
And gathered, here and there, some golden ore—
From Cape de Vela to Darien's bay,
But failed to find the riches of Cathay.
Ojeda, and Vespucci, sailed anew
To swell the knowledge of these regions new,
And chose a course they deemed unploughed by man,
Which might—who knew?—lead on to Hindostan,
But when   they   reached—disheartened—Hayti's
    shore,
They found their course Bastides-ploughed before;
And little wealth, or glory, either won
By aught on this exploring voyage done:
But still the ardor for adventure spread,
And all believed the sea to riches led.
To Newfoundland a fleet of fishers sped,
And reaped the finny harvest of the deep,
Which—off the Banks—is rarely prone to sleep.
From France, and Spain, and Portugal, they sailed
To work a mine of wealth that never failed.
There Denys mapped the sea, and shores around,
While haply the St. Lawrence, Aubert found,
And back to Gaul conveyed an Indian bride,
Who'd wandered on the margin of its tide.

To find that Western passage to the East—
On which their eyes were destined ne'er to feast—
From Seville, now, with Solis, Pinzon sped;
And to Brazilian shores their voyage led,
Where bright *La Plata* on their vision shone—
A stream, ere this, the white man ne'er had known.
The woods primeval there adorned the view.
Beside the feath'ry, tall, and straight bamboo,

Cecropias in beauty—slender—grew,
And to the breeze their lofty branches threw
A hundred feet above the weeds below,
While humming-birds were wand'ring to and fro,
And captive led the wond'ring gazers' eyes,
And arborescent ferns of mammoth size
With spreading fronds looked up to court the sky,
While mistletoes their tendrils flung on high.
Lobelias with spikes of azure bloom
Relieved the mighty forest's sylvan gloom,
And capheas, with purple blossoms bright,
Their odor shed, and charmed, the while, the sight.
Acacias, and bromelias, displayed
Their wealth of leaf in varied tints arrayed,
While mangroves, and bignonias, were seen
Among the lowlands, dense and grandly green,
With golden maize, the Red Man's native fare,
In patches o'er the landscape, here and there.

Ere long to Yucatan they ploughed their way,
And gazed on spots where ruined cities lay,
Whose builders, too, had like them passed away,
Nor left a trace on Time's eternal tide.
At length, beside *La Plata*, Solis died—
For he, again, from Seville sailed away
To seek that mythic channel to Cathay—
And on that second voyage he was slain
Where glides the river to embrace the main,
While comrades round him shared his tragic end
And vainly strove existence to defend;
For savage hosts in warlike fury rose,
And capped the climax of their earthly woes.

VIII.

Columbus died, but Spanish conquest spread,
And more, and more, the Indians filled with dread.

The poor untutored natives of the soil
The Christians treated as their lawful spoil,
And made them serve as slaves where they had ruled
Ere by their cruel tyrants they were schooled.
They fell like wheat before the reaper's hands,
Invasion's blight careering o'er their lands.
Exhaustion, Famine, Pestilence and Strife,
Left Death triumphant o'er barbaric life :
And when their numbers dwindled to a few,
Their place was filled with slaves of ebon hue,
Who, torn away from Africa—their own—
In bondage ever after lived to groan :
But one among the Spaniards fought for Right,
And took in righteous deeds a keen delight,
And strove to shield the savage from his foes—
To wrest from slavish bonds, and countless woes ;—
And Mercy o'er his name a garland throws—
Bartholomew Las Casas of Castile.*
He labored long, and well, with patient zeal,
And for his fellow-man his heart could feel.
For fifty years he bore this noble toil
To serve the Indian on his native soil,
And to the New World, sadly, bade good-by,
And mourned the wrongs from which he ne'er
    could fly.

---

* Bartholomew de las Casas, (pronounce Las Cassas) a native of Seville and a priest, was appointed in 1516, by Cardinal Ximenes, who acted as regent after the death of King Ferdinand, to the office of Protector of the Indians at his own solicitation. He had accompanied Columbus on his second voyage to the New World, and saw how horribly the Indians were oppressed by the Spanish yoke, and sought to ameliorate their sufferings. In 1551 Las Casas, after having zealously labored for fifty years in behalf of the " Liberty, Comfort and Salvation " of the Indians, returned to Spain, a disappointed man, in the seventy-seventh year of his age. He died there in 1566.

May he to fame—Las Casas—long be known—
The Red Man's friend, whose cause he made his own.

IX.

Columbus in the New World lived anew
When to its shores Don Diego's squadron drew.*
He sailed while, still, Ovando sat the throne,
Which once his father's, now became his own,
And Hayti shone with splendor erst unknown.
Then, burning with the glow of enterprise,
He toward the mainland turned his eager eyes—
Resolved adjacent coasts to colonize—
But, quickly, squadrons reached the isle from Spain,
Encroaching on Don Diego's wide domain.
The King had cut the continent in twain.
One half, Castile—the Golden—he had named,
Whose ruler Nicuesa was proclaimed ;
The rest New Andalusia he called,
And in command Ojeda, then, installed.
The two commanders—rivals—sailed away
To bring the savage land beneath their sway,
And naught of this their mission Diego knew
Till they at San Domingo met his view.
Ere long they bade to Hayti's shores adieu,
Ojeda steering east, his rival west,
And each with hope, and courage, in his breast.
Pizarro—yet to conquer in Peru—
Was one, among Ojeda's fiery crew ;
And Cortez—yet in Mexico to shine—
Disease compelled the voyage to resign.

Ojeda steered to Carthagena's shore,
Expecting wealth to reap in golden ore,

---

* Don Diego Columbus, the son of Christopher Columbus,
succeeded Ovando in the government of Hayti, in 1509.
† Pronounce Nee-que-essa.

And revel in a paradise of charms—
But landing, faced a multitude in arms.
He then advanced, and bade the priests proclaim
His holy mission and his lofty aim,
And they, in stately form, began to read
What Spain's divines and jurists had decreed;
And thus the solemn formula was phrased :—
" Jehovah's name—O savages !—be praised !
Behold a captain of the realm of Spain,
Who o'er your native land has come to reign,
And o'er your idols raise the Cross, divine !
Idolatry—ye heathen !—then, resign.
The Pope, who holds on earth St. Peter's sway,
All savage lands, from here, to far Cathay,
Has on the Christian monarchs well bestowed ;
And we, their servants, come to point the road.
Acknowledge, then, the Christian doctrine true ;
Revere the Pontiff, and for favor sue,
And to the Spanish Crown allegiance swear,
And you may, each, a crown of glory wear;
But fail in this, and woe to all of ye !
From wrath like ours 't were vain to strive to flee ;
The sword shall work its havoc, far, and wide,
And desolation travel like the tide ;
While all your tribes as slaves shall ever toil,
And all your riches be our lawful spoil ! "
The wond'ring Red Men heard the strange address,
Which threatened thus to curse, if not to bless,
But on their ears it fell as empty sound.
The tongue was new—the argument profound.
Thus Spain designed to sanctify her crimes—
Her Christian warfare in barbaric climes.

Submission was demanded, but in vain.
The Red Men spurned the proffered hand of Spain,
For Carthagena's sons were strong and brave,

And fiercely, to the soldiers, battle gave.
Three hundred men in three light brigantines
Were actors in the midst of warlike scenes;
And poisoned arrows winged their fatal way
From naked hosts assembled for the fray.
Ojeda—ever daring—drove them back,
And made their masses reel in each attack,
Advancing, further inland, day by day,
And vigilant assailing foes to slay.
At length, when he his conquest deemed complete,
He met with overwhelming, dire defeat.
His scattered forces went in search of spoils,
And fell into the foe's destructive toils,
And, save himself, of all who'd landed there
Not one was left, the story back to bear.
He cut his way through hosts of fighting braves,
Who surged around him like engulfing waves,
And, 'neath the friendly mantle of the night,
He sought escape in swift, and shoreward, flight.
Then, with the dawn, he hid himself in trees,
And to the Virgin prayed on bended knees,
Till Night again with darkness veiled the land,
When he renewed his journey toward the strand;
And in a mangrove thicket down he lay
When in the east he saw the break of day.
Those on the ships, the while, had anxious grown,
For naught, on board, of those ashore was known;
And when they searched, their search was all in
   vain,
Save learning this:—their comrades, lost, were slain.
'T was as they neared the beach to re-embark,
And flee the coast ere shining day grew dark—
That one among them—halting—uttered—" Hark!"
And pointed where the mangroves thickest grew,
Then, stooping, peered the swampy thicket through.
All near the spot, with eyes dilated, drew,

And saw a Spaniard's form reclining there.
"Ojeda!" cried the foremost, "I will swear."
Yes! on the mangroves' matted roots he lay,
But, though alive, his strength had ebbed away,
And not a word the famished knight could say;
Yet on his shoulder still he bore his shield,
And in his hand the sword he could not wield.
His comrades placed him gently on the sand,
And prayed for help from the Almighty's hand,
But ere they bore him, shipward, from the strand,
They saw his rival's fleet advancing near,
And with their great surprise was mingled fear,
For he, and their commander, now, were foes.
He came, perchance, intent on striking blows.
Ojeda whispered—"Go, and leave me here
Till he, again, has left the harbor clear:"
But when Nicu'sa heard the dismal tale
He said—"A crippled foe I'll ne'er assail,
But aid him as a brother in distress!
Though once a foe, I'm not a friend the less!"
The two, no longer rivals, met once more,
And Vengeance vowed on all that savage shore.
Four hundred men were landed, ripe for blood,
And marched, in darkness, through the primal wood,
While startled parrots vented screaming cries—
As if intended to anathemize.
At length they reached the village they had doomed,
When all around them they with flames illumed,
And slaughtered either sex—the young, and old,
And stripped them of their ornaments of gold.
Not one escaped that fatal night attack,
And of the village, naught was left but wrack—
The hamlets where the Spaniards had been slain.
Triumphant o'er the savage, now, was Spain!
The two commanders parted, soon, as friends,
Each to pursue his own ambitious ends,

Ojeda east, his comrade to the west,
Adventure craving with an equal zest.

X.

Ojeda landed on a spacious bay,
And, to the Virgin, knelt he there to pray,
And San Sebastian, called the spot he chose,
While all around were arrow-flinging foes.
He sent a ship to Hayti for recruits,
And lived, the while, on roots, and scanty fruits.
A ceaseless battle here he found his life,
And fast his forces perished in the strife,
While hunger, and disease, were ever rife.
Men welcomed death as yielding sweet relief
From horror, and despair, and bitter grief.
At length, one bright and hope-inspiring day,
As sorely wounded—helpless—there he lay,
While tropic vegetation round him bloomed,
A sail above the clear horizon loomed,
And Gladness banished Sorrow from his heart,
And of his wounds he nigh forgot the smart.
He deemed it brought him succor, and supplies
To push anew his daring enterprise ;
And toward it all directed joyful eyes,
And gave unfettered play to wild delight
As by degrees it swelled upon their sight.
It anchored where the camp o'erlooked the sea,
While on the shore prevailed unbridled glee,
And starving men indulged in dreams of bliss :
But what a ship, and what a crew was this !
'T was not the promised bark Ojeda thought,
Though succor she to dying Spaniards brought,
And though from Hayti's isle her course had been,
She came a stranger on the troubled scene,
And bartered food for gems, and plates of gold,

Her crew a horde of desperadoes, bold,
Who cried—" A lawless, pirate gang are we ! "
A stolen ship, with stolen freight, was she,
With Talavera o'er her in command,
Aspiring for the riches of the land.
Time passed away, and all she brought had gone,
The camp, the while, still dwindling, one by one,
And clamor, and dissension, rife within :
Yet still Ojeda treasure strove to win,
And daily hoped for succor, ne'er to come.
At last he said—" The oracles are dumb ;
So I, myself, to Hayti's isle will sail,
Nor to return, with plenty, I shall fail ;
And o'er you all I'll leave—my trusty band—
Pizarro—Don Francisco—in command.
The pirate's ship will bear me on my way,
And here, the while, my faithful comrades stay ! "
The pirate crew for home began to yearn,
Nor, with Ojeda, trembled to return,
So certain death, by ling'ring there, appeared.
For Hayti's isle, with him, they gladly steered,
And deemed escape from such a coast a boon :
But he with Talavera quarrelled soon,
And by the gang was fettered to the deck.
Ere long they feared their bark would prove a wreck,
And then they freed him, and implored his aid.
The storm that raged appalling havoc made,
And some despaired of reaching Hayti more,
But in the end were cast on Cuba's shore,
The caravel unfit to longer sail—
A leaky vessel shattered by the gale.
Against their lot the crew began to rail,
But overland Ojeda led the way—
A toilsome march that filled them with dismay—
And many perished ere the task was done
Beneath the fervor of that torrid sun.

At length the wand'rers gained the eastern coast,
And met, with joy, a friendly Indian host,
And saw Jamaica's mountains far away,
For distant twenty leagues the island lay.
The natives told of Spaniards there, by signs—
Men who, for gold, were prone to search the
    mines ;
And thither sent Ojeda a canoe
For succor, from his countrymen, to sue.
Don Diego there had placed a trusty band
To colonize, and cultivate, the land,
With Esquibel—Don Juan—in command,
And, when Ojeda's message reached his hand,
A vessel spread her sails for Cuba's strand ;
And all were thus to fair Jamaica borne.
The pirate crew embraced it as their bourn.
Ojeda, only, on to Hayti sailed,
But there in finding succor sadly failed,
And died, ere long, in San Domingo, poor—
So poor he found a pauper's grave, obscure ;—
Neglected as an unsuccessful man—
He who had oft so proudly led the van.
Thus, as a gourd, his glory passed away,
And he, to disappointment, fell a prey.
The dauntless spirit grief, at last, o'ercame,
And briefly he survived the wreck of fame.
The chivalry of ocean, he adorned,
And, splendid in his courage, cowards scorned,
Yet perished like the meanest of mankind,
The world to all his ancient prowess blind—
Alonzo de Ojeda, reckless, brave—
And none could tell where lay his humble grave.
Ere this the pirate crew were captive made,
And on the gibbet Talavera swayed—
Fit end to his adventurous career,
Whose moral, like its infamy, is clear.

XI.

Don Diego turned his thoughts to Cuba's shore,
For rumor made it rich in golden ore,
And there he sent a bold exploring band,
And to Velasquez gave the chief command.
Three hundred strong, the Spaniards ranged the
    isle—
A Christian host and yet satanic, vile—
Nor one of all their number there was slain
Ere Cuba passed a conquest o'er to Spain.
They swiftly swept the native race away;
And at their feet a groaning people lay
And cursed their blighting and tyrannic sway.
They fell as falls the grass before the scythe,
And on the stake, too oft, were seen to writhe.
A chieftain who from Hayti's shore had fled
Was to the verge of flaming fagots led,
And asked if he'd the Christian faith embrace,
And win thereby in Paradise a place.
" Will such as you," the savage spoke, " be there ? "
The priest responded with a solemn air—
" All righteous Spaniards to that bourn repair."
" Then," said the chief, " I thither ne'er will go,
For that would be a heritage of woe.
Than with that race accursèd ever dwell
I'd rather live eternally in Hell."
The priest in holy horror raised his eyes.
" Torment him," cried Velasquez, " as he dies."
A moment later flames around him roared,
And he was cut to pieces by the sword;
But ere he died Velasquez raised his voice,
And said—" The holy angels all rejoice
To see the writhing infidel expire,
And winds from heaven are sent to fan the fire."

When such as he Invasion's vanguard led
Well might the name of Spaniard kindle dread,
And isles of beauty reek with dusky dead.

XII.

When from wild Carthagena's gory shore
Bold Nicuesa's squadron westward bore,
Rude, baffling storms assailed him day by day,
And left the bark he sailed a castaway—
A stranded wreck—one dark, and awful night ;
And when the morning shed its welcome light
No more her sister vessels met the sight.
With thankful hearts, her crew escaped to land,
And saw her broken timbers strew the strand,
And all she carried swallowed by the tide;
And o'er her hapless fate, in anguish, sighed.
With scanty raiment, minus arms, and food,
They found themselves in savage solitude,
And wandered westward by the ocean's verge—
And listened, as they journeyed, to its dirge—
But sought the missing squadron all in vain.
A sailless waste of billows was the main.
Thus days, and weeks, in fruitless toil were passed,
And some before the prospect stood aghast,
And some who seldom mourned were seen to weep.
Their only boat beside them skimmed the deep,
And, few by few, in this they crossed a bay
That in their course along the sea-beach lay,
And, landing, found their resting-place an isle,
A gulf beyond it stretching many a mile.
They longed to flee the spot ere fell the night,
But day already showed declining light,
And so they camped upon its marshy soil,
And sought in slumber rest from anxious toil ;
But when the morrow broke no boat was there,

And sunken cheeks grew livid with despair.
Were those who manned her, like her, now no more?
Or had they steered her to some other shore,
And left their helpless comrades there to die?
Long, weary weeks again went slowly by,
And famine, and disease, and wearing grief
Made lives as prone to wither as a leaf;
And thus they saw their numbers dwindle fast,
While only shadows on their lot were cast.
Some uttered groans, and lamentations, loud,
And some in mute despair were sadly bowed:
Some called on God for succor, and for grace,
And some were Death, impatient to embrace.
At length one morn on ocean's wrinkled face
They saw a sight that filled them with delight—
A swelling sail that shone with golden light.
No bounds their transports in that moment knew.
On toward the shore the distant vessel flew;
And yet the isle might well escape its view;
But nearer came the welcome, speeding ship,
And prayers for rescue rose to ev'ry lip.
'T was of the missing fleet—a brigantine,
And in her boat the missing crew were seen.
They rowed ashore, and told their stirring tale:—
How they had left the isle, to eastward sail,
Expecting thus the squadron, soon, to find,
And prove their motive for desertion, kind:
How when the river Belen met their eyes,
They felt rewarded for their enterprise,
And saw the squadron's ruins crumbling there,
And on the shore their comrades in despair: •
And how they thus with succor reached the isle,
And turned the frown of Fortune to a smile.
The crews embraced on meeting, and with tears,
For sorrow makes us kindred, and endears;
And all together sailed for Belen's stream.

The rescued saw the future brightly gleam,
So great the change that o'er them came appeared,
But those who rescued, worse disaster feared,
For they had dwelt where Belen's waters flowed,
And all their features woe, and famine showed.
They reached the camp—a sorry, dismal scene—
And saw their comrades haggard, wan, and lean,
Four hundred less than when they landed there,
And in their eyes, dejection, and despair.
Three hundred still survived, but wrecked in health,
And disappointed of their promised wealth.
Olano* o'er the squadron held command,
And welcomed Nicuesa to the land,
But he his false lieutenant met with scorn,
And cried—" To be a traitor you were born !
You o'er the squadron longed for boundless sway,
And from the bark that bore me steered away,
Nor sent a single craft to learn my fate.
Such base desertion merits more than hate.
Go wail in bondage o'er your cruel crime,
And I will slay you at the fitting time ! "
And as a traitor he was seized, and bound,
While all his fellow captains stood around.
" You, too," their chief in indignation, cried,
" Are with the stain of crime as foully dyed,
Or ye'd have searched the sea, and ranged the
    shore ! "
"We deemed," said they, "yourself, and ship, no
    more ;
That she—alas !—had foundered in the gale,
And all our search, in finding her, would fail : "
. So he, at length, was won to Mercy's side,
And by his act not one offender died.

---

* Lope de Olano, Nicuesa's first-lieutenant.

XIII.

Disease, and Famine, were the Spaniards' foes,
And native hosts allowed them no repose.
Their hunger forced them, once, to rob the grave,
And eat the putrid body of a brave,
And thirty perished by the foul repast.
Then Nicuesa stood, again, aghast,
And from the mournful spot resolved to flee,
And trust his damaged fortunes to the sea.
Two brigantines, alone, were left him now,—
Save what Olano built—a masted scow,—
And he, with these, his way began to plough;
But there a few were forced to linger still,
And bow submissive to their Maker's will.
Due east along the coast he led the way,
And reached, ere long, a small sequestered bay.
" Here, in the name of God," * said he, " we'll land,
And plant the Cross, devoutly, in the sand !"
But Indian foes, and famine, mowed them down,
And Fortune, still, was only seen to frown.
All living things they welcomed as their food—
The alligator, and his slimy brood,
And all the crawling reptiles they could find,
And loathsome snakes, regardless of their kind.
A bark was sent for those they'd left behind,
Yet but a hundred met when all were joined.
And sick, and wasted, these, with sadness groined.†

---

* From these words it took its name—*Nombre de Dios.*
It was the port which Columbus had previously named
Puerto de Pastimientos, or Port of Provisions. Nicuesa had
previously louched at Porto Bello, and been driven off by the
Indians.

† Groin was used by Chaucer as the equivalent of groan,
although the word is now obsolete.

The craft to Hayti sailed for fresh supplies,
But fatal proved, alas! the enterprise,
For ne'er again it reached a friendly shore,
Or e'er was heard of, by the Spaniards, more.
Time wore away, and horrors greater grew,
Till, lo! the hundred dwindled to a few,
And these too weak to guard the fort by night,
Or sally forth, assailing foes to fight.
Of all that noble squadron's gallant host,
Which of so much, of yore, could proudly boast,
These—these alone—remained the tale to tell
How to the world their comrades bade farewell.

XIV.

Before Ojeda San Sebastian left—
To seek for much of which he stood bereft—
His friend Enciso * sailed to lend him aid,
But ere he sailed, alas! too long delayed.
When Hayti's palms had vanished from his view,
And sky, and ocean, met in kindred blue,
He heard a strange, sepulchral voice arise,
And cast around a look of wild surprise,
But sought the speaker, o'er, and o'er, in vain.
" Perchance some saint addressed me from the
    skies!"
He whispered to himself, and raised his eyes,
" Or from the deep some warning angel spoke.
Oh! may the Lord His blessings ne'er revoke,"
And on the sea, in silence, down he gazed,
And with his lips the holy trio praised.

---

* Bachelor Martin Fernandez de Enciso, a lawyer of San
Domingo, who had been induced by Ojeda, before sailing, to
promise to fit out a vessel at his own expense, and join him
in the new colony.

Again the voice was heard, but hoarse, and near,
And then the Spaniard showed a trace of fear,
And deemed that Satan—not a Saint—was there.
" A Spanish oath," Enciso cried, " I swear ! "

Yet once again it caught his list'ning ear,
And then a blow was heard, resounding, clear,
While from a cask the head—projected—flew,
And in its place another rose to view—
A human head—a Spaniard's face, and form.
Enciso seemed himself a gath'ring storm
As he surveyed his strange, mysterious guest—
One like a poor, but gay, hidalgo dressed—
And rudely, then, assailed him where he stood,
And asked his mission ere he shed his blood.
" This stratagem," the stranger well replied—
" May good to you, but ill can ne'er, betide,
For I have come to join your daring crew,
And this my advent you, nor yours, will rue.
I own myself a fugitive, to you,
But to your cause you'll find me stanch, and true.
My creditors—rapacious—rabid, grew,   ·
And to appease them naught but gold would do,
And I, alas ! of that had none, I knew.
Thus deep in debt, and light of heart and purse,
I vowed to flee the isle that seemed my curse.
I'm Vasco Nuñez de Balboa—yea,
A seeker for the riches of Cathay !'
I with Bastides left the shores of Spain,
Expecting wealth, and great renown, to gain ;
Yet, now, behold me poorer than before,
But strong, ambitious, brave, I still may soar.
I speak the truth, nor falsely e'er averred ;
And though—as from an egg escapes a bird—
I here appear to seek adventure, new,
And for your favor thus to meekly sue—

My callow days are numbered with the past,
And I aspire to win renown at last!"
Enciso's anger quickly died away,
And Vasco Nuñez, once again, was gay.

XV.

The ship to Carthagena found her way,
And anchored in its deep, and sheltered bay.
The natives brandished weapons on the shore,
And feared Ojeda's troops had come once more :
But when the Spaniards made them friendly signs
They banished with their wrath their fierce designs,
And then displayed a calm, pacific mien—
So easy 't was their hearts from war to wean—
And, hospitably, toward them nearer drew,
Though Spaniards there, before, their kinsmen slew,
Unmindful of their sex, or yet their age,
And hamlets burned, and ravaged, in their rage.
They rose above the spirit of revenge,
Nor sought their wrongs, terrific, to avenge.
As there the vessel lay, a sail was seen,
And into port there sailed a brigantine.
Enciso marvelled much at such a sight,
And some, on board, surveyed her with delight,
While others feared the stranger boded harm,
And yielded to suspicions, and alarm,
For in those lonely seas a sail was rare.
Some deemed a phantom ship was sailing there :
But on she came, and anchored by their side,
While from her prow a Spaniard "Welcome!" cried.
From San Sebastian's shore she'd ploughed her way,
Nor longer there her starving crew could stay.
Ojeda failed to bring them back supplies,
And for a sail they, vainly, strained their eyes.
Two brigantines were left, and these were filled,

But both were light, and fragile, in their build,
And one, ere long, went down with all on board,
Who, from their comrades, help, in vain, implored.
Of all Ojeda's squadron naught remained,
Save this lone, feeble craft, by tempests strained,
And those she bore—the last surviving few
Of his once proud, and truly gallant crew;
And o'er them, still, Pizarro held command,
And ruled with kind, and yet determined, hand.

XVI.

Enciso would to San Sebastian go,
Despite the tale he heard of thrilling woe,
And on Pizarro he, at length, prevailed
To backward turn; and both, together, sailed:
But to his own, and comrades', bitter cost,
Just as he reached the port his ship was lost,
And with her all—but human lives—she bore,
While breakers lashed, and roared, along the shore.
The fortress, and the huts, in ruins lay,
And hostile natives filled him with dismay.
'T was now that Vasco Nuñez forward came,
And said that with Bastides—known to fame—
He years before had voyaged past the coast,
And found the Indians there a friendly host,
And rich in food, and gold, the country round,
While with a ring of gold the chief was crowned.
The spot was by Darien's stream, and west,
Where palm-trees threw their shadows on its breast.
There went the Spaniards in the brigantine,
And charming to the eye appeared the scene.

The green enamelled leaves of koo-chook trees *
Were whisp'ring softly in the tropic breeze,

---

* Caoutchouc, or India-rubber.

While from the gramalott—high water-grass—
And tabaquills—the weeds of the morass—
Aquatic birds, from time to time, arose—
Snipes, herons, pipers, fishers, and the rest,
Each with a touch of beauty on its breast ;
And crocodiles lay gilded by the sun—
Grim monsters sunk in slime, and long and dun.
Where mangroves in the swamps luxuriant grew
The manatus—the sea-cow—met the view ;
And cormorants were wand'ring to and fro,
Or diving in the liquid depths below,
And venting screams discordant, harsh, and shrill,
Save in the noontide heats, when all was still ;
And in his swinging hammock Man reposed,
And on the world his eyes—contented—closed.
Atrato's waters in the sunlight gleamed,
And with the finny tribe—disporting—teemed,
While in their champas natives skimmed it o'er.
Great caves and grottoes, marked the ocean's
    shore,
Where waves were wont, when tempests raged, to
    roar;—
And boil, and foam, and fret, and plunge, in
    storms ;—
For Neptune here had carved fantastic forms—
The work of ages and the sportive brine—
The tapestry of rocks, of strange design—
The sculpture fashioned by the hand divine.

XVII.

The forest seemed alive with plumaged throngs,
And here, and there, they sang their sylvan
    songs—
The cardinal, and tropeo, and more—
While turkeys, toucans, parrots—score on score—

With gaudy colors, flamed before the eye ;
And crested, white macaws were heard to cry,
And mocking-birds to warble in the shade,
Where agile monkeys in the branches played.
Majestic trees their lofty branches twined,
And formed arcades, as if by man designed—
Vast avenues, of architecture grand—
Their arches, with capricious vines festooned,
And Nature's harps æolian there attuned.
The Cordilleras rose against the sky,
A mighty background—grand, eternal, high—
With splendid vegetation gayly dressed,
The verdure reaching almost to their crest,
While over all the sun resplendent shone,
Diffusing lustre from his dazzling throne.
The nights were vocal with the sounds of life—
The forest with the hum of voices rife :—
The night-birds screamed and hooted on the air ;
The frogs, in concert, told that they were there ;
The monkeys cried, and chattered to the moon,
And herons spoke from river, or lagoon,
While shining stars—the flow'rets of the skies—
Looked down on dancing, gleaming, fiery flies.

XVIII.

Enciso, landing, stormed the Indian town,
And slew the monarch with the golden crown,
And drove his people from their wild domain,
Or left them, where they'd bravely battled, slain ;
Then plundered where he'd conquered, and, behold !
Ten thousand castellanos gained, of gold.
He, then, Darien named the spot, and there
Began to rule as the alcaldé mayor :
But in the Spaniards' midst, dissensions rose.
Enciso found them, one and all, his foes,

And Vasco Nuñez fanned the fire of hate,
And—with his comrades—stripped him of his state,
But ere his place, a new commander filled,
And ere the tumult of the camp was stilled,
The sound of distant cannon caught the ear.
Men paused to list in wonder, and in fear.
Then from the brigantine a gun replied,
And toward the shore a ship was seen to glide;
Another, too, behind it, soon, was eyed—
Two barks for Nicuesa, with supplies.
The sight moved all with gladness, and surprise.
O'er these one Colmenaris held command,
And claimed the coast as Nicuesa's land,
To whom for aid the camp resolved to look,
And, with him, Colmenaris envoys took,
Who found his chief where last we left his band,
With hollow cheek, and eye, and shrivelled hand,
And only sixty left of all he'd ruled—
Men bitterly in want, and warfare, schooled—
And begged him to their camp to take his way,
And o'er it hold a rightful ruler's sway.
He felt as one restored from death to life—
As one who'd proved a victor in the strife—
But indiscreetly made prophetic signs,
And spoke, in vaunting tone, of harsh designs.
The envoys heard, and quickly took alarm,
For words like his foreboded naught but harm,
And speeding back before he left the land
They cried—" Beware ! you court a knave's command ! "
Then all were sad to contemplate their deed,
From which it seemed too late to, now, recede ;
But Vasco Nuñez said—" No more despair !
For you the evil work can, soon, repair
By not receiving him for whom you've sent.
He naught can do but rage with discontent."

His comrades deemed his counsel truly wise,
And toward the ocean turned expectant eyes,
And saw, ere long, the promised bark appear ;
Then gathered on the beach when she was near,
And warned him—Nicuesa—from the shore.
He marvelled much, and felt exceeding sore,
And—night approaching—steered again to sea,
But in the morning back, once more, was he.
He, then, was asked to parley on the beach,
And found himself ensnared within their reach,
For as he touched the ground he felt their blows :
But he was fleet, and fled his angry foes.
He gained the friendly woods, by these pursued,
And wandered there, awhile, in solitude.
When Vasco Nuñez* saw the people's rage
He tried their stormy passions to assuage,
Repenting of the fury he'd aroused,
While those around on native wine † caroused :
But all in vain he counselled measures, mild.
His comrades seemed with indignation wild.
They seized on Nicuesa in the wood,
And threatened there, and then, to shed his blood ;
But, in the end, resolved his life to spare
If he'd to Spain without ado repair.
In fear of death, the promise asked he gave,
Though he was, like his nation, proud, and brave.
They forced him on a leaky brigantine,
Which sailed away, but ne'er again was seen,
Nor one survived her tragic fate to tell.‡
Thus Nicuesa bade the world farewell.

---

* After Enciso had been deprived of his office, Vasco
Nuñez de Balboa, and another, were appointed alcaldes.

† Made from maize, and the pineapple.

‡ Nicuesa sailed on March 1, 1511.

XIX.

The hapless bark had vanished from the view,
But on Darien's strand contention grew.
Enciso tried, condemned, and sent to Spain,*
Left Vasco Nuñez o'er the band to reign,
Who frank, and fearless, and of courteous ways,
Had won his comrades' confidence, and praise.
Tall, strongly built, and full of manly grace,
With auburn locks and prepossessing face,
And young, though verging on the noon of life,
He looked a leader, born to conquer strife,
And soothe the angry passions of his band
By ruling with a firm, but gentle hand.
He labored, now, success, and gold, to win—
For these he deemed atoned for ev'ry sin—
And prove his skill, and fitness for command
By deeds of valor, and achievements grand.
He heard of regions rich in precious ore,
And sent Pizarro thither to explore,

---

* The bachelor Enciso was charged with usurping the powers of alcalde mayor on the mere appointment of Ojeda, who had no authority over this territory, it being included in the province assigned by the Crown to Nicuesa. He was found guilty, and imprisoned, while his property was confiscated ; but afterwards he was released, and allowed to return to Spain, where he made representations concerning these harsh measures at the Court, which greatly prejudiced King Ferdinand against Vasco Nuñez de Balboa, and led to the appointment of Don Pedrarias Davila as governor of Darien, who ultimately caused the execution of Vasco Nuñez. The latter, however—then about thirty-five years of age—succeeded to the command of the colony after the departure of Enciso, and his own fellow-alcalde, Zamudio— who went with him to counteract any injurious representations he might make in Spain—and this command he retained until the arrival of Pedrarias.

And when Pizarro back, defeated, came—
And left behind a comrade sick, and lame—
He made him feel the bitterness of shame.
He, then, returned, and so the comrade saved,
Though countless perils in the task he braved.
To those who'd Nicuesa's fortunes shared—
At Nombre Dios—brigantines repaired,
And to Darien's camp the remnant bore ;
And glad were they to leave that fatal shore.
Two Spaniards, who'd deserted long before,
Were by them found arrayed in Indian guise,
And leaders in barbaric enterprise—
The guests of Coyba's chief—Careeta named,
And for his might, and prowess, justly famed ;
And these, returning, Vasco Nuñez told
Of all his stores of food, and pearls, and gold,
Betraying him who'd sheltered them of old.
Then Vasco Nuñez planned his overthrow
By striking, in the night, a crushing blow.
'T was done, and he—the chief—was plunged in
     woe.
He saw himself, his wives, and children, bound,
And gazed, in sadness, on the scene around.
When Vasco Nuñez met his pensive eye,
The captive clanked his chain, and heaved a sigh,
And thus, in mournful accents, slowly spoke :—
" Why bow me down to such a cruel yoke
When I, nor mine, have ever done thee wrong ?
'T is true I'm weak, and thou, and thine, are strong;
But I have seen the Spaniard in his need,
And succored him, and proved a friend indeed.
When first I saw thee near my dwelling-place
I met thee not with anger in my face,
But welcomed thee with brotherly embrace,
And gave thee of the best that I possessed.
Yet thou wouldst, thus, from me my freedom wrest !

Oh ! set me free, and I, and mine, will be,
For ever, faithful friends to thine, and thee,
And all thy wants supply, from time to time,
And show thee all the riches of the clime ;
And as a pledge of friendship, true, sincere,
I'll give thee one I hold supremely dear—
Yea love, and cherish as I would my life—
My daughter—Vasco Nuñez—as thy wife ! "
Before his eyes the damsel captive stood—
A lovely form in life's expanding bud—
Dejected, trembling, beautiful, and chaste,
And by the charms of nature only graced—
A Venus with a wealth of raven hair.
To Vasco Nuñez she was wondrous fair,
And to Careeta's offer he replied—
" I'll take the maiden gladly as my bride,
And naught you ask to you shall be denied,
For I would turn my native foes to friends ;
And wise is he who Cross, and Crown defends ! "
That captive fair the captor captive led,
For to his heart a dart from Cupid sped,
And in the beauty's smiles he found delight,
And ne'er before had eyes appeared so bright.

PART II.

THE PACIFIC OCEAN DISCOVERED.

I.

DON VASCO NUÑEZ kept his promise true,
And he and King Careeta friendly grew.
He served the chieftain's friends, and fought his foes,
And brought his war with Ponca to a close ;

For Ponca—like himself a great cazique—
Was in the mountains forced to shelter seek,
His country ravaged, and his people slain
By Vasco Nuñez and the troops of Spain ;
Who, then, adventured on Comagre's plain,
And reaped a harvest, rich, of virgin gold.
A tale to Vasco Nuñez there was told,
Which fired with ardor, new, the Spaniards' breast,
And widened Spain's dominions in the West.
A young cazique—with south-extended hand—
Said—" See those mountains yonder, tall, and grand!
Beyond them lies an ocean, deep, and wide,
Where ships with sails—like yours—are seen to
    glide, *
And, with their oars, their course the rowers guide.
There—on the shores that stretch along the main—
Proud kings, in garments, o'er their people reign,
And eat, and drink, from vessels wrought of ore,
Which glitters on each river's sandy shore.
There that—the yellow gold you precious deem—
You'll see where'er you go before you gleam,
For earth with shining treasure there doth teem !
But you will need a thousand men at least
Ere on its fruits, and riches, you can feast ! "
These welcome words, that Vasco Nuñez heard,
His heart with joyful expectations stirred.
He then resolved to win this dazzling prize,
And crown his life with fruitful enterprise.
He hastened to Darien to prepare,
And found Valdivia †—with provisions, there.

---

* He doubtless referred to the bolsas of Peru—large rafts,
nearly square, and each with a single mast, and sail. These
vessels are still used on the west coast of South America.

† Valdivia, who was chosen Regidor of the colony after the
deposition of Enciso, had been sent to San Domingo, for provisions, and recruits, on the departure of the latter, who was
to touch at that port on his way to Spain.

" To San Domingo back," said he, "repair,
And this dispatch to Hayti's ruler bear,
Which tells him of a region, rich and new,
That I am eager—Regidor—to view.
Solicit him to ask the King for aid,
Describing all the progress we have made:
And take the treasure with you for the Crown—
The royal fifth that we have melted down—
And have it sent without delay to Spain ;
For gold may win when words are all in vain ! "

II.

Valdivia sailed, and Vasco Nuñez mused,
And, then, along the coast, for booty, cruised.
He heard of rich Dobayba's golden fane,
And sought it long, impelled by thirst of gain,
Yet found it not, but met with countless foes,
And gave, and took, a hurricane of blows
Ere he, with spoils, and captives, journeyed back
To find Darien threatened with attack.
A secret plot, the native hosts had formed.
Darien they determined should be stormed.
'T was then that Vasco's lovely Indian bride
Proved unto him, and his, a faithful guide,
For from her brother's tongue the plot she gleaned,
And, this divulging, Vasco Nuñez screened.
The plot was foiled, and all its leaders slain,
And still triumphant o'er the land was Spain :
But factious discontents again arose,
And from the camp was banished all repose,
While hunger pressed, and no relief appeared.
Valdivia's loss, or treachery, was feared.
At length two caravels from Hayti came,
And fanned, with succor, Hope's expiring flame,
While they to Vasco Nuñez tidings brought,

Which in his mind a revolution wrought;
But of Valdivia's fortunes naught was known,
Nor he the island reached, to claim his own.

Enciso's tale had reached the Sovereign's ear,
And Vasco Nuñez learned he'd much to fear.
His hopes, and fortunes, seemed already crushed,
And with chagrin and rage his features flushed.
One chance remained—to find the Southern Sea,
And let the world his grand achievement see—
Before the royal mandate reached the land
To rob him—and for ever—of command.
Such great success would surely favor win,
For crimes atone, and cover ev'ry sin.
A thousand men were needed, it was true,
And to his standard he could call but few;
Yet fame, and fortune—life itself, perchance—
Hinged on that enterprise—that single chance.
The ships had brought recruits to swell the throng,
From which he picked the resolute, and strong,
And then with scarce two hundred in his train—
And bloodhounds, each submissive to a chain—
He led the way, a splendid realm to gain,
With friendly natives bringing up the rear.
He knew his danger, though he felt no fear.
A brigantine, and nine canoes, in line,
Receded, from Darien, o'er the brine,*
And reached, in safety, Coyba's welcome shore,
Where gold, and pearls, the chief—Careeta—wore.
He met his daughter—Vasco's beaming bride—
As one who felt a father's loving pride,
And gave to Vasco Nuñez greeting, kind,
And precious gifts, their friendship more to bind;

---

* Vasco Nuñez embarked, with 190 Spaniards and a
number of Indians, September 1, 1513.

And there the Spaniard left his fleet behind—
With half his force to guard it where it lay—
And toward the mountains, then, pursued his way:
But ere he left the coast he knelt in prayer,
And Mass was said to all who gathered there.
With armor, and with weapons, loaded down,
The Spaniards journeyed toward the mountains'
    crown.
Through forests dense, and passes deep, and wild,
The valiant band intrepidly defiled,
And bravely toiled up precipices steep,
And, here and there were fissures forced to leap.
With splendid fervor shone the tropic sun,
Whose scorching rays the toilers sought to shun,
And numbers sank exhausted by the way:
But not for these would Vasco brook delay.
He bade them back to Coyba slowly go,
While he advanced, and left them far below.
At length a warlike host appeared in view,
And yelled, and menaced, as they near him drew:
Then—armed with bows, and arrows, clubs, and
    spears,
And with no outward sign of inward fears—
They on the Spanish band, with fury, rushed,
And, for a moment, deemed the strangers crushed;
But when they heard the arquebuses roar,
And saw their comrades slain, or flecked with
    gore
They felt they fought with demons, thunder-armed,
Whose lives against assailing foes were charmed,
And in dismay—pursued—away they fled,
And left behind them full six hundred dead,
Their chieftain Quaraquah among the slain.
O'er all the fleeing, Terror held its reign.
The bloodhounds tore their victims with their fangs,
Who perished in excruciating pangs,

While swordsmen, with their weapons, · hundreds
   slew,
And lancers pierced unnumbered bodies through.
A group of chieftains—clad in robes of white—
Ere long were overtaken in their flight,
And by the dogs of war to pieces torn,
With none around, their hapless lot to mourn.
The victors from the vanquished gathered spoil,
And then renewed their journey, and their toil,
Save those who—sick, or wounded—helpless lay,
Or fell to hunger, and fatigue, a prey.
But sixty-eight remained of all the band
To scale the heights, and view the ocean strand.
Emerging from the forest, with their guides,
They climbed the naked mountain's rocky sides,
And, in the pure, and balmy, morning air,
Beheld the summit near them, gray, and bare.
"Halt!" was the cry of Vasco Nuñez then,
And not a step beyond advanced his men:
But he kept on with palpitating heart—
Resolved to play alone his mighty part—
And from the mountain-top the prospect eyed—
A scene that white man ne'er before descried.
With rugged mountains, and savannas green,
And forests dense, and wand'ring streams between,
There, far below, the promised ocean lay—
A mirror shining in the beams of day,*
Extending far as human eye could reach
From where he stood above the rocky beach.
In gratitude, and rapture, Vasco knelt,
And strove, in prayer, to picture all he felt,
And uttered thanks, impassioned, and sincere,
To Him whose guiding hand had led him here.

---

* This was on September 26, 1513, twenty days after the
departure from Careeta.

Then, calling on his comrades to ascend,
Before the Throne of Grace he bade them bend.
"Behold !" said he, "this grand, and glorious sight
That fills me with unspeakable delight !
Let us to God our thanks, devoutly, give,
And pray that we to conquer all may live—
The world so new that here before us lies,
And ne'er till now was seen by Christian eyes !
Let us this heathen realm evangelize,
Nor ever shrink from holy enterprise,
But preach the gospel wheresoe'er we wend ;
And to His glory may our actions tend !
To me—my comrades !—be ye staunch, and true,
And wealth ye'll reap, whose like ye never knew,
While great will be your service to the King—
So great that poets of your fame will sing !
Eternal glory, too, on high, you'll gain,
For winning this barbaric world for Spain,
And to the Faith converting all within—
Idolaters who, now, are steeped in sin.
A new career—my soldiers !—we begin !"
The Spaniards, then, embraced him as their friend,
And vowed devotion ne'er, on earth, to end,
While one—a priest—devoutly raised his voice,
And said—"My brethren, let us here rejoice,"
And chanted the *Te Deum* loud, and clear,
Which made the heroes feel that God was near ;
And, kneeling, all the rest, with hearts sincere,
Took up the sweet, the grand—majestic—strain,
And tears of joy among them fell like rain.
With pious fervor each the anthem sung,
And inspiration seemed on ev'ry tongue ;
And ne'er oblation purer rose on High,
Than from this mountain top, beneath the sky—
An altar thus so richly sanctified.
The Spaniards rose, and—wond'ring—looked awide.

Was this some sea embraced by lands unknown,
Or some vast ocean, stretching zone to zone,
Or that which washed on Oriental shores,
Where Marco Polo gathered precious ores?
Was *it* untraversed save by Indian arks,
Or was it swiftly ploughed by splendid barks,
Whose sails were spread—like theirs—to catch the
    wind,
And were they laden with the wealth of Ind?
Was *it* bedecked with islands rich in spice,
And gems, and gold, and pearls, surpassing price?
What golden realms were those of which they
    heard,
And which their breasts with strange emotions
    stirred?
A thousand questions seemed at once to rise,
To which Imagination gave replies;
And in conjecture all were lost who gazed.
The revelation held them rapt, amazed.
Then from a stately tree a cross was wrought,
And to the spot by zealous toilers brought,
And when uplifted, there a shadow threw—
The symbol of the faith, divine, and true,
And of the Saviour's blood on Calv'ry spilt.
A monument of stones was round it built,
And on the tree was carved the Sovereign's name—
The outward mark of Spain's indubious claim—
While Vasco Nuñez said—"I now proclaim
This ocean, and its realms, belong to Spain,
And may its monarchs o'er it ever reign!"
The great Pacific Ocean thus was found,
And Vasco Nuñez felt himself renowned.

He, with his band, descended, now, the slope,—
Each one elated—buoyant, gay—with hope,—
And toward the ocean boldly led them on;

But ere he'd far on this his journey gone,
A native host appeared in warlike guise,
And warned him back with loud, defiant cries.
In Indian terror Spanish safety lay,
And Vasco Nuñez opened, then, the fray,
And filled the savage mind with wild dismay.
The arquebuse's flash, and deaf'ning sound,
And the impatient bloodhound's fatal bound,
Spread consternation through the naked throng—
The victims of Invasion's blighting wrong—
Who through the forest fled to shun their foes,
To them, forever, lost their old repose :
But Peace, ere long, o'er brutal War prevailed,
And Cheeps, the chieftain, Spanish guests regaled,
And calabashes brought them, filled with gold,
Which gladdened Vasco Nuñez to behold ;
Who, in return, gave mirrors, beads and bells,
Which charmed the unadorned barbaric belles,
And made the chieftain feel unwonted pride,
While all his people, too, for baubles sighed.
Those left behind where Quaraquah was slain
Were ordered on, their comrades to regain,
While scouts were sent by Vasco to explore
The shortest way to reach the sea-beat shore.
Alonzo Martin reached it ere the rest,
And there embarked on ocean's tranquil breast,
And said—" The first of Spaniards here am I !
Such glory reconciles a man to die ! "
Then Vasco Nuñez with a chosen few—
A band of twenty-six, well armed, and true—
Advanced until he gained the ocean's verge *
And heard, in whisp'ring tones, its sullen dirge.
He knelt beneath a tufted palm-tree there,

---

* He left the village of Cheeps, or Chiapes, on the 29th of
September, and reached the ocean on St. Michael's day, and
called the spot St. Michael's Bay.

And thanked the Holy Trinity in prayer.
The rising tide to meet him seemed to run,
And shone like molten metal in the sun ;
And when it reached his feet, he cried aloud—
" Of this achievement I am truly proud ! "
And, with the Virgin's banner in his hand,
He rose, and left his comrades on the strand,
Unsheathed his sword, and wading to his knees,
Said—" Mark ! I take possession of the seas,
And all the coasts, and isles, they'll yet reveal,
For Arragon, and Leon, and Castile—
For Ferdinand, Juana, and the Crown !
Long live the King, and Queen, of great renown !
This gulf I name, as 't is St. Michael's day—
In honor of the saint—St. Michael's Bay.
Spain here—henceforth—shall hold eternal sway,
And, while the world endures, let all obey ! "
Those on the shore responded with applause,
And vowed, as Spaniards, to defend her cause :
Then tasting of the waters, rising near,
" Each drop," said they, " doth savor of a tear.
We taste the ocean in the sparkling brine.
The hand that led us is the hand Divine.
Thank God once more, to whom the glory be,
For guiding Christians to this mighty sea ! "
Then crosses on the trees they carved with care,
And Vasco Nuñez knelt again in prayer,
For Chivalry, and Faith went hand in hand—
The Sword, and Cross—among the daring band,
Whose minds were tinged with superstitious hues,
And prone to conjure too romantic views.

III.

The Spanish chief the country round explored,
Inspiring terror of the Christian's sword,

And adding daily to his golden hoard,
While natives told him tales of old Peru,
And fired his ardor for adventures new.
At length he said—" I'll venture on the deep,
And gold, and pearls, in other regions reap,"
Though warned the stormy season had begun,
And of the risk canoes at sea would run.
With sixty men, and nine equipped canoes,
And stalwart braves to constitute his crews,
He started on his enterprising cruise.
Across the bay the small armada steered,
But those on board ere long the danger feared.
For winds blew high, and waves tumultuous rolled,
And quicker beat the hearts of e'en the bold :
But ere the night they reached an islet's beach,
And said—" Once more for help we God beseech ! "
They sank to rest, but ere they'd slumbered long
The winds, and ocean, sang a wilder song.
The waters foamed, and rose by swift degrees,
And breakers rushed, and roared, and lashed the
    trees,
And one by one their topmost boughs submerged.
The night was dark ; the skiffs were fast below,
With billows o'er them dancing to and fro.
The ocean round the islet wildly surged,
And, fleetly, foot by foot it smaller grew
Until at last it vanished from the view ;
Yet still the waters round the Spaniards rose—
Who felt despairing, agonizing throes—
And reached their girdles where they, trembling,
    stood.
The breakers seemed to clamor for their blood,
And sounds appalling drifted o'er the flood.
"To Father, Son, and Holy Ghost, I cry—
And to the Holy Virgin—ere I die,"
Said Vasco Nuñez :—" Let their will be done,

But still I trust my course has not been run,
And that I'll live to see another sun."
Just then the moon above the waters shone,
A welcome sovereign on her silver throne—
And less terrific grew the winds and waves.
" Behold, His children thus Jehovah saves ! "
The Spanish chieftain cried to those around :—
" In realms above each Christian here is crowned !"
The waters slowly ebbed, and land was seen,
Touched by the Queen of Night with mellow sheen ;
And all rejoiced where all had mourned before,
Their awful peril from submersion o'er.
When on their Ararat had dawned the day
They found their food and clothing washed away,
With all that, erst, in their flotilla lay,
And shattered wrecks alone of this remained.
The spectacle the Spaniards deeply pained.
They—faint, and weary—gazed in mute despair.
But each for safety spoke, at heart, a prayer.
Then Vasco Nuñez said—" We'll these repair,"
And with their girdles some were braced, and
    bound,
But few canoes that still could float were found,
And some in splintered fragments strewed the
    ground.
The cracks, and holes, were caulked with pounded
    weeds,
And covered, here and there with riven reeds ;
And all embarked in these surviving arks—
Four fragile, crippled, overladen barks—
Which on the bounding waters rose and fell,
And trembled in the vortex of the swell.
Sunk almost to the foaming verge were they
And those within were dashed with flying spray,
While ev'ry yawning gulf between the waves
Suggested to the gazers wat'ry graves.

All day they toiled, both hungered and athirst,
And some in silence, Vasco Nuñez cursed;
But as the sun forsook the western sky,
They reached the land, and gave a joyful cry.
"T was midnight ere they gained the Indian town,
Where Vasco Nuñez preached the Cross and
    Crown,
But unsubmissive found the native host,
Who warned him, through his guides, to leave the
    coast;
Whereon he let the raging bloodhounds loose,
And fired his arms till all had cried a truce,
When he his booty found in gold and pearls,
And beauty saw, in all the native girls,
While in abundance fruits, and homely fare,
Were garnered in the habitations there.
The morning proved the land divinely fair.
There plantains, and bananas, clustered, grew,
And sweet ananas showed their golden hue,
And pear-like cherimoyas pendant hung,
And cocoanuts were nestling in the trees,
And yellow maize was waving in the breeze,
And pomegranates seemed to blush within.
Perchance 't was such that tempted Eve to sin.
A wilderness of fruit and bloom was here,
And harvest-time for man was all the year.
But now, behold! the Red Man's doom was near.

IV.

The Spanish leader sent his Indian guides
To seek the chief along the mountain sides,
And him—Tummakko—there, at length, they found,
And begged he'd meet the Spaniards, so renowned,
Who served their friends, but punished all their foes.
He, with them, sent his son to peace propose,

And when with gifts the young cazique returned,
No more with wrath the injured father burned.
Thus friendly actions hatred soon dispelled,
And Indians in the Spaniards gods beheld.
The chieftain added largely to their spoil,
While they in pleasure found relief from toil.
Two hundred pearls he gave them, great in size,
Which kindled signs of rapture in their eyes,
And then he told them where he gathered these—
The precious jewels fashioned by the seas.
Five leagues away the pearly islands lay,
And he dispatched his divers there for more,
And with them journeyed Spaniards, to explore.
" Beyond them, further south," said he, " there lies
A country that invites your enterprise,
Where gold abounds, and lamas burdens bear.
Great houses, built of stone and brick are there ;
And garments you may see the people wear ;
While o'er the realm a mighty monarch reigns,
And all is done that he—the chief—ordains."
Thus of Peru again Don Vasco heard,
And glowing thoughts, once more, his bosom stirred.
The chieftain traced, with inartistic hand,
The outline of a lama in the sand.
" A camel!" cried Balboa. " 'T is the East,
For only there is found that noble beast.
How much I long this ocean to explore,
But I must first return, the mountains o'er,
And gather strength to conquer as I go,
For Kubla Khan may prove himself a foe.
Behold, my comrades, what Columbus sought !
Who knows with what this great event is fraught ? "

To him Tum-mak-ko gave a vast canoe,
Hewn from the tallest tree, the country grew,
And manned by Indians, o'er a hundred strong.

A hundred feet, and ten, the craft was long,
And all its paddles were with pearls inlaid,
While in its centre rose a roof for shade.
In this the Spanish leader left the shore,
Beyond the bay, the seaboard to explore,*
And landing there again, with sword in hand,
He cried—" I take possession of the land ! "
And wading deep—his banner o'er him raised—
Said—" Father, Son and Holy Ghost be praised ! "
The pencilled forms of islands met his view .
Against the mighty vault of heavenly blue—
The Isles of Pearl that later famous grew—†
And .with a wistful eye he scanned them o'er,
Athirst to glean the harvest, rich, they bore ;
But he was wisely warned not there to go
When winds were prone in sudden gusts to blow,
And—prudence-led—refused to venture far,
For he was born beneath an evil star,
And deemed it rash, too much to test his fate.
Still later he Tum-mak-ko bade adieu,‡
And steered to Tee-o-kan his great canoe,
Where he, the chieftain captured, and despoiled,
And, then, for gold, and pearls—his plunder—
    toiled,—
And deemed his duty to his country done,—
Yet o'er to friendship, soon, the savage won ;
For something in his courtly manner charmed,
And enmity in native breasts disarmed.
He, now, prepared to leave this Southern Sea,
But, ere he journeyed, bent, in prayer, the knee,
And asked protection from the Holy Three.

---

* This was on the 29th of October, 1513.

† Vasco Nuñez named the group the Pearl Islands, and the central and largest one of the number Isla Rica.

‡ He left on the 3d of November, 1513, for the province of the Cazique Tee-o-kan, or Teaochan.

His course across the mountains, backward, lay,
And up the steep ascent he led the way,
With all his band, and friendly native guides :
But as they climbed the Cordilleras' sides
They searched for water, day by day, in vain,
And vainly, too, devoutly prayed for rain.
The burning sun above them brightly shone ;
And tortures made the panting toilers groan ;
While many sank exhausted to the ground ;
And by their thirst all former ills were crowned.
At length they found a fountain in a glen,
And felt a joy unpictured e'er by pen.
The chieftain here was Poncar, rich in gold—
Of whose great wealth they long before were told—
And to the village, where his wigwam rose,
The Spaniards hurried, heedless of repose :
But he had fled, distrustful of his foes,
Though, in abundance, gold he left behind—
Three thousand crowns of precious shining ore—
Which only served to make them long for more ;
And so they sent their guides to bring him back—
To coax, and soothe, or threaten with attack—
And Poncar came, with three exalted braves.
The Spaniards said—"Your flight has made you
     slaves !
Reveal your mines, or perish where you stand ! "
They told whate'er they knew of this their land,
But those who questioned, doubted as they spoke,
And into angry speech before them broke,
And tortured them new riches to disclose,
Then added brutal murder to their woes ;
For they were torn by bloodhounds where they
     stood ;
And Innocence—defenceless—shed its blood.
Foul be this blot on daring Vasco's fame ;
And yet he did it in the Saviour's name.

V.

Where Poncar died they tarried thirty days,
And chanted morn, and eve, Jehovah's praise,
And met the comrades they had left behind—
To whom they found that Fortune had been kind—
And gathered gold where'er it met their sight,
And wooed the native maidens with delight.
Then, through Comagre, by its river, wild,
O'er rugged mountains, slowly, they defiled ;
And precipices climbed that crossed their course,
And heard the condor's cry—above them—hoarse;
And into deep, umbrageous valleys passed,
While Famine forced them long, at times, to fast ;
And those—the natives—who their burdens bore,
In numbers sank, alas ! to rise no more.
At length, they reached a village, and supplies,
And raised, in prayer, to God their grateful eyes.
Though prone to sin their faith was deep and strong,
And faith they thought atoned for ev'ry wrong ;
And by the sword they deemed they served the
    Cross ;
And saw salvation in their golden dross.
By bigotry, and superstition swayed,
The Spaniards sinned, and then for pardon prayed,
And for their crimes implored Almighty aid.

VI.

They now advanced to meet a great cazique,
Whose name the guides with terror seemed to
    speak—
Tu-ban-a-ma, whose deeds had won renown—
And forced a march upon his mountain town.
With sixty men—the strongest of his band—

Balboa swiftly reached the chieftain's land,
And stealthily, and suddenly, by night—
When he, and his, were unprepared for fight—
Descended on his primitive abode,
And blood from unoffending bodies flowed.
The chieftain, and his household gathered there,
Were captured, as if led into a snare,
And he—astounded—groaned in wild despair.
To learn the secret of his golden store
Balboa told him he should rule no more,
And gave the order—" Tie him hand, and foot,
And give him to the dogs before his hut !"
And anger with the trembling savage feigned,
Who asked the charge on which he stood arraigned.
"Take all my gold, and bid me find you more,
But spare my life—great swordsman—I implore !"
In touching accents, spoke the mountain chief,
While all his wives, and people, shared his grief.
Don Vasco, yielding, said—" Your life I spare !
Now let your braves your ransom hither bear !"
Three thousand crowns in gold, at dawn, they
    brought—
Ore into forms artistic rudely wrought—
And—later—yet three thousand crowns beside.
The Spaniards with delight the treasure eyed,
And, Vasco Nuñez set the chieftain free.
" This much," said he, " he well deserves from
    me !"

Ere long the way-worn band the march resumed,
But some to death by fell disease were doomed,
And health no more in Vasco's features bloomed,
For Fever's burning hand had touched his brow,
And to the tyrant he was forced to bow ;
But, quickly, he regained his wonted air,
And in the toilsome journey bore his share.

The sick, in hammocks, followed in the rear,
And these he strove to comfort, and to cheer,
While down the rugged slope he led the way,
And longed once more to sight Darien's bay.
The broad Atlantic glittered far below
As on they marched with weary steps, and slow,
But in the end they reached the northern shore,
With all their pearls, and all their golden ore,
And haggard faces looks of pleasure wore.
They through Comagre passed to Coyba's coast,
And met Careeta, and his friendly host,
And told their story grand to comrades there,
Who longed their glory, and their gold, to share.
The brigantine lay waiting on the strand,
And Vasco, there embarking, left the land,
And reached Darien ere the morrow's eve,*
Where some the wondrous tale could scarce be-
    lieve :
But when they saw the wealth of pearls, and gold,
No more they doubted aught their comrades told.
" The ocean that Columbus sought I've found,"
Don   Vasco   cried—" Success   the   search   has
    crowned !
The riches of the Orient are ours,
And we, ere long, shall gaze upon its towers,
And gather spoil in Mangi, and Cathay,
And o'er the East extend the Christian's sway ;
For, soon, again I'll seek the other shore,
And far and wide that Southern Sea explore !"

VII.

Don Vasco wrote the tidings to the Crown,
And felt he'd won the laurels of renown,

---

* The 19th of January, 1514.

And to his monarch's favor paved the way.
Before him, now, a world of promise lay.
He sent the royal fifth, and more, to Spain,
And waited for rewards he hoped to gain.
His caravel, howe'er, was slow to sail,
And—later on—was crippled by a gale,
So ere the gold, and tidings, reached the Court,
Enciso there had made an ill report,
For with his wrongs his nature bubbled o'er,
And hate he, toward his rival, Vasco, bore,
Who governed but, said he, by force, and fraud,
And who had been in Hayti's isle outlawed.
"Another I will send to rule the land,
And supersede Balboa in command,"
Exclaimed the King, and Davila* he chose
To journey west, Don Vasco to depose,
And strip him of the honors that he claimed.
A soldier, for his martial prowess famed,
This Davila—Pedrarias—was brave,
And yet, at heart, a tyrant, and a knave.
Zamudio—Don Vasco's friend—in vain
For him—Balboa—favor strove to gain,
Though he had with Enciso bade him sail
To counteract at Court his evil tale.

'T was then that Colmenaris home returned,
From whom the monarch cheering tidings learned—
The secret of the mighty Southern Sea.
"A thousand men," wrote Vasco, "send to me,
That I may cross the mountain range between,
And conquer that which Christian ne'er hath seen."
Ambition, av'rice moved the monarch's breast.
"A fleet," said he, "shall voyage to the West,
With Davila—the gallant—in command;"

---

* Don Pedro Arias Davila, commonly called Pedrarias.

And fifteen ships, and caravels, ere long,— *
Manned by chivalrous souls—two thousand strong—
Sailed down the Guadalquivir, westward bound,
To seek the sea Don Vasco erst had found.
A little later Vasco's caravel—
That came his story of success to tell—
Was borne upon the Guadalquivir's swell.
Her captain—Arbolancha†—sought the King,
And said—" O Sire ! to you I treasures bring,
And tidings of a sea before unknown,
And regions that with gold, and pearls are sown—
All which are now beneath your righteous sway.
That sea, methinks, doth lead to rich Cathay.
Don Vasco Nuñez 't was who gained the prize—
The splendid fruit of noble enterprise—
And he is eager still for conquests, new,
And fain would reach an empire called Peru,
Where cities rise in grandeur on the view,
And ships with sails career o'er ocean's blue,
And camels bear their burdens to and fro,
And gold like vegetation seems to grow.
He only waits to swell his valiant band
Ere he returns to conquer all the land,
And gorgeous Oriental shores explore,
And harvests reap of gems, and golden ore."
The monarch heard the tale with glad surprise—
Which gave a diamond glitter to his eyes—
And sore repented of the deed he'd done.
Don Vasco Nuñez great renown had won,
And yet the fleet that westward ploughed its way,
Ere long, would leave him shorn of all his sway.

---

* This fleet sailed from San Lucar on the 12th of April, 1514.

† Pedro de Arbolancha, a firm friend of Balboa's, who had been in the expedition to the Pacific.

Had Vasco's vessel sooner come to Spain,
Triumphant would have been the hero's reign—.
So much on little oftentime doth hinge,
And moments, with their stain, may ages tinge.
Castile resounded with Don Vasco's praise,
And King, and country, wreathed his name with
  bays.

VIII.

In peaceful toil he passed his days the while,
And made the earth with blooming orchards smile,
And fashioned fields, and gardens, fair to view,
Where in abundance all he planted grew;
And awed, or won, the natives, far and near,
Till sons of Spain from these had naught to fear.
His band was, now, five hundred strong, and more,
And all the look of gallant spirits bore.
They built a city on Darien's shore,
Which prospered well beneath their leader's sway,
Who looked for coming ships from day to day,
Resolving there to wait for news from Spain
Ere he rsturned to range the southern main.
At length, in June, one splendid moonlit night,
Castile's armada slowly hove in sight,
And anchored, from the coast, two leagues away.
Pedrarias an envoy sent to land,
Announcing his arrival, and command,
Who marvelled at Don Vasco's simple state—
One whose pretensions he had heard were great—
An unassuming man in homely dress,
But with a courtly mien, and grand address.
Don Vasco felt chagrin, and some surprise,
Yet none betrayed before the envoy's eyes,
And answered—" Tell the Don he's welcome here,
Where all the holy Cross, and Crown, revere ;

And he will find me willing to obey;
And to his hands I, now, resign my sway."
But many cried—" Invaders we'll repel.
Against them all 't is virtue to rebel.
Don Vasco rules : his banner we'll sustain,
And o'er us ne'er this new recruit shall reign !
Long live the King,—long live the Queen—of
   Spain ! "
But Vasco said—" Your duty is to yield.
Reserve your prowess for a fairer field ; "
And all were, then, submissive to his will,
Though some exclaimed—" The signs, indeed, are
   ill,"
And felt their blood with indignation warm.
Each floating hive disgorged its human swarm,
And o'er two thousand Spaniards landed there,
With flags, and music, floating on the air,
While at their head Pedrarias was seen,
His wife beside him, gorgeous as a queen,
And pomp, and splendor glitt'ring all around.
Balboa bowed with rev'rence deep, profound,
And said, " I yield obedience, and love,"
And wished him countless blessings from above,
Then led him to the wigwam where he dwelt,
And Nature's garden gifts—abundant—dealt.

The new commander friendly feelings feigned,
And from Don Vasco all his secrets gained,
But only then to own himself a foe,
And strike a paltry tyrant's cruel blow.
He charged him with Enciso's overthrow,
And Nicuesa's death, and minor crimes,
And vengeance vowed in hatred sundry times,
So jealous felt he of his great renown.
With petty spite he strove to beat him down,
And meant, in chains, to send him back to Spain,

But fearing this might prove the captive's gain,
And Vasco be a hero none the less,
In other ways he labored to oppress.
He tried to colonize the southern coast,
That this might ne'er become his rival's boast,
And hide, or filch, the laurels he had won—
The glory of the deeds that he had done :
But Retribution followed him with speed,
For Pestilence around him sowed its seed,
And nigh a thousand perished of his band,
While he was stricken, too, by Fever's hand,
And Famine stalked, the while, throughout the land.
About the huts, and roads, in dire array—
A ghastly sight—the dead unburied lay.
Gaunt Hunger triumphed where disease had failed.
A carnival of death, and want, prevailed.
He said, at length—" All those who will may flee,"
And many sought a refuge on the sea.
Some steered for Cuba's shore their caravel,
And, homeward-bound, some bade the West fare-
    well,
Of ruined health, and fortunes, tales to tell.

IX.

When from his couch Pedrarias arose,
He found his people still oppressed by woes,
And bade them o'er their sorrows cease to brood,
And range the country far, and near, for food,
Else they would perish in the wild domain.
The work was done, nor proved the task in vain.
Then other bands were sent in search of gain,
Who wheresoe'er they wandered havoc wrought,
Nor gave to native rights a single thought,
And marred the plans Don Vasco had designed,
By making hostile those who erst were kind.

X.

At length there came a ship direct from Spain,
Whose tidings filled Pedrarias with pain.
It bore a note to Vasco from the king,
Which seemed his rival's heart with rage to wring.
The monarch praised him for his daring deed,
And honors, rank, and offices decreed,
Which left him nigh co-equal with his foe.*
Pedrarias was staggered by the blow.
He sought, himself, the letter to retain,
And time, by wily subterfuge, to gain,
But he was foiled in this ignoble aim ;
And, then, he tried to further blast his fame,
And justify refusal to obey.
" 'T would wrong the king," said he, " to yield him
    sway,
And I should be as nothing where I stand—
A ruler with but little to command."
A compromise, howe'er, at last was made
By which he gave the titles, and the grade,
But not the right to govern in the land
Till this was granted at the tyrant's hand.
Don Vasco placed his trust in Time, and Right,
And prophesied a future grand, and bright,
But with his title, friends around him came,
Which roused his foe to blacken more his name.
He charged him with conspiring to rebel—
Yet in substantiation naught could tell—
And, seizing him, condemned him to a cage,
So great was the suspicious dastard's rage.

---

* Balboa was appointed Adelantado of the South Sea, and
governor of the provinces of Panama and Coyba, but subordinate to the general command of Pedrarias, who was, however, ordered to consult him on all matters of importance.

From this, howe'er, the captive soon was freed
Ere sentence had been followed by the deed :
But Vasco Nuñez, persecution-stung,
Grew poor in purse, and felt at heart unstrung.

XI.

The Southern Sea Pedrarias allured,
And to the Isles of Pearl his heart was moored,
For there he hoped unbounded wealth to reap
In jewels formed and cradled in the deep.
Like Venus, in her beauty, from the foam,
They came perfected from their wat'ry home,
Or, as Minerva from the brain of Jove
They left their shells—the ocean's treasure-trove.
He knew Don Vasco best could lead the way
To where those isles of boundless riches lay,
But that would yet distinguish him the more.
And add a chaplet to the bays he wore.
He bade Morales—Gaspar—journey there,
And named Pizarro, too, the task to share,
For he—Francisco—by their shores had been—
An actor with Don Vasco on the scene.
With sixty daring spirits, born of Spain,
They led the van across the mountain chain,
And paddling from the Southern Ocean's shore,
Their country's banner, to the islets bore :
And there they shed, in battle, native gore,
While arquebuses spoke with rattling roar,
And loosened bloodhounds bayed in hot pursuit,
And, Man, in terror, fled each angry brute :
But Peace, ere long, o'er cruel War prevailed,
And those who erst were foes as friends were hailed.
" A wealth of pearls, but little gold have I,"
The chieftain said, with candor in his eye ;
" But yonder lies a region where it grows,

And gilds the course of ev'ry stream that flows,
And glitters in each river's sandy mouth,"
And as he spoke he pointed toward the south—
Along the line of mountains tall, and grand,
That stretched, till lost to view, beside the strand.
Pizarro heard the story, old, anew,
And saw with mental eyes the land Peru,
And o'er its marvels nigh ecstatic grew,
For wealth, and fame, resolving there to sue.

The   Spanish   throng—triumphant—gleaned   the
    spoils,
And.deemed themselves repaid for all their toils,
Exclaiming—" Fortune's favored ones are we ! "
Well freighted with the jewels of the sea
They left the isles, again to cross the chain,
And tell how great had been their country's gain:
But hard indeed they found their journey back,
And fierce the Indian warriors in attack.
Biru—a great cazique—assailed the band,
And forced them, in dismay, to flee the land,
And, as they fled, pursued them day by day;
Then other hosts of Indians gave them fight,
And added to the horrors of their flight,
And to the awful perils of their plight.
A number perished in the bitter strife,
And thirst, and famine, in their midst were rife.
Back to the Southern Sea their wand'rings led,
Where in canoes from seeming death they sped
To climb again the Cordilleras' slope;
But fresh reverses nigh extinguished hope.
Their journey proved a long-continued fray.
At length the remnant reached Darien's Bay,
And spread their pearls before astonished eyes,
While all forgot their perils in their prize.

XII.

Pedrarias, the while, the land explored,
And tried to rule by terror, and the sword.
He made the natives, far and near, his foes,
And banished from the settlement repose.
The Spaniards felt by day, and night, alarm,
So much the signs around them boded harm.
They watched the plains, the mountains, and the
    sea,
And danger seemed, where'er they gazed, to see.
The green savannas waving in the breeze,
The silver streams, and patriarchal trees,
For lurking foes, by anxious eyes, were scanned,
And oft, in prayer for safety, knelt the band.

XIII.

While thus with cares Pedrarias was vexed,
And by his feud with Vasco much perplexed,
The *Padre*—yea, the Bishop—of the fold
His plan for peace to him—the leader—told.
"Why quarrel thus," said he, "with one so bold,
And make a foe when you might win a friend—
One who could either punish, or defend,
And serve you well, or work you grievous ill?
The bitter cup for him why further fill,
And strengthen more your people's evil will?
One course remains to blot the past from view,
And this, I pray, with willing heart, pursue.
You've daughters fair: on Vasco one bestow,
And blessings on your head from this will flow.
A popular hidalgo in his prime,
And with a record splendid, and sublime,
He'll shed his lustre on your own career,

And while—infirm—you fail from year to year
He in the noon, and vigor of his days—
And favored by the King with grateful praise—
Can guide affairs, and mitigate your toil,
And pour on Faction's waters soothing oil."
Pedrarias by argument was won,
And said—" I'll take Don Vasco as my son."
His spouse consented ere the day was done,
And Vasco found his courtship had begun—
A happy ending he had ne'er divined.
The tender vows of marriage, soon, were signed,
And Vasco gave his promise to be true :
But naught of this the daughter chosen knew,
Nor had Balboa e'er the maiden seen.
The broad Atlantic rolled, the two, between,
For she was still a happy girl in Spain,
Though summoned now, in haste, to cross the main.
The suitor viewed the prospect with delight,
For sorrow fled, and all around was bright,
Though he remembered he'd an Indian bride—
A faithful friend, companion, slave, and guide—
And o'er the thought of parting faintly sighed.
The Bishop deemed his triumph truly great
To turn to love such jealousy, and hate,
And said—" My friends, I each congratulate ! "

XIV.

Pedrarias—thus won to friendship's side—
In Vasco Nuñez felt a sudden pride,
And, erst a foe, became his dearest friend.
His proffered favors seemed without an end,
And all to his aggrandizement to tend.
He for the past was eager to atone,
And linked Don Vasco's fortunes with his own.
He gave him leave to search the Southern Sea,

And left him in his enterprises free,
Which gave ambition to achieve, a zest.
His cherished project Vasco forward pressed,
And planned to launch a fleet of brigantines
To navigate through ultramontane scenes.
The timber, and the rigging, he prepared,
And then, with zeal, for transportation cared.
Across the mighty mountains these were borne
By negroes from their native Guinea torn,
And Indian braves, who perished by the way.
The task stupendous filled them with dismay
As on they toiled, and struggled day by day.
At length they reached a river by the sea,
And Vasco knelt, and thanked the Trinity :
But worms, alas ! were boring through the wood,
And all, ere long, was swallowed by a flood.
Yet Vasco, undiscouraged, planned anew,
And stately trees he felled that near him grew,
And o'er the Andes sent for fresh supplies,
And saw success attend his enterprise.
Two brigantines on Bolsas river lay,
In which the brave explorer sailed away
Triumphant o'er the obstacles opposed.
In fervent prayer again his eyes were closed,
While in the Faith his confidence reposed.
Appalling oft his daring task had seemed,
But through the gloom the light of Hope had
    gleamed,
And, now, he felt for all his pains repaid,
And asked for triumphs new, Almighty aid.
Before him stretched the vast, mysterious sea—
The restless emblem of Infinity ;—
But who could tell to where its waters led ?
A world unknown before his vision spread,
And Fancy, and Imagination fed.

XV.

To Isla Rica, and the isles around,
Don Vasco, first, in search of pearls, was bound,
And there designed yet other barks to build,
Which he, in thought, with glist'ning treasure filled.
He reached the group, and soon the work began ;
Then down the seaboard south, and eastward, ran :
But, twenty leagues beyond St. Michael's Bay,
His crews beheld what filled them with dismay—
A school of whales, each spouting on its way.
They deemed them rocks, and breakers, in the night,
And anchored till the morn had shed its light,
Intending, still, their voyage to pursue ;
But when it dawned the wind against them blew,
And with it Vasco Nuñez changed his course,
And landed at Chuchama all his force,
Avenging there a troop of Spaniards slain— *
To glorify the Cross, and Crown of Spain—
Till blood had stained the mountains, and the plain,
And bloodhounds made a hecatomb of dead.
Then to the Isles of Pearl again he sped,
Nor knew how much his altered course had cost.
By that event, to him, Peru was lost,
For had he onward kept his wat'ry way,
Perchance he'd soon have found that new Cathay ;
And all his future might have thus been changed,
And he, a victor, o'er an empire ranged.

XVI.

On went the work of building brigantines,
And Isla Rica witnessed busy scenes,

---

* A party of ten belonging to the expedition of Francisco
Pizarro and Gaspar Morales.

While Vasco sent from sea to sea again
For fresh supplies—a gang of fitting men.
Then tidings from Darien reached his ear,
Which made him eager further news to hear.
Pedrarias was ordered back to Spain,
And, in his stead, another sent to reign.
A new commander might his work undo,
And, more to learn, he more impatient grew,
He chose a comrade he esteemed as true,
And said—"Across the mountains journey you,
And—as your outward purpose—seek supplies,
And act with prudence as becomes the wise.
If he—Pedrarias—still ruleth there,
A courtly message to the courtier bear.
Tell all we've done, and all that lies before,
And of munitions ask a further store;
Say, too, of soldiers, that we need some more;
Explain delays, and promise greater speed,
And take of all he says respectful heed:
But if a ruler, new, has come from Spain,
Not there a moment, ere you turn, remain,
And hasten back, the tidings to impart,
That we, ere orders come, may hence depart,
And eastward sail, the country to explore,
And gather as we go the golden ore:"
But Garabito—such was he by name—
Resolved to blight his noble leader's fame.
Toward Vasco, long he'd felt a secret hate,
And, now, said he—"On me depends his fate!"
Vindictive, dastard, foul, and base at heart
He gloried in revenge—his cruel part.
Ere this he'd warned Pedrarias by stealth
That Vasco aimed alone at power, and wealth,
And meant to act with independent sway,
And make himself the ruler of Cathay,
Nor e'er designed his daughter fair to wed

As by an Indian beauty he was led.
Pedrarias—the jealous, and the proud—
On reading this, his wrath expressed aloud,
And all his old suspicions rose anew,
And with the lapse of time but deeper grew,
While Vasco's foes—of whom he numbered few—
Of this distrust, were quick to fan the flame,
And strove his name—in malice—to defame.

XVII.

Perfidious Garabito!—why so base,
And yet a loving friend to Vasco's face ?
Know then Careeta's daughter charmed his eye,
And words between the friends had once run high ;
And those which Vasco spoke in angry heat
Were cherished as a morsel—bitter—sweet.
Malignant in his spirit, this was bliss,
And yet, like Judas, he could Vasco kiss.

XVIII.

Pedrarias, he found commander, still,
Though one, ere this, had come, his place to fill,
But in the harbor, ere he landed, died.
To rouse suspicion Vasco's envoy tried,
And thus was summoned to the ruler's side,
And captive held, his purpose to disclose.
His capture broke the colony's repose,
For all exclaimed—" Behold, the ancient feud
'Twixt Vasco, and Pedrarias, renewed ! "
Then Garabito told whate'er he knew,
And much beside it wilfully untrue—
All he suspected, and surmised, and more,
To gratify the malice that he bore.
On this a friend of Vasco's felt alarm,

And warned him that his foes designed him harm,
And bade him put to sea without delay,
Nor trust to Don Pedrarias a day,
But look to the Jeronymites * for aid
If charges e'er against him should be made;
For these—the Fathers—would, in Hayti's isle,
On this, his expedition, gladly smile,
Believing 't would the holy Faith diffuse,
And Spain would gain what infidels would lose.

The note was intercepted on its way,
Which filled its hapless writer with dismay,
And he was seized, and in a dungeon chained.
Pedrarias a love of justice feigned,
And said—"A plot! Behold my knowledge
  gained!"
His aim was, now, Don Vasco to secure.
He, therefore, sought his victim to allure,
For force would on the Southern Sea be vain
With valiant spirits in the hero's train.
Dissembling feeling he to Vasco wrote—
Nor conscience e'er the simulator smote—
And asked him to Careeta to repair,
And promised, when he came, to meet him there,
Expressing friendship as he'd done before:
But fearing Vasco would his note ignore,
He sent Pizarro, with a chosen troop,
To seek Don Vasco at the island group,
And bring him, if he could, the mountains o'er—
A fettered captive to Careeta's shore.

---

* Through the representations of Las Casas with respect to
the cruel treatment of the Indians, Cardinal Ximenes, in 1516,
had appointed three Jeronymite Friars to proceed to San
Domingo, and remain there, to remedy all abuses connected
with the treatment of the natives; and the exercise of their
authority had a powerful effect for good in the New World.

Balboa's friends to warn him felt afraid,
Lest they should captives, too, for this, be made,
And Terror seemed among them all to reign.
The friendly Bishop erst had left for Spain,
Or he—perchance—would here his voice have
 raised,
And, as a friend, the valiant Vasco praised.

PART III.

. The Fate of Vasco Nunez de Balboa.

'T was night at Isla Rica—lustrous night,
And brightly shed the moon her silver light,
Illuminating grandly sea, and land—
The lesser isles, and continental strand,
And far away, but vivid to the eye,
The Cordilleras, vast, eternal, high—
While stars with scintillations filled the sky.
The tranquil waters like a mirror shone,
And Night's Sultana sat a dazzling throne.
Don Vasco stood, a gazer on the scene,
His figure lighted with the splendid sheen,
And looking upward saw a luckless sign.
"'T is strange," said he, " a star doth yonder shine,
That tells me I'm in peril of my life ;
Yet naught around me seems with danger rife.
In health, and strength, I feel I've naught to
 crave,
Nor fear I, yet, I'll fill an early grave.
Three hundred men have I, well armed, and brave,
And brigantines—aye, four of these—beside
With which to navigate this southern tide,
And wealth, and glory, waiting where I go.

What more could man aspire to here below?
Yet Micer Codro told me years ago
That when that star shone where it shineth now
Death might condemn me at its shrine to bow.
How vain are these predictions," and he smiled,
" And yet how oft by such are men beguiled!"
'T was on the morn succeeding eve so bright,
While Vasco viewed his future with delight,
That ultramontane tidings reached the isle,
And that ensnaring letter, full of guile.
Don Vasco—unsuspicious—read it o'er,
And all unconscious of the fate in store,
Or of a wrong, to kindle wrath, he'd done,
Obeyed the summons ere another sun,
And left his force to wait his quick return ;
For he was slow his danger to discern.
A faithful few, from those who held command,
Alone he chose of all his valiant band
To cross the Andes to the northern strand.
'T was as they climbed the lofty mountain chain—
And far below them saw the glitt'ring main—
That those who brought the tidings, feeling kind,
Told Vasco what Pedrarias designed.
He marvelled much, and scarce the truth believed.
He felt as if his senses had deceived.
What cause so great a change, so soon, could work ?
What secret in this sudden wrath could lurk ?
Some transient ire—perchance—had moved to hate,
Or foes had labored envy to create,
But this his presence, soon, would dissipate.
Could he who'd pledged his fairest daughter's hand,
Her suitor seek to ruin in the land ?
Thus musing he continued on his way,
Nor sought his forward movement to delay,
Though on his course he might have turned the
    while,

And journeyed backward to the southern isle,
And there repelled pursuers from the shore,
And sailed upon his voyage to explore.

II.

As Vasco climbed the Cordilleras' side,
And led the way, his comrades' valiant guide—
While Echo to his mountain song replied—
He saw a troop, Pizarro at its head,
And faster—to embrace him—onward sped:
But in his greeting he was strangely cold,
And, then, on Vasco's arm laid sudden hold.
His story, by the action, he had told.
"I come," said he, "to take you back in chains;
You're branded as an enemy of Spain's."
Don Vasco looked, astonished, in his face,
Then yielded to be manacled with grace.
"Is this," said he—reproachful in his tone—
"The way that you, to serve a friend are prone?
Francisco, ah! Francisco, we were friends:
Remember God the innocent defends!"
Then he was led to Acla on the coast,
Where dwelt Careeta, and his swarthy host,
And in a dungeon there was left to mourn,
From all his rights, and freedom, rudely torn.

III.

Pedrarias pretended friendship still,
And said—"Toward Vasco I've no evil will;"
Then visited the captive in his jail,
And told him a dissimulator's tale.
" Feel not," said he, "oppressed by this, my son;—
Not less could I, in duty, now have done
In view of accusations that were made;—

Nor of this transient rigor be afraid;
Your innocence will, doubtless, soon be proved,
And these suspicions of your guilt removed—
Your loyalty established to Castile,
And to your king exhibited your zeal: "
But while he thus to soothe his victim spoke,
And hope within his drooping breast awoke,
He turned to Espinosa,* of the law,
And said—" Indict the wretch, without a flaw,
For treason to King Ferdinand of Spain—
Conspiracy to filch the southern main—
And those—his comrades—who are with him, too :
Methinks that to the Crown they're all untrue."
'T was done, and Vasco's trial soon began.
He stood before the court an injured man,
While Garabito swore to heartless lies,
And showed the love of vengeance in his eyes,
And falsehood in the movement of his hand.
Its progress by Pedrarias was scanned,
And when the perjured villain told his tale—
" Ha, ah," said he, " not, now, will justice fail ! "
And sought again the victim of his wiles
But he no more bestowed upon him smiles.
He pulled the mask of kindness from his face,
And showed a foe without a Christian grace.
" Till now," he spoke, with fierce, upbraiding tone,
" I deemed you true and loyal to the Throne,
And unto me, the servant of the Crown :
But in your thirst—ambitious—for renown
I find you've been rebellious in your aim
And on your name, and mine, have cast a stain.
For you no more affection I can bear,
Nor can you e'er the flagrant wrong repair.

---

* Gaspar de Espinosa, the alcalde mayor, and only lawyer
and magistrate in the colony.

Henceforth you'll find I'll treat you as a foe,
And Justice may return you blow for blow."
Don Vasco's indignation flushed his cheek,
And he began in self-defence to speak.
" Had I been conscious of my guilt," said he,
" Would I for this have left the Southern Sea ?
Was my confiding frankness proof of wrong
When I was there with barks, and comrades, strong ?
What need had I, if aught had I to fear,
To journey o'er the Cordilleras here ?—
To trust to mercy at your cruel hands
When straight before me lay inviting lands?
If I had been rebellious in design
The fitting opportunity was mine,
For ships, and men—an ample force—had I,
To win my way and all my foes defy.
I'd but to spread my sails, and forward press—
Beseeching God the enterprise to bless—
To reap a golden harvest far away
In regions independent of your sway.
Yet in my simple guilelessness of heart—
My innocence—I played this fatal part,
And at your mere request, in friendly guise,
Put off my promised southern enterprise,
And came to meet you, willing to obey :
And yet behold me where I am to-day—
Degraded, slandered, dungeoned, and in chains.
What else for me but death itself remains ? "
But all in vain Don Vasco thus appealed.
He found the tyrant's heart to mercy steeled,
For he exasperation showed the more,
And multiplied the manacles he wore,
And urged with malice, and indecent speed,
The inquisition faster to proceed,
And all the ancient charges, then, revived,
And at conviction with his foes connived :

But still the trial slowly dragged along,
For Espinosa recognized the wrong,
And felt aversion for the task imposed.
At length his judicative labors closed,
And GUILTY Vasco Nuñez was pronounced;
But as this cruel verdict was announced
He said—" To mercy, Vasco I commend,
For empire he has labored to extend,
And shed unfading lustre on the Crown,
While for himself, achieving great renown,
And this will live, and brighter grow with time.
The written law convicts him of the crime,
But guiltless still his motives may have been:
The hearts of men by God alone are seen.
I, too, advise permission to appeal
From this our court to that of old Castile."
The sentence on his comrades was the same, *
Though guiltless, too, of treasonable aim.

IV.

Pedrarias with unrelenting hate,
Impatient felt to seal his victim's fate,
Exclaiming—" No appeal I'll tolerate,
Nor mercy more for such as he have I.
If he is guilty, let the traitor die,
Nor ere his death must needless moments fly.
To execution bear the wretch away."
In Vasco's death he deemed his safety lay,
For he had gone too far to e'er retreat,
And, with the proverb, said—" Revenge is sweet."

---

* Three of his officers—Valderrabano, Munos, and Botello
—and Hernanda de Arguello, who had written the intercepted letter. Garabito, the informer and perjurer, was,
however, pardoned. The trial and execution took place in
the year 1517.

He'd ever as a rival Vasco viewed,
And Garabito's tale his hate renewed—
The hate the marriage articles had lulled—
A contract thus by death to be annulled.
To spurn his daughter, and dispute his sway,
Was, to his mind, the part he meant to play:
But Vasco ne'er designed his pledge to break—
The soon expected maiden to forsake,
But gladly would have wed her when she came,
While ne'er was he a rebel in his aim,
Though, once embarked upon the Southern Sea,
He meant his course of action should be free,
Resolved capricious orders to discard,
Nor let, by these, his enterprise be marred.
Though he designed his conquests but for Spain—
Nor toward her felt an atom of disdain—
His own deserts, the favor of the throne,
The jealousies and obstacles he'd known,
The offices the Sovereign had bestowed,
The love and friendship that compatriots showed,
Alike encouraged boldness of design,
And made him long with lustre, new, to shine.

V.

O'er Acla, gloom and horror seemed to reign,
When Vasco, and his melancholy train,
Emerged upon the populace's view,
While still, and breathless, the observers grew.
The scene of execution was the square,
And all the Spaniards congregated there,
And few were they whose eyes were unbedewed.
The spectacle with sorrow all imbued.
They thought of Vasco's gallant deeds of arms,
His noble mien, his chivalry and charms,
The persecution he had calmly borne,

The rights of which they'd seen him rudely shorn,
The dauntless, daring enterprise he'd shown,
The Southern Sea—a triumph all his own,
The glory for the Cross and Crown he'd won,
The grander deeds expected, but undone,
The coming maiden, ne'er to be his bride,
Pedrarias, his tyranny, and pride ;
But such was of the tyrant, now, the dread
That from each bosom native courage fled,
And none for Vasco dared a voice to raise.
Hushed, under terror, was the tongue of Praise.
The crier, thus proclaiming, led the way—
" A traitor, and usurper, dies to-day,
One who aspired himself a crown to win.
Behold him reap the penalty of sin !
'T is by the King's command the deed is done.
All ye who hearken learn his crime to shun."
As Vasco heard the words he cried—" 'T is false :
I ne'er rebelled, whate'er have been my faults,
Nor harbored of the crime a single thought,
But loyally to serve my Sovereign sought,
And ever strove to widen his domain.
God knows of my fidelity to Spain ! "
His dying words were uttered there in vain,
But all who heard them spoken knew them true,
Though naught could they, to save the culprit, do.
The Cordilleras pierced the southern sky.
Toward these he gazed as if to say good-by,
Then turned away, in sadness, with a sigh.
He knelt before the crucifix to pray,
Confessed his sins, and felt them washed away,
Received the holy Sacrament, divine,
And on his bosom, made the Saviour's sign ;
Then, strong in faith, reliant on his God,
The scaffold with a step courageous trod,
The block with calm demeanor boldly faced,

And laid his head where he the cross had traced.
A moment more revealed a headless trunk.
Before the sight the startled gazers shrunk—
All save the tyrant who, in secret, saw ;
And said—" At last triumphant is the law ! "
Then one by one his comrades forth were led
Till three were, like him, numbered with the dead.
A fourth remained—Hernando, Vasco's friend,
Whose warning note involved this fatal end.
Some interceded even now for him
And sought the tyrant in the twilight, dim,
But he was stern, and cruel as before,
And said—" Why ask for pardon o'er, and o'er.
I'd sooner die than one of them should live.
No other answer 't is for me to give,"
And in the tropic twilight's gath'ring gloom
The stroke was heard that sealed the victim's doom.
The concourse vanished in the fading light,
And lamentations ushered in the night :
But even this to soothe the tyrant failed.
" The traitor's head," said he, " I wish impaled ;
Erect a pole within the public square,
And place it as a ghastly warning there.
Whate'er he left I confiscate to Spain.
Triumphant over Treason Law must reign."
For days the breeze caressed the victim's hair,
And fanned the features, picturesque, and fair,
While daily there a plaintive moan arose—
A woman's groan, suggestive of her woes.
Careeta's daughter mourned her idol dead,
And o'er his fate her heart—in anguish—bled.
The promised bride came radiant from the sea
Expecting her hidalgo, brave, to see,
Instead of which she heard the awful tale
That made her turn, with sick'ning horror, pale,
And then she wept, and cried—" Oh, why was this ? "
And found to sorrow turned her hopes of bliss.

VI.

Thus passed away the hero in his prime—*
A guiltless victim, branded deep with crime—
Arrested midway in his grand career,
Yet meeting death without a trace of fear,
His greatest blemish he deserved too well.
He bade the world regretfully farewell—
The prey of base, perfidious designs :
But o'er his grave the myrtle ever twines.
Unjustly dealt a cruel death he died,
And o'er his fate all but his murd'rer sighed,
For Garabito felt at last remorse,
And shed a tear o'er Vasco's headless corse.

PART IV.

The Story of Valdivia.

I.

Valdivia's tragic fate can soon be told.
When he for San Domingo sailed with gold†
Fair blew the winds to waft his caravel,
And till he saw Jamaica all was well.
A gale—a wreck—and he, and twenty more,
A sailless boat directed toward the shore,
But they were tossed nigh half a month at sea
Ere they beheld a country on their lee,

---

* At the time of his execution Balboa was in his forty-second year.

† This was in 1512, on his voyage from Darien—of which he was Regidor—under the orders of Balboa.

And soon were stranded on its verdant coast,
Where round them gathered an unfriendly host,
Who dashed their boat in pieces where it lay,
And bore them captive—to the chief—away.
'T was on the eastern coast of Yucatan.
They heard the name, and thought it Kubla Khan.
Fourteen alone—a famished crew—were left,
And these of all but scanty garb bereft.
The chieftain gave them banquets of the best,
And, in their bondage, they were blessed with rest,
While thankful for escaping to the land.
They saw in this the Lord's protecting hand :
But Terror o'er them soon resumed its sway.
The chief selected five he meant to slay—
Valdivia of the number—and they died,
For all in vain for mercy 't was they cried.
Before the native idols they were bled,
And on their bodies those who slew them fed.
The nine surviving heard their comrades' groans,
And saw anon their flesh-divested bones,
And from their cage, and death so awful, fled,
And in the woods a life of hunger led.
Another chieftain captured them at length,
And made them daily toil beyond their strength,
And one by one they died till two remained—
Gonzalo, and Jeronimo, a priest.*
The first despaired of succor from the east,
And hung his nose, his ears, and lip, with rings,
Tattooed his form, and copied native kings,
And won a chieftain's daughter as his bride.
The other took his calling for his guide,

---

* Gonzalo Guerrero, a sailor, and Jeronimo de Aguilar—a priest. The former became a great warrior, and married a native princess, and the latter was rescued by Cortez, whom he accompanied in his expedition to Mexico, acting in the capacity of interpreter.

And, meek, and chaste, his way to favor found,
And for his wondrous virtues grew renowned.
The chief besought him oft to choose a bride,
And brought the fairest damsels to his side,
But he as oft the proffered boon declined,
And said—"To single life I'm well resigned,
And marriage would to me—a priest—be sin."
The chief could ne'er the priest for woman win,
Though he was left to virgin charms, and wiles,
And wooed to bask in loving Beauty's smiles.
He gently all caressing nymphs rebuked,
Nor e'er with lover's eyes on maiden looked.
By patient houris he was fondly wooed,
But all in vain bewitching woman sued.
Jeronimo preferred his solitude.
Though loving looks, and sighs, on him were rained,
He zealously from wedded life refrained,
And faithful still to priestly vows remained.
Years passed away: Cordova's squadron came, *
But though escape had been his constant aim
The coast was distant, and his captors keen,
And ne'er by him the Spanish ships were seen.
A year, and more, and ships again appeared—
Grijalva's † squadron—but to flee he feared,
For he was still by jealous eyes deterred,
And naught Grijalva of the Spaniards heard.
Another year, and Cortez reached the strand,‡
And, gleaning tidings of Valdivia's band,
A greeting penned, and sent it o'er the land.
An Indian bore it to the Spaniard's hand.

---

* Francisco Hernandez de Cordova sailed along the coast on his voyage of discovery. This was in 1517.

† Juan de Grijalva, who coasted Yucatan in 1518.

‡ This was in 1519.

..e read the welcome missive with delight,
And at the moment meditated flight.
The natives stood around with wond'ring eyes,
For much the speaking paper roused surprise.
Jeronimo said—" Here are mighty men,
With ships, and arms, that far surpass your ken.
The thunder and the lightning they can mock,
And fill the country with the awful shock.
They bless their friends, but all their foemen slay.
Propitiate them then without delay."
" Jeronimo," the chief replied, " depart,
And win for me their great commander's heart."
He sent Gonzalo word, but he replied
He'd evermore in Yucatan abide.
He went, and reached Cozumel's isle at last,
And—naked—told the story of the past,
Though half forgotten seemed his native tongue.
A crimson cloak around him Cortez flung,
And warmly gave him welcome to the fleet.
The long lost wand'rer's heart with rapture beat,
For he'd despaired of meeting Spaniards more,
And cried—" At length, my savage life is o'er."

PART V.

THE ADVENTURES OF PONCE DE LEON.

I.

ROMANTIC and chivalrous sons of Spain
Delighted in adventures on the main,
And none of all the best and worst of these
More loved to range the islands and the seas,
Than Ponce de Leon, who, with storied name,
Passed through a long knight-errantry to fame.

In Moorish wars inured, at first, to arms,
A warrior's life to him was full of charms,
And in Granada many a tilt had he
Ere he embarked his fortunes on the sea.
The second time Columbus sought the west
He bore him out a rover on its breast,*
And when Ovando ravaged Hayti's isle,—
And o'er his work of slaughter seemed to smile,—
Don Ponce de Leon—foremost in the fray—
For gold, and glory, battled day by day,—
As quick to fight as he was prone to pray,—
And cried—" 'T is holy, infidels to slay ! "
When Peace, o'er War at last regained its sway
He looked around for wild adventures, new,
And Porto Rico's island met his view.
From Hayti 't was but forty miles away,
And on its lofty mountains green, and gray,
He saw the sun—in light, and shadow—play.
From native tongues he learned that gold was
    there,
And begged Ovando he might there repair.
He landed on its deeply wooded shore,
And o'er him saw the scarlet heron soar,
And gathered in the streamlets shining ore,
And learned that far away were golden mines.
The sycamore, and cedar, clad with vines,
Grew grandly with the ceiba, and the palm,
While willows waved, and blossoms shed their balm,
And through the groves the cardinals were heard,
And tropeos, and many a mocking-bird;
And fields of yuca, interspersed with maize,
Looked golden in the sun's effulgent rays.

---

* Ponce de Leon accompanied Columbus on his second
voyage in 1493, and was made lieutenant-governor of the Province of Higuey, in Hayti, by Ovando, after its subjugation.

To friendly speech the natives coined their breath,
Nor saw in him the harbinger of death;
And gifts the chief in rich profusion gave,
Nor knew how near the stranger brought the grave.

For Hayti's Isle he spread his vessel's sail,
And told Ovando his attractive tale,
Who Porto Rico's conquest then designed,
And boundless riches there aspired to find:
But ere for this he found the martial means
His thoughts were swiftly turned to other scenes.
Don Diego came to govern in his stead,
And back to Spain the fierce Ovando sped,
And praised his friend De Leon to the Crown,
And told how great, for prowess, his renown,
Whereon the King, admiring all he'd done,
Said—" For himself the island's rule he's won,"
And sent him word to govern there for Spain,
Nor should Don Diego e'er dispute his reign.
" Behold my rights invaded," Diego cried,
" Though I, in Spain, so long for justice tried ! "

II.

A bloodless triumph Ponce de Leon gained,
For Porto Rico peaceful still remained,
Though, with his forces, he was ruling there;
Yet storm impended while the sky was fair.
Oppression roused to wrath the native breast.
" The Spaniard," said the chief, " is but a guest;
Yet like a master he to rule us aims,
And—mark me—I repudiate his claims.
Is he—my people—an immortal man,
Or is his lifetime measured by a span?
If mortal, we can take him by surprise,
And spear him, and assail him, till he dies;

But if he's everlasting, woe to all,
The honey of our lives is turned to gall.
To test his immortality we'll seek,
And if he dies, then, vengeance we shall wreak ! "
A Spaniard slain the mortal story told,
By which the savage heart was rendered bold,
And all the chiefs and native hosts combined
To execute the fatal work designed.
At night the warriors met in painted throngs,
And sang—in groves—areytos—battle-songs,
And danced the war-dance round their fagot fires,
And blew their shells, and twanged their native
    lyres.
A Spaniard, hearing, joined them, painted too,
And seemed himself an Indian to the view,
And, from their language, and suggestive signs,
Their plot divined, and all their foul designs.
With speed he warned his comrades quartered near,
Who marvelled much of such a plot to hear,
And scarce believed that all they heard was true.
Don Christoval * howe'er distrustful grew,
For he a chieftain's daughter there had won,
And she had warned him massacre to shun,
But he from fondness deemed her fears arose,
And not till now believed her kinsmen foes.
He hastened to Caparra far away,
Where Ponce de Leon with his army lay,
But slain was he—with comrades—on the way,
While all the towns by Spaniards built were razed,
And fires upon the mountain summits blazed.
All saving those who to Caparra fled
Were left by the avenging warriors dead.

---

* Don Christoval de Sotomayor, who had been for a time
alcalde mayor under Juan Ponce de Leon.

A hundred Spaniards perished at a blow,
And from the fort no soldier dared to go : *
But Ponce de Leon sent to Hayti's shore
Don Diego's help in peril to implore,
And forces fresh responded to the call.
Then Ponce de Leon from his fortress wall
Cried—" Christ, and Santiago, sally out !
The Christian's sword the Infidel will rout ! "
" Christo y Santiago ! " was the cry
That oft repeated made the echoes fly,
And Ponce de Leon must'ring ev'ry man,
And shouting—" Adelanté ! " led the van.
The Indians gazed in wonder at the sight,
And consternation moved their hosts to flight.
Once more alive they deemed the Spaniards
    slain,
Or why such numbers in De Leon's train ?
With men immortal battling seemed in vain.
By swift degrees the Spaniards trod them down,
And Ponce de Leon basked in fresh renown.
The race of Red Men passed like gourds away,
To all the ills invasion brought a prey—
Toil, sickness, famine, cruelty, and woe—
The tares the Spaniard wearied ne'er to sow :
But Ponce ere long was shorn of all his sway.
" Don Diego," said the King, " let all obey,
For unto him that favored isle belongs.
His rights must not be recognized by wrongs ;
And Ponce de Leon, though he's nobly done,
Must yield to him—the great explorer's son.
Thus I a wrong committed now repair : "
And Diego after that was ruler there.

---

* There were in the fort, besieged, at this time, a hundred
Spaniards, and a bloodhound.

III.

Don Ponce de Leon dreamed of conquests new.
Another world he pictured to his view,
And in imagination conquered this,
And reaped renown, and everlasting bliss.
The Indians told him of a land of gold,
Where none of all its people e'er grew old,
And Pleasure reigned and pain had ne'er been known,
And where the sun on beauty ever shone,
And flowed the river of eternal youth.
The eager Spaniard deemed 't was all the truth,
And sought this splendid region of delight,
Where hearts were glad and eyes forever bright,
And only beauty met the ravished sight.
He felt his youth, and prime, already past,
And life too short for enterprises vast,
But could he reach this youth-restoring stream,
No longer life a fleeting thing he'd deem.
Rejuvenized, and yet with all he knew,
What thought could compass all he still might do?
So credulous, and fanciful was he
That he embarked, for this to search the sea,
His youth renew, and gather golden ore.
He found his comrades eager to explore,
For like him they believed the fiction true,
And, in imagination, glowing grew.
A fairy-land before them seemed to lie,
And there in fancy all were wont to fly.

Three caravels, with hope-exalted crews,
Their canvas spread on this Quixotic cruise,
And, northward steering, passed from isle to isle,*

* This fairy-land, the Indians said, lay far north, but an
island called Bimini, much nearer, was similarly endowed.

All eyes in expectation strained the while.
The green Bahamas one by one were passed
Until they reached San Salvador at last,
Where first Columbus trod the western world,
And by its shores his sails—rejoicing—furled :
But all in vain the pilgrims sought the land,
And drank of ev'ry stream from strand to strand,
And in their waters bathed with zealous zest,
With youth, and riches, hoping to be blessed.
Yet Ponce de Leon—hopeful none the less—
Northwestward, still, his way resolved to press,
And sailed till land, and palms, again were seen—
A country splendid in its garb of green,
Where Flora revelled in undying bloom,
And from the shore was wafted sweet perfume.
"This is," said he, "the paradise we seek.
A monitor, I hear within me speak."
'T was on a Sabbath * in the blush of spring,
When through the forest, birds were wont to sing,
That, crucifix in hand, he landed there,
And with his comrades knelt awhile in prayer,
Then rising said—"So flow'ry are the trees,
And with such fragrance freighted is the breeze,
That I the region Florida baptize,
And may its waters all rejuvenize."
He cruised for weeks along its flow'ry coast,
But met where'er he went an angry host,
Nor found the promised stream, nor golden ore,
Though still a garb of splendor Nature wore.
"Alas!" he cried, "that clime so fair as this

---

* It was Palm Sunday, (Pascua Florida), March 27, 1512,
in about thirty degrees north latitude, and both from this
circumstance, and the flowery aspect of the vegetation, Ponce
de Leon named the country Florida, its Indian name being
Cautio. The coast had, however, been discovered in 1498 by
Sebastian Cabot.

Contains not that perennial source of bliss—
The stream of beauty, and eternal life,
For which I've longed and sought through toil, and
    strife.
A river famous in barbaric lore—
And which, if found, would bless me evermore—
Might fitly grace a paradise so bright,
And crown with glory all that meets the sight.
Oh! Life's Elixir! Lives there such a thing
To free this body from its mortal sting?"
Before him in magnificent array
The earth revealed its splendors to the day;
But vainly Flora lavished all her charms,
And round him threw her close-embracing arms.
He sighed for something more than she could yield,
And in his thoughts surveyed a wider field.
There the palmetto, ever graceful, grew,
And spread its fan-like leaves to catch the dew;
The date-palm's plumes, majestic, waved on high,
And borrowed lustre from the beaming sky;
The breeze, the feather-like acacias wooed,
And birds, with music, filled the solitude;
Magnolias, with creamy blossoms gay,
And glossy leaves bedecked, adorned the way;
The guava and a fruit of scarlet hue,
In tempting beauty blushed upon the view;
Fantastic moss in hoary ringlets hung
From cedar, oak, and cypress, while there sung
The cardinal and tropeo, on high,
And mocking-birds were heard both far and nigh.
The fig, the lemon, and the peach displayed
Their dainties in the sunlight and the shade;
The citron there exhaled its rich perfume,
And roses seemed the pine-woods to illume;
The yellow chaparelle there, too, was seen,
With the verbena, and the myrtle, green,

While eglantine and jessamine were found
In beds of blossoms, carpeting the ground.
A silent river through the forest wound,
Where sailed the pelican in stately pride,
Where, too, the milk-white heron loved to glide,
And by the reedy margin of its tide
The pink crane wandered, and the thirsty deer
Came down to drink ; and there the waters clear
Reflected them upon its tranquil breast,
While all around was eloquent of rest ;
And pillowed on their velvet leaves, were spread
The graceful lilies in their liquid bed.
The balmy air was fragrant of the woods ;
The sun bathed all the earth in golden floods ;
The sky was bright, and beautiful, and blue ;
And when the Night its sable mantle drew
Across the scene, the gleaming, fiery flies
Vied with the shooting stars before the eyes ;
While brightly shone the placid, silver moon,
As if to rival Phœbus at his noon.

IV.

The Seminoles the pilgrims forced to flee,
And Ponce de Leon.ranged again the sea,
The fabled river eager still to find,
And fondly to the legend's falsehood blind.
Once more his barks from isle to isle careered,
But all in vain : no wondrous stream appeared,
Nor Bimini—the fairy isle—was seen.
Don Ponce de Leon felt at last shagreen,
And back to Porto Rico made his way—
But grave of mien where he before was gay—
Though he a comrade bade the search pursue
Till that enchanted island met his view.
'T was found ere long, but not the stream of life.

Delusive proved the stories that were rife.
'T was rich in palms, and brooks, and crystal springs,
And birds with golden breasts and scarlet wings,
And all its face was picturesque, and fair,
But no rejuvenizing stream was there.

V.

De Leon, stung by disappointment, sighed
For other lands to conquer ere he died,
But found them not, and wounded felt his pride.
Awhile he languished 'mid the fragrant isles,
And prayed in vain for Fortune's cheering smiles.
He mourned the day he left his native clime,
And uttered lamentations time on time,
With deep regrets, and sad forebodings, too,
For all his thoughts wore Melancholy's hue.
The fountain of eternal youth no more
Could fire him with the ardent hopes of yore,
For bitter mem'ries round the fable hung,
And he no more to hopes delusive clung.
He courted in forgetfulness repose,
And felt that thorns grew even with the rose.

VI.

Discouraged, Ponce de Leon sailed to Spain,
And honors from the Sovereign sought to gain.*
Then he returned the Carib hosts to fight,
But Guadaloupe his forces put to flight,
And he again to Porto Rico sped,
And then for years a life inactive led,

---

* He was made adelantado of Bimini and the supposed
island of Florida, and appointed to command a fleet of three
ships which sailed in 1514 to destroy the Caribs, who had been
making descents on Porto Rico.

Till Cortez roused him from his long repose,
And made him long to meet barbaric foes.
Once more his eyes to Florida were turned,
For, ripe for conquest, he for booty yearned,
And there he, now, the continent discerned,
Though but an isle he deemed the land before.
With ships equipped to colonize the shore,
And thoughts in realms of fancy prone to soar,
He westward sailed, ambitious of renown,
And eager after laurels from the Crown.
With buoyant hope he trod the flow'ry coast,
And—" Here I'll conquer ! " was his sanguine boast.
The Seminoles, howe'er—a warlike host—
Assailed with fury the invading band,
And wheresoe'er they went along the strand
Thick flights of poisoned arrows coursed the air,
And goaded Ponce de Leon to despair.
A battle fierce, and bloody, then was fought,
And havoc rude on either side was wrought.
He saw his soldiers in the combat slain,
And " Jesu Christo ! " cried with sudden pain
As arrow-struck he—tott'ring—reached the ground.
His bleeding wound his faithful comrades bound,
And bore him to his waiting caravel,
When to the coast he bade a long farewell,
And sailed to Cuba where ere long he died
With fevered body, and with humbled pride—
A disappointed, broken-hearted man,
Whose life was measured by the common span—
One who had hoped to cheat the tyrant Death,
But who to Jesus gave his latest breath —
A brave, chivalrous knight, but proud, and vain,
Who loved the Cross, and next his native Spain—
His early fame eclipsed by grander deeds,
The garden of his life o'errun with weeds,
His body poisoned by the arrow's sting,
And no one near him left, his praise to sing.

PART VI.

THE SEA THE REGION OF ROMANCE.

I.

THE region of romance was now the sea,
And o'er its waste of waters, vast, and free,
The paths of glory, ever widening, led,
And nations watched each wand'ring bark that sped,
And waited long—unwearied—its return,
All eager of the universe to learn—
The world they saw expanding on their view.
Enthusiastic, wond'ring Europe grew.

II.

Once more Sebastian Cabot sailed—with Pert—*
Far western shores in search of wealth to skirt.
They to Brazilian waters ploughed their way,
And later steered to Porto Rico's bay;
But spare success their noble efforts crowned,
Though in their brave example England found
The good which slowly ripened into deeds.
They sowed of ocean enterprise the seeds,
And Britons on the sea with Spaniards vied,
And Albion's commerce spread its sails awide.

III.

Ambitious of renown, and golden ore,
Velasquez sent his ships from Cuba's shore,

---

* Sir Sebastian Cabot, and Sir Thomas Pert, sailed from Bristol in 1516 with two ships fitted out by merchants of that town, and visited the coast of Brazil and touched at Hayti and Porto Rico. The voyage resulted in no profit to the adventurers, but it extended English navigation and nautical knowledge.

And with Cordova—Francis—in command
They steered by Yucatan's inviting strand,
Where erst had landed wrecked Valdivia's band ;
And there he battled hard, but met defeat,
And to his squadron turned in swift retreat,
Then sorely wounded—back to Cuba sailed,
And dying cried—" My enterprise has failed."
Velasquez, then, still other ships supplied,
And bade Grijalva there his forces guide,
And he explored in Yucatan anew,
And with remorseless arm the heathen slew ;
Then Mexico, in sailing onward, eyed,
And, gazing, felt a first discov'rer's pride,
While Montezuma's fame his wonder raised,
And all he heard but left him more amazed.
He hastened back the tidings rare to tell,
And felt his breast with aspirations swell.
Pinedo from Jamaica's sunny isle
Had sailed, and sighted Mexico, the while ;
But he was forced the angry shore to flee,
And seek a refuge on the open sea ;
And of his ships but one escaped the land,
And reached again Jamaica's palmy strand.
Of Mexico, with joy, Velasquez heard,
And with ambition soaring like a bird—
And by the love of gold, and glory spurred—
He to Hernando Cortez, turning, said—
" Here go, my comrade, and the gospel spread !
Assail the heathen of this savage shore,
And reap a harvest of their golden ore.
There plant the Cross, and gospel truths proclaim,
And put the godless infidels to shame,
Nor e'er return until thy work is done,
And thou the triumph I foresee hast won."

BOOK THE SECOND.

THE
CONQUEST OF MEXICO.

[Period 1519 to 1523].

PART FIRST.

I.

THE chivalry of ocean found its vent
In daring deeds along the continent,
And glory was the Spaniard's dream of hope.
For this the New World gave unrivalled scope:
This—linked with gold—allured him far and wide,
A bold crusader o'er the ocean's tide.
He lived for gold, for glory, and the Cross,
And all beside he counted only dross.
In Mexico Velasquez viewed a prize
Toward which he looked with keen, and wistful eyes,
And to its shores his own armada planned—
An armament with Cortez in command—
He but alcaldé of a Cuban town,
Unknown to fame—a stranger to renown,
Yet who was destined, soon, to win a name
Which through Castile was greeted with acclaim.
He well was fitted for the pilgrimage.

Of middle stature and nigh middle age, *
Of pale complexion, with a speaking eye,
Which at a flash could flatter or defy ;
In frame robust, and lithe, and strong of limb,
His comrades found a leader bold in him.
Inured to toil, and in privation schooled,
No fitter chief could o'er his camp have ruled ;
In manner frank, but truly strong of will,
With warlike tastes, and all a soldier's skill ;
Not fond of banquets, nor yet prone to wine,
But proud of rank, and—dress—its outward sign,
And with a hero's yearning after fame—
For deeds of glory—an undying name.
Such then was Cortez, ripe for dauntless deeds,
Whose motto was—AUDACITY SUCCEEDS :
But ere he sailed Velasquez grave became,
And Cortez held, for actions done, to blame,
And of his course, too late, repented sore.
" I feel," he cried, " in Cortez faith no more,
For—daring, and ambitious—he will soar.
And aim to rule where he should strive to serve.
Not such as he supreme command deserve."
Thus deeply jealous, and distrustful, grown,
He chose a new commander, tried and known,
Who'd labor well, nor for himself alone,
Nor dare to call the glory all his own :
But Cortez from Saint Jago fled by night—
Though ships and crew were found in sorry plight—
And left Velasquez in a savage mood
O'er thwarted plans, and blighted hopes, to brood. †

---

* Hernando Cortez, according to Gomara, was born at Ned-
ellin, in Estramadura, in 1485, and was therefore between
thirty-three and thirty-four years old when, in 1519, he first
landed in Mexico.

† Cortez sailed, clandestinely, early on the morning of November 18, 1518, from St. Jago, Cuba, with an ill-provided fleet,

A fav'ring breeze the squadron seaward bore,
But ere receded far the island's shore
Velasquez—from his slumbers roused—appeared,
And, on the beach, the sailing vessels neared,
And cried to Cortez loudly—"Come to me,
Nor dare in ships of mine to put to sea!"
And in the moonlight wildly waved his hands,
And, with excited motions, trod the sands:
But Cortez left Velasquez raving there,
And saints, and Virgin, thanked for wind so fair.
In flight alone, he knew, his safety lay.
"'T would fatal be," he murmured, "to obey.
Whate'er I have of wordly wealth is here,

---

for the port of Macaca, fifteen leagues' distant, where he obtained supplies and additional volunteers. Thence he sailed to Trinidad, a larger town on the southern coast of Cuba, and secured fresh supplies and reinforcements, Cristoval de Olid, Alonso de Avila, Juan Velasquez de Leon, and Gonzalo de Sandoval, afterward conspicuous in the Conquest, among the number. His fleet afterwards proceeded to Havana with the same objects in view. Before he left St. Jago, however, Velasquez, the governor of the island, having repented of appointing him to the command of the expedition, in vain tried to arrest his departure and subsequent progress. On the 10th of February, 1518, the squadron, consisting of eleven sail, varying in size from open brigantines to vessels of seventy, eighty, and a hundred tons burden, steered for Cape St. Antonio. Landing there, Cortez delivered a stirring address to his followers, and placing his fleet under the protection of St. Peter, his patron saint, sailed on the 18th of February, 1519, for the coast of Yucatan. His forces at the time numbered one hundred and ten sailors, and five hundred and fifty-three soldiers, thirty-two of whom were cross-bowmen, and thirteen arquebusiers. In addition there were two hundred Cuban Indians, a few of whom were women, designed to perform menial labor. The expedition carried ten heavy guns, four brass falconets, an abundant supply of ammunition, and sixteen horses, the latter of inestimable value. The expenses of the squadron prior to its departure from St. Jago were borne by Velasquez and Cortez, who invested all the moderate means at his command in the purchase of ships and supplies.

And death ashore, if I return, I fear."
Saint Jago vanished slowly from the view,
And Cortez found his comrades stanch, and true.
From port to port he sailed along the coast,
Increasing as he went his motley host—
A reckless band, crusaders in their type,
But all for war, and wild adventure, ripe;
And brigantines were added to the fleet,
While Cortez vowed he'd ne'er endure defeat.
Ten fragile barks, beside his own, had he—
And o'er six hundred sons of chivalry—
With which to launch his fortunes on the sea.
Velasquez strove to seize him as he sailed,
But all he did to thwart, or capture, failed.
Supplied, and manned, from Cuba sped the ships—
Each Spaniard with a prayer upon his lips—
And steered for Yucatan's inviting shore.
" Adieu ! " said Cortez, " Cuba evermore ! "

II.

Thus led by greed of conquest, and of gain,
From Cuba's isle he wooed the open main.
The daring hero, bent on bold emprise,
Sailed full of hope, ambition, enterprise,
With lust of wealth, and battle, in his eyes,
But thus he spoke ere land was left behind,
The closer to himself his men to bind :—
" Within your reach a prize not all of gold,
But gold and glory—Comrades—now behold !
Ere long ye'll be the favored sons of Fame
Who'll trumpet to the world each soldier's name,
If strong in faith ye bravely fight for Right
With Sword, and Cross, against the pagan's might;
And God against barbaric foes will shield
All ye who meet them on the battle-field ;

And riches yours—whate'er ye crave—shall be,
And Spain will give ye welcome from the sea.
Extend ye, then, her sway o'er regions new,
And to yourselves, and me, be ever true ! "
Then Mass was said ; Saint Peter's aid was prayed,
And 'neath the Saint's protection all was laid.
Ere long a storm assailed his speeding fleet,
When from the blast he turned in swift retreat,
And in Cozumel's island found repose,
Though there awhile beset by Indian foes.
'T was then he heard from Yucatan the news
That on its coast had landed shipwrecked crews
Which made him seek them with exploring zeal,
Both for their own, and for their country's weal.
'T was there the meek Jeronimo appeared,
When from his captors he so gladly steered,
In whom he found a servant, and a friend—
One whose interpretations served an end
That of itself to conquest paved the way,
And built on Aztec ruins Spanish sway.*
" Jeronimo," said Cortez—" yet once more
Come spread the gospel on a heathen shore."

III.

Along the sunny shore of Yucatan
Intrepid Cortez led the Spanish van,
And there he landed, fearless of his fate,
With music, banners, and the signs of state.*
The hills, and valleys bloom, and verdure, wore,

---

* Jeronimo de Aguilar served as interpreter and ambassador to Cortez in Mexico until the final conquest of the country, when he was appointed regidor of the city of Mexico as a reward for the valuable services he had rendered.

* Cortez landed at the river of Tobasco on the 13th of March, 1519.

And earth her fruits through all the seasons bore.
The wand'rers gazed in unrestrained delight,
And felt a charm in all that met the sight.
But warlike throngs assailed them where they stood,
Then vanished in the deep primeval wood,
And Cortez called his troops at once to arms,
Who dwelt no longer on the prospect's charms.
Canoes were marshalled on Tobasco's stream,
Which seemed with hostile multitudes to teem,
And there in force the Spaniards found their way
On foot, in boats, and mounted for the fray.
"Saint Jago! Christo!" Cortez loudly cried,
And native blood the flowing river dyed.
Then dusky legions fought with might and main,
And grappled wildly with the boats of Spain,
And Spaniard after Spaniard there was slain,
While mother earth drank human blood like rain.
Both Infidel, and Christian, dyed the sod,
And Spanish lips were moved in prayer to God.
The Indian arrows bird-like—whizzing—flew,
And Spanish arms by thousands foemen slew.
Their strength with guns the arrows tried in vain,
And when at length, the horsemen reached the plain,
And charged the foe in battle's stern array
The native squadrons fled—pursued—away,
For man and horse seemed monstrous to their eyes,
And roused alike their terror, and surprise.
Believing both to one existence wed
They felt—nor strangely—overwhelming dread,
For ne'er the horse had met·their view before,
Nor e'er, till then, they'd heard the cannon's roar.
They left the Spaniards victors in the fight,
And all Tobasco subject to their might.

Next morn, in cotton garments darkly clad,
Caziques approached, submissive, meek, and sad,

And prayed the boon of taking thence their dead.
O'er these a solemn Mass the Spaniards said
When they—the chiefs—had kissed the cross di-
    vine,
And of allegiance made a fitting sign :
And with them twenty blooming maids they brought,
As gifts to those they'd erst so bravely fought,
Nor such as these the Spaniards failed to win,
For they were prone to sentiment and sin ;
But sighs, and tears, from breaking hearts escaped
As there they stood like statues all undraped,
Ere from their native land they turned to go
Where'er the winds the Spanish fleet might blow.

Down by the river where the mangroves grew,
Its ample shade a lordly ceiba threw,
And here his sword Hernando Cortez drew,
And with it thrice its mammoth trunk he smote,
And thus the legend of his conquest wrote—
A conquest that was fast and far to spread,
And fill an empire with appalling dread.

IV.

Not long the daring victors lingered here,
But re-embarked, their course again to steer
Toward Mexico, whose shore was blooming near ;
And soon San Juan's island met their view—*
Like some bright vision—in a sea of blue.
There Cortez landed in triumphant mood,
His mind with conquest, and with prayer, imbued.
Before him rose an empire vast, and great,
Whose oracles had long foretold its fate—

---

* The island of San Juan de Uloa nearly opposite the modern Vera Cruz.

A pagan people, civilized withal,
Predestined by Invasion's blight to fall.
Where this dark Egypt of the New World lay
He saw bright promise of a new Cathay.

Macaws, and parrots, screamed among the trees,
And fragrant of the forest was the breeze;
The dusky buzzards flew in search of prey,
The monkeys climbed, and gambolled, all the day;
The luscious cherimoya pear-like hung,
And to the locust, passion-flowers clung;
The yellow cedar shed its sweet perfume,
And oleanders stood arrayed in bloom.
Ananas, rich in scent, and gold and green,
With welcome fruit adorned the sylvan scene,
And beards of moss festooned the lofty pines,
While scarlet blossoms beautified the vines.

The squadron by the isle at anchor lay
Within the shelter of a bending bay,
And high the mainland backed the splendid view
Beneath a beaming sky of azure hue,
From which canoes, with tawny paddlers, came
Attracted by the white invaders' fame.
The wond'ring natives brought them fruit and gold,
And of their country, and its marvels, told,
And Cortez gave them trinkets in return,
And tried from these whate'er he could to learn.
Jeronimo was versed in Mayan lore,*
And knew the language of the Mayan shore,
But Aztec strove to comprehend in vain,
And Cortez viewed his ignorance with pain.
'T was then he saw a houri on the deck

---

* That part of Yucatan where Jeronimo was wrecked was
called Maya.

Fall weeping on a greeting Aztec's neck,
And utter words all Aztec like his own,
And claim him one her early youth had known
Ere bitter griefs her tender heart had wrung.
Yet she, like him—her kinsman—still was young.
From Mexico, and home, she'd erst been torn
In Yucatan—a captive child—to mourn.
Ere this her father—scarce remembered—died,
Whose relict, then, became another's bride,
And bore a son for whom her fondness grew,
While ne'er for her—her daughter—love she knew.
She stole for him the wealth designed for her,
And av'rice proved to crime the ready spur.
In secret she was sent from home away,
And sold to traders one eventful day.
While in her stead her parent placed a corse,
And feigned distress, nor o'er it felt remorse,
And called the lifeless form her daughter dead.
The child was soon to far Tobasco led,
And by the traders sold for lucre there.
A budding beauty she was, fresh, and fair
With winning eyes, and lustrous raven hair,
And fairy form, and winsomeness of face,
And movements witching in their artless grace.
She fascinated Cortez by her charms,
And wished success, and glory, to his arms.
He felt that here indeed he held a prize,
And on her features cast admiring eyes,
And deemed she'd prove, whate'er betided, true.
She spoke the Aztec, and the Mayan, too,
And eager seemed an active part to play,
And, as his own interpreter, obey,
While in the priest Jeronimo of Spain
Was one to whom the Mayan tongue was plain.
Through strange adventures thus the maid had
  passed

To reach again her native land at last.
Thenceforth Marina—so by Cortez named—
The Spaniards served, and lived both loved and
    famed.

V.

When to the neighb'ring coast the squadron sailed,
With plenty there the troops were all regaled ;
And there they camped 'tween sea, and mountain-
    land—
Out on a level plain with hills of sand,
And all around them picturesque, and grand.
Before them nightly flashed the gleaming flies—
Like fiery phantoms—dazzling to their eyes,
While humming-birds, and butterflies by day,
With gaudy flashes, made the prospect gay.
There sang the tropeo his joyous lay,
And piped the oriole his roundelay,
While sky and ocean blended far away.
Ere long they called their camping-ground a town,
The Vera Cruz that since has won renown.
The natives marvelled more than e'er before,
And daily thronged to see them on the shore,
While from their sov'reign gifts, and greetings,
    came,
By noble envoys known to Aztec fame.
Great Montezuma in his native vale
Had heard with wonder of these wand'rers pale,
These bearded strangers from a land unknown,
Whose ships by winds o'er ocean's breast were
    blown,
And, half in fear, their friendship sought to gain,
Yet begged them soon again to sail the main,
For from Tobasco tidings grave had he
Of these intrepid rovers of the sea.

Time fled, and there the Spaniards lingered still
Though much against proud Montezuma's will.
Yet gifts again by noble hands he sent
With kindly words of Aztec compliment,
For he to win them o'er from wrath was bent,
But prayed they'd soon be gone, the daring band,
Nor venture more to spy the Aztec land,
And desecrate the soil oe'r which he reigned—
A soil till now by strangers unprofaned.
No nearer they to where he dwelt could draw,
Nor linger longer, by his country's law.
The wily Cortez heard the envoys through,
And then replied " Believe my friendship true,
Nor e'er my advent here you'll live to rue ;
But I would fain a realm so wondrous view,
And to your sovereign pay the rev'rence due.
A monarch truly great, I hear, is he,
And gladly I'd his court and person, see,
So, with the help of God, I'll onward press,
And trust that He the enterprise will bless."
Then all the Spaniards to the tolling bell
On bended knees in deep devotion fell.
Before the Cross they asked Almighty aid,
To execute the plans their chief had made,
To give them strength, and weaken all their foes,
And leave them at the mercy of their blows.
Faint on the air their supplications rose.
The envoys looked in wonder on the scene
With placid but a strange inquiring mien.
Then priests, and Cortez, told by word and sign,
The story of the Christian faith, divine,
And deeper still barbaric wonder grew
Ere to the camp the envoys bade adieu..

Still later chiefs from Cempoalla came
Attracted by the pale invaders' fame,

And told how they were Aztecs but by name,
A tribe subdued by Montezuma's hosts,
Which overran their valleys, and their coasts.
Totonacs, they were rich in ancient lore,
And sighed for independence as of yore.
"Our lord at Cempoalla dwells," said they,
"And fain would see you thither take your way,
Where gardens blush with roses all the day,
And orchard-trees with fruit, and bloom, are gay."

VI.

Time passed away, and Cortez lingered still
Though much against the Aztec monarch's will;
But o'er his fortunes oft the leader sighed,
For he his ranks contention saw divide.
In insubordination troops arose,
And, erst his friends, became his open foes.
The cry was—"Back to Cuba we'll repair,
For well may we of conquest here despair,"
But Cortez said—"The enterprise is grand;
Why leave behind so rich, and fair, a land
With riches—mark me! Comrades—close at hand?
With trust in God, and courage, strong are we.
Why back to Cuba, then, despairing, flee?
Dispel your fears, and bravely follow me!"
Their courage rose, their clamors died away,
And all resolved in Mexico to stay.
They laid their plans to colonize the shore,
And faith in Cortez as their captain swore,
And Villa Rica * where they camped they named,
And all the region for their monarch claimed.
Ere long howe'er a fairer spot they chose

---

* The full name was Villa Rica de Vera Cruz—the Wealthy
Town of the True Cross.

Where they the camp could screen from native foes,
And where the ships would find a sheltered bay,
And all the beach was like a sandy quay :
So to the north careered the Spanish fleet
From winds, and waves, to seek the calm retreat,
While Cortez with his men—a martial host—
Marched full in view along the shelving coast
Where Orizaba in the distance rose,
Its summit hoary with eternal snows,
With mountains massed—a rugged chain—below,
Bathed in the shining sun's resplendent glow.
O'er dreary plains for miles the army toiled,
And time on time from grim remains recoiled,
Where men had erst in sacrifice been slain
Within the portals of some Aztec fane.
The Spaniards gazed—astounded—on the sight,
And vowed to shed the gospel's holy light
This deep, barbaric darkness to dispel,
And of a purer faith—the Christian's—tell.
But from a sandy waste to living green
Ere long, by Cempoalla, changed the scene.
The country, far and near, was grand to view,
And all the sky a bright, and mottled, blue,
Its sweeping sides the Andes baring still,
While nearer—seaward—hill succeeded hill,
All clothed with vegetation flecked with bloom,
Which on the balmy air exhaled perfume.
Each glance disclosed new beauties to the eye
Down from the peaks that pierced the azure sky
To where the spreading sea, with glitt'ring breast,
Lay—type of God's immensity—at rest.
Here Nature's face was wondrous fair and bright,
And of itself existence seemed delight.
With light festoons the stately trees were gay,
And these with ev'ry breeze were prone to play,
While Flora painted earth with colors gay,

And purple grapes were clustered on the vines—
Which wove on high their intersecting lines—
And honeysuckles clambered up the pines.
The prickly aloe, and the rose, were twined
With vegetation of a kindred kind,
A rich, and tropic, undergrowth around,
And fadeless green to beautify the ground.
In herds the timid deer were seen to run,
And parrots flashed, while flying, in the sun.
Sweet warbling notes by mocking-birds were
   trilled,
Whose woodland songs the gorgeous forest filled,
And cardinals, with scarlet plumage bright,
Made vocal sounds from early morn till night.
The cocoa-palms were bending with their fruit,
And tall bamboos returned their proud salute,
While turkeys, wild,* and pheasants, sought their
   shade,
Or basked, and chattered, in the leafy glade,
And stately cottonwood, and almond-trees
Soft whispers uttered in the idle breeze,
Cacãos † with their red and golden pods—
Rich theobromas bearing food for gods—
And, with their snowy blossoms, thickly flecked,
Rose in the shade, with purple leaves bedecked,
While, tall and straight, organos tapered there,
And on the hillsides bloomed the prickly pear.
The cotton-plant its bursting bolls revealed,
And golden maize adorned the open field,
While fell tobacco's large and lustrous leaf—
Whose fumes imparted solace, and relief,
Long ere the conquest, to the Aztec race—
Disclosed its vivid green with bending grace.

---

* The turkey was first introduced into Europe from Mexico.
† Chocolate-trees.   Pronounce Ka-kā′os.

With long, coarse leaves the juicy maguey grew,
A plant from which the natives nectar drew,
Whose sap—fermented—into pulqué turned,
And few were they who ne'er for this had yearned,
For in the cup intoxication lurked,
And, through the brain a strange enchantment
    worked.*
'Twas to the Aztecs an exciting wine,
And in the aloe they beheld their vine,
While now, as then, the fluid freely flows,
Where in Mexico the aloe grows.
It spreads its poison o'er the hapless clime,
And stimulates to vice, and deeds of crime.

VII.

The town of Cempoalla met the sight,
Its temples, and its dwelling-places white.
Of sun-dried brick, and sandy stone were they,
And thatched with palm-leaves, bleached to sober
    gray.
Young maidens came to greet the Spaniards there,
And with their songs of welcome filled the air,
And on their leader's helmet chaplets hung,
And in their native tongue his praises sung.
They lavished roses on his charger, too,
And floral favors to the soldiers threw,
While picturesque, and fair, were they to view.
They, like their swains, in cotton robes were clad.

---

*The sap of the maguey, or great aloe, was gathered by cutting off the centre shoot of the plant, in the hollow of which it formed a basin, holding about a pint. This filled two or three times a day, and was drawn off by mouth suction, through a reed, and after being discharged into a skin, or other vessel, was allowed to ferment, when it became pulqué. The custom still prevails.

And seemed, to meet the mailed invaders, glad.
In ears and nostrils, rings of gold they wore,
Which all could see were made of golden ore.
On these the Spaniards cast their eager eyes,
And in each jewelled maid beheld a prize.
They marvelled much a cultured race to find,
And deemed for this they'd been by God designed.

Through Cempoalla's narrow streets they passed
When from their trumpets rang a martial blast.
The chieftain met them as became a brave
With friendly motives, but with features grave,
And entertained with native fare the troops,
Who broke from solid columns into groups.
Their captain to the native leader turned,
And from his lips the nation's story learned.
He told how weak was Montezuma's sway,
And how he longed to see it swept away,
A feeling o'er the country thousands shared,
Though none their discontent to whisper dared.
Here Cortez found to great success the key,
And murmured " Jesus ! help I ask of Thee !
Let Montezuma's foes in strength arise,
And strive the Spanish arms to aggrandize
That we may thus the land evangelize.
Though yet we've scarce the noble work begun,
By Grace divine the prize will soon be won.
Against itself divided what can stand?
I trust, O Lord ! to Thy protecting hand ! "

VIII.

Four leagues from Cempoalla northward lay
The chosen spot, and deep but sheltered, bay.
So Cortez onward soon resumed his way,
While Cempoalla's braves his burdens bore

To where the ships were anchored off the shore.
There Cempoalla's lord was borne in state
With all the pomp environing the great,
And while he lingered with the Spaniards there
Within a native market-place or square,
They saw approach them men of high degree,
Who said—" We come Totonac's chief to see."
Then when they reached his palanquin they bowed
But with the air of equals—great, and proud—
And spoke in tones of censure, and command—
" Why treat you thus the strangers in the land
When Montezuma bids them leave the strand ?
We twenty men, and maids, for this demand,
And these ere long—a sacrifice—shall die !
Henceforth to Spaniards all relief deny ! "
The chief prepared the mandate to obey,
But Cortez, when he heard it, bade him stay,
And seize the nobles ere they went away,
And this, though with reluctance, soon was done.
On these as captives sank, that day, the sun,
But, ere the night succeeding quite had flown,
Hernando sought these envoys from the throne,
And o'er their plight distress was quick to feign.
And said— " I'll see your freedom you regain.
Go tell your monarch he's a friend in me,
And that, ere long, I hope his face to see,
For which I've journeyed far across the sea.
Totonac's braves would slay you where you lie,
But from their wrath, in secret, you shall fly.
The time has come for hasty flight.—Good-bye ! "
Thus Cortez sought their monarch's smiles to win,
And on Totonac throw the weight of sin.
Against her Montezuma's ire he'd raise,
And both in turn, to serve his purpose, praise,
For with Totonac, and the monarch, foes,
He saw his way to strike triumphant blows.

The morrow found Totonac wrapped in gloom,
Her people apprehensive of their doom,
For Montezuma's wrath was feared by all.
" No harm on you," said Cortez, " here shall fall.
Embrace the Cross ; allegiance own to Spain,
And Montezuma's rage shall, then, be vain."
With one accord Totonacs bowed the knee,
And sought in these invaders from the sea
A shield from Montezuma's scourging hand.
Thus rent in twain the Spaniards saw the land.
The while his nobles toward the monarch sped
As from Totonac—halting ne'er—they fled—
With.glances backward, still pursued by Fear,
And told their tale in Montezuma's ear.
With anger flashed his black, and lustrous eyes,
And all his features spoke his great surprise,
But fear amid his indignation rose,
And, timid still, a peaceful part he chose.
Once more he sent ambassadors in state
On Cortez, and his warlike band to wait,
And bid them on his shores no more delay,
Nor hesitate his mandate to obey,
And as a golden bribe, in peace, to go—
For friendship toward them still he aimed to show—
He sent them other presents, rich, and rare,
Which only laid his wealth, and weakness, bare,
And made the Spaniards as they eyed them swear
They'd march ere long to conquest, or would die
Beneath the splendors of that glowing sky.
To Cempoalla's lord the monarch sent
A message grave, and solemn in intent,
With threats, and warnings for his guilty course—
. His blind adherence to a hostile force.
But ill Totonac's troubled chief could bow
To aught beside the fierce invaders now.

Disposed to please, eight damsels he bestowed
On those who—in command—with Cortez rode.
All chieftains' daughters, richly clad were they,
With female slaves to fan them as they lay.
" But these," said Cortez, " Spaniards ne'er can wed
Till to the Christian altar they've been led,
And been, with water, there baptized, and named,
And, in the faith, with solemn pomp proclaimed;
Nor yet till all your gods are overthrown,
And in their stead the Cross your priests enthrone,
And till your shrines are, with your idols, waste,
And by the Virgin and the Child replaced!"
" Baptize, and name," Totonac's chief replied,
" But in our temples let our gods abide.
The Cross, with these, we'll worship day by day,
And, like yourselves, before your emblem pray."
The Spaniards felt the spur of Christian zeal,
And gave the cry of " Jesus, and Castile!"
And marched to Cempoalla's grandest fane,
And called on Christ to bless the cause of Spain,
Then moving forward tore the idols down,
And   cried   aloud—"Huzzah! for Cross,   and
    Crown!"
To arms Totonac's chieftain called the town,
And sudden sounds of tumult filled the air.
The priests—Totonacs—wailed, and tore their hair,
And uttered frantic protests all in vain.
The fiery Spaniards met them with disdain.
Then Cortez captive made the great cazique,
And bade him words to calm his warriors speak.
Exclaiming—"If Totonac strikes a blow
Your blood in expiation here shall flow.
Remember Montezuma is your foe,
And if you forfeit Spain's protection, lo!
Your land will know the bitterness of woe!"
" The gods," he cried, with anguish in his face,

"Will soon avenge their horrible disgrace,"
And then he mourned o'er all his people's loss.
No blow was struck. The Spaniards raised the
   Cross,
And where Totonac's idols erst had been
The Virgin Mary and the Child were seen.
A long procession, bearing lights, was formed,
And Mass the priest—Olmedo—there performed,
When Cortez set the captive chieftain free,
And cried—" Triumphant thus we'll ever be ! "
The people deemed their gods were weak indeed
When strangers thus could break them like a reed,
And of the Spaniards greater grew their fear.
"A Christian shrine I leave," said Cortez, " here,
And pray you'll learn its teachings to revere.
You'll find in me—Totonacs all—a friend,
Who'll fight your rights, and dwellings, to defend
If ye but prove to all your pledges true,"
And, then, to Cempoalla bade adieu.
The Bible, and the sword, went hand in hand
Where'er the stern invaders trod the land.
*Fast Villa Rica, labor-planted, grew,
And in its midst a chapel met the view.
It formed the centre of a fruitful plain
Where summer seemed eternally to reign,
And walls, and ramparts, all around it rose
To bid defiance to aggressive foes.
There native thousands toiled from day to day—
The while submissive to the Spaniard's sway—
And looked on Montezuma as their bane,
And welcomed in their midst invasion's reign.
They gladly saw beneath their native sky

---

*The spot selected for the future town of Villa Rica de Vera
Cruz is called Quiabislan by Solis and Robertson, and
Chiahuitztla by Prescott.

The city's walls, and turrets, rising high,
And hoped therein protection long to find
From all who ill to them and theirs designed,
Ne'er thinking it a harbinger of woe,
And that one arm would crush both friend and foe,
With all their ancient glory trampled low.

" 'T is time," said Cortez, " now to write to Spain,
The Crown's approval of my acts to gain,
For well I know Velasquez is my foe,
Who'll strive where'er he can, to drag me low,
And fain would consummate my overthrow.
I'll all the tidings glad my sov'reign tell,
And show I've served my native country well.*
I'll send him all the treasure that I've stored—
Yes all my own, and comrades', glitt'ring hoard,—
And not his meed—the royal fifth—alone,
For this would scarce add lustre to the throne,
Or well befit an enterprise so grand.
Let Spain behold the riches of the land!
Velasquez, then, will strive to thwart in vain,
For in the hearts of Spaniards I shall reign!"
Each man of all his soldiers gave his share
When Cortez said—"Awhile from wealth forbear
That we may reap, as heroes, great renown,
And win unfading laurels from the Crown."
The wealth they'd won they yielded for applause—
To glorify their enterprising cause—
And labored on with self-denying zeal,
Their motto—"Gold, and glory, and Castile!"

Ere long the ship they freighted passed from view,
And Cortez cried with eyes bedewed—"Adieu!"

---

*In allusion to the first letter of Cortez, which was undoubt-
edly written, but cannot be found.

Four Aztec braves had joined her Spanish crew,
And welcome gave each seaward wind that blew.
No dread of leaving home, and kin, had they,
But eager felt to wend their wat'ry way,
Athirst to see the wonders of the world.
Ere long in Spain they saw her canvas furled.

IX.

Some still there were who o'er their lot repined
And crafty flight from Aztec shores designed,
But Cortez foiled them ere they left the shore,
When some were maimed and some were seen no
   more.
" The day," said he, " for cowards' plots is o'er,
For mark me close to all escape the door.
By stratagem I'll sink my floating fleet,
And those who can may then, by sea, retreat."
Cut off were they—his comrades—at a blow,
And down their features tears were seen to flow
When first the startling tidings reached their ears,
And kindled in their breasts appalling fears,
While indignation mingled with their woe.
How now to home, and country, could they go
With ne'er a caravel to seaward sail ?
How now could they to reap disaster fail ?
Their murmurs, discontent, and grief, were great,
And all on Cortez vented rage, and hate.
The stoutest hearts before the prospect quailed,
And with dismay their dismal lot bewailed.
His danger Cortez knew, but calmly stood,
And tried to soothe the anger in their blood,
And win them by Persuasion's gentle art,
Afraid, as yet, to play a bolder part.
" The ships destroyed are mine," said he, " alone,
And these unfit to sail the sea had grown,

While by their loss a hundred men we gain—
Who've—guarding these—been stationed by the
main—
To join us here, and swell our marching train.
To look for succor e'er from ships how vain
When far behind we've left the murm'ring sea.
Let all resolve from foemen ne'er to flee!
To contemplate escape would woo defeat,
And cowards only deem that flight is sweet."
His arguments impressed his hearers well,
And made their breasts with rising courage swell.
Resentment fast, like morning vapor, fled
When, sun-like, Hope its cheering radiance shed,
And few were they who, then, denied him wise,
Though keen regrets expressed themselves in sighs.
" My firm resolve," said Cortez, to his band,
" Is here to die, or conquer all the land.
Our hearts with hopes delusive ships would buoy,
And so, a spirit whispered 'These destroy;'
No refuge ours if we defeated be,
But conquest waits on all who follow me!"
His comrades, warming, cried "To Mexico!—
To Mexico—with willing hearts—we'll go!"

PART SECOND.

I.

FROM Villa Rica's walls the march began
With Cortez, gayly mounted, in the van.
Four hundred Spaniards, and a group of steeds—
With food, and powder, to supply their needs,
And loaded guns, and music in the air,
And on the lips of each a whispered prayer—

Composed the martial host that moved away—
A glitt'ring line—one sunny August day.*
Their comrades left behind to guard the town
Cried "On ye ne'er may Fortune cast a frown,"
And valiant Escalanté, in command,
Said—"Here till glory crowns our work I'll
   stand!"
The troops at Cempoalla paused for rest,
And once again with garlands these were dressed
By maiden hands, ambitious but to please,
While roses gave their fragrance to the breeze.
But tidings came that ships were hov'ring near,
And Cortez of Velasquez felt in fear.
To Villa Rica's beach he hastened back
Prepared to welcome friends, or foes attack,
And saw the squadron sailing by the shore,
But these no evil sign about them bore,
And to the strand a boat with Spaniards came
Who told they'd gold, and glory, for their aim,
And from Jamaica's isle had ploughed their way—
Commissioned to explore, by Don Garay—†
And Cortez, and his comrades, warned away.
But he the boat, and Spaniards, captive made,
And plans to capture all the squadron laid,
When those on board perceiving peril nigh
Bade Vera Cruz, ere fell the night, good-bye.
Then back to Cempoalla Cortez rode,
While in his eyes his burning ardor glowed,

---

* The horses referred to numbered fifteen and the field-pieces seven.

† Francisco de Garay, governor of Jamaica, who had equipped four vessels at his own expense to make discoveries, Spain having previously given him authority over any new lands he might discover.

And Sandoval, and Alvarado, * cried—
"We welcome thee compatriot, and guide !"
The morning showed the march again begun,
And arms, and armor, glistened in the sun,
While Cempoalla's sons advanced in line—
Two thousand strong—the whole a pageant fine.†
"On !" Cortez cried, with pleasure in his glance,
And waving in the air a Spanish lance,
"On ! comrades, on ! to Mexico we go,
And soon we'll leave the tropic plain below,
And cross the heights that yonder court the sky,
With hearts courageous, and our trust on High.
We march beneath the Saviour's guiding eye,
And wheresoe'er we meet with heathen foes
We'll—God assisted—strike triumphant blows.
The ancient Romans great achievements wrought,
And battles oft victoriously fought,
But greater deeds than ancient Rome could boast
Will shed their lustre on our Christian host.
We'll fight for gold, for glory, and the Cross,
And all our gain will prove but Satan's loss !
No refuge save our arms, and Christ, have we,
But one continued triumph I can see.
On ! on ! my comrades, on ! to Victory !"
"We'll all obey !" with one accord they cried,
"And conquest's ours with Jesus on our side.
We'll follow on where'er you choose to lead.
The Christian's arms must—God sustained—suc-
    ceed !"
Here in a land of beauty flashed their steel,

---

* The two officers whom he had left in command of the
troops at Cempoalla.

† The march from Cempoalla toward the City of Mexico
began on August 16, 1519, and 1,300 Indian warriors, and
1,000 *tamanes*, or porters, to drag the guns, and carry the baggage, accompanied the little army led by Cortez.

Where the vanilla, and the cochineal
Were native to the clime, and flowers bloomed
The seasons through, and all the air perfumed;
Where fruits in one unbroken circle grew,
And, gay with scarlet plumes, flamingoes flew;
Where insects with enamelled wings were seen
That flashed like diamonds on the sunlit scene.
Here, climbing up the mountains' sweeping slope,
Their hearts were light with rapture-kindling hope,
And when Xalapa's city met their gaze
They murmured to their Maker words of praise,
And looked upon the paradise below
With eyes that seemed with ardor keen to glow,
Its silver streams, its woods, and meadows green,
All warmly bathed in bright Apollo's sheen,
With here and there a village like a gem
Set, clear and sparkling, in a diadem,
While on the far horizon, lo! a line
Told of eternal ocean's restless brine
Beyond which home, and kindred, distant lay.
Who'd see them e'er again?   Ah, who could say?
Above, there swelled the grand, and steep ascent
O'er which the army's rugged way was bent.
Far on the right Sierra Madre rose—
Its summit whitened by a wreath of snows—
Girt with a belt of low, and sombre, pines,
And dusky hills in long uneven lines,
While in the south, alone and far away,
The mighty Orizaba, dark, and gray,
In grandeur rose—a thing sublime—on high,
And like a giant spectre pierced the sky.

II.

Still up the mountain slope the army wound—
And food for thought where'er they ventured found—

In battle order massed by night and day,
And ever prone, by night and day, to pray;
Alert to danger, watchful of surprise,
And looking forward with expectant eyes.
The more they climbed the more the climate changed,
And through a region bleak, and wild, they ranged.
From mountain heights there blew a chilly blast.
Hail, sleet, and rain, descended on them fast,
And Cempoalla's children stood aghast,
And one by one beneath their burdens died,
While vainly all for sultry valleys sighed,
And supplicated oft, in prayer, for aid.
There earth and sky alike were cast in shade.
The rich banana's dark and glossy leaf
No longer gave the wearied eye relief,
But still the golden maize its harvest spread—
Kind Mother Nature's sweet unfailing bread—
And fields, and hedges, of the cactus grew,
And great organums, tow'ring proudly, too,
While aloes, huge, with stems of vivid green,
And golden bloom, in clusters graced the scene,
And yuca plants, and native pepper-trees—
The Ægis of the Aztec—spiced the breeze.

Through towns, and hamlets, on the Spaniards
    pressed—
And on their journey seldom paused for rest—
Exciting wonder through the country round,
And consternation by the trumpet's sound.
Their arms, and dress, their prancing steeds and
    dogs,
Their bearded faces, and their Spanish hogs,
Made Aztecs marvel, as at something weird,
For ne'er before had men like these appeared,
And native eyes saw e'en in such as swine
Mysterious things with attributes divine.

III.

While far before it spread its flying fame
To Tlascala the marching army came.
There Cortez said to Cempoalla braves,
"Go tell the chiefs that here my banner waves,
And I would fain their land adventure o'er,"
But tidings ne'er to Cortez back they bore,
For they were captured, and condemned as spies
By those they'd rashly ventured to apprise.

Know ye for war that Tlascala was famed,
And independence long ere this proclaimed
Of Montezuma's empire, and alone—
A fierce republic—still it held its own.
It now prepared, believing Spaniards foes,
To strike them down with overwhelming blows.
So loudly blew each chief his warning shell,*
And on the bold invaders armies fell
In battle line, a hundred thousand strong—
A picturesque, but nigh appalling throng,
With bows, and arrows, jav'lins made with springs,
And spears, and darts—all copper barbed—and
    slings,
Which sped their missiles as if borne on wings,
While blazoned banners in the distance waved.
The Indian masses thus the Spaniards braved,
The soldiers with a simple girdle clad,
Their bodies painted and their war-songs glad,
While drums and trumpets, sounded o'er the roar
Of swaying numbers as they onward bore.
Each captain was arrayed in feather mail,
Whose tints were richer than the peacock's tail,

---

* The conch-shell, which, when blown into, produced a loud shrill summons to battle.

And—half concealing this—a vest of gold—
A bright cuirass whose wearer's station told—
And leathern boots, or sandals, silver trimmed,
While from his helmet rose a plume or crest,
Whose colors dimmed the lustre of the rest,
And here and there a leader wore a mask
Grotesque in form, which made the Spaniards ask
If they were men, or demons in disguise,
Who in this guise Satanic met their eyes.
Then, as the morning sun illumed the scene,
And gilded moving hosts with dazzling sheen—
Where Christians fighting infidels were seen,
While back its rays cuirass and helmet flashed—
The horsemen, at a signal, forward dashed.
" *Christo y Santiago!* " loudly rang
Above the battle's far-resounding clang,
And *"Adelanté! Adelanté!"* too,
And fast their lances pierced the heathen through.
With headlong pace they ploughed the human tide,
And earth where'er they went with slaughter dyed,
And by despair emboldened " Conquest ! " cried.
The while the Spanish infantry defied
The nation's gathered armies with their swords,
And cut their battling foemen down like gourds.
The foremost in the fray was Cortez there,
And " *Jesu Christo!* " filled at times the air,
While oft his lips were seen to move in prayer.
The natives paused, and wavered ; then they fled,
And left behind them, on the field, their dead,
But ere retreating far—pursued, and sore—
While in their ears they heard the cannon's roar—
They turned, and stood, defiantly, at bay ;
Again advancing fought, and lost the day.
With cruel carnage sore repulsed were they.
The Christian troops had closely serried stood,
And there the shock of all their arms withstood.

Their panoplies of steel a shelter gave
From darts, and spears, and ev'ry heart was brave,
Though round in tumult warriors wildly surged,
Their shattered ranks by valiant leaders urged.
The ancient Greeks and Persians, seemed once more
To fight their battle as in days of yore.
The cannon boomed and filled the field with slain,
And arquebuses threw their leaden rain
Till Tlascala, defeated, cried—"'T is vain
To longer combat with the bearded foe
Who thus with death can down our columns mow."
So back they fell again to music low.

Embroidered on the standard of the state,
Which—thus repulsed—now trembled for its fate,
A golden eagle spread its shining wings*
As if to soar from this to better things,
While near it—white—the heron on a rock†
Waved undisturbed by war's tremendous shock,
And other banners here and there were seen—
Red, white, and yellow, purple, blue, and green.
One last resort to arms—a night attack
Still brought these legions to their foemen back,
But they were vanquished more than e'er before,
For Spanish steel, alas! slew thousands more.

IV.

Ambassadors were sent ere passed the night
To tell the chiefs how great was Christian might,
Inviting peace ere dawned the morning's light.
The Spaniards—all—were wounded in the strife,

---

*The banner of the Republic of Tlascala was emblazoned with a golden eagle with outstretched wings.

† The white heron on a rock was the standard of the house of Xicotencatl of Tlascala.

And passed had some—through mortal wounds—
   from life,
While clamors rose which Cortez grieved to hear.
" We'll seek the sea," they cried, " for death is here ! "
But Cortez answered—" Comrades, banish fear,
For Christ our prayers, where'er we are, will hear."
How glad were they when ere the day there came
Submission in the fierce Republic's name,
Which left them free triumphantly to go
Through Tlascala, and on to Mexico.
The great caziques extended welcome aid,
And with the victors there a treaty made—
Declaring thus allegiance firm to Spain—
And sanctioned in their clime the stranger's reign ;
While Cortez cried—" From ill I'll shield you all.
Bear witness now Saint Peter, and Saint Paul ! "
So he to steadfast allies turned his foes,
And in their leading city found repose,
And tarried like a monarch twenty days,
Receiving homage, and awarding praise.
Alas ! they little knew the depth of woe
To follow this their country's overthrow,
Or yet how soon the victors they'd have been
Had they their strength, while strength availed them,
   seen,
Against the few invaders of their soil—
Athirst for conquest, and the victor's spoil.
'T was strange their legions thus should come to
   naught
When bravely they for life, and country, fought.
They deemed their fierce assailants' lives were
   charmed,
And all with thunder, and with lightning armed.

In Tlascala—the city—Cortez cried—
" Your idols spurn, or else ye woe betide,

And Christ, and Virgin, in your hearts enthrone,
Nor dare to worship gods to us unknown ! "
But priestly words the leader's hand restrained,
And blood no more the soil beneath him stained.

Six blooming maids, as brides, were tendered there,
All chieftains' children, richly dight, and fair,
But Cortez said—" Ere Spaniards these can win
Freed they must be—baptized—from ev'ry sin,
For Christians ne'er with heathen wives can dwell."
And to the rite then bowed each Indian belle
Ere to the city Cortez bade farewell.

V.

When Montezuma heard the tidings true
Invasion's cloud to him portentous grew.
In fear and haste he sent four nobles more
With gifts superb which they to Cortez bore—
Three thousand ounces weight of golden ore,
And fabrics, rich, a monarch well might wear,
But prayed from further havoc he'd forbear,
Nor nearer to his city e'er advance,
For ill might there o'ertake his arms, perchance.

VI.

Toward Mexico the army moved again,
And in its ranks six thousand native men.
These Cortez placed from prudence in the van,
And with them wide the country round o'erran.
Ere long a city vast—Cholula—shone
Before his vision, built of brick, and stone—
A sacred, and a consecrated place,
For to this Mecca pilgrims came for grace.
A mighty mound—a pyramidal form,

Which had for countless ages braved the storm—
High on its summit reared a jewelled shrine,
And there they prayed to gods they deemed divine.
From this exalted temple all was grand
As Cortez gazed upon the smiling land.
Far to the west a rocky barrier rose
Designed the mighty valley to enclose—
The charming gem of charming Mexico,
Which he beheld with admiration's glow—
While high above two mountain peaks were seen—
A freak of Nature seeming on the scene—
Like sentinels to guard this splendid vale,
Which looked to him like an enchanted dale.
Far to the east still Orizaba's cone
Among the clouds stood barren, bleak, alone,
And nearer Mount Malinchè shadows threw
O'er plains below where maize, and aloes grew,
The mountains—all volcanoes—ermine crowned,
And wide o'erlooking all the region round.
Below, the holy city peaceful lay,
Its turrets sparkling in the beams of day,
Its groves, and gardens, stretching far away,
Its pinnacles resplendent in the sky.
Such is the prospect still that meets the eye
Which o'er the plain of Puebla wanders wide,
And all the Spaniards viewed the scene with pride.

VII.

Cholula gave them welcome with her praise,
And strewed their path with fragrant bloom, and
　　bays,
While music rose, with incense, on the air,
And songs were sung by maidens young and fair.
In art, and science, she no rival knew,
But, indisposed to fight, her wars were few,

Yet there—" A plot !—A plot ! " was whispered
  low,
And Cortez cried—" I'll strike a crushing blow.
I'll lead the heathen masses to the square,
And slay them while they struggle in the snare."
No plot was known among the native throng,
Yet felt they all the lash of cruel wrong.
The deed was done : the signal Cortez gave
Which ushered sinless creatures to the grave.
The troops—prepared—a dreadful volley fired
From arquebuse, and crossbow, then retired
A step, again to load, while forward flew
The cavalry, and pleading masses slew.
Like grain before the reaper's fatal sweep
They fell, and Death enfolded them in sleep,
While Phœbus brightly from his burnished throne
On that terrific scene of carnage shone.
Some tried to scale the walls, but wounded fell ;
Some perished at the gateways with a yell,
The victims of the pikes that pierced them there.
'Mid agonizing shrieks that filled the air
Some burrowed under piles of reeking slain,
But all from slaughter sought escape in vain.
Yet " Jesu Christo ! " Spaniards spoke in prayer,
Unmoved by cries of anguish, and despair.
Outside the walls that girt the fatal square
The people ran their kinsmen there to save,
But some who strove to succor found a grave,
For on them, lo ! the cannon, now were turned,
And homes, and fanes, by Spanish hands were
  burned.
The Tlascalans—their foes—upon them sprang,
And thrilling blasts from conches round them rang,
And swelled the tempest which still wilder raged
As Indian flew on Indian, there, enraged.
The flames, and carnage, and the dying groans,

The cries for mercy, and heartrending moans,
The musket's rattle, and the cannon's roar,
The spectacle of ruin, and of gore,
The pandemonium of sights, and sounds—
Where evil passions knew no common bounds—
Filled all the scene; and horror, and dismay,
Spread through Cholula on that awful day.
Then as the storm of battle died away,
The troops for plunder through the city sped
While o'er six thousand lay—their victims—dead.
All this beneath a Christian flag was done.
Could worse have acted Vandal, Goth, or Hun?
Yet ere the night the victors kneeling prayed,
And, looking upward, asked for heavenly aid,
And crossed their breasts devoutly in the Mass,
Nor grieved that deeds so foul had come to pass.
But still there rests on Cortez, and on Spain,
This wanton massacre's revolting stain.
" Let Christian faith," said Cortez, " supersede
The doctrines of Cholula's ancient creed,"
And where the jewelled shrine on high had stood,
Before this hurricane of fire and blood,
A mammoth cross was built of lime, and stone,
Nor more Cholula's idols there were known.

VIII.

When Montezuma heard this tale of woe
He trembled for his fate, and Mexico.
With rage, and consternation, deep, he saw
The fierce invader toward his city draw,
And envoys sent again to meet the foe,
And warn him back to ocean's breast to go,
Yet friendship feigned withal, and presents sent
To win to this—how vainly!—his consent.
In mind he weakly wavered which to do—

Oppose him foe-like, or for favor sue.
Unable yet to make him flee the soil
He feared he'd find in Mexico his spoil,
And cried—" My reign, perchance, will soon be o'er
When thus Cholula's bathed in Aztec gore.
Yet still I'll try to stop the foe's approach,
For whose advance not I deserve reproach."

The Spaniards soon their lengthy march resumed
To meet him—Montezuma—now foredoomed.
But Cempoalla's braves the monarch feared
The more as they his island city neared,
And said, " O Master! let us homeward fly,
Nor lead us into Mexico to die,
And Cortez—with reluctance—yielding this
They found in nearing home, and kindred, bliss.

IX.

The road awhile through green savannas lay,
And rich plantations stretching far away.
But soon they climbed the bold Sierra's sides,
Which Mexico's from Puebla's plain divides.
Its frosted crest above them grandly rose,
While condors o'er it soared, and carrion crows.
On up the steep ascent the troops defiled
Between the two volcanoes, lofty, wild,*
Which there in grandeur pierced the vault of blue,
And lent majestic beauty to the view.
The loftiest peak some daring Spaniards scaled,
Yet, then, to reach the belching crater failed,
But Cortez sent a troop in later days

---

* Popocatepetl —" The hill that smokes "—rising 17,852
feet above the level of the sea, more than 2,000 feet higher
than Mont Blanc, and Iztaccihuatl—" the white woman,"—so
called from its robe of snow.

To glean the sulphur from its walls—ablaze,
" For we," said he, "can turn to powder this."
They heard the deep volcano roar, and hiss,
And saw its fires beneath them, strangely bright,
Which touched the crater's walls with lurid light.
Down this abyss four hundred feet or more,
Their lot was then a Spaniard, bold to lower—*
A valiant deed that filled them all with pride.
Volcanoes thus with powder Spain supplied.

X.

Through gorge, and cañon, on the army filed,
And soon—the summit gained—the valley smiled
In blooming beauty—an enchanting vale—
As bright as e'er was sketched in fairy tale.
Before them there the Mexic garden lay,
Bright, picturesque, colossal, green, and gay,
Its noble forests stretching far away,
With cultured fields, and orchards here and there,
Distinct, though distant, in the lucid air.
Its shining lakes, and far-extending plains,
Its cities with their turrets, and their fanes,
And dusky hills, and meads of yellow maize,
Appeared before their rapt, admiring gaze,
While in the centre of the valley stood—
Borne on the bosom of Tezcuco's flood *
Great Mexico where Montezuma dwelt,
And equal laws to all his people dealt—
The stately Venice of the Aztec realm,
Which they—so few—were soon to overwhelm.

---

* They cast lots, and it fell on one Montano to descend in the basket.

* Lake Tezcuco in the centre of which the city of Mexico was built.

High o'er it all the Royal Hill was seen
Crowned with a cypress-grove, gigantic green—
The home of Montezuma, and his race,
Their cradle, throne, and sacred resting-place.
A speck, beyond the waters of the lake—
Half screened from view by intervening brake—
Told of Tezcuco's city, like it grand,
Backed by a porphyritic belt—a band
Which girdle-like around the valley wound—
A setting meet for all the gems it bound.

The Spaniard's breast with warm emotion swelled
As he at last the promised land beheld,
And Cortez felt as Moses felt of yore
When he from Pisgah viewed the happy shore.
The fairest scene was this that e'er he'd seen,
Bathed in the morning sun's resplendent sheen.
But while it charmed it awed the band he led,
And while the wealth he saw his av'rice fed
His comrades quailed, so great seemed Aztec might,
Whose signs where'er they journeyed met the sight.
"Oh! backward," some to Cortez pleaded, "turn!"
But all such pleadings he was quick to spurn.
For spoils so rich his ardent spirit yearned,
And Christian zeal for Aztec converts burned :
Nor failed he languid courage to revive.
"For conquest, and conversion," cried he, "strive,
Nor, Comrades, e'er of great success despair.
The Christian's safety is the Virgin's care!"
And so emboldened, down the mountain-side
The army marched with reawakened pride.

XI.

From many a hamlet startled peasants came
To see the White Gods—they had won the name—

And down the valley, far, had spread their fame.
All anxious seemed to do whate'er would please,
And wond'ring crowds grew denser by degrees.
Ambassadors ere long once more appeared
From Montezuma who their prowess feared,
And these to Cortez rendered gifts of gold,
And of their sovereign's might and grandeur
  told,
Yet begged he'd turn, and all his steps retrace,
Nor e'er again from ocean turn his face.
But Cortez said—" To him—your king—I go,
For to his friendship much, methinks, I owe,
And I would gaze awhile on Mexico,
And more of Spain I ween he'd gladly know."

When Montezuma heard the tidings, lo !
He felt a sense of deep, impending woe.
The bold Sierra's topmost height was scaled,
And all his arts to stay the march had failed.
That lofty and defensive screen was leaped,
And he in sorrow found his spirit steeped.
His martial courage left him, and he cried—
"Oh ! that ere this—my destiny—I'd died !
But as so far they've journeyed o'er the plain
And all resistance seems, to check them, vain
I'll now extend a welcome as a friend,
And envoys, new—with gifts—to meet them send.
Necessity a virtue thus may seem,
And I would fain my course they'd friendly
  deem."
The envoys met their guests by Chalco's lake,
And said—" Of all we bring you come partake.
We wish you welcome from your distant clime,
And Montezuma, whom we call sublime,
His gifts, and kindly greetings, bids us bear.
To Mexico he prays you'll now repair,

And in the monarch's name the way we'll lead."
"On! Comrades," Cortez cried, "with quickened
  speed!"

The blooming cacti, and the maguey green,
And oaks, and ceibas, beautified the scene;
And woodlands plumed with palms, and clad with
  vines,
And hung with moss in countless strange designs—
Where sycamores, and willows, rose on high—
In patches, here and yonder, met the eye.

Across the lake—along the causeway grand—
The army marched—a small but gallant band—
With water stretching far on either hand,
And floating gardens blooming on its face
Borne by the restless winds from place to place,
While round the margin of the lake were towns—
Besprinkled with the palm-trees' spreading crowns—
Whose limits ran beyond the solid land—
The views around diversified, and grand—
And rose on piles above the placid flood,
Which skirted league on league of field and wood,
And o'er whose surface in the noontide glow
A thousand light canoes shot to and fro.
So picturesque, and bright, and fair a scene
Had ne'er before by Spanish eyes been seen.
To Iztapalapan at length they came—
Still, as they marched, preceded by their fame—
Where, in the palace, all were entertained,
And there, with sumptuous cheer, the night remained
And wandered through its gardens, vast and gay,
Where Flora made a prodigal display,
And trees and shrubs—each species in a row—
Were gathered from all over Mexico,
And as the sun sank grandly in the west

His beams the city's minarets caressed.
The tongue of Cortez uttered words of praise
As Mexico, the famous, met his gaze.
There shining bright in those inspiring rays
Were *teocallis*,* palaces, and spires,
While on the distant hills blazed beacon-fires
To signalize the presence of the band
Whose advent spread such wonder through the land.

PART THIRD.

I.

THE morrow came : the march was then resumed,
While trumpet blasts were heard, and cannon
　　boomed
To fill the Aztec multitude with awe,
And make them marvel at the things they saw.
Like some bright fairy vision shone the scene,
With tints of gold and crimson, blue and green.
Scarce now four hundred sons of old Castile
Advanced in line with arquebuse, and steel,
With full six thousand allies in the rear—
No man of whom but felt a twinge of fear—
To overthrow an empire, and a throne,
And claim the country, and its wealth, their own.
Along the giant causeway, built of stone,
Extending through a broad and placid lake,
Not slow were they their onward way to take,
For straight it led them to the city's gate,
And who could tell what there would be their fate ?
Here floating isles of verdure, and of bloom
Displayed their beauty and exhaled perfume,

---

* Temples.

And villages, and hamlets, built on piles,
The sparkling waters half-concealed for miles,
While swift chinampas * here and there were seen,
And wondrous fair was all that sunny scene.

II.

A host of nobles soon were met who came
Great Montezuma's advent to proclaim.
These cotton skirts, and mantles—woven—wore,
And some with feather-work were blazoned o'er,
And round their necks and arms mosaics shone,
While from each nostril hung a precious stone,
And underlips, and ears alike displayed
Rich pendants, both of gold and turquoise made.
Ere long the monarch's glitt'ring retinue,
Around his palanquin, appeared in view.
"The Aztec sovereign," Cortez cried, "behold!"
'Mid blazing feather-work, and burnished gold,
Beneath a canopy with silver fringed—
While all around his faithful vassals cringed—
Borne on the shoulders of his lords he came.
The mighty Montezuma known to fame,
Whose word was law throughout his rich domain,
Who'd battles fought, and seldom fought in vain—
The sovereign ruler of a warlike race—
Here met the white invaders face to face.
Alighting from his splendid palanquin,
Which brightly sparkled in Apollo's sheen,
He stepped to where the Christian leader stood,
While shone on either side Tezcuco's flood.
In slavish adulation forms were bowed
As Montezuma passed among the crowd.
He wore his nation's ample cloak and skirt,

---

* The canoes on Lake Tezcuco.

And gaily-colored, much embroidered shirt,
And sandals, for his feet a fitting shield.
His raven hair a helmet half concealed—
A crown in which—*Cappilli*—* stood revealed—
Whereon an eagle, soaring high, was wrought
Which lustre from the beams of Phœbus caught,
While from its centre rose a royal plume
That rivalled in its beauty richest bloom.
His garments, too, with gems were thickly set—
The *chalchuite*,† the ruby, and the jet,
And ornaments of gold of strange design.
In stature tall—and thin—with look benign
He seemed a man by nature formed to shine ;
While pale of skin, the fairest of his race,
His keen and ebon eyes illumed his face,
On which there grew a scant yet comely beard,
And seldom such on Aztecs e'er appeared.
Both dignity and ease his port combined,
And culture gave refinement to his mind.
Bright silver casques and plumes his warriors wore,
And mantles—gay *tilmatli's*—‡ red as gore,
But trimmed with fur, and thickly jewelled o'er,
And quilted tunics, cotton-wove, and blue,
And sashes of a like cerulean hue.

To Cortez Montezuma soon was shown,
Who to the Spaniard made his mission known.
" I come," said he, " with welcome on my tongue,
Ye men of whom the oracles have sung ! "

---

* The name of the Aztec monarch's crown.

† The Mexican emerald.

‡ The *tilmatli* was a mantle of blue-tinted cotton worn over
a lightly quilted cotton tunic by the Aztec men generally, but
in the case of those of high degree it was of crimson color,
jewelled, and trimmed with fur. The sash which bound it
was also of cotton and called the *maxtlatl*.

The Spanish chief dismounted at his side,
And through Marina to his words replied,
With great respect, and reverence profound.
A necklace round his throat the Spaniard wound,
And then embraced the monarch where he stood,
Exclaiming—" I esteem thee great, and good ! "
But those in waiting on their sovereign cried—
" From mighty Montezuma stand aside ! "
And showed by looks their wonder and alarm,
But Cortez answered—" Children, fear no harm,
For I embrace your chieftain as a friend,
And ne'er may friendships thus cemented end."

Surprise was pictured in each Spaniard's eyes
As Montezuma praised their enterprise,
And feigned to welcome those he held in dread,
Whose coming through the clime had wonder spread.
Strange men were those he now before him saw,
And on their forms the monarch gazed with awe.
Their advent in his valley had of old
Been by his sacred oracles foretold,
And more than human all their prowess seemed.
" Yes these," he sighed, "are those of whom I
    dreamed,
Predestined to my country overrun.
Such men are surely smiled on by the Sun."
The hue of superstition tinged his mind,
And, like a bigot led, he wandered blind.
His oracles inspired his anxious dread—
While with delusions all his fears were fed—
When first he heard of this invading horde
Who came from ocean armed with fire and sword.
These oracles of fell invasion told
By strangers from the waters—strong and bold,
And prophesied they'd speedy triumphs gain,
And ever after in the land remain.

Resistance, then, by him might prove in vain,
And why should man of destiny complain?
He felt them his superiors in race,
In weapons mighty, and like gods in face.
These surely could no other be than those—
The wonder, and the terror, of their foes—
Predicted by the oracles—whose sway
Would sweep for ever Aztec rule away;
And so he yielded—rather than defy,
Nor dared to sound his country's battle-cry.
It might be, too, some providence had sent—
The God, perchance, that starred the firmament—
These pale, and bearded men to scan the land
For some great purpose none could understand,
And good might come from evil things at last,
And turn to joy the mourning of the past.
Thus o'er their advent Montezuma mused,
And none of wrong, or cowardice, accused.

Amid a prostrate multitude of braves,
Who gladly owned themselves their monarch's
    slaves,
His royal wand great Montezuma waved—
While those around; his blessing humbly craved—
And stepped into his palanquin in state,
And thus returned he to his palace gate.
He bade his brother onward lead the guests,
Who marched with hope rekindled in their breasts;
And so with flags and music, soon, they came
To Tenochtitlan,* great in Aztec fame.

---

* The Aztec name of the city of Mexico, signifying a tunal
(a cactus) on a stone—so called by the first settlers there,
about 1325. The name Mexico by which the city and country have always been known to Europeans, was derived from
that of the Aztec war-god called Mexitli by the Spaniards,
but more properly known as Huitzilopotchli—the Mexican
Mars.

III.

The city's grandeur, now, the Spaniards saw,
And admiration ripened into awe.
The street they trod was stately, long and wide,
With massive buildings ranged on either side—
Both fanes and dwellings built of reddish stone—
Whose roofs with blooming plants were half o'er-
    grown,
While gardens lay between them here and there,
Diffusing fragrance through the balmy air.
Great open squares—*tianguez*—met the eye,·
And pyramidal temples rose on high,
Colossal in their bulk, with blazing fires—
On altars built for solemn fun'ral pyres—
Which ever burned in darkness, and in light,
And crowned each sanctuary's topmost height.
Vast Aztec crowds were gathered by the way—
The sight of which made ev'ry Spaniard pray—
The pale invaders, as they came, to see,
But not a sound was heard of revelry.
They thronged the roads, the windows, and the
    roofs,
And started at the sound of horses' hoofs,
That clatt'ring trod their pavements smooth and
    clean.
Such monsters, huge, they ne'er before had seen.
The music seemed unearthly in their ears,
In some awaking mirth, in others fears,
For instruments of theirs had never thrilled
Their hearts like these, whose strains their city
    filled.
Bright falchions flashed, and bonnets made of steel,
And cries arose of "Jesus and Castile!"—
While in the shining sun the armor glanced—
As on the troops with stately tread advanced.

Close in the rear the Tlascalans appeared
At whose approach the Aztecs—groaning—sneered.
For these—their safety—Cortez gravely feared,
For each the other hated, and with hate
That time could ne'er—nor circumstance—abate.
O'er bridge on bridge o'er broad canals they passed
On which canoes were gliding thick and fast,
Each bearing market burdens to and fro,
Whose paddlers sang at times in voices low.
At length the army halted in a square
Where high the war-god's temple pierced the air—
The largest fane that rose in Mexico
Since Cortez laid Cholula's structure low,
And facing this a royal palace stood,
While in the distance shone Tezcuco's flood.

IV.

Here Montezuma came his guests to meet,
And gladly seemed their chief again to greet,
And round his neck a string of jewels placed,
And with a scarlet plume his helmet graced.
Then pointing to a palace near his own,*
Where long before his father sat the throne,
He said—" In peace, I pray you there abide,
And daily all your wants I'll see supplied."
The Spaniard in return his thanks expressed,
And Montezuma, and his empire, blessed,
While beads of glass, and baubles, he bestowed,
And ardor thus to gain his favor showed.
But though so calm, and peaceful, all appeared
The Spanish chief surprise, and danger feared,
And guns, and troops, disposed in such array

---

 * The palace of Axayacatl, Montezuma's father, built about
fifty years before, but not occupied by Montezuma.

The palace grounds they guarded either way.
A banquet soon was served to all the guests
Who murmured—"Thank the Lord!" with grateful
  breasts,
And then the sweet siesta these enjoyed—
A boon that Spaniards ne'er themselves denied,
And which they found as needful as their food,
For this repose exhausted strength renewed.
Anon came Montezuma prone to speak,
And said—"Of Spain I more of knowledge seek,
And gifts I bring to all who've gathered here,
Who well deserve the best of Aztec cheer.
Each gift's a pledge of friendship unto ye,
Ye pale-faced rovers from a distant sea."
Each Spaniard in the army took his share
Of gold, and silver, gems, and garb to wear,
And when the monarch with his train withdrew
All praised him for this proof of friendship new,
And cried—"The tales we heard were all untrue.
Munificence like this who ever knew?
His foes, perchance, their falsehoods yet will rue!"
That eve their cannon thundered in the square
In celebration of their advent there,
And smoke as from volcanoes filled the air.
The Aztecs—superstitious—felt afraid,
And Montezuma looked like one dismayed.

V.

The morning dawned, and Cortez, grave with thought,
The Aztec monarch in his palace sought,
"For there," said he, "I fain would pay my court."
He found it vast, and fashioned like a fort—
The buildings low—a long uneven file,
But built of stone, and picturesque in style,
With fountains in their yards, disporting high,

And touched by rays that brightened earth and
   sky,
While running o'er a hundred baths to fill.
Floods from Chapultepec's deep basin'd hill
Thus found their way within the palace walls.
Hernando Cortez crossed the outer halls—
Mid servitors—to Montezuma's throne,
Which like a jewel in its splendor shone,
While clouds of incense from the censers rose.
Magnificence was blended with repose.
In *nequen* robes the servitors were dressed,*
Each anxious to obey his King's behest,
And Montezuma wore his royal crest—
The gay *capilli*, yea, the Aztec crown.
His features seemed to wear a passing frown
As unfamiliar footsteps caught his ear,
But to his herald he " Admit " replied,
And Cortez soon was standing at his side.
He welcomed him, and asked him why he came.
Then Cortez, in pursuance of his aim
To make a convert of the nation's head,
Explained how Jesus on the Cross had bled,
And died for all mankind, who thus were saved
If they by grace their own redemption craved.
A crucifix he held before his eyes,
And said—" Embrace, I pray, the Christian's prize,
Nor let barbaric learning sway your mind.
In this you'll bliss, and life eternal, find.
The scheme of man's salvation I'll explain : "
But all his exhortation proved in vain,
For Montezuma to his gods was true,
His faith unshaken still by doctrines new.

---

* The *nequen* was a coarse white garment made from the
fibre of aloes, which was worn by courtiers, and others, in the
presence of Montezuma.

VI.

Marina as interpreter had served,
And well the praise of Cortez she deserved.
"Why from his faith has not the monarch
   swerved?"
He asked in disappointment. She replied—
"His faith is that in which his fathers died.
He scorns whoe'er would faith so true deride.
His nation's gods he loves, respects, and fears,
And ne'er will he renounce what he reveres.
Lo! danger lurks in efforts to convert.
He handles fire who'd Aztec gods subvert!"
Marina loved her lord, as well he knew.
Her warning voice he heeded and withdrew
From Montezuma's presence ere he spoke
Another word his anger to provoke.
But, ere he left, the monarch gifts bestowed,
And friendly feelings toward the Spaniard showed,
And sent his soldiers more of gems and gold,
And jewels of a strange, fantastic mould.
"Such gifts as these," he said, "become the
   bold!"

VII.

To Cortez all was new, and strangely grand,
That met his eye where'er he viewed the land,
And far surpassing all he hoped to find.
The mighty city Art had well designed,
And strength with beauty there was well combined,
While in the realm an engine vast he saw
By reason guided, disciplined by law,
And ruled by one whose edicts all obeyed.
To fight it well might Cortez feel afraid.
His little band had ne'er more helpless seemed

Than when the city first before him gleamed.
That city like a citadel was planned,
And screened by water from the neighb'ring land.
A drawbridge here, and there a dike, were seen,
And long canals that basked in sunny sheen.
It insulated stood from all around.
The houses rose like castles from the ground,
And who could tell but Montezuma's nod
Might send them to the presence of their God?
With odds so great could skill and science cope?
Yet plans strategic gave the Spaniards hope.

VIII.

A week of calm in Mexico had flown
When Cortez said—"The monarch I'll dethrone.
The royal favor may to fury turn,
And where before he flattered he may spurn.
The Mexicans may weary of their guests,
For secret hatred rankles in their breasts.
The bridges raised, where then can we retreat?
And we may meet—we know not how—defeat."
Thus in the leader's mind distrust arose
Which tended much to rob him of repose.
To Montezuma's palace he would go
To capture him, or strike the monarch low.
He bade his captains come in straggling groups,
While at their call should wait their bravest troops,
To turn his palace to a battle-field
If Montezuma there refused to yield.

IX.

The morning came for meeting, and they met,
When Cortez murmured—"Ere the sun doth set
The monarch's fate, and mine, perchance I'll seal,

For God is good, and trusty is my steel ! "
Addressing Montezuma, Cortez spoke
As one resolved to wrathful words provoke,
But he to rouse his indignation failed,
And found himself with gifts again regaled.
He none the less, howe'er, with threats assailed
The friendly sov'reign seated on the throne,
Whose word might then have all his arms o'er-
    thrown ;
But Montezuma still from wrath refrained,
And with his foe serenely peace maintained.
A pretext for his contemplated act
Found Cortez in a city he had sacked,
Where of his soldiers two were seized, and slain.
"Of this," said he, " I now and here complain,
And blame you, Montezuma, for the deed.
Let death to all who slew them be decreed.
To show your friendship come with us reside
Till, like their victims, slaughtered, they have died,
And in the palace we will treat you well.
A pleasant place it is in which to dwell."
Amazement Montezuma then displayed,
And o'er his visage passed a sombre shade,
And then with indignation he was flushed.
A moment more, he trembled, and was crushed.
He saw his awful fate before him rise
With thoughts which seemed his soul to agonize.
He deemed resistance vain against the foe
Who stood prepared to strike a deadly blow,
Whose might, he knew, had filled the land with woe.
He lost his strength by yielding to despair,
Which laid his craven heart, before them, bare.
Still wore his mind its superstitious hue.
The God supreme, who ruled the world, he knew
Had sent these wondrous beings thus to do,
And whatsoe'er Mexitli had decreed

He'd gladly do, nor for protection plead.
Yet from his palace walls he ne'er would
    go
To make himself the scorn of Mexico.
" No degradation such as this for me,"
The monarch cried—" No, leave me—Spaniards—
    free,
And justice fairly dealt to all I'll see."
In altercation full two hours had passed,
And Montezuma sat his throne aghast,
When one among the Spaniards—Leon named—*
Impatient of the long delay, exclaimed—
" Why waste on this barbaric hound our breath ?
In this attempt, if not the deed, is death
To all our hopes if we but falter here.
We've gone too far—my comrades—to recede,
So let us do whate'er we do with speed.
We'll spear him through and through if he
    resists,
And still to linger where he is persists.
Arrest him now, and tear him hence away,
Or we have lost in Mexico the day !"
Marina into Aztec turned the threat,
And Montezuma's brow grew cold and wet,
While sadly he with grief, and terror, sighed.
" I would," said he, " ere this that I had died,
Ere in the dust was crushed my native pride,
And on my country this affliction fell.
The oracles have conquest long foretold
By fierce invaders, like these Spaniards bold,
But few believed the sage prediction true.
Tezcatlipoca † thus why dost thou do ?"

---

* Velasquez de Leon, the leader of a hundred men, and a kinsman of Velasquez, the governor of Cuba.

† A god supposed to have been the creator of the world.

X.

Pride came at last to Montezuma's aid.
" Let preparations now," said he, " be made
To bear me in my palanquin to dwell
Where lodge the strangers, more I cannot tell."
Then he was carried through the palace gate
With all the pomp attending royal state,
And passed within the barracks of his foes.
The people near in tumult nigh arose
Believing Montezuma captive made,
But he exclaimed—" No need have I of aid,"
And—Cortez-prompted—then, with bearing proud
Addressed his sons—a dense, excited crowd—
As in the palmy days forever gone,
Yet felt dismayed, and looked in visage wan.
He said—" My children, angry passions calm,"
And in his words they found a healing balm.
Thus he to rescue closed the open door
Lest he should perish ere the strife was o'er.
Weak, superstitious, craven-hearted too,
He bowed submissive to a tyrant few
With stony hearts, and fierce as beasts of prey,
Whose impulse was to plunder, and to slay.
They feigned respect, for Montezuma now,
And Spaniards as they passed him paused to
  bow,
And gave him freedom in those narrow bounds
Prescribed by safety and his prison grounds,
But guarded him by night and day from flight,
For well they knew that this would be their
  blight,
While, through his fears, in bondage he'd remain
The friend of Cortez, and the hope of Spain.
Through him they'd hold the Aztec realm in awe,
For still his word in Mexico was law.

XI.

" *Tezcatlipoca!* " Montezuma cried—
" Ere this occurred I would that I had died ! "
He called the *teotuctli* * to his side,
And said—" Methinks I'll here awhile abide,
And take the *teomoxtli* † for my guide,
And to the sea-god—*Halo*—daily pray
To take the white invaders far away.
In all the *teocallics* ‡ in the land
Invoke *Mexitli's* all-protecting hand
To screen us from the dangers of the day,
And make our foes of *Mictlan* § soon the prey.
To ev'ry *teule* ‖ in ev'ry garden bow,
And ask of *Quetzal* ¶—mark me !--wisdom now.
To each *teotl* * *—ev'ry household shrine—
A prayer address, and make the sacred sign,
And let *tamanes* † † bear you to and fro
To do the work appointed here below,
And o'er the lake in swift *chinampas* ‡ ‡ speed,
And in the signs around the future read."

His fav'rite game of *totaloque* §§ no more
He played with golden balls, as oft before,

---

* The chief priest.

† The Aztec bible.   ‡ The temples.

§ The Aztec hell, symbolized by the owl.

‖ An image of a god generally placed on a pedestal in a garden.

¶ *Quetzalcoatl*, who taught agriculture and wisdom.

** The image of a god to be found in a niche in every house.

†† The porters employed to carry palanquins—the carriages of those of high degree.

‡‡ The canoes on Lake Tezcuco.

§§ One of the amusements of Montezuma—played with

But brooded sadly o'er his fallen state,
And *tunas,* * and the *choclat* † only ate,
Nor drank of *pulqué* though his heart was sore ;
Yet *nequen* still his vassals round him wore—
To show that he was monarch o'er them still—
And all their actions hung upon his will.

Time passed until at length one morn there came
An Aztec chief ‡ that Cortez held to blame—
An escort with him worthy of his fame.
He came to answer Montezuma's call,
As yet unconscious of the monarch's fall.
" Two.Spaniards in your country have been slain,
And death alone can wipe away the stain,
So you and all your nobles here must die.
Apply the torch, and pile the fagots high."
Thus Cortez to his answer made reply.
The chief, his son, and fifteen nobles died,
And o'er their fate a gazing concourse sighed,
Who deemed that Montezuma doomed to death
Those who in torments thus resigned their breath ;
But while the palace-yard was red with flame
The captive   monarch   groaned   with   grief   and
    shame,
For manacled and chained thus soon he lay.
He felt at last he'd lost his sov'reign sway.
He saw himself insulted and despised,
And stripped of all he cherished, loved and prized—
A captive where he'd ruled—a helpless slave.
Less bitter would to him have been the grave.

---

golden balls—which he relinquished after the invasion of his
empire.

   * Figs.
   † Choclatl—chocolate.
   ‡ Quauhpopoca, an Aztec governor of a province.

Deep in his soul the dagger entered then,
And clear were all things to his mental ken.
"These fetters are," said Cortez, "but your due.
Your honored chief—no more—the Spaniards
    slew,
And guilty, with your chief, perchance are you,
But I will now unloose your binding chains,
For mercy is an attribute of Spain's."
The monarch gave him thanks, and gifts of gold,
And of his friendship for the Spaniards told—
He Montezuma yesterday so great,
Who ruled a realm, and lived in splendid state :
So mighty then, so abject now, so low.
A sad romance was this of Mexico.
To tyranny, and fate, he humbly bowed—
He who had erst been proudest of the proud.
The burning of the chief, and all his train,
The valley filled with terror, and with pain,
And all the Aztecs marvelled o'er the deed,
Nor failed in this still greater woes to read.

XII.

One who the city near—Tezcuco—ruled,
And who in native war was deeply schooled—
A kinsman * of the captive monarch, too,
Indignant with the fierce invaders grew,
And vengeance vowed on all who'd gathered there,
Nor one of these, his country's foes, would spare.
But Cortez said to Montezuma—" Lo!
Your kinsman—yea, your nephew—is my foe,
And ere he strikes, this hand must leave him low.
For him I bid you swiftly weave a snare,
Or you no more may breathe your native air : "

---

    * A nephew.

And by the snare, by Montezuma laid,
The prince who sought his rescue stood betrayed,
And chained, and bound, to Mexico was borne
O'er cowardice, and perfidy to mourn,
But with his Aztec pride unbroken still,
And dauntless courage, and unyielding will,
While like him, too, by Montezuma's aid,
His comrades in the league were captive made.
The monarch thus the Spaniards' favor won,
And Cortez owned he'd noble service done.
Of his—his captor's—wrath he lived in fear,
And sold for life what others held more dear.
Lo! on the necks of princes conquest's heel
Was planted 'neath the banner of Castile.
The priests in solemn prayer their thanks expressed,
And to their lips their crucifixes pressed.

XIII.

"Allegiance, Montezuma, I demand
From you and all the princes in the land,
And all must render tribute unto Spain,
And glorify the Spanish sovereign's reign."
Thus Cortez spoke, and thus the king replied—
"Crushed in the dust is all my former pride.
A captive can but follow where you guide."
He summoned, then, his leaders to his side,
And begged them all allegiance to declare,
And love fraternal toward the Spaniards bear.
Amazed, but still submissive, they complied—
Though o'er the degradation, deep, they sighed—
And tribute sent in silver and in gold
To which the monarch added wealth untold.*

---

* The whole was valued at about six millions, three hundred thousand dollars or £1,417,000, exclusive of the previous presents.

The spoils with avaricious eyes were viewed,
And o'er their distribution rose a feud,
While those who quarrelled gambled with their
    gains,
And angry blood went coursing through their veins.
Ere long, as oft before, the luckless swore—
With every *peso* lost—they'd play no more.

XIV.

Achieved the conquest of the country seemed,
And of a reign of triumph Cortez dreamed,
But this still lay through bloody fields remote :
Nor yet the Aztecs had their tyrants smote.
The Aztec faith in Aztec breasts remained
Though Aztec temples Christian hands profaned.
Misguided thousands still devoutly stood
In prayer, at altars red with human blood,
And sacrifices—human—in their eyes—
With tragic scenes designed to agonize—
Alone their wrathful gods would satisfy,
And some there were with longings thus to die.
" Idolatry like this," the Spaniards cried,
" We pray you leave—with one consent—aside,
And Father, Son, and Holy Ghost address,"
But they idolaters were none the less.
With angry eyes the Spaniards on them looked,
And oft were they, with Christian zeal, rebuked.
" *Mexitli's* shrine," said Cortez, " shall be Thine :
Where idols are I'll raise the Cross divine,
And in the fane in which barbaric rites
Present by night and day revolting sights—
And earth itself by these are now defiled—
I'll bow before the Virgin and the Child."
And there, where Aztec pagans idols praised,
A Christain altar richly dight was raised,

And side by side the Christians, prone to prayer,
And pagans, prone to slaughter, worshipped there.
This formed a strange, and inconsistent scene,
Which ne'er had erst in heathen lands been seen.
Wild chants, and shrill, before the war-god's
   shrine *
Were heard above the Spanish hymns divine.
Not discord thus to concord e'er could lead,
Nor in the spirit aught but anger breed.
The profanation of their sacred fane
The Aztec priesthood filled with hate of Spain.
These on their people called the foe to smite,
And put the pale invading host to flight.
All but this outrage on their sacred fanes
The Aztecs bore in silence ; e'en the chains
Of captive princes, and the fun'ral pyre
Had ne'er aroused their deep and deadly ire
Like this foul insult, which united all.
They by their gods resolved to stand or fall.

XV.

On Tenochtitlan seemed to fall a pall
Of darkness and of gloom, as when a squall—
Before it bursts in fury—shrouds the sky,
And warns the sailor of the danger nigh,
Presaging thunder, lightning, wind, and rain,
And foaming billows on the angry main.
Then Montezuma Cortez warned to flee
From wrath to come, and shelter seek at sea,
" For all," said he, " will rise at one command,
And slay the pale invaders of the land.

---

* The great *Teocalli*, or Sanctuary, of Mexico was dedicated
to Mexitli, or Huitzilopotchli, the war-god of Anahuac, or
Mexico.

If you, Malinché *—list—would shun the fight
From Tenochtitlan speed ere comes the night."
Surprised, and startled, but with courage armed,
No sign he gave that Spaniards felt alarmed.
He calmly to the monarch's words replied,
And wisely pondered ere he all defied.
"'T would pain me much so quickly hence to fly,"
The Spaniard spoke, " and, then, no ships have I
To bear me o'er the vast, cerulean main
To tell the tale of Mexico to Spain.
But if from Tenochtitlan I should go
'T would only swell the measure of your woe,
For on the march a captive you'd remain,
And suffer an infinitude of pain.
Then spare yourself the journey, and the toil,
By pouring on the troubled waters oil.
Tell all your sons they'll find my friendship true,
And ne'er the Spaniard's advent here will rue."

XVI.

Still darker Montezuma's brow became
On comprehending the invader's aim.
A captive on the march he feared to be,
And longed to be from Spanish thraldom free.
He asked how soon new vessels he could build,
And if in building such his men were skilled,
And when he heard from Cortez in reply
He said, with kindling lustre in his eye,
" I'll all the help your men may need supply,
To fell the trees that nearest court the sky,
And build the barks to bear ye from the soil.
The builders of the ships began their toil

---

* The name bestowed upon both Cortez and Marina by the
Mexicans.

At Villa Rica, near the ocean's tide—
The Spaniard and the Aztec side by side—
While Mexico in sullen mood surveyed,
And Spanish lips for God's protection prayed.

In Tenochtitlan—Mexico—no more
Time passed serenely as in days of yore,
For hatred slumbered in the nation's breast,
And all around was ominous unrest.*
The Spanish army seemed to stand at bay :
Its sentinels were doubled night and day,
And many a brave hidalgo feared a doom
More dreadful than consignment to the tomb—
A death upon the sacrificial stone,
Where oft was heard some dying victim's groan ; †
But boldly there the Christians stood their
  ground,
While signs of siege were gath'ring all around.
Six months had passed—since first they came—
  away,
And dark the prospect now before them lay.
" Ere long from Spain a fleet may find its way,"
The trusting Spaniards oft were heard to say,
And oft for this they bent their knees to pray.
With fresh supplies, and comrades, new, to
  cheer
They felt of future conquest scarce a fear,
But minus these, the future who could tell?
And some to Hope were prone to cry farewell.

---

* This was the condition of affairs early in May, 1520,
six months after the arrival of the army in the capital.

† The victim of sacrifice was placed on a large flat stone
on the summit of the temple of the war god, and slaughtered by a priest making an incision in the breast and pluck-
ing out with his hands the reeking heart.

PART FOURTH.

I.

'T WAS then from Villa Rica tidings came—
Which filled the camp with gladness, and acclaim—
That there a Spanish fleet one morn appeared,
And straight for Villa Rica's shelter steered.
But soon to apprehension joy was turned
When of the strange armada more was learned.
Nine hundred men and eighteen caravels,
As ancient writ the simple story tells—
In days like those a mighty armament—
From Cuba's shore Velasquez there had sent
To take from Cortez all his former sway,
And force his band Velasquez to obey.
O'er this armada Narvaez * held command,
And cried—"Surrender!" when he touched the
    land,
And all his men exclaimed—"With Cortez down!"
And camped in peace in Cempoalla's town.
"Surrender! Cortez," cried they, "now your sword,
Your gold and silver—all your precious hoard;
Surrender! ye at Villa Rica, too,"
But to their trust, and Cortez, they were true,
And shouted in defiance—"Spaniards, nay,
We'll ne'er surrender while our chief's away!"

In Tenochtitlan Cortez heard the news,
And then resolved to perpetrate a ruse.
"You, good Olmedo, both my priest and friend,†

---

  * Pronounce Narvaz.

  † Father Olmedo, who through the campaign had shown
himself able and discreet in secular as well as spiritual
affairs.

To Narvaez with the olive-branch I'll send.
A welcome to my rival I'll extend,
But all my rights as captain still defend.
I'll greet him as a comrade where he stands,
But spurn his chief, and all that chief's demands.
He'll ne'er, I know, consent to this—not he.
Let this, howe'er, your mission seem to be,
And keep concealed your object from his ken—
To gain adherents there among his men;
For we, with these divided, ne'er can fail
Success to reap when we his ranks assail.
The diplomatic task with speed begin,
And strive by words from anger these to win.
Go seek the camp and turn our foes to friends.
Be rich in promise, so to serve your ends,
And scatter gold through all the hostile camp,
Nor tardy be a wondrous tale to vamp
Of Mexico—a great and dazzling prize—
The fruit of our unrivalled enterprise—
Whose like has ne'er in other lands been seen—
And from its riches all who come can glean."
Olmedo went, and served his leader well
Ere out of favor he with Narvaez fell.
Then he was seized and, guarded, sent away,
No more within the hostile camp to pray.
But ere he left he'd sown dissension's seeds,
Which were anon to germinate in deeds.
The new commander spurned his rival's claims,
And uttered threats of sentence to the flames
If Cortez bade defiance to his sway,
But promised much if he'd his rule obey.

II.

To Tenochtitlan back Olmedo sped,
And told to Cortez all that Narvaez said,

And all he'd done adherent troops to gain—
To serve the cause of Jesus, and of Spain.
Then Cortez saw with some chagrin, and pain,
In Tenochtitlan he must now remain
To meet the onset of this daring foe,
Or boldly to his camp—to battle—go.
A scanty force had he to charge him there,
But fruit Olmedo's words perchance would bear,
And, though the bolder course, he'd this pursue,
And Alvarado leave—a soldier true—*
In Mexico the garrison to rule,
And warn him to be prudent, firm, and cool.
He left him forty and a hundred men †
To guard the fallen monarch in his den,
And overawe a nation prone to arms—
A land already rife with wild alarms.
The dike across the silent lake he trod,
While prayers he breathed of gratitude to God.
" I go," said he, " with scanty troops to fight
In what I deem the sacred cause of Right.
But sixty-nine intrepid souls have I
With which imposing numbers to defy.
Yet on their arms for triumph I rely.
They're of my army's chivalry the bloom,
And fear no more their foemen than their tomb.
May Samson's strength to ev'ry arm be lent!"
Great Montezuma with the Spaniards went
In royal state beyond the city's gate,
Then parted with no outward sign of hate,

---

* Pedro de Alvarado, the *Tonatiuh* of the Mexicans.

† In addition to this number of Spaniards there were left in
the garrison on the departure of Cortez from the city of
Mexico about 6,500 Tlascalans, and Cempoallans. He left
about the middle of May, 1520, more than six months after
his arrival there.

Escorted to his prison by his foes
To meditate again o'er all his woes.

III.

Ere long Cholula met the Spaniards' view,
And long-expected comrades near them drew.
De Leon * first, then Sandoval, appeared,
And loudly the approaching columns cheered.
The little band now nigh quadrupled pressed
Right on to meet the foe, nor paused for rest,
But at the dead of night the camp surprised,
And, rushing in, the troops demoralized.
Then Narvaez, springing from his hammock bed,
Was captive made, and up to Cortez led.
"Surrender!" was the victor's thrilling cry.
And—"We surrender!" was the camp's reply.
Thus many yielded quickly to the few,
And in the fight but little blood they drew.
The victors and the conquered one became,
And followed Cortez, sharers in his fame.
The vanquished leaders were alone consigned
To such a fate as they'd for him designed,
And sent to Vera Cruz in chains to toil,
All helpless now his daring schemes to foil.
Capricious Fortune played fantastic tricks,
Nor slow was she the bitter draught to mix.

Around them lay a region of delight
Where earth and sky with tropic tints were bright.

---

* Velasquez De Leon, who had previously been sent by
Cortez to form a colony, with a hundred and twenty Spanish
troops, joined Cortez at Cholula, and Sandoval, soon afterwards, with sixty men from the garrison at Vera Cruz. The
army of Cortez now numbered two hundred and sixty-six
men, five of whom were mounted.

To yellow cedars passion-flowers clung,
And birds amid their wealth of verdure sung.
Silk-cotton trees their lengthy branches spread
Umbrella-like—fantastic—overhead,
And threw around their buttresses to shield—
The strangest forms in Flora's fertile field.*
Macaws and parrots, rich in many a hue,
Both in and out of leafy bowers flew.
The monkeys frolicked in the almond-trees,
And cherimoyas trembled in the breeze.
Where water-lilies grew the heron soared,
And pomegranate boughs revealed their hoard,
While, far and near, a wealth of maize was seen,
And here, and there, palmettos graced the scene.
Ananas, and bananas—gold and green—
In rich profusion, charmed the searching eye,
And gorgeous insects wandered idly by
To sip the nectar from the rose's bloom,
And revel in the jessamine's perfume.
The glossy-leaved magnolia arose,
Its sweet and creamy blossoms to disclose,
While mangoes waved among the nodding palms,
And aromatic shrubs diffused their balms.
The tamarind, with elephantine trunk,
From all the wild-fig's close embraces shrunk,
But shrank in vain : it climbed it to its crown,
And, swaying in the wind, threw blossoms down.
The land was clad with verdure to the shore,
Where, too, a tinge of green the ocean wore,
Though far away its color changed to blue,
And on the line which bounded human view
It softly blended with the bending sky,
As deep and clear as indigo in dye.

---

* The silk-cotton tree throws out its flat buttresses, and spreads its branches one or two hundred feet in diameter.

IV.

Across the mountain range the tidings flew—
Which Cortez found were but, alas! too true—
That slaughter was in Tenochtitlan rife,
And all the city filled with sounds of strife.
He to the army's valor now appealed,
And into line with one acclaim they wheeled—
A thousand foot, a hundred horse, with spears,
While martial music lulled their rising fears.
On toward the mountains, looming high, they
    marched,
And 'neath the burning sun with thirst were
    parched.
At length they climbed the steep Sierra's slope,
With wearied limbs, but full of ardent hope,
And saw above them rise volcanic smoke,
While on their view a charming prospect broke.
Dark forests of the cedar and the pine,
With here and there a cypress and a vine
Around them grew; through which they, now and
    then,
Caught glimpses of a chasm, or a glen,
Or sweeping valleys in the depths below,
Refulgent with a semi-tropic glow.
Then from the Cordillera's crest they gazed
Upon a scene that all, with pleasure, praised.
The broad expanse of country they had crossed
Before them spread, till far away 't was lost
In fair Cholula's plains of living green,
While to the west the valley's charms were seen—
Its lakes still trembling in the shining light,
And on their bosom towns and hamlets, bright ;—
Its fanes surmounted by a gleam of fire, *

* The *teocallis* had blazing fires on their summits night and
day.

Sustained by hands that never seemed to tire ;—
Its cultivated slopes and sombre hills,
Its blooming orchards, and its sparkling rills ;
While at their feet, 'yond groves of cypress,
    lay
Tezcuco, † flashing in the beams of day,
And in the distance Mexico reposed,
Its varied splendors to the eye disclosed.

V.

As down the western slope the troops defiled,
No longer on their ranks the natives smiled,
For hatred and distrust inspired them all,
And by their country they would stand or fall—
Fight to repel the fierce invading foe,
Whose deeds had plunged all Mexico in woe.
No longer to their banner thousands flocked,
And, there disporting, nigh their pathway blocked.
A sullen silence ev'rywhere prevailed,
Nor were they, as before, with cheer regaled.
The people fled their presence, as a pest,
By dark forebodings, wrath, and grief oppressed.
So unopposed they gained the palace yard,
Where Alvarado's troops were still on guard,
Awaiting their commander's slow return
With anxious hearts that never ceased to yearn.
There Cortez sought the story of the strife,
Which nigh had ended ev'ry soldier's life.
The storm had for the moment lulled, but lo !
Like an avenging angel, sure if slow,
Came Famine to destroy ; and slumb'ring fires
Might soon—perchance—be turned to fun'ral pyres.

---

† The city of Tezcuco, by which the Spaniards, on this
occasion, entered the valley.

VI.

In Tenochtitlan one inspiring day—
When earth was loaded with the bloom of May—
The Mexicans had gathered in their fane,
Where worshipped, too, the heroes born of Spain.
A festival they'd met to celebrate—
Mexitli's day—the war-god's solemn *fête.*
The Aztec nobles gathered there in state
All unsuspicious of their coming fate,
And worshipped, with the throng, before the shrine,
The God *Mexitli*, whom they deemed divine.
For this his sanction Alvarado gave,
And old and young were there—the fair and brave—
The high, the low, the giddy and the grave.
Their gala costumes, and their jewels bright,
Were picturesque and comely to the sight,
And in the dance, exciting, music wild
Wailed through the mighty temple like a child.
A signal, and with suddenness there sprang—
While cries of terror through the building rang—
The armored Christians on the heathen mass,
And slaughtered right and left until—alas !
Six hundred slain lay wel'tring in their gore
On that great temple's tessellated floor.
Not one escaped of all within the walls
To tell of deeds whose chronicle appalls.
The Aztec nation's proudest nobles fell,
And through the land was heard their doleful
    knell,
This wanton carnage roused its sons to arms—
For they were stung by losses, griefs, alarms,—
And all resolved the slaughter to avenge—
To seek through blood, a terrible revenge.
Cholula's dreadful massacre had paled
When they this awful sacrifice bewailed.

The ruthless soldiers plundered all the dead,
For av'rice to the cruel carnage led;
Though Alvarado, too, had deemed it wise
To fill the land with terror and surprise.
He safety hoped in Aztec fears to find,
But to his duty proved he foully blind.

With one accord the Aztec people rose
And crowded round the palace of their foes,
Who battled hard to hold them all at bay.
Their superstitious dread, before displayed,
Had passed away.   No more they seemed afraid
Of Spanish shot, and bright Toledo steel.
Relentless fury it was theirs to feel.
Some tried to scale the walls, or lay them low ;
And some to strike by other means a blow.
But while they stormed the battlements, be-
    hold !
Great Montezuma, looking as of old,
(He thus to do, was by his captors told,)
Appeared in sight to mollify their rage,
Nor slow was he their anger to assuage.
" I'll lose," said he, " if you persist, my life ;
So pause, my sons, in this appalling strife."
They ceased   to storm   the   Spanish quarters
    more,
But not their struggle with their foes was o'er.

To starve them to surrender, now, they tried,
And, by blockading, all their arts defied.
Both food and water were, alike, cut off,
And at their sorry plight they learned to scoff ;
But Alvarado's soldiers found a spring !
" The Virgin sent," they cried, " this precious
    thing ! "
And this averted death, perchance, to all,

Though wounds and sickness, still might well
   appall.*
Their only hope was now their chief's return,
The battle tide against their foes to turn.
He came while, thus beleaguered, they invoked
The mercy of the nation they'd provoked.

VII.

When Cortez heard the tragic story through,
He cried, " 'T was simple folly thus to do !
You, Alvarado, will your rashness rue.!
You ne'er Conciliation's arts employed,
But peace, by useless carnage, you destroyed,
And that when all for warfare unprepared.
To disobey my orders—mark !—you've dared,
Nor yet for those you governed have you
   cared.
All Mexico we've now, perchance, to fight,
And we alone may refuge find in flight.
'T is well that we are stronger than before ;†
But hark ! what's that ?   I hear a sullen roar !"

With terror breathless, in a picket rushed—
His body wounded, and his helmet crushed.
"Once more the city's all in arms !" he cried,
"And toward us rolls a surging human tide !
The dikes are open, and the bridges raised !
The Virgin save us, and her name be praised !"

---

* Seven Spaniards and many Tlascalans had died and there
was hardly one of either nation who had not received several
wounds.

† The army within the fortress was at this time composed
of about twelve hundred and fifty Spaniards and eight thousand native warriors, chiefly Tlascalans.

VIII.

The hoarse and sullen sound to clamor grew
As nearer to the garrison it drew,
Till from the summit of the outer wall
The scene was one to sadden and appall.
The highways seemed with warlike masses dark,
Whose weapons had the fortress for their mark.
Slings, spears and arrows they, with courage bore ;
And shrill their music rose above the roar,
While all the roofs around, with crowds, were filled,
Who in the use of native arms were skilled.
As if by magic these had risen up
To make, in blood, their foes of sorrow sup,
And there their missiles brandished high, and threw.
Thick in the palace yard their arrows flew !

The silence that prevailed when Cortez came
Thus proved to be strategic in its aim.
With all the Spanish forces here enclosed,
And all the channels from the city closed
The Aztec triumph seemed already gained,
For time would do the work that still remained.
The prelude to an awful storm behold !
Around the palace walls the masses rolled !

PART FIFTH.

I.

THE Spanish trumpets called the troops to arms.
The stirring blast, which cowardice disarms,
Aroused the camp to action.   Ev'ry man
Was at his post before the strife began :—

The cavalry, well mounted for the fray,
Prepared, with gleaming swords, the foe to slay ;
The gunners at their guns, with eager eye,
That seemed the Aztec nation to defy ;
The musket-men* and archers, rank on rank,
And native allies massed upon their flank.

The Aztecs onward came in columns bright,
Their spears and helmets gleaming in the light,
Their banners waving o'er the moving tide—
Which spread before the vision, far and wide,—
Their whistles wildly rising, shrill and clear,
And falling, like an echo, on the ear,
Above the sound of atabal and shell,
And clanging copper—the avenging knell.
Then, from their hands, a storm of weapons flew—
Stones, darts and arrows, and some lances, too—
Which, thick as rain, on the beleaguered fell ;
While from the roofs and terraces as well,
Came volleys, dense, with savage fury thrown.
The storm a roaring tempest now had grown !
When hark ! the cannon boomed, the missiles flew,
And ploughed the ranks of the besiegers through.
They sank by hundreds into Death's embrace,
But still fresh thousands swelled into their place,
Though, with bewildered looks, all stood aghast
Before the horrors of this roaring blast—
This deadly hail, this all terrific fire !
Again the cannon boomed, and carnage, dire,
Their masses swept, in long and gashing lines ;
And o'er the bodies of their comrades dead
They struggled on, and bravely fought and bled ;
While piercing cries they uttered as they rushed
To strike the foe, ere falling they were crushed !

---

* Arquebusiers.

The guns still thundered, and their thousands slew,
But nearer to their mouths the Aztecs drew,
With broken ranks, and mangled limbs, yet brave,
Determined, if they could, their land to save.
To boldly scale the parapet they tried,
But ere they reached the other side they died.
Their comrades followed over piles of slain,
The inner courtyard of the fort to gain,
And like them perished on the rampart's height.
Yet, undismayed, none shrank before the sight.
To make a breach within the wall they strove,
And, ram-like, fallen trees against it drove,
But failed in this ; next, burning arrows threw
To fire the buildings, when there rose to view
A cloud of smoke, with tongues of lurid flame,
Which all the Aztecs hailed with one acclaim.
This fresh disaster all within deplored ;
No water they, to quench it, could afford,
And so the dreaded conflagration spread—
By stables, sheds, and barrack-houses fed—
While consternation through the ranks prevailed.
Another foe their safety now assailed.
The palace, built of stone, alone escaped,
And that was with a shroud of blackness draped.
Within the outworks raged the roaring fiend,
And none were from its growing fury screened.

" Down with the wall, and stay the march of fire,
Or we shall be o'erwhelmed with losses, dire ! "
Cried Cortez, with a glance that swept the scene :
" Plant cannon in the breach, and musketeers,*
And for the rest, my comrades, have no fears ! "
Then with revengeful fury rushed the foe
To storm the gap, and strike their tyrants low,

---

* Arquebusiers.

But they were mowed by Death's relentless scythe,
Or, wounded, left in agonies to writhe,
As fast as, forward, to the breach they sprang,
While yells terrific from their masses rang,
And groans amid the battle-cries were heard.
Then, through the air, a cloud of arrows whirred,
And fiercer still the bloody battle raged.
Through fire, and smoke, and thunder, it was
    waged
From morn to eve, throughout the livelong day.
Then, with her sable wings, Night hushed the fray,
For darkness lulled the Aztecs to repose ;
And there they lay, on arms, before their foes,
Awaiting vengeance, and the morrow's dawn,
Their crowded ranks in martial order drawn.

II.

Then Cortez to Marina turned, and said—
" Not only have I fought this day, but bled,
And so, methinks, have all that I have led.
I ne'er had dreamed, against a force so great,
The Aztec foe would prove so obstinate.
For ne'er before they showed unflinching front,
Or braved the battle's devastating brunt
With courage so undaunted and sustained,
And skill, which shows that they to war were
    trained.
Why rose they not their sov'reign to defend,
When to my will I made him humbly bend ?
This inconsistency is strange indeed ;
But of fresh courage they will soon have need.
Such fire as theirs must quickly burn away !
But, while it lasts, their thousands I will slay.
To-morrow's morn will see me sally out,
And with my troops their countless legions rout ! "

Marina listened with a pensive air,
And features touched with anguish, grief, and
  care,
While in her eyes Hope struggled with Despair :—
So black, and lustrous, and withal so sad,
They looked as though they'd nevermore be glad.
Her glossy, raven hair caressed her breast,
Which swelled, and sank, with feelings of unrest,
And o'er her beauty mourning threw a veil :
She felt her nature 'neath the struggle quail.
"Alas !" she cried, "our doom, I fear, is sealed.
We need for our defence, a stronger shield
Than any we possess. The war-god's rage,
When once aroused, can hardly be assuaged,
Save by the blood of those who braved his hate.
I dread, Malinché, our impending fate.
'Twas folly to provoke him to the strife—
Involving such dread sacrifice of life—
When you, and all who followed where you led,
Were by the people reverenced, and fed.
Our only hope of safety lies in flight—
Flight under cover of the shades of night—
And woe to you, and all within these walls,
If you neglect the warning voice that calls !
I love you well, Malinché, as you know,
And hence would save you from this pending woe.
Till death in life I'll ever faithful be,
And with you, where you go, I'll gladly flee."

The brow of Cortez darkened as he heard
These warning words. "I know," said he, "I
  erred
In leaving Alvarado in command,
For he in blood, by rashness, plunged the land,
But ne'er will I give way to woman's fears,
Nor from my course be moved by woman's tears.

For me there's nought remaining but to fight,
And only if compelled I'll take to flight."

III.

To Spanish eyes the morrow's dawn revealed
A vast besieging army in the field—
More vast than on the last preceding eve,
And massed in swaying columns, deep, and dense,
Awaiting word, the battle to commence ;
Not in disorder, as they first appeared,
But as a foe well ordered, to be feared,
With banners flying, and by leaders led,
Each with a feathered casque upon his head,—*
A metal plate from harm to shield his breast,
And in a coat of plumage, brightly dressed.
High Anahuac's † standard waved o'er all—
An eagle on its prey about to fall,
That prey an océlot emblazoned there—
While cries, for vengeance, floated on the air.
Save sashes round their loins, no raiment wore
The sea of troops ‡ that swelled, the view before,
But they were armed with maguas, § slings, and
    spears,
And courage, which divested them of fears.

The battle opened with the cannon's roar,
And through their ranks the balls, and bullets tore.
Confusion followed, then the sortie came,
Which devastated like a sheet of flame.

---

* The casque resembled the head of some animal, over-
hung with brilliantly colored plumes.

† Anahuac was the Aztec name of Mexico, and this was its
ancient banner, showing an eagle pouncing on an ocelot.

‡ The common soldiery.

§ The *maguahuitl* was the Aztec tomahawk slung at the back.

The gates flew open, and the cavalry
By Cortez led—who gave his battle-cry—
Rushed out at flying gallop. Then came on
The infantry, well armed, who fought as one ;
And after them the Tlascalans deployed.
All these were in the fierce attack employed.
The foe were trampled down by horses, fleet,
And writhed beneath the native allies' feet—
Cut by the lance, the dart, the spear, the sword—
While still the loud-mouthed cannon round them
    roared.
Pierced by the speeding, deadly, leaden ball,
They fell as only battling heroes fall—
Fell striking for their altars, and their fires,
Fell in defence of country, and their sires—
Fell with unbroken courage in their eyes,
While to the last defiant were their cries.
They died, but not despairing of the end,—
The sacred cause they struggled to defend,—
And left their comrades to prolong the fight,—
To strike for life, and liberty, and Right ;
And bravely they returned the tyrants' blows,
And sank by thousands in the battle's throes ;
Nor one for mercy e'er the foe beseeched.
The routed Aztecs rallied as they reached
A barricade that stretched across the road,
And made a gallant stand, while onward rode
The cavalry in haste, but here were checked,
And not till cannon came, the screen was wrecked.
But all around the Aztec army hung,
And at the Spanish troops their weapons flung,
While to their horses' legs some bravely clung,
Esteeming vengeance dearer far than life,
And perished in the thickest of the strife.
Some from their saddles riders strove to tear—
Moved by ferocity, revenge, despair—

And woe to those thus captured. They were slain
Upon the spot, or in the war-god's fane,
Beneath the Aztec's sacrificial knife,
Where all around was eloquent of strife.

A storm of stones, and missiles from the roofs,
To Cortez gave, of havoc, painful proofs.
He saw his soldiers from their horses fall;
He heard, from roof to roof, the battle call,
And still the volleys poured. "The torch!" he
  cried,
And to the buildings this was soon applied,
When, though of stone, they succumbed to the fire,
And every house became a fun'ral pyre,
For all within, combustive, felt the flame,
While Spanish voices rose in loud acclaim.
But still the progress of the flames was slow,
Canals, and bridges, intersected so,
Yet hundreds of the habitations fell,
Ere the invaders ceased the work of hell.
Though backward forced the Aztecs kept the field,
Prepared to fight, and die, but ne'er to yield.
In sallies, and retreats, they spent the day—
The native army still in dense array,
The Spanish forces lessened by the fray.
At length by toil, and hunger, overcome,
With carnage sated, too, they heard the drum,
Which, to their quarters, ordered quick retreat,
But harrowed were the troops along the street
By tens of thousands, who with flights of stones—
And flying arrows, and derisive groans—
Saluted the receding cavaliers,
While bitter were the taunts that reached their ears.

The troops rejoined their comrades in the fort,
And, of their woes, their foes made savage sport,

And uttered threats of sacrifice, and death,
To which some listened with abated breath.
The dying day sank in the arms of Night,
And with the darkness ceased the bloody fight,
But all around the fortress camped the foe
In numbers vast—no less they seemed to grow—
Another dawn awaiting, undismayed,
Nor of the fate of those no more, afraid.
Through seas of blood, they stood prepared to wade,
Nor cared if they, in dust, were, like them, laid,
If only they could rescue Mexico
From all her deep, unutterable woe,
By trampling the invading army low.

IV.

Exhausted by the turmoil of the day,
And wounded sorely in the awful fray,*
The Spanish leader brooded o'er the scene,
And to Marina told his anguish, keen,
While tenderly he gazed into her eyes:—
"Dark is the prospect that before us lies,
Sweet *Senorita*, and our enterprise
Is menaced with destruction. You were wise
In counselling retreat, but I mistook
The signs, and now your words my acts rebuke.
Such fury I am helpless to restrain.
But Montezuma lives, and not in vain
I'll turn, perchance, to him, the storm to calm,
And to this ghastly scene bring healing balm.
He languishes, we know, alone, and sad,
Yet when he learns to leave that we'll be glad
If he'll but open wide for us the way—

---

* Cortez sustained a severe wound in the left hand during
the action.

Nor linger where we stand another day—
He'll feel again in spirit bright and gay.
Should he refuse to pacify the crowd,
I'll threaten him, nor idly, with a shroud,
And on to-morrow's eve prepare for flight,
Protected by the raven wing of Night."
Marina, in his language, found delight;
" Malinchè " * she replied, " you think aright.
To persevere, to linger longer here
Would be like self-destruction—madness clear,
Yet who can say 't is not too late to fly ?
Before to-morrow's eve we all may die !
We're standing on volcanoes, so beware,
Though for a moment, feel not thou despair.
'T is well to Montezuma to appeal,
But trust thou more thy bright unfailing steel.
He may with thy request, in fear, comply,
And yet, their king, the people may defy.
To thee they deemed him craven thus to yield ;
Another leads his forces in the field,
And he, no more, doth here his scepter wield.
Their fury was, through him, restrained at first,
But now the pent-up hurricane has burst.
It rends my heart to see my kinsmen slain ;
To find thee wounded, too, it gives me pain ;
To see us all in peril grieves me more,
But I am thine—come what may—evermore."

V.

Cool, clear, and gray, another dawn appeared—
A day, whose sequel all the Spaniards feared—
And soon the sun in all his glory rose

---

* Marina, like other Mexicans, addressed Cortez by the name given to him, and her, by the Aztecs.

To shed impartial light on friends, and foes,
And wake the armies from their night's repose.
The hills with rich and vivid rays were crowned,
And only man upon the prospect frowned.
The Aztec host were first to open fire,
And with redoubled energy, and ire,
As if the sortie of the yesterday,
More eager made them for the coming fray—
Not waited they the Spaniards' fierce attack,
Ere they essayed the fort to storm and sack,
And in the fury of their wild assault
Scaled ramparts high, and, with a fearless vault,
Reached where were gathered all the Spanish band,
Who fought in desperation, hand to hand.
A moment, and it seemed as if the place
Was captured by the heroes of their race,
So frantic was the desolating strife,
So awful was the sacrifice of life.
But, rapidly the battle's stormy tide
Turned to the pale and mailed invaders' side,
And all ere long, who scaled the works, had died,
While Mercy o'er the scene of horror sighed.

'T was now that Cortez sent a prompt appeal—
Impelled by danger, he was quick to feel—
To Montezuma, who in bondage lay,
And urged him to arrest the fatal fray.
The monarch answered in a friendly mood.
"All that I crave," said he, "is solitude.
Toward me but hate Malinché* e'er has shown.
To all the fort his deep contempt is known,
And o'er my lot in spirit oft I groan.
I've heard, and seen, with grief these battles fought,
And shrink before the havoc wild they've wrought.
What with my country's curse have I to do,
Except their baneful presence here to rue?

I ne'er Malinché wish to meet again,
Or longer live, imprisoned, in this den.
My only earthly longing is to die,
Nor care I from this wreck, abased, to fly.
To what a state I stand reduced to-day—
My freedom and my crown both thrown away !
No heart have I to Aztec braves to speak,
Nor hearing me, less vengeance they would
    wreak.
They'll ne'er again believe a word of mine—
Who, like a coward, could a throne resign—
Nor one false word, or promise of the foe,
Who's trampled me, and Mexico, so low.
They'll ne'er escape these reeking walls alive,
Do what they may—no matter how they strive."

A troubled look the face of Cortez wore
When this reply Olmedo backward bore.
"Go back," said he, "and urge him more and
    more
To face the mighty throngs and bid them pause,
And humbly bow to him, and Aztec laws,
Nor longer we'll remain to fight and die;
And tell him, hence, it is our wish to fly."

By loud entreaty moved, and waste of blood,
And hoping thus to work his country good,
By sending off the fierce invading horde—
Who'd devastated it with fire, and sword—
And in the land his freedom thus regain,
And once again, perchance—a monarch—reign,
He, none the less, said he'd address the mass,
Although at heart he sighed " Alas! alas!"
With awe his gathered army to impress
He clothed himself in rich imperial dress.
The gay *tilmatli*—mantle—white, and blue

Clasped by a gem of emeraldine hue *—
(While other gems profusely were displayed
All o'er the garb in which he stood arrayed)—
Hung on his shoulders, and his feet were shod
With golden sandals, while he held a rod—
The emblem of his rank—and on his head
There rested the *capilla*—green, and red—
The Aztec diadem—a jewelled crown,
But on his features grief hung like a frown.
Thus, in the purple fitted for a throne,
He to the turret walked, but not alone :
Some Aztec nobles, and a Spanish guard,
Attended Montezuma, so ill-starred—
The abject monarch of a fated land,
Who feared before the populace to stand.

A sudden change : the ruler rose to view,
Advancing with his royal retinue
Along the battlements, in solemn line.
He, for a moment, seemed a thing divine,
So great a charm his presence worked on all,
While thousands on their knees were seen to fall.
They saw 't was Montezuma at a glance,
And watched him slowly, like a god, advance.
The clang of instruments, and warlike cries
Were hushed in rev'rence, and in strange surprise,
And death-like stillness o'er the concourse crept,
While Montezuma turned aside, and wept.
The tumult wild and fierce, that raged before,
The shoutings of assailants, and the roar
Of battle, could be heard, or seen, no more.
As if by magic thus the scene had changed,
While Montezuma's eye the prospect ranged.
He felt his people, still, with slavish awe,

---

* The green *chalchivitl.*

Believed that he personified the law,
And deemed him still the monarch he had been,
Ere white invaders in his clime were seen.
While gazing there his confidence returned.
"Not yet," he murmured, "Montezuma's spurned."

He raised his voice in accents calm, and clear,
Designed to reach the heart as well as ear,
But in dissimulation more than truth—
To turn away the Spaniards' wrath forsooth
As well as thus his craven heart to hide,
Which, well he knew his warriors would deride.
He feigned a freedom that he'd lost, alas!
And—"Blame me," cried, "for all that's come to
     pass."
Thus spake he to the breathless thousands there,
Prepared to list—revering—as to prayer:—
"Oh! why my children are ye here in arms,
Disturbing Tenochtitlan with alarms?
Why gather ye, these palace walls around—
The palace of my fathers, so surround?
Is it that ye your sov'reign think confined,
And to release him thus have all combined?
If so ye've acted well; but ye mistake.
I'm not in bondage;—to this fact awake,
For I am free to leave when e'er I choose.
My guests—the strangers—I would not abuse.
Have ye to drive them from the city come?
How vain when, at a signal from the drum,
They mean from Tenochtitlan to depart.
But ope the way, and lo! you'll see them start.
Return ye to your homes, deserted long;
Lay down your arms nor sound the battle-song;
Show now to me—I claim it as a right—
Obedience in Tenochtitlan's sight.
The Spaniards to their country will return

And peace for all my children I discern.
All yet, with us, my people, will be well.
Believe, obey, and do ye as I tell."

As Montezuma thus himself proclaimed
The friend of those who'd brought the land to
　　shame,
A murmur through the mighty concourse ran.
Could words like these e'er come from Mexican
When Mexico lay bleeding at the hands
Of these invaders from the distant lands?
Could Montezuma, from his high estate,
Descend so low as, now, to palliate
Such crimes as theirs?—how craven, and how base!
Against him rose the passions of his race,
Which swept their ancient reverence away.
" Unworthy son of worthy sire," they cried,
" Where is thy Aztec monarch's courage, pride?
Lived all thy warlike ancestors in vain,
Nor taught thee how thy honor to sustain?
Degenerate, and cowardly, art thou
Thus weakly to thy country's foes to bow.
At heart a woman, born to spin, and weave,
Yet with no soul o'er woes of ours to grieve,
'T is not for thee to counsel us to yield.
Behold the horrors of this battle-field!"

And while the murmurs floated on the air,
And Montezuma trembled, in despair,
A cloud of stones, and arrows, reached the spot,
And lo! he fell, by three such missiles shot—*
Fell bleeding, and unconscious, to the ground
Before the Spanish guard, that stood around,

---

* One of which, a stone, struck him with such force on the
head, near the temple, as to leave him senseless.

Could shield him from the unexpected storm.
His nobles bent above his prostrate form,
And bore him—like a lifeless thing—away,
While they were filled with horror and dismay.
The strange revulsion shocked the cavaliers,
Whose fears, and pity, moved them nigh to tears.
The hopes they had on Montezuma built
Were dashed to naught—like hoarded water spilt—
And who could tell how soon the Aztec horde
Might overwhelm the wielders of the sword?
But, suddenly, 'mid consternation, lo!
There rose a dismal rushing sound of woe,
And, as in panic, all the Aztecs fled—
Their cries, by those who threw the volley, led.
Alarmed at this, their sacrilegious act,
And by remorse, regret, and terror racked,
They ran in all directions, till the scene
Looked bare, deserted, as it e'er had been:
Not one was left in all the spacious square,
Of all the host that erst had gathered there.

VII.

When Montezuma's consciousness returned,
He murmured—"I'm degraded, hated, spurned."
A sense of rage, and wretchedness, he felt,
And, into tears, his eyes were prone to melt.
From Degradation's bitter cup he drank,
And in Humiliation's valley sank.
Reviled, rejected, by his people stoned,
He o'er his blighted life in anguish groaned.
The meanest of his race had dared to throw
The missiles which, alas! had struck him low.
The world no longer wore a charm for him.
No longer fair it seemed, but foully grim—
A region changed from paradise to hell,

And who could of the darksome future tell?
He, now, had naught to live for :—he would die,
And from its terrors, thus, forever fly.
To reconcile him, vainly some essayed,
For unto none he sign, or answer, made,
And resolutely he refused their aid,
And brooding, sat, with sad, dejected look,
Nor aught to nourish, or sustain, he took,
But from his bleeding wounds, each bandage tore,
Sighed long o'er days of majesty, no more,
And all his crowding miseries reviewed,
With agony of eye, and attitude.
That he'd survived his glory well he knew,
Yet meant he to his country to be true.
He mourned his timid nature as his bane,
And owned a coward quite unfit to reign.
But still he showed a spark of Aztec pride,
When he himself, all further help denied,
Resolved to perish, rather than endure
That wounded honor, naught he knew could cure.
But from this painful scene, the trumpet called,
And dangers, new, the Spanish troops appalled.

VIII.

Before the fortress stood the war-god's fane, *
From which the Aztec arrows fell like rain ;
And hosts of Mexicans, of high degree,
Massed on its walls, the Spaniards now could see.
The spot had ne'er been fighting-ground before,
For that was sacred in the nation's lore,

---

* The *teocalli* of Huitzilopotchli—or Mexitli, the Aztec war-god—a pyramidal mound, crowned by sanctuaries—rising to the height of 150 feet, and completely commanding the palace of Axayacatl occupied by the Spaniards, which was only a few rods distant.

And this diversion of itself, proclaimed
How Aztec hearts with angry passions flamed.
But though the weapons thus, so thickly, flew,
The temple's walls, the archers screened from view.
This Cortez saw, with something like dismay.
To longer where his troops were quartered stay,
These foes, he knew, he'd have to drive away.
A force to storm and capture he despatched,
Which soon returned defeated—overmatched—
Repulsed with slaughter by those lion hearts,
Who stung them with their spears, and stones, and
    darts.
Then with three hundred chosen cavaliers,
And thousands of his native volunteers,
Intrepid Cortez rushed upon his foes,
Who staggered as he dealt terrific blows,
But step by step, all up the terraced height,
His way disputed with redoubled might ;
And close and bloody was the awful fight.
Four times the terrace, round the temple, led,
O'er which defenders, and invaders, bled,
Ere he the flat and ample summit gained,
While some below, to guard the gate remained.
" *Christo y Santiago !* " then he cried.
His buckler to his wounded arm, was tied,
And with the other hundreds he defied.
A dripping sword his hand—the right one—held,
And ev'ry stroke some dusky foeman felled,
While all the priests, around him, wildly yelled ;
And there he, with his comrades, battled hours,
And cried—" We'll fight until the day is ours ! "
But fast their numbers dwindled in the fray,
Though faster far, 't was theirs the foe to slay.
In mortal combat, on the temple's crown,
The races strove, and hurled each other down
From this aerial, reeking battle-field

To earth below.   Foe grasping foeman reeled
Together o'er the precipice, whose edge
Was bare of rampart, parapet, or ledge,
While all within the fortress raised their eyes
To view this tragic duel in the skies;
All o'er the city, too, 't was plainly seen—
A thrilling, ghastly, horrifying scene.
For three long hours the bloody fight went on
With undiminished fury, till not one—
Of all the Aztecs there—alive remained,
Except the   priests   whom   Cortez   spared,   and
    chained. *
Their lifeless forms the broad arena stained,
And crimson currents washed the outer walls,
And leapt the heights, like mimic waterfalls †

"Down with the Aztec altar!" Cortez cried,
And to the shrine the daring Spaniards hied—
Where they an idol—great Mexitli—found,
With reeking hearts before it, on the ground.
With shouts triumphant, this they trampled low,
And, in completion of its overthrow,
The monster hurled from off the terraced height,
And filled the startled Aztecs with affright.
Then to the building, they, the torch applied,
And, o'er the flames, all Tenochtitlan sighed.
Bright, fiery tongues up slender turrets crept,
And, demon-like, from wall and rafter leapt,
While all the city shone with lurid light,
And all from lake, and valley, viewed the sight,—

---

* Two or three priests were led away in triumph by the victors.

† The number of Aztecs slaughtered in the temple was about six hundred.   The Spanish loss included forty-five of the best men, and nearly all of the remainder engaged in the conflict were more or less wounded.

Far as the girding mountains—tall, and grand.
Deep horror thrilled the sore afflicted land !

The Spaniards down the temple's winding slopes
Returned, with buoyant step, and ardent hopes,
And through the spaces passed into the square ;
Nor met they from the foe resistance there,
But safely reached the welcome palace gate,
With great success—though dearly bought—elate.
That night advantage further still they pushed,
For when in sable shrouds the earth was hushed
They sallied forth, and struck the sleeping foe
A cruel and a desolating blow.
A sortie then was made, and fire, and sword,
Went hand in hand till conflagrations roared,
Where'er advanced the mailed invading horde,
And full three hundred homes were wreathed with
    flame,
Nor felt the Spanish heart a twinge of shame.
The Mexicans had battled ne'er by night,
And horror overcame them at the sight,
While none escaped but those who took to flight.

IX.

" Methinks," said Cortez, when the morrow came,
And to Marina turning, " I will tame
These Aztec spirits ere my work is done.
Already, I believe, a peace I've won,
If I but pause to parley with the foe ;
So I will call the chiefs of Mexico
Before these battered palace walls, to-day,
And offer, down, both sword, and torch, to lay,
If they will yield submissively to me !
And—mark me !—to these terms they'll all agree."
Marina looked with doubting eyes, and sighed—

"The foe is here unbending in his pride,
And though disaster overwhelms the land,
He by its fortunes still will bravely stand.
This valley's warlike sons more courage show
Than we have met before in Mexico.
Their prowess through the region round is known,
And they, in strength, and valor, stand alone."

The chieftains gathered in the open square,
And legions, with them, too, assembled there,
In answer to the call by Cortez made,
Who to address them from the fort essayed.
He stood where Montezuma stood before,
And, there, a look of proud defiance wore.
Marina, young and beautiful, was near,
With sparkling eyes, and all-attentive ear,
Prepared in Aztec words the throng to tell
What from the lips of Cortez—speaking—fell.
The concourse eyed her with an earnest look,
But not a word they uttered in rebuke,
Though to the Spanish cause they deemed her true,
And well her sway o'er all the Spaniards knew.
Thus spoke she, as an echo, to the crowd
In accents clear, and musical, and loud :—
"All, now, must be convinced that 't is in vain
For you to longer cope with mighty Spain.
Your helpless gods in dust are trampled low ;
Your land is filled with desolation, woe ;
Your homes are burned ; your altars broken lie ;
Your bravest sons have fought us, but to die.
Yet some would, still, our righteous rule defy !
Upon yourselves this chastisement you've brought ;—
The evils that afflict you, ye have sought
By taking arms against our sov'reign king.
Yet if you'll now, aside, your weapons fling,
And to submission once again return,

Nor seek Castile and Arragon to spurn,
We, whom you've thus so wantonly assailed—
And whose misfortunes Aztecs ne'er bewailed—
Will stay the hand uplifted to destroy,
And Spain will give you welcome back with joy;
But if ye, now, this proffered peace reject
Ye'll—like your temple—see the city wrecked.
Yes, Tenochtitlan shall in ruins lie,
And ev'ry soul that peoples it shall die !
Not one we'll leave to mourn its awful fate :
Be warned—beware !—before 't is all too late ! "
But threats like these were lost upon the throng,
In whom a tempest slumbered, born of Wrong.
" 'T is 'true," they cried, " our temples ye've de-
     stroyed,
And thousands of our bravest men have died,
And thousands more may like them perish yet,
But ne'er can we, for freedom, this regret,
If we for ev'ry thousand comrades slain,
Can slay but one of those who come from Spain.
Behold, still thronged, our terraces and streets,
As thronged as ere we suffered our defeats !
Far as the eye can reach our ranks extend
Prepared, through life, our country to defend.
Our losses on our numbers hardly tell,
For new recruits the masses daily swell,
But yours, remember, cannot be replaced ;
You cannot bear, like us, the battle's waste.
From hunger, and from sickness, you must die ;
Already you for food, and water, sigh.
'T is vain to think that hence ye e'er can fly.
We daily wait to glory o'er your fall.
The gods for vengeance, and your corses call !
Think not that ye can e'er escape your fate ;
For flight, across the lake, 't is far too late !
The bridges all are broken down, and Death

Waits eagerly to catch your final breath!"
And as they ended in defiance, lo!
Each chieftain shot an arrow from his bow,
And, from the turret, those assembled fled,
By disappointment stung, and full of dread.
The fierce, and heedless, courage of the foe,
Their dauntless fire, and patriotic glow,
At once amazed them, and awoke dismay.
All they had suffered, night, and day, and done—
The perils braved, the bloody battles won—
Had gone for naught, and been of no avail!
The bravest of the troops began to quail!

PART SIXTH.

I.

As, sometimes, when a ship is wrecked, the crew
Are to their pledges, and the law, untrue,
And, in their mutiny, no more obey
Those who, above them, held a sov'reign sway,
So, now, the Spanish soldiers stood aghast,
And like the mutineers before the mast—
To all subordination lost—defied
Their leader, and for liberation cried.
No longer they would in the fortress fight,
Where death was certain.   They demanded flight;
And lamentations loud, and curses, deep,
They uttered; while, in sorrow, some would weep,
Despairing of again beholding home,
And wishing they had ventured ne'er to roam.
But still—among the staunchest troops—a few
Urged amity:—subordination, too,
And saw how much they'd grave dissensions rue,

And rallied all to hold to Cortez true.—
Reflection brought them to this sober view.

Cool, calm, courageous, Cortez eyed the scene,
Nor showed his apprehension in his mien.
" 'T is sad," he mused, " to contemplate retreat,
And find success thus turned to dire defeat—
To leave behind the treasures dearly won,
And find myself pursued, abased, undone.
What greater triumph could my foes desire?
Could I to conquest after that aspire?
And what a sorry end to all my vaunts;
My comrades well may sting me with their taunts.
But if humiliation here I'd shun,
And make each man stand firmly by his gun,
And threaten death to all who urge retreat,
What brighter prospect do I, gazing, meet?
Already Famine's gnawing at his prey,
And sickness finds new victims ev'ry day;
The breaches in the fort grow wider, fast,
And little longer will our powder last.
To linger here 't would, therefore, fatal be.
For life, I fear, that we shall have to flee."

The question, now, was how to cross the lake,
And by what causeway he his troops should take?
He reconnoitred, made a feint or two,
And then decided what 't was best to do.
Three *Mantalets* with musketeers, he manned, *
Whose galling fire the foe   uld ill withstand,
And sent them out to belch their leaden hail,

---

* These were called *Mantas*, and built, after the fashion of
the *Mantalets* of the Middle Ages, to protect the arquebusiers
within. They had been in process of construction for some
days before Cortez decided to retreat. They were dragged on
rollers by the Tlascalans.

Each sheltered musketeer encased in mail.
But these the broken bridges failed to pass,
And, soon, their roofs fell—shattered—in, like glass,
Beneath the stones from ev'ry house-top hurled,
While smoke no more from each embrasure curled,
And those who drew them swiftly left the world.
Before the sting of death their spirits fled
To join the mighty army of the dead.

II.

The shortest of the causeways Cortez chose *
As that by which he'd flee his angry foes.
A wood to this extended straight, and wide,
And oft canals † athwart it rolled their tide—
Though ev'ry bridge o'er these was now destroyed—
And then—two miles in length—it spanned the lake.
"O'er this," said he, "by night I'll take my way.
'T would folly be to choose, instead, the day."
No pause he made a single bridge to build,
But all the yawning gaps, with ruins filled,
While stones, and arrows, thickly round him flew,
And Spaniards, and their toiling allies, slew.
At ev'ry bridge the Aztecs bravely fought,
And havoc in the ranks opposing wrought—
Till faint through loss of blood, and craving food,
The worn Castilians mourned the day they came
To seek, in Anahuac gold, and fame.
At length, by unremitting toil, the work was done—
Two days of labor had the triumph won—
And troops were placed to guard the open way.
But soon the Aztecs swarmed in dense array,

---

* Namely, that known as Tlacopan, or Tacuba.
† Seven canals intersected the great streets of Tlacopan, and communicated with the lake.

And laid their work on all the bridges waste
Where Spanish skill had nigh the gaps effaced.
Then to the rescue fast the Spaniards rushed,
And cavalry the heathen masses crushed,
While Cortez gave his ringing battle-cry—
"*Christo y Santiago !* at them fly !"
And hotly raged the battle till the night
When with the light the natives took their flight.

III.

There in the dusky solemn even-tide—
With Cortez bruised, and bleeding as their guide—
The troops, returning to the fort, deployed—
Each both in spirit and the flesh annoyed—
Not as exulting victors in the fray,
With streaming pennons, and with trappings, gay,
But with dejected look, and motion slow,
With hunger fainting, and oppressed by woe,
With battered armor, and their weapons hacked,
While weariness and wounds their bodies racked ;
And there they heard the tidings, sad to them,
That vacant was the monarch's diadem—
That Montezuma's sorrows now were o'er,
And on the earth his shadow fell no more.
A broken-hearted captive he had died,
His faithful nobles weeping at his side ;
And o'er his fate his mourning captors sighed.*
But ere his spirit left this mundane sphere,
A Christian priest spoke softly in his ear,†
And offered him, to bliss, a title clear,
If he would but renounce his gods on earth,

---

* Father Olmedo.

† Montezuma died on June 30, 1520, about forty-one years old, of which he reigned eighteen years.

And seek, in Christ, a new—a second—birth;
And kneeling, held a crucifix on high
To guide him to the realms beyond the sky,
And prayed him to embrace the sacred sign
Of man's redemption, holy, and divine.
But no! the proffered boon he coldly spurned,
And to his ancient faith for succor turned.
Apostasy he held in high contempt,
And asked why priests conversion should attempt.
The gods his fathers loved he'd ne'er reject;
For these he'd naught but rev'rence and respect.
He murmured low, " My children, I have left—
Now that of all but life they seem bereft—
Sunk in their deep unutterable woe—
To his protection—his Malinchè's—oh!
May they receive a father's care from Spain.
Let this be my reward for all my pain—
For all the friendship I, her sons, have shown,
A fatal friendship—who can this disown ?—
And one to which my woes are due, alone.
The loving children of the wives I love,
Should be, through life, all common wants, above.
These are the precious jewels I adore,
Though lost to me are they for evermore !
I care not for myself :—my race is run,
But these I would not have, like me, undone." *

Thus perished one, who in his youth had been
A warlike actor on the busy scene,
Whose martial prowess early gained him fame,

---

* Montezuma left a numerous progeny by his several wives,
most of whom were lost in obscurity after the conquest.
Two of them, however, a son (baptized Pedro) and daughter
(baptized Isabella) embraced Christianity, and had titles and
estates bestowed upon them by Spain, and became the found-
ers of houses whose scions—the Counts of Montezuma and
Tula—intermarried with the best blood of Castile.

And who, as monarch, won a lustrous name;
But who, as time advanced, less warlike grew,
And raised his empire into splendors new;
Who to Invasion fell an easy prey,
And saw his glory—dream-like—pass away;
Whose superstition filled his mind with fears,
His country blasted, and cut short his years.
Behold the transient grandeur of the world
In Montezuma from his station hurled,—
A captive, and an outcast, when he died,
And trampled in the dust his ancient pride!

His body, in his royal robes arrayed,
Was on a bier within the fortress laid,
Whence 't was upon his nobles' shoulders borne—
The faithful few, who lived his loss to mourn—
Beyond the prison walls, to seek the tomb,
Where slept his ancestors amid the gloom
Of cypress wreathed Chapultepec, and, lo!
A distant sound of wailing, wild, and low,
Soon floated on the air, then died away,
Drowned in the murmurs of the pending fray.
But where they placed the lifeless monarch's
  form *
No Spaniard knew; and in the awful storm
Which swept the ancient landmarks from the
  sight,
And turned the Aztec day to hopeless night,
All traces of his sepulchre were lost,
As in the spring dissolves the winter's frost.

---

* Whether Montezuma was buried at Chapultepec, or, after
his body had been burned to ashes, in the burial-place of the
city named Copalco, or elsewhere, is uncertain. What became of his body after it left the Spanish quarters never indeed transpired to the Spaniards.

IV.

Without a pause—the Spanish chief—appalled
By scenes he saw around—a council called,
When, quickly, all agreed that night to fly,
And, by the causeway, o'er the lake, to hie,
Then onward march, across the mountain chain
Till once again they trod Cholula's plain.
But some there were who grave misgivings felt,
And down, before their crucifixes knelt,
For well they knew the dangers of the way;
Yet worse would wait them, were they here to stay,
And none their flight, were willing to delay.
To guard the treasure Cortez first prepared.
In this he, with the Crown, and army, shared—
But, in such rich abundance it was stored,
He ne'er could carry all his precious hoard,
And left it strewn about the fortress floor—
Bright, shining heaps, and bars, of golden ore.
"Take what you will," said he to all his troops,
As round the spoil they stood, in longing groups,
"But let the soldier, who for lucre stoops,
Remember that the lighter be his load
The safer he will travel on the road."
Of this the wary, and the wise took heed,
But many lost their prudence in their greed,
And pining for the riches they beheld—
While visions of delight before them swelled—
Oppressed themselves with burdens hard to bear,
And found their wealth brought only toil, and care.
The order of the march was, next declared,
And Cortez cried: "My comrades, stand prepared!"
The trusty van by Sandoval was led—
Two hundred Spanish troops, to danger bred;
The centre, Cortez chose, himself, to guide—
And with Marina, mounted, at his side;—

The third command, he Alvarado gave,
Because, though rash, he knew him to be brave.
The army's strength, in infantry, was here,
And native allies followed, in the rear.
Some captive nobles were arranged in line—
And Cortez deemed their punishment condign—
While of the fallen monarch's children, three *
Were clustered where Marina loved to be.

V.

'T was midnight, and the solemn Mass was o'er,
As under àrms the troops, so rich in ore,
Passed through the fortress gates without regret—
Plunged into night, dark, cloudy, wild and wet.
In silence, and deserted, lay the square,
And only piles of slain were gathered where
The recent conflict had been thickest fought—
The wildest carnage of the day was wrought.
Along the street that to the causeway led—
Across canals that lay like polished lead—
The army marched, and not a foe appeared
Till they the lake they sought, yet dreaded, neared,
Although the tramp of horses, echoes woke,
And rumbling trains, and wagons, silence broke.
But as the causeway came in sight, a cry
Rose, from the native sentinels, on high,
Which, soon, repeated, all the city round,
Swelled into a portentous, roaring sound.
The watchful priests on ev'ry temple's height—
Where dimly burned the changeless, sacred light—
The tidings caught, and clanged resounding shells,
And uttered shrill, demoniacal yells,
While from the war-god's ravaged fane there pealed,

---

* Two daughters and a son.

Like floods of light where darkness had concealed,
The clangor of the gong-like drum that thrilled
The Aztec heart, and all the city filled.
The people sprang from slumber to the fray,
As if awakened by the God of day.

VI.

Three bridges in the dike * had spanned the lake,
'Neath which canoes were wont their way to take,
But now three yawning chasms met the eye,
And seemed the Spaniards' progress to defy.
But Cortez in the van a bridge had brought—
A substitute with grave disaster fraught—
A platform to be moved from gap to gap,
Yet, as the sequel proved, a fatal trap.
Across the first canal it, quickly, fell,
And o'er it rushed the infantry, pell-mell—
Amid a storm of arrows, darts, and stones,
And, from the sorely wounded, dying moans—
Then, cavalry, artillery, and gold.
But while the army onward moved, behold!
The mighty, rushing, swelling sound drew near,
And filled the flying troops with rising fear,
While, on the lake, the plash of paddles told
Of armed canoes, and made the blood run cold.
Louder, and louder, to a tempest grew
The clamor of the hosts night hid from view.
Faster, and faster, Aztec missiles flew,
But not a sword, as yet, the army drew,
Save where an arm was raised to ward a blow.
All sought to flee, and not to fight the foe.
The countless legions swarmed o'er land, and lake,
And with their cries the earth appeared to shake.

---

* The causeway.

On through the driving storm the Christians pressed,
While on each side, upon the water's breast,
The war-canoes against the causeway ran,
Whence leaped their crews upon the army's van,
And fought till hurled into the lake again,
Alive, or dead—one Spaniard to their ten.
The van had reached the second breach before
The crowding rear had passed the first one o'er,
And there it halted 'mid the pelting sleet—
The hail of missiles from the Aztec fleet.
Before it yawned the open, deadly breach,
And over this the bridge alone could reach.
" Send on the bridge—the bridge—or else we die !"
Was Sandoval's impatient speeding cry,
But vainly he for needed succor cried ;
The bridge the strength of all the troops defied.
Within the chasm tightly wedged it lay,
Nor aught availed to move it either way.
Stones, darts * and arrows in a torrent fell
Upon the workmen as they labored well
Till all were wounded who had not been slain,
And all exclaimed—" Our labor is in vain !"
The bridge was then abandoned, in despair,
While yells, and groans, terrific, rent the air.

The dreadful tidings spread from man to man,
And quickly through the helpless army ran,
When high arose a cry of wild dismay,
Which drowned the howling thunder of the fray.
Cut off from all retreat they feared the worst,
And Cortez, and their lot, in fury, cursed.
Each man to save himself, in haste, prepared,
Nor for his gold, or dearest comrade, cared,

---

* The darts were generally attached to strings held by the throwers, who pulled them back every time they threw them, thus tearing the flesh of the wounded.

But sought to save himself whate'er the cost.
Subordination was, in panic, lost.
Self-preservation was the law of all,
And no man heeded his commander's call.
The weak were trampled under by the strong ;
The wounded found no mercy in the throng.
Alike were trodden down both friend, and foe,
And men rushed, shouting madly, to and fro.
The leading files pushed onward by the rear—
And even goaded by the sword, and spear—
Were forced into the open breach to leap.
Some swam the gap, and gained the other steep,
But hundreds perished in the waters, deep.
The horsemen, on their steeds, plunged with the rest,
And strove the waters of the lake to breast,
And, like them, either sank, to rise no more,
Or struck the other steep ascending shore,
Then, overturned, rolled down into the flood,
Where floating thousands clamored for their blood ;
Or scaled the bank in safety, but to face
Again the fury of the Aztec race.
Along the dread *calzada* * carnage, dire,
Raged wildly 'mid a fierce unbroken fire
Of weapons from the concourse of canoes ;
And fiend-like battled their exulting crews.

The combat thickened as the moments flew,
While hotter the appalling conflict grew,
And o'er it rose the wild, discordant sounds
Of tumult, and of fury minus bounds.
Shrill shouts of vengeance, loud and dying groans,
The screams of women,† and despairing moans,

---

* The Spanish equivalent of causeway.

† Several women, both Spanish and native, had accompanied
the Spanish camp, the native wives of the cavaliers, before
mentioned, among the number.

With invocations of the goodly saints—
And, to the blessed Virgin, frantic plaints—
Were mingled in the darkness, nor a ray
From moon, or star, shed lustre on the fray.
Foe grasping foeman, rolled together down
The causeway's side into the lake, to drown,
Or to be rescued by the natives there—
A fate for Christians harder far to bear,
For they were borne away, and sacrificed,
While o'er their slaughter all around rejoiced.

Marina fought not, save to parry blows,
But others of her sex, like soldiers, rose
In self-defence, and combated their foes.
Maria De Estrada, one of these—
Who, from her native clime, had crossed the seas—
There battled with the broadsword, and the shield,
As bravely as the bravest in the field,
Though to such arms unused, for danger stirred
All those, to fury, who the conflict heard.

At length the wreck of matter formed a ridge
Above the water-line—a ghastly bridge
Of men, and horses, wagons, gold, and guns,
And Montezuma's presents—tons on tons—
O'er which there clambered an excited mass,
All eager to the other side to pass.
Here Cortez crossed upon his faithful steed,
And, vainly, tried his bleeding troops to lead,
And order bring from their confusion, wild.
He found himself as helpless as a child :—
His voice was lost in all that roaring strife,
And, like the rest, he battled for his life,
And hurried onward with the human tide,
As if the storm, and whirlwind he would ride.
He of his army's vanguard went in quest

And forward with a chosen number pressed
Until the third—last—gap he gained, and saw
His comrades round him, like dark shadows,
    draw.
There Sandoval appeared, undaunted still,
With lion heart, and steadfast iron will,
And on the chasm's verge—both deep and wide—
He all the rage of Mexico defied.
Into the yawning lake they plunged once more—
Those gallant horsemen—'mid the battle's roar,
And swam the gulf as they had done before :
And, so emboldened, others took the leap,
Which plunged them in Tezcuco's waters, deep,*
And tried to scale the causeway's stony steep.
Some crossed in safety, but the many sank
Ere they had reached—to them—the distant bank ;
Some to the horses, and their riders clung,
And there were slain, or rudely from them flung,
Or perished with them in a common grave.
Few, who were willing, had the strength to
    save,
Yet Cortez, Sandoval, and more as brave,
When tidings came the rear would soon be crushed,
Back to the help of those surviving rushed—
Across the breach, and onward—fighting—sped—
Through blood, and water, and o'er piles of dead—
And rescued Alvarado from his foes
Ere he—unhorsed—was overwhelmed with blows ;
Then with him fled, like arrows, to the van,
And o'er the breach again the blockade ran ; †
But some of those who ventured, ne'er returned
To hear the praise their chivalry had earned.

---

* Lake Tezcuco encompassed the ancient city of Mexico,
and fed the numerous canals which traversed it.

† The blockade of canoes, seeking to intercept those crossing.

When Alvarado reached the brink—pursued
By an excited, savage, multitude—
He through the breaking dawn beheld, below
Canoes—death-dealing—moving to and fro,
And feared—dismounted as he was—to swim
O'er an abyss so threat'ning, and so grim.
His only arm was now a lance. 'T was long,
And oft had proved a weapon keen and strong,
And this he firmly planted in the breach,
And, as the furies came within his reach,
He forward sprang with all his might and main
To clear the gap, nor made the leap in vain.
At one astounding bound, from shore to shore,
The yawning chasm there he vaulted o'er,
And wonder-struck alike both foe and friend,
Who scarce could deed so daring comprehend;
And to this day the miracle is told
Of Alvarado's leap, so vast, and bold.
" He truly is the offspring of the sun,
This triumph over distance to have won ;
None could, save *Tonatiuh*, thus have done,"
Exclaimed the Aztecs, cheated of their prey :
" 'T was wondrous   he   should   thus   have   flown
    away." *

VII.

The cold gray light of early morn reveaied
The tragedy that night before concealed.
The lake was flecked with countless war canoes
O'er which there gleamed the weapons of their
    crews—

---

* The width of the breach at the time is unknown, but the
wonderful exploit is still commemorated by the name given to
the spot—*Salto de Alvarado*—Alvarado's Leap.

With copper, and volcanic *itztli*, barbed—
These, saving cotton tunics, all ungarbed,
While far along the dike dark masses fought
And ev'ry moment further havoc wrought,
Each struggling for the mastery, and life,
O'er that confused, and writhing scene of strife,
Until the very causeway seemed to shake,
And earth itself—beneath the shock—to quake.

The thunder of the cannon, now, was hushed,
For all the gunners at their guns were crushed.
Pushed on by those behind, the ranks in front
Swept like a torrent, with resistless brunt,
O'er all the monsters belching leaden hail;
And what could even courage here avail?
Abandoned were artillery, and spoil—
The fruit of battles, enterprise, and toil,
The treasure Montezuma had bestowed;—
And like them left, and scattered, on the road,
Were arms, and ammunition, banners, crests,
The army's records, and the baggage chests,
For life was dearer than the world beside
To all borne onward by that swelling tide,
And he who travelled lightest, swiftest fled.
Whoso to Mammon clung, the carnage fed,
And—treasure laden—fell among the dead.
From breach to breach the mangled army passed,
The while by the pursuing foe harassed,
But, as the long *calzada's* end was neared,
Pursuit grew fainter where they most had feared,
And from the causeway to the land the troops
Marched in disorder, singly, or in groups,
With few molesting from the lake, or rear.
'T was well for them the fury of the fight
Subsided with the progress of the flight,
And well the Aztecs paused to gather spoil—

Exhausted, too, by their unwonted toil—
And left the remnant of their foe to flee,
As if they failed to there and then foresee
How from the ruins of this awful night
The hated tyrants would arise in might,
Nor saw that by pursuit—a crushing blow—
They'd lay the whole retreating army low—
So crippled, and so helpless, and so cowed,
Had now become the phalanx erst so proud.
'T was well for Cortez, and his gallant band
The dusky foe thus stayed his gory hand,
But sad was it for all the Aztec band
That they escaped on that eventful morn—
Torn though they were, and crippled and forlorn—
For, as the future showed, the tide of blood
Not yet had reached its horrifying flood.

VIII.

As from the lake the struggling troops defiled,
The rising sun upon the mountains smiled,
And to the gaze revealed their dismal plight—
Torn, wretched, bleeding, and a sorry sight.
With bitter thoughts, and anguish in his eye,
Their leader scanned them as they passed him by,
Before a stately temple, rising high
As if to court the God that ruled the sky.
There on its steps, dismounted from his steed,
Which sniffed within his reach a growing weed—
The jaded friend that bore him through the fight,
Through blood, and darkness, to the morning
   light—
Sat Cortez, not despairing, even yet,
But full of disappointment, and regret.
Those broken files their tragic story told.
Not always is the battle to the bold.

With feeble limbs, the infantry dragged on,
Their crests, and banners, and their muskets, gone,
Their mail and garments, shattered, wet and torn,
And, they, of all their pride and glory shorn,
Their wounds and bruises by their rents revealed—
Nor was their anguish by their looks concealed;—
And, with them horseless cavalry appeared,
Stripped of their arms and tattered, and besmeared.

The eye of Cortez brightened as in view
Came Sandoval and Alvarado—two
As brave as ever fought with Spanish steel.
O'er their escape he only joy could feel,
But gladness inexpressible he felt—
And into tears his eyes were seen to melt—
When one he loved—Marina—near him drew,
For he had ever found her fond, and true.
"To God!" said he, "your presence here is
    due!"
Aguilar, too, her co-interpreter,
Escaped the dangers of the night with her,
And Martin Lopez, skilled in building ships,
Saluted, with a prayer upon his lips;
But brave De Leon * nowhere he could see,
From which he knew no more on earth was he.

Remounting, Cortez to Tacuba † rode,
And cheered his weary comrades on the road,
Then halted with the army in the street,
But soon resumed—for safety—the retreat,
For still he feared pursuit, and worse defeat,
So small his forces were, the foe to meet;

---

* Juan Velasquez De Leon, who with Alvarado com·
manded the rear.

† Sometimes called Tlacopan, a city of the valley, and
prior to this period the capital of an independent principality.

And these in wild disorder still advanced,
And at each Aztec cast a startled glance.

Not distant rose a green and lofty hill*
Crowned with a monument of human skill—
A native temple built of wood and stone.
" Come on, my men, this shrine shall be our own ! "
Cried Cortez to the wounded and the weak.
" We die, unless we here a refuge seek,"
And though disheartened, stupefied, and sad—
Exhausted, too—to follow they were glad.
The temple, stormed, soon fell an easy prey—
For its defenders fired, then fled away—
And there each others' wounds the captors dressed,
And found both food, and temporary rest:
And this was all now left of that array
Which fled from Mexico but yesterday.
Where now were all the dreams of vast success?
All ended in far worse than nothingness.
But Cortez in this famished, bleeding horde—
Armed only with the cutlass, or the sword—
Found hope, his ruined fortunes to retrieve,
Though none could deeper o'er disaster grieve.
In death four thousand of his allies slept,
And o'er his comrades,—now no more,—he wept—
For nigh five hundred sons of Spain were lost
Ere, on that fatal night, the lake was crossed : †
And Montezuma's children where were they ?

---

* The hill of Otoncalpolco, but sometimes called the hill
of Montezuma.

† Gomara and Camargo state the loss in killed and missing, of the Spaniards on the *noche triste*, or melancholy night,
to have been four hundred and fifty, of which forty-six were
cavalry, reducing the number in this division of the army to
twenty-three, in addition to four thousand of their Indian
allies, chiefly Tlascalans.

Too good, perchance, were they on earth to stay,
And perished with the captives on the dike—
Too young, and sad, in self-defence to strike :
And with the captives died Tezcuco's chief,*
Steeped in the bitterness of hate, and grief.

PART SEVENTH.

I.

In Mexico,—while here the army lay—
The Aztecs cleared the wreck of war away—
Removed the dead that rose in ghastly piles
Along the streets—where they had fought—for
    miles,
And from the causeway bore the mangled mass
Of friends, and foes, some yet alive, alas!
And sacrificed their captives at their fanes,
And glorified their countrymen's remains.

Again Night o'er the earth her mantle threw,
And Cortez round him all his soldiers drew,
And strove, their hearts, with courage to imbue.
That soon the foe might follow him he knew,
And, he was anxious, eager, to press on
Till further from the tragic scene he'd gone.
" At midnight, comrades, we our march resume,
So live in hope, and cast aside your gloom.
We'll journey to the smiling Land of Bread,†
And banish from our minds despair, and dread.

---

* Cacama, Montezuma's nephew.

† Meaning Tlascala, a name signifying " land of bread,"
from the abundance of maize grown there.

Who knows what from our ruins yet may rise—
What triumphs still await our enterprise,
And which disaster to success will turn,
And make anew, our waning ardor, burn!"
His words rekindled hope in languid breasts,
And all obeyed his soldierly behests,
And at the midnight hour they moved away,
And, unmolested, marched till dawned the day.
Then like a cloud of locusts, on their rear,
The natives, in the distance, swarmed, but near
Few ventured to dispute their toilsome way,
And to the front the mighty mountains lay.
Not from the city had these hosts pursued,
But hostile was the people's attitude.
The tidings of the night retreat had flown,
And gladness spread where'er the news was known.
No more as gods the Spanish troops were feared,
No longer as divine were they revered.

Up the Sierra's sweeping slope they passed,
By the pursuing multitude harassed,
And turning oft to battle with their foes,
And carnage leave where'er they struck their blows.
From heights above, among their ranks, were
    thrown
Huge mountain missiles—timber, rock, and stone—
Which striking, killed, or wounded, those below,
While hunger filled their bitter cup of woe,
And flights of darts and arrows coursed the air,
And met them here, and there, and ev'rywhere.
Thus day by day they climbed the steep ascent,
And nightly camped, the sky above them bent,
Or shelter found in hamlet, or in town—
Some spot which seemed to wear a bitter frown—
Deserted by its people, stripped of food,
And silent as a barren solitude.

Thus Famine stole upon them by degrees.
They'd naught save what they gathered from the
    trees,
With, now and then, a stalk of golden maize,
For which, to God, they uttered grateful praise;
But, when a horse was killed, they paused to feast,
When vanished, like a gourd, the faithful beast.
Faint with fatigue, and hunger, one by one,
They fell, expiring, as they journeyed on.
The few who to their golden spoils had clung
Through all their perils, now, their burdens flung,
As worthless things, away, for life to them
Was dearer than earth's richest diadem.

II.

'T was on the seventh morning of the march—
While skies above them formed a lustrous arch—
That, from the summit of the mountain chain,
They looked below, upon Otumba's plain,*
Which, toward the Land of Bread, stretched leagues
    away,
Resplendent in the flashing beams of day;
And full in view two pyramid's arose—
Their origin, and history, who knows ?— †
One sacred to the sun, and one the moon; and nigh,

---

* This was on the 7th of July. They were only nine
leagues from the capital, but having come by a circuitous
course, they had marched more than thrice this distance.

†. The pyramids of Teotihuacan—with the exception of the
temple of Cholula, the most ancient Mexican remains—were
found by the Aztecs on their entrance into the country. One
was dedicated by them to Tonatiuh—the sun—and the other
to Meztli—the moon. Both were four stories high, but the
former was by far the largest, being six hundred and eighty-
two feet long at the base, and one hundred and eighty-two
feet high.

Great numbers—smaller—met the searching eye *
In stately lines arranged, and built in rows,
Where found the dead their undisturbed repose :—
And to the stars were dedicated these,
While o'er them waved gigantic cypress-trees.
There still their ruins stand upon the plain,
All that of those who built them doth remain—
The monuments of kings who passed away,
And left no record of their early day,
Long ere the Aztecs came to rule the land,
And built by slow degrees a city grand.

Who, now, the highest pyramid will climb,
Will find around him native scenes sublime : —
The hills of Tlascala, southeastward rise,
While fields of grain, surrounding, greet the eyes,
And in their midst a dwarfish village lies
Where once a city wooed to enterprise.
Still further to the south the Puebla plains
Reveal the summits of their Christian fanes,
For Puebla's churches, grand, and famous, still,
All who upon them gaze, with wonder fill ;
And to the west, extending far away,
The splendid valley † blushes in the day—
With Mexico, that once from ruins rose,
Spread out below, new beauties to disclose,—
Encompassed by its hills umbrageous, bold—
Which gather round it as they did of old,—
And by its shrunken lakes that shine like gold.

---

* These were seldom more than thirty feet high, and had served as sepulchres for the great among those who built them—a people lost in the mists of tradition at the time of the conquest. The plain where they stand was called by the Aztecs *Micoatl* or the Path of the Dead.

† The valley of Mexico.

Who e'er can on that lovely prospect gaze,
And not recall the scenes of other days?

III.

As the Sierra's crest the army turned,
A mighty host, below them, they discerned *
Arrayed in snowy cotton mail, and armed
With weapons which the Spanish scouts alarmed.
The Aztec braves from all the country near—
Each with his darts, his arrows, and his spear—
Had gathered to attack the fleeing foe,
And crush the hated tyrant at a blow.
Obedient to the monarch's call † they'd come—
With clanging shells, and hollow-sounding drum—
Their country's wrongs, and insults, to avenge,
And wreak, in blood, a terrible revenge.
Far as the eye could reach their banners waved.
Such odds not even Cortez e'er had braved;
But he and all his little army, knew
That great success alone, would bear them through,—
That dire defeat would carry death to all—
A thought which might the stoutest hearts appall,—
That from the conflict there was no retreat,
And this emboldened all, the foe to meet.
A restless sea of helmets, shields and spears,
Lay stretched before the way-worn cavaliers.
Where they had hoped for peace, and rest, they
    found
Another, and an awful, battle-ground.

The dispositions for the fight were made,
And Cortez, then, invoked Almighty aid,

---

* Estimated to have numbered two hundred thousand men.
† Cuitlahua, Montezuma's successor.

And prayed the Virgin, and Saint James to shield
All soldiers of the Cross, who took the field.
Next, turning to his troops, he said—" My men !
Your lot it is to face the foe again—
The foe that you have vanquished oftentime
With Christian courage, dauntless and sublime,
When numbers nigh as great as those we see
Contended with you for the mastery.
Be not dismayed by multitudes : we know
That God is with us wheresoe'er we go,
And He who, through our perils, brought us here
Is still our guide, to succor, and to cheer.
The infidel must fall beneath our swords !
The Cross will triumph o'er barbaric hordes,
And with our lances we will dye the plain
With Aztec blood, and strew it o'er with slain ! "
Then straight against two hundred thousand foes—
Whose cries for vengeance from the valley rose—
He led his little, but determined band—
A solemn, thrilling spectacle, and grand.
Down from the mountains to the plain they passed
In silence, and in battle order massed,
Their twenty horsemen mounted in the van,
And as they marched the Aztec army ran
To meet them with discordant yells, that rang
Among the hills, and rocks and peaks—a clang
The Andes echoed back, while missiles flew
So thickly as to hide the stormy view.
The Spanish soldiers vanished in the crowd,
And " Christ and Santiago ! " cried aloud.
A river in an ocean had been lost,
And on its billows wrecks were wildly tossed.
Soon, in the Aztec ranks a breach was made,
On either side of which the masses swayed,
As charged the mounted men at flying speed—
The spirit of the rider in his steed.

Confusion followed as they backward fell,
And then the infantry supported well.
The breach was widened, but again to close,
And they, once more, were lost among their foes.
But like an islet in an angry sea,
Or, 'mid the shock of arms, as stands a tree,
They stood unmoved, unflinching, firm, and true,
And, with their swords, and lances, thousands slew.
They fought with desperation, knowing well
Defeat would be a sacrificial hell.
Their native allies mingled in the fray
As eager as themselves the foe to slay,
And man to man they struggled, each for life,
Amid a roaring hurricane of strife.

Long hours of bloody warfare passed away,
And high above them rode the God of day,
And poured his fervent beams upon the plain,
Where Cortez fought, as yet, his foes, in vain.
His comrades, all, were wounded in the fray,
And some around him dead and mangled lay.
Still round him surged the sea of native braves
That ebbed, and rose, and dashed like mighty
    waves,
Fresh masses beating wildly to the front.
Could he much longer bear the battle's brunt?
His wearied troops ere this began to flag,
And some their feeble limbs could hardly drag.
The horse fell back, and crowded on the foot,
And boldly both essayed their way to cut
Through—as before—the host that gathered round,
But like a wall it seemed their course to bound.
Faint with fatigue, and loss of blood, at length
They felt, nor failed to show, their waning strength.
The natives with redoubled force assailed,
And wild with rapture coming conquest hailed.

They saw the weakness of their wearied foe,
And strong with ardor each one aimed his blow.
High ran against the Sword and Cross the tide—
While "Santiago!" loudly Cortez cried—
And all the Spaniards now could do was still
Their fighting foes at every blow to kill,
And sell their lives as dearly as they could,
Then fall, expiring, in a sea of blood.
Against them seemed to point the hand of Fate,
And all believed they fought at Glory's gate.
Their leader's eye impending ruin saw,
And from the vortex sought, his troops, to draw,
And rising in his stirrups, scanned the field
In search of what might aid, or refuge, yield,
When, suddenly, far distant, he descried
A great cazique, with nobles at his side,*
Borne in a palanquin in robes of state.
None else in all the throng appeared so great,
And Cortez said, "'T is he who holds command.
I'll seize him, and demoralize his band."
His surcoat was of gorgeous feather mail
That well became his color—tawny—pale—
While scarlet plumes high o'er a coronet—
And over that a staff, and golden net †
To hold a banner—rose above his head—
Though to the winds the flag was rarely spread—
A strange device—the symbol of his sway,
And round him all was picturesque and gay.

With glance triumphant Cortez turned, and cried
To those—his captains ‡—fighting by his side—

---

* This was Cihuaca, the Aztec commander.

† A short staff was attached to his back, and—bearing a golden net for a banner—rose above the *panache* of plumes, set in gold and gems, which formed his head-dress.

‡ Sandoval, Alvarado, Avila and Olid.

"There lies our mark! Straight onward let us ride!"
And with his war-cry sounding clear and loud,
He spurred his steed, and bounded through the
    crowd.
The native legions fell—disordered—back,
Dismayed and daunted by the fierce attack,
While with his lance he pierced opponents through,
And, 'neath his charger's hoofs, more crushed, and
    slew.
His mounted comrades followed in the rear,
And felt, though bold and brave, a sense of fear.
On, with the fury of the storm, they went,
Through solid ranks, which they asunder rent,
Their pathway strewed with dying, and with dead—
The path that straight to Ci-hu-a-ca led,
On whom with lance in hand Hernando rushed,
And, ere he paused, the chieftain felled, and crushed,
His guardsmen fleeing, trampled down, or killed,
And all around with consternation filled.
So sudden and appalling, was the blow—
Which turned the tide, and struck their chieftain
    low—
That all the Aztecs reeled beneath the shock,
And fled like sheep, when wolves assail the flock.
With lightning speed the woeful tidings spread
That he who erst had led them now was dead.
A panic seized on all that mighty throng,
Which seemed till then so fearless, and so strong.
Their terror to their own confusion led.
Their numbers but intensified their dread.
They knew their foes pursued them as they fled,
And trod each other down as on they sped.
The sudden change, so marvellously wrought,
Refreshed the victors, who, like demons, fought,
For vengeance eager, dealing death around,
Till, in a flood of gore, the plain was drowned,

And twenty thousand bodies strewed the ground.*
Long they the flying foe pursued, with haste,
And with their wondrous victory elate.†
Then—when with slaughter sated—they returned
To glean the golden spoils for which they yearned
And filch barbaric splendors from the dead—
The chieftains who their native hosts had led—
The sun was sinking in the western sky,
When prayers arose to Jesus throned on high,
In gratitude for boon so vast and great—
For this escape from dire impending fate.
They falsely deemed the heathen ne'er had rights,
And that Jehovah sanctified their fights—
That all the blood they spilt for Him was shed,
Who bade them, with their swords, the gospel spread.
Such was the spirit of their age, and race,
And they, in conquest, saw a Christian grace.

IV.

The troops resumed their march ere died the day,
Across the plain which, now, deserted lay,
And just as night with darkness draped the land—
Succeeding an effulgent sunset, grand—
They reached a temple, standing on a height,
And camped till morning shed again its light.
Once more in the ascendant was the star
Of Cortez in the tragedy of war.
Defeat had into victory been turned,

---

* The number estimated to have been slain.

† The battle was fought on the 8th of July, 1520, and was
the most remarkable victory ever achieved by the Spaniards
in the New World, considering that they had lost the *prestige* of success, that they were without cannon or firearms of
any kind, and wasted by disease, famine and prolonged suffer-
ing, and bearing in mind the immense disparity of the forces.

And all the Aztec host, in triumph, spurned.
War's glorified uncertainty behold!
Chance rules it still, as in the days of old.

Save clouds of skirmishers that came and went—
While throwing volleys at their foes intent—
Naught menaced on the morn that broke anew,
Nor near enough for battle these e'er drew,
And as the forward march was soon resumed—
While, far and wide, the sun the earth illumed—
They vanished in the distance, one by one,
Till, from the shining landscape, all had gone.

That day they camped within the Land of Bread,*
Where friendly greetings dissipated dread.
The fierce republic—Montezuma's foe—
Had gloried in his woes, and overthrow,
And grieved o'er the disasters of the night
When Cortez, and his army, took to flight.
They welcomed him with hospitable cheer,
But thousands wept o'er missing kinsmen, dear,
Who went, as allies, to return no more.
Life's battle thus, too soon, for them, was o'er.
The loving mother mourned her slaughtered
　　child ;
The warrior's wife gave way to frenzy wild ;
The tender maiden, who had loved, and lost,
Was like a flower nipped by winter's frost ;
And father, sister, brother, sadly sighed—
While in their anguish sons and daughters cried—
O'er those who in the war had bravely died.
By grief and disappointment hearts were wrung,
And songs of sorrow plaintively were sung.

---

* The Republic of Tlascala, hostile to the Empire of Mexico, and known as the Land of Bread.

V.

Here found the shattered army peace, and rest,
But many by their wounds were sore oppressed,
And Cortez lingered at the door of death,
So near, he hardly seemed to draw his breath ;
But health o'er sickness triumphed, and he rose
Resolved again to battle with his foes.
Not so his comrades, save a few, were prone.
The thought of further bloodshed made them groan,
For they were eager Mexico to flee,
And once again on Cuba's shore to be.
Thus discontent among them grew apace
When *he* proclaimed that he'd his steps retrace,
In triumph, to the city left behind,
So soon as he could reinforcements find,
And loud, and deep, the sullen murmurs grew.
"Let us," said they, "our homeward march renew,
Till Vera Cruz, and ocean, meet our view.
To strive for conquest longer would be vain,
And we should, soon, be numbered with the slain ! "
He saw that yielding to his troops' appeal
Would end his dream of glory in Castile,
And unaccomplished leave the great emprise,
Which he awaited, yet, with longing eyes.
" No, I will reap where I have sown," he cried,
" Nor leave ungathered harvests at my side
For other hands to garner. Wealth is ours
And glory, too, if we exert our powers ;
But to abandon conquest is defeat,
And I will ne'er retreat with willing feet !
Let those who would, like cowards slink away,
But all the brave will, resolutely, stay,
And share, as heroes, in the great renown
With which success, our enterprise, will crown ! "
His vet'ran troops around him gathered then—

A reckless band of brave and trusty men—
And swore that they'd to him be ever true,
And called on all their comrades thus to do,
Convinced their course, they ne'er would live to rue.
This silenced disaffection for awhile,
But many longed for Cuba's sunny isle,
Nor sighed they less for this when dangers new,
Confronted them, and formidable grew.
Not all the chiefs were friendly to their cause.
One asked—"Why feed we those who break our
    laws,
Who have our sons consigned to early graves,
And who would fain make Tlascalans their slaves?
Let us destroy the monsters while they're weak
Ere they their vengeance on us all can wreak,"
And even Cortez apprehensions felt;
He saw 't was on volcanoes that he dwelt.
Just then ambassadors, of high degree,
From Tenochtitlan came, the chiefs to see,
And urge the fierce republic to unite
With Mexico in fighting for the right;
And they—the chiefs—in council met to solve
The question—on their future course resolve.
Thus spoke the chief ambassador : " Behold !
Like wolves the white men linger in your fold !
With us arise, and slay them ere they flee.
Your gods to see them here, must wrathful be,
For they your sacred fanes have rendered waste,
And all your ancient glory nigh effaced.
If ye to their support, and friendship trust,
Remember how they ground us in the dust,
And warning take from Tenochtitlan's fate
Before ye find it—countrymen—too late.
Join hands with us, and we'll forget the past,
And make these Spanish despots stand aghast.
The sacrificial block awaits them all,

If ye respond to this our monarch's call.*
All Anahuac's nations should combine
To death, these dreaded tyrants to consign."
The younger chiefs were eager to unite
With former foes, the greater foe to fight,
But those of riper years had deeper hate
For Mexico—the mighty Valley State—
Than they had dread of Cortez, and his band,
And so resolved alone that they would stand.
'T was fear, they said, that prompted this appeal,
But they would court the friendship of Castile.
Could Fortune more have favored Cortez? No,
For Tlascala could, now, have struck a blow,
Which would have laid the bold invaders low.
'T was only by divisions they could hope
To find for action a sufficient scope,
And, with no native allies in the land,
Soon would have perished all the Spanish band.
No longer, the republic, Cortez feared,
For friendly to his cause all now appeared.
The malcontents were hushed, and Spaniards slept
Where they before had nightly vigils kept.

VI.

In action Cortez saw that safety lay,
For idleness gave discontent its play.
Some neighb'ring tribes had Spanish soldiers slain,
And he would march against them o'er the plain.*

---

* Cuitlahua, brother and successor of Montezuma, who died
of small-pox—brought into the country by the Spaniards—
after he had reigned only four months.

‡ Tepeaca was a province of Mexico—the Aztec Empire—
adjacent to Tlascala, and the Tepeacans had previously massacred twelve Spaniards on their march from Tlascala to the
capital.

Tepeacans to Tlascalans were foes,
And both were ripe to strike each other blows,
So Tlascala would join him in the fight
Against Tepeaca, and show its might,
And thus his army prestige would regain,
By causing blood the fertile fields to stain,
And piling up huge monuments of dead.
To battle, then, his soldiers, Cortez led,
With hosts of allies marshalled in the rear—
Who rent the air with whistles, shrill and clear.
Two fierce engagements, desperately fought,
The writhing region to subjection brought,
And victory, in savage slaughter, won.*
The brutal work of conquest quickly done,
The foe surrendered, and allegiance owned.
The people 'neath the brand in anguish groaned,
For they by Cortez were condemned as slaves; †
And here to bondage first consigned were braves
On this great Western Continent—a doom
Which those enslaved soon likened to the tomb,

---

* The army of Cortez in this encounter has been estimated at 50,000 men, one-half of the fighting force of Tlascala. Two pitched battles were fought before the enemy tendered his submission.

† The inhabitants of the places implicated in the massacre were branded with a hot iron as slaves, and, after the royal fifth had been reserved, were distributed among the Spaniards, and their allies. This was the first instance of slavery on the American Continent, but the punishment was afterwards disapproved by the Spanish Government. The Tepeacans were charged with rebellion because, when the Spaniards first marched through the country they swore allegiance to them, but after the disasters in the capital, transferred this back again to the Aztec Empire, and hence the severity of the sentence inflicted on those who had added murder to their political crimes. The system of *repartimientos* in the West India islands suggested this enslavement of the people.

Their crime resistance to Invasion's yoke,
And pledges of allegiance which they broke.

Hence, Cortez marched to join a traitor chief,
Who longed to see his country plunged in grief.*
He, with his people, humbly bending down,
Declared allegiance to the Spanish crown,
And drove the Aztec army from the town,
The Tlascalans, like bloodhounds, in pursuit,
While Mercy in each soldier's breast was mute.
The allies and the Aztecs fought, and slew,
And wild, then wilder still, the conflict grew,
While thousands—slaughtered—weltered in their
    gore,
And thirsting Vengeance clamored, yet, for more.
The suburbs blazed along the line of flight,
And now and then the Aztecs turned to fight.
Still thirty thousand strong, and brave, were they,
With captains rich in opulent display,
When Cortez charging, routed them, and lo!
Like water blood was made again to flow,
And, of that army, few escaped to tell
How it was butchered in the mountain dell,
And how the victors gloated o'er the spoils
Of all who fell within their deadly toils.
Another blow at Mexico was dealt;
Another pang was through the Empire felt
As Itzocan surrendered, deep in blood,
A town that had for days the siege withstood,
And here the spoils, in treasure, found were great,
While sad and stormy was its people's fate.

---

* The cazique of Quauhquechollan, a city in the Aztec Empire of thirty thousand inhabitants, at the foot of a range of
mountains, about twelve leagues from the Spanish quarters
in Tepeaca, where a large Aztec army had assembled, against
which the people fought on the arrival of Cortez.

Then to Tepeaca—the conquered—back
The army marched, still eager to attack,
And all the cities of the foe to sack.
On expeditions it was sent afar,
And o'er the country spread the flames of war,
Till from the mighty Volcan on the West,
To where bold Orizaba bared her breast
Far in the East, and from the mountains' base,
To where the ocean lay, with furrowed face,
The knee to Spain, 'mid massacre, was bowed,
And mourning fell on conquest like a shroud.
Beneath the sword of Cortez thus there grew—
Each day becoming larger to the view—
An empire, fertile, populous and wide,
With which he all the Aztec arms defied.

VII.

To Mexico 't was, now, that Cortez turned—
The prize for which his restless spirit yearned—
But to the causeways he would trust no more.
In brigantines he'd sail the waters o'er,[*]
And Martin Lopez these, with speed would build,
For he in building caravels was skilled.
To Tlascala, as ordered, he repaired,
And for his task with diligence prepared.
The forest round him yielded ample wood;
To do his bidding natives ready stood;
From Vera Cruz he sails, and rigging drew,
And bolts and nails and copper-sheathing, too,
And pitch from pines that on the mountains grew,
And e'er the army deemed the work begun,
The sturdy builder cried, " Behold it done ! "

---

[*] A number of these vessels had been constructed under
his orders in Montezuma's time, but they were subsequently
destroyed by the populace.

Thirteen stout brigantines, in parts, he made
To be upon the backs of natives laid,
And so borne o'er the mountains to the scene
Of battle, with the shining lake between.*

The white disease—a desolating plague—†
Of which the people's knowledge was but vague—
Mowed down the native populace like grass,
Alike in valley, and in mountain pass—
A bitter scourge which ne'er was known before
The stern invaders landed on their shore.
It plucked the Aztec monarch from his throne,‡
And claimed the greatest chieftains for its own.§

VIII.

Success and plunder made the army glad,
And those were joyous now who once were sad,
But some hidalgos still for Cuba sighed—
As sighs the lover for his absent bride—
And unto these their leader said—" Begone,
If ye would not, with me, still battle on ! "
And so they journeyed to their chosen isle,

---

* Lake Tezcuco, surrounding the city of Mexico.

† The small-pox.

‡ On the death of the Emperor Cuitlahua—Montezuma's brother and successor—his nephew Quauhtemotzin,—or, as the Spaniards corrupted the name, Guatemozin—who had married Tecuichpo, Montezuma's daughter—ascended the throne. He was then in his twenty-fifth year.

§ Among these was Maxixca, the principal chief in Tlascala, and the stanchest friend the Spaniards had met with there. Father Olmeda was sent to him, and he died in the Christian faith (?) declaring that the Spaniards were the great beings whose coming into the country had been predicted by the oracles. Montezuma, it will be remembered, labored under a similar impression.

Where Nature wears eternally a smile.*
Their loss was followed by a speedy gain.
Two ships arrived which showed the flag of Spain,
Both by Velasquez sent with stores for those
Who came to treat compatriots as foes.
Instructions came with these to Cortez seize,
And send him on for trial o'er the seas.†
The unsuspecting crews were seized instead,
And to the distant camp of Cortez led,
Where they were in the army's ranks enrolled,
And told that Fortune favored but the bold.

In dire distress, two other ships arrived,
Whose crews, at seizure, with the troops connived,
And willingly the band of Cortez joined,
While Fancy for them boundless riches coined; ‡
And soon there still another vessel came—
Attracted by the country's budding fame—
From the Canary Isles and Cuban shores,
With welcome arms and military stores.
The ship, and cargo, Cortez bought with gold,
And cried aloud—"These blessings I foretold,"
While fresh recruits were furnished by its crew.
The army's prospects brightened to the view.

---

* They sailed from Vera Cruz in one of the ships of the fleet commanded by Narvaez before his capture by Cortez.

† The ships were sent to Vera Cruz for the relief of Narvaez by Velasquez, governor of Cuba, and bore among other despatches one from Bishop Fonseca, the Spanish colonial secretary, instructing Narvaez to send Cortez to Spain for trial if he had not already done so.

‡ These ships had been sent by Garay, governor of Jamaica, to plant a colony on the river Panuca, north of Vera Cruz, in contempt of the claims of Cortez. Three had sailed but one had foundered, and the expedition came to an end in the manner described.

So providential seemed this help in need
That all ascribed it to the Lord indeed.
" He that," said they, "the raven's young doth feed
Has succor sent to those who fight for Him,
And never may the sword His glory dim."

IX.

'T was now that Cortez, full of hope, and pride,
With exultation coming conquest eyed,
And to Marina, ever at his side,
Exclaimed—" Ere to the capital I go,
I'll tell my Sov'reign more of Mexico—
All I have seen, and done and mean to do,
And how, to Spain, I've never been but true.
I'll tell him that Velasquez is my foe,
And disappointed, aims to strike me low,
And court investigation by the Crown.
Castile I know will praise, not crush me down ! "
And, eager all his actions to defend,
This second letter to the throne he penned,
And prayed the Monarch would his cause be-
    friend : *
And where he wrote, a colony he planned,
The second he had founded in the land,
And called the spot Segura, hoping there—
Where all in Nature was divinely fair—
Security to find from all his foes,
And those twin blessings, plenty and repose.*

---

* The Emperor Charles V. was then on the throne of Castile, and this, the celebrated second letter of Cortez, was the
first full and authentic account received in Europe of the populous Empire of Mexico, his first letter having been dispatched
from Vera Cruz before he had penetrated into the interior.

† The full name given to the settlement—the second Spanish colony in Mexico—was *Segura de la Frontera*, or Secu-

In view of wants the future might disclose,
A trusty cavalier Hernando chose*
To sail to San Domingo for supplies,
And gave him ships, and gold, for his emprise,
And bade him for his army find recruits,
And tell how rich were Conquest's golden fruits.
Then to the Land of Bread, twelve leagues away,
The Spanish army marched, in dense array,
While Cortez, in his glory, led the van,
And to behold the sight the people ran.
With trophies, and with banners, spoils, and slaves,
All battle-captured from the Aztec braves—
The pageant of a conqueror, it passed
Through towns and villages, until at last
The grand procession reached its journey's end,
While cheers and songs, in peace were heard to
  blend—
The friendly greetings of a conquered race.†
The saddened heart reproached the smiling face.
There Cortez drilled his allies in the art
Of fighting with the arrow, spear, and dart,
And for his march to Mexico prepared.
" 'T is ours," he cried, " if I am only spared,
And we shall have revenge for all the blood
That mingled, by the causeway, with the flood."
Five months from that sad night had scarce gone by,

---

rity of the Frontier, and it was situated in what was previously the province of Tepeaca. It rose to importance soon afterwards, but nothing now remains to commemorate the flourishing Indian capital of Tepeaca, but a small village which bears its name.

* Alonzo de Avila, who also bore conciliatory dispatches from Cortez to the Royal Audience at San Domingo. The expedition consisted of four vessels.

† The march of the army was through Cholula to Tlascala and took place about the middle of December.

When all seemed lost, and Death was hov'ring
   nigh—
When Ruin like a stern avenger came,
And left the army little but its fame :—
Yet now behold !—how wondrous was the change !
'T was like romance, improbable, and strange,
Or stranger still some inconsistent dream,
Where all may real, yet fantastic, seem.
The shattered wreck became a mighty host,
Whose sway was from the mountains to the coast.
New armies, as by some enchantment, rose,
And Cortez ruled, triumphant, o'er his foes.*

PART EIGHTH.

I.

In Mexico's proud capital 't was known
That Cortez scon would claim it as his own,
And strive to drive the monarch from his throne,
And crush his ancient empire in the dust.
In Might not Right all knew he placed his trust.
So Quahtemozin—he who wore the crown†
Since Death had struck his predecessor down—
Resolved to perish, or to reap renown—
Prepared the threatened storm to bravely meet,
And force the fierce invaders to retreat.

---

  * Although, however, the native army of Cortez—estimated
as high as 150,000—was as large as he could desire, his own
troops numbered, at this time, less than six hundred men,
forty of whom were cavalry, and eighty arquebusiers or cross-
bow-men. The infantry were armed with sword and target,
and the copperheaded pike of the country. His artillery was
limited to nine cannon of moderate calibre.

  † The name is also written Guatemozin.

He called his noble vassals to his side,
And in their breasts roused patriotic pride;
Reviewed his troops as one who knew them well,
And urged them all as soldiers to excel;
The useless, and infirm, dispatched away,
And bade his people the invaders slay
Wherever found, in darkness, or by day;
Built new defences, and with warlike zeal,
Made Mexico his youthful ardor feel,
While to his God he prayed to scourge the foe,
And on him bring unutterable woe.
The Aztec realm no bolder spirit knew,
Nor—to his native country—one more true.
Such was the leader Cortez had to brave,
For whom no terrors had a bloody grave,
Whose purpose was his monarchy to save—
By force a throne, that tottered, to uphold,
And rival, with his arms, the feats of old.
Well worthy he, the sceptre, was to wield;
And in him Mexico herself revealed.

The time to march on Mexico had come,
And through the camp of Cortez rolled the drum.
The army passed him quickly in review,
And in the van his old campaigners, true.
To these he said—" Brave soldiers of Castile,
Trust in Jehovah, and your polished steel.
We go to fight for riches, Cross, and Crown,
Imperishable glory, and renown;
To punish rebels to the realm of Spain,
And foes who've treated Jesus with disdain;
To wipe away the stain of our retreat
By overwhelming them with dire defeat;
To all our wrongs, and injuries, avenge,
And show how terrible is our revenge;
To win the brightest prizes earth can give,

And when we die in Paradise to live,
For on our work the eye omnific looks,
And whoso fails in duty it rebukes !
Go then, ye conq'ring heroes, on your way,
And all the infidels ye capture slay ! "
The troops with acclamation filled the air,
And answered " We no infidels will spare ;
The enemies of Christ, in blood, must die,
And ne'er again from Mexico we'll fly.
We'll conquer, or we'll perish as we fight,
And join our comrades of the awful night ! "

Then passed the allies, like them, in review,
And splendid was the pageant to the view.
Battalions with banners filled the plain,
With here, and there, a chieftain with his train,
With surcoat of gay feather-work, and plumes—
Bright as the brightest floweret that blooms—
High waving o'er his richly jewelled casque,
Which served, whene'er he chose it, as a mask,
And sandals trimmed with precious gems, and gold.
The scene was fascinating to behold.
To these spoke Cortez, through Marina, thus :—
" We fight your battles, and you fight with us ;
Fight then as soldiers worthy of renown,
And from your ancient foeman tear his crown ;
Fight to sustain the glory you have won,
And like a tempest o'er your valley run ;
Let none my banner follow, but the brave,
Prepared to conquer, or to find a grave,
To battle with me till the work is done,
Nor for a moment danger ever shun.
Not all here gathered with me I shall take,
But those I leave must follow to the Lake—*

---

* Lake Tezcuco.

And bring the brigantines—at my command;
Then ye shall shed fresh lustre on your land,
And riches reap, amid achievements grand!"

This over, Cortez led his troops away—
'Mid loud huzzahs, and martial music, gay,
With banners waving all along the line—
A spectacle strange, picturesque, and fine;
While anxious thousands hung upon the rear,
To take a parting glance at kinsmen dear,
And offer words of comfort, hope, and cheer, *
Imploring gods their righteous arms, to bless,
And lead them to victorious success.

II.

Three routes into the valley open lay,
And Cortez wisely chose the roughest way,
As one most likely to be guarded least,
Though hard he found the road for man and beast.
The mountain range dividing west from east—
And one great plateau from a kindred plain—
The army traversed, while above them rose
A lofty peak that wore a crown of snows.†
The winter torrents channels deep had made,
And trees had been across their pathway laid.
The piercing cold contrasted with the glow
Which—semi-tropic—warmed the plain below,
And thin and sombre forests of the pine
Were seen instead of sycamore, and vine,

---

* Cortez took his departure from Tlascala for Lake Tezcuco
on the 26th of December—leaving most of his allies behind,
however, to await his orders to advance with the brigantines.
This was done on account of the difficulty of provisioning so
large a force.

† Iztaccihuatl, or "The White Woman."

While overhead voracious vultures flew.*
At length the valley burst upon their view,
Though intervening woods and hills concealed,
In part, the splendors further on revealed.
As down the bold Sierra's slope they passed—
By barricades of timber still harassed—
The climate, and the vegetation changed,
And beauty met the sight where'er it ranged.
The graceful pepper-tree refreshed the eye—
With berries loaded, of a crimson dye—
And gaudy creepers climbed the sturdy oak,
While mocking-birds the woodland silence broke.
An open level reached, the valley lay
Before the vision in its bright array,
Bathed in the golden radiance of the day.
It lay embosomed in its hills that rose
As sentinels, to guard its sweet repose,
And like a jewelled cluster on its breast
Tezcuco's city seemed to be at rest.
To some the prospect seemed a tale to tell,
Which, like a knell, upon their senses fell.
They vividly recalled the fatal night
When carnage followed their disastrous flight ;
But admiration kindled in their gaze,
And moved their lips to utter words of praise,
As they beheld the splendor of the scene,
Magnificently touched with gold, and green.
"To victory, or death 'tis now we go,
Let all prepare to meet, and crush the foe !"
Cried Cortez with defiance in his tone,
And that resolve each soldier made his own.

'T was now the hill-tops blazed with beacon fires—
To telegraph by flame instead of wires,—

---

* Flocks of the *Zopilote*, the native vulture, or buzzard.

The news that the invading host had come ;
And thundered in each fane the warning drum.

At ev'ry turn they looked for some surprise,
And searched the hills, and dales, with watchful
    eyes,
But only dusky multitudes were seen,
From time to time, with distance great between.
That night the Spaniards, unmolested, camped—
With hope and courage on their features stamped—
Within the shadow of a leafy wood,
And but three leagues from where Tezcuco stood—
A noble city with a storied name,
And second to the capital in fame.
Ere he attacked the great metropolis,
The plan of Cortez was to capture this.

III.

The morrow dawned, and still no foe appeared—
The hosts that all night long the army feared—
But soon ambassadors with flags of gold *
Approached the camp their mission to unfold.
"We come," said they, "your mercy to implore !
Our city spare, and plunge us not in gore !
Seek shelter, if ye will, within our walls,
But needless slaughter save us !—that appalls.
Our Lord, and master—the cazique—will swear—
In his own palace when you meet him there—
Allegiance—as a vassal—to the Crown,
And to your arms submissively bow down ;
Yet we would till to-morrow pray you wait,
For he would meet you in becoming state."
In Cortez, joy was equalled by surprise,

---

* The flag of truce.

But neither he betrayed to Aztec eyes.
His feelings he dissembled, and replied,
With seeming anger, and offended pride—
" Where lie the Spanish soldiers that ye slew—
The forty-five who put their trust in you ?—
And where, too, are the spoils ye gleaned from
   them ?
This massacre, and plunder, I condemn,
And on the restitution of their gold
I now insist, nor dare ye that withhold ! " *

"Nay, blame the monarch, and not us," they cried,
For by his orders 't was the soldiers died,
And he received the treasure that they bore.
The sovereign then is now, alas ! no more,
But his successor may the spoil restore."
Not heeding their petition to delay,
The Spanish chief continued on his way
And soon into the ancient city rode,
And chose a palace for his troops' abode. †
'T was like a voiceless city of the dead,
For from its precincts— overwhelmed with dread—
The people had, by lake and mountain, fled,
And with them Co-an-ac-o—the cazique,
On whom had Cortez vengeance vowed to wreak.
" A barren victory is this," cried he ;
" Pursue, and capture, those that yonder flee,
And see if the cazique among them be.

---

* The forty-five Spaniards referred to were on their way
from Tlascala to the city of Mexico when the disastrous retreat took place, but before they were made aware of that
event they were captured in the Tezcucan territory, and afterwards sacrificed on the altars of the metropolis. Cuitlahua,
the successor of Montezuma, was then on the imperial throne.

  † Cortez at the head of his army entered Tezcuco on the
31st of December, 1520.

Those envoys sought to throw me off my guard,
And, by a day, my progress to retard,
Through promises as false as they were fair,
And, in that day, to strip the city bare,
And refuge seek in less disordered flight;
But I will ere there comes another night
Dethrone the hostile, fugitive cazique—
Who would his promises, and pledges, break—
And on another place the vacant crown,
One who will bow obediently down."
So from the few, who still remained, he took
A youthful noble, with a comely look—
A brother of the chieftain he deposed—*
In whom he—Cortez—confidence reposed,
And—when baptized—he placed him on the throne,
And cried, " Behold ! the Province is your own,
To rule for Spain, whose vassal you are now,
No more to Aztec Emperors to bow !
See that you rule it well, and to Castile
In all humility, and friendship, kneel ! "

The story of Te-co-col's reign is brief.
He died—'t is said he fell a prey to grief—
Ere many days the sceptre he had swayed,
And with his fathers in the tomb was laid.
The leader of his arms—a kinsman—next
Assumed the crown, and with its cares was vexed.
A fast, and zealous friend he then became—
Of Cortez—and won military fame—
The glory, or the infamy, of deeds
Whose record like a tale of horror reads.
He more than all the chieftains of his land,

---

* Tecocol by name. He reigned only a few months, and
was succeeded by his brother Ixtlilxochitl, the general of his
armies.

Against his country raised his gory hand,
And labored harder to enslave his race,
And all their ancient splendors to efface.
In Aztec lore who else appears so base,
Or merits such—both deep and foul—disgrace ?
But in the Spanish chronicles his name—*
Aloof from condemnation, blame, or shame—
Is spoken with Castilian acclaim.
He played the hero on Invasion's side,
And waded deep in Conquest's bloody tide.

IV.

The army camped, as if in time of peace,
And from the battle's turmoil found release.
The fugitives by slow degrees returned,
When of the city's quietude they learned,
And' of the proclamation Cortez made,
That he would all who came, protect, and aid.
These the defences were employed to build,
Or left to labor, each as he was skilled.
A watchful eye on the cazique was kept,
And on the people one that never slept.
A deep canal—to float the brigantines—
Was dug amid the busiest of scenes.
For half a league, from camp to lake, it ran,
With width enough two brigantines to span.
From local valley chiefs, around them, came—
Moved by their dread of the invader's name—
Meek offers of submission to the foe,
For they began to fear a sudden blow.
" Before my Monarch, then, in me, bow low,"
Said Cortez in reply, " and hither send—

---

* Ixtlilxochitl, brother of his two predecessors, at the head
of the territory of Tezcuco.

If ye would ne'er his Majesty offend—
All fugitives that linger in your land
In needless dread of vengeance at my hand,
And all who from the capital are there
Or yet may come.   Protection these shall share."
'T was done, and with the many came a few
Brave Aztec nobles, to their country true.
To these spake Cortez—" To your monarch go—
To him who holds the fate of Mexico—
And say I, bitterly, the war regret,
And all the past will willingly forget,
If he will yield, submissively, to Spain,
But, otherwise, the plain I'll fill with slain !"
The offer was unanimously spurned,
And Tenochtitlan for the battle yearned.
United, all as one, the city stood,
And frowned defiance o'er Tezcuco's flood.

V.

" My plan," said Cortez, to his men, " you know
Is, ere I march on haughty Mexico,
To lay all other cities round her low,
If they submission to the Crown refuse,
And thus support from others she will lose ;
And fall the sooner when the siege begins,
To rise no more, till purged of all her sins.
The city I shall first in force attack—
And when subdued, with satisfaction, sack—
Is Iztapalapan six leagues away.
'T was once our lot within its gates to stay—
For it has sworn the capital to aid,
And preparations to resist us made.
A week since we Tezcuco reached has passed
In peace and comfort, but this cannot last.
We'll march to-morrow at the break of day,

And woe to those who meet us in the fray."
So Cortez with two hundred sons of Spain,*
And nigh four thousand allies in their train,
Marched forward on their warlike enterprise,
With courage, and defiance, in their eyes.
The camp was left in Sandoval's command
With this injunction—" Ever ready stand ! "

Along the lake, by towns, and hamlets, bright,
Beneath the morning sun's inspiring light—
Past groves of cypress, and of cedar-trees,
And gently fanned by the refreshing breeze,
The army marched in picturesque array,
While Cortez, and Marina, led the way,
For she was ever with him in the van,
Nor feared she danger more than any man.
Two leagues were they from Iztapalapan,
And, in the distance, from the waters rose
The valley's Queen, † in grandeur, and repose,
When suddenly an army on them sprang,
While loud, and wild, their war-cries round them
    rang.
The Aztec forces would their way dispute,
And they were fiercely brave, and resolute,
And fought like tigers when they, wounded, fly
At their pursuers, ere they sink to die.
But fury, wild, by fury, wild, was met,
And with their gore the reeking plain was wet.
The native allies demon-like attacked,
And by the Spanish troops were boldly backed.
The sight of these, their ancient Aztec foes,
Made terrible their passions, and their blows,

---

* Two-hundred infantry and eighteen cavalry, and between
three and four thousand Tlascalans,
† The city of Mexico.

And, in disorder, soon, the Aztecs fled
Ere from the field they bore away their dead.
The victors forward marched, in eager chase,
With thirst for vengeance written in each face,
Until to Iztapalapan they came,
And o'er it swept—like the destroying flame
Which followed in their devastated track,
Till all the city was, with ashes, black.
The native allies plundered ere they burned;
Then fiercely to the combat they returned,
Nor spared they either sex, or any age,
But slaughtered all in wild, satanic rage.
Men, women, children, babes, alike were slain
Beneath the Christian Cross of saintly Spain.*

Out on the lake—along the shore for miles—
Were human habitations built on piles,
To which the people—seeking refuge—flew.
Like bloodhounds, then, they saw the foe pursue,
And to the lake the battle was transferred,
While sounds of tumult on its breast were heard.
Up to their waists, and girdles, in the flood
The forces fought, and dyed it with their blood.
More desperate the struggle, now, became,
More murderous each battling soldier's aim;
But all in vain the Aztecs fought their foes;
They fell, defeated, 'neath their cruel blows:
And all, too, in those habitations died,
Though they—defenceless there—for mercy cried.

Before the strife was o'er the shades of night
O'erspread the scene.   But still a lurid light
From burning buildings brightened lake, and sky,

---

* The slain on the Aztec side numbered more than six
thousand. Cortez tried to restrain the ferocity of the Tlascalans in this indiscriminate slaughter, but failed.

And added horror to what met the eye.
Resistance at an end—the battle o'er—
The victors sated with their victims' gore—
The avaricious troops to pillage turned,
And stripped of wealth, where they before had
  burned.
'T was while they plundered that a cry arose—
" The dikes are broken, and the water flows ! "
And, like a gale which through a forest blows,
There near, and nearer, came a rushing sound
Of floods that washed, and rippled, o'er the ground,
And stretched as far as eye could see around.
Then deep, and deeper, grew the bubbling tide,
And men who erst were brave stood terrified.*

The inaudation o'er the valley spread,
And filled the army with appalling dread.
The trumpet called them to their leader's side,
And then—" All follow me ! " he loudly cried.
With booty laden, wading deep they went,
Alone, now, on escape their efforts bent,
The salt floods gaining on them by degrees,
Oft rising to their waists, and sinking to their knees.
The conflagration threw a lurid light
Upon the waters as they took their flight,
But faint, and fainter, as they sped it grew,
Till all around them was of ebon hue.
As they advanced, in strength the current gained,
And ev'ry nerve was desperately strained.

---

* The Aztecs had cut through the mole which fenced in the great basin of Lake Tezcuco in order to inundate the city, and that portion of the valley in which it was situated, and destroy the Spanish army by drowning. Iztapalapan had contained fifty thousand inhabitants, and was built on the narrow tongue of land which divided the waters of the Great Salt Lake from those of the fresh.

'T was hard to breast the flood, but Spanish blood
Its whirling depths, and plunging force withstood,
And where to walk they failed, they boldly swam
Till they had passed beyond the broken dam.
But many of the allies vainly tried
To breast that loosened, angry, swelling tide,
And, swept away, beneath its waters died.
All lost their spoils, preferring life to gold ;
All shivered in the night wind, rude, and cold,
And found it hard to drag their weary limbs.
" Disaster such as this our glory dims,"
Said Cortez, to Marina, as he rode,
While on his heart he bore a weighty load ;—
" Our powder spoiled, our arms and trappings wet,
Our allies dwindled, and our souls afret ;
Our conquest thus by vengeance snatched away,
What profits it our triumph won to-day?
Our flight, methinks, through floods like these, will
    seem
As wondrous as the marvels of a dream."
To which Marina answered—" Stand prepared,
He never won, who never bravely dared !
'T is true, Malinchè, that the struggle's long,
But in the end the battle's to the strong.
I would this carnage had been spared us all—
For scenes so bloody, horrify, and appall—
Yet, if the fate of Mexico is sealed,
'T were well 't were quickly to her sons revealed."

VI.

The lake at dawn was swarming with canoes,
While arrows flew, in thousands, from their crews,
And stones, and other missiles, thrown from slings,
And darts that coursed the air with feathered wings,
And carried with them cruel, deadly stings.

Troops in the distance fired upon their ranks,
Disquieting the Spanish army's flanks.
But Cortez had no spirit for attack :
Tezcuco wooed him, like a siren, back,
And ere, by night, the land again was veiled,
He, by his comrades, in the camp was hailed.

Alas ! for Iztapalapan ;—its fate
In Aztec breasts aroused still deeper hate,
While terror through the valley, wide, it spread,
Till even hatred was o'ercome by dread.
Though cursing their invaders, envoys came—
From towns, and cities, great in wealth and fame—
Submission to the white men to proclaim,
And, as their vassals, their protection, claim.
The Aztec rule had long oppressed them all,
And they might thus, perchance, escape its thrall.
From loyalty they—disaffected—swerved,
And those they should have fought they basely
    served.
The ancient city Chalco * was of those
Who thus surrendered to their country's foes,
While still an Aztec garrison was there.
" To Chalco you, then, Sandoval, repair ;
The garrison destroy, and all who dare
Your forces to defy ; and in the name
Of Cross, and Crown, our government proclaim,"
Said Cortez to his comrade, and he went
On conquest of the city sternly bent ;
But ere he reached it legions blocked his way,
And nigh his army perished in the fray ;
But finally he routed all his foes,
And found in Chalco welcome and repose :
Then, with two nobles, to the camp returned,

---

* It was built on the eastern extremity of Lake Chalco.

And from their lips the simple story learned
That the cazique—their father—ere he died,
Had bidden them espouse the Spanish side,
For oracles had prophesied of old
That from the East strange beings—strong, and
　　bold—
Would some day take possession of the land,
Whose prowess Mexico could ne'er withstand,
And woe to those who battle gave to these
Pale-faced invaders from the Eastern Seas!

VII.

Though, to the foe, allegiance had been vowed,
Not always, to the yoke, the people bowed.
With watchful eyes the Aztec armies saw,
One after one, the cities round withdraw
From Aztec rule—the empire's ancient sway,
And, when the Spanish troops had moved away,
They swept—like hawks, when pouncing on their
　　prey—
Upon those hapless cities, to avenge
Disloyalty, and revel in revenge.
Then for protection these to Cortez cried,
Who to their succor with his forces hied.
Between contending armies thus they lay
In danger of re-capture, day by day,
For Cortez could no garrisons bestow,
To bid defiance to the Aztec foe.
His troops so scanty, scattered, could but
　　yield
Whene'er they met an army in the field,
Yet concentrated they could well withstand
Whatever force they met in all the land;
Still, to retain the cities he had gained,
He nerve, and muscle, and resources strained.

At length from parts beyond the valley came
Some messengers from chiefs with friendly aim,
Who saw upon the mountains beacon fires,
Which kindled in their breasts—for war—desires—
Just as the sight of blood, to beasts of prey,
Inflames their passions till they spring to slay—
And these, fresh troops would o'er the mountains
   send,
The cause of the invaders to defend.

" No more of fighting allies I require,"
Said Cortez in reply, " but I desire
A garrison each city to protect ;
And if to furnish these your chiefs elect
Across the mountains let them hither come,
And I will welcome them with fife, and drum ! "
" Alas ! but we abhor these valley tribes,
Nor could we tolerate their jeering jibes,"
The messengers responded with a sigh,
A look of anger, and a flashing eye :
" Beneath the Aztec banner they have fought,
And havoc in our ranks of old have wrought,
For we were to the empire, ever, foes,
And so received, and then returned, its blows ! "
On Cortez, then, a bright idea flashed.
His allies with his allies, even, clashed,
So much divided was this fated land.
Against itself—could such a nation stand ?—
To reconcile, and fuse them, he resolved,
And in his mind the plan he well revolved.
To all beneath his flag he said, " Behold !
Together banded ye are strong and bold !
Let not divisions, then, your strength impair,
But with each other wisely learn to bear.
Forget your ancient wrongs in brotherhood,
For ye are all—remember !—one in blood,

And vassals of one monarchy ye stand!
Unite then, heart to heart, and hand in hand,
To sweep the tyrant from your native land!"
They listened, pondered, finally embraced,
And ancient hatred, Cortez saw effaced.
United allies, and divided foes—
Behold the Empire in its dying throes!
Who knows that Cortez would have conquest
    wrought,
If these had not—in concert—bravely fought?
More mighty than the Spanish arms were they
In paving, to victorious ends, the way.
In unity they battled for the flag,
Which in the dust both friend and foe would
    drag,
And crush beneath one juggernaut the two—
Those to their country false—those to it true.

VIII.

Again sent Cortez, to the Aztec crown,
Some envoys he had captured, of renown.
To whom he said—"Go Quahtemozin tell
That all with Mexico will yet be well,
If he to his allegiance will return,
Nor longer dare the olive branch to spurn.
If he this proffered peace should, now, embrace,
He still shall be the ruler of his race,
And all beneath his sceptre shall once more
Be free, and happy, as in days of yore!"
To this the monarch, proud, no answer gave,
For he was dauntless, resolute, and brave.
He, still, to death put all his captured foes,
And struck, where'er he could, aggressive blows,
Against defections keenly sought to guard,
And to preserve his Empire struggled hard.

To him SURRENDER was a word unknown.
While life remained he'd battle for his throne.

IX.

'T was now to Sandoval that Cortez turned,
For he, in him, rare virtues had discerned.
" The brigantines are ready. Go ! " he said,
" And bring them hither from the Land of Bread.
Two hundred foot, and fifteen horsemen take,
And on your way a dread example make
Of those who slew our comrades—forty-five—
And of the rest who with them dared connive ! " *
In Zoltepec—a small Tezcuco town—
The soldiers had, ere this, been stricken down,
And there some relics of the slain were found,—
A temple's walls—as trophies—hung around ;
But ere the troops approached the people fled—
And little blood upon the field was shed,
Though wheresoe'er they captured fleeing braves,
They tortured, and then branded them as slaves.
Then to the fair republic they advanced,
And scarce within it had their chargers pranced,
When lo ! they saw an army's banners rise
Among the mountains, to their great surprise,
And this was turned to joy when, soon, it neared,
And in its midst the brigantines appeared.
Yes, 't was the allies' army that deployed
Before their vision, and the fleet convoyed.
" But twenty thousand of the host I need,
With me, to Lake Tezcuco to proceed,"
Said Sandoval, " save those who burdens bear ;
The rest may to their camp again repair."

---

* These were the forty-five Spaniards, before referred to as
having been massacred in the territory of Tezcuco.

This done, with slow and painful steps, they toiled
Up the ascent, and through the glens defiled,
And worked their way o'er eminences, steep,
And waded mountain torrents, wild and deep ;
Then, scarce molested, trod the valley slope—
Elated with their enterprise, and hope—
Marched to the sound of atabel, and flute,
And to the horn's wild, melancholy toot,
And reached the camp, in safety, with the fleet.
Thus was achieved a memorable feat
Nigh unexampled ere Balboa tried
To so transport to the Pacific's tide
Four brigantines o'er twenty leagues of land,
Of which but two e'er reached the ocean strand.*
The convoy was with acclamations hailed,
And with the best Tezcuco gave regaled.
"Long live Castile, and Tlascala !" they cried.
And in their gladness with their comrades vied.
Long would have Mexico † its foes defied,
If ne'er the fleet had kissed its waters, wide ;
Nor might it e'er have yielded where it stood,
Surrounded by the deep, protecting flood.

---

* Vasco Nuñez de Balboa, the discoverer of the Pacific, tried
the experiment referred to in 1516, across the Isthmus of Darien, and this may have suggested a like effort to Cortez.   A
similar transportation for a short distance, had previously
taken place, on two occasions, at Tarentum in Italy, once
under Hannibal and again under Gonsalvo De Cordova.

† The city of Mexico.

PART NINTH.

I.

THE allies were athirst for Aztec blood,
And Cortez deemed the time for battle good.
To reconnoitre Mexico he planned,
And, on the way, spread terror through the land
By scourging the most active of his foes,
Who took delight in breaking his repose.
His host of swarthy children of the soil—
Brave war-worn Tlascalans, inured to toil,
Who, after blood, were eager most for spoil—
And fifty, and three hundred sons of Spain—
The rest in camp were ordered to remain *—
The Spanish leader boldly forward led,
With banners waving—yellow, blue and red.
'T was early spring, but balmy and serene, †
And all the valley looked superbly green,
Save where the lakes were rippling in the sun,
Or cities rose—white, massive, gray, and dun.
Behold a skirmish ere they'd journeyed far !
An Aztec force strove hard their way to bar,
But overwhelmed, at last, it—routed—fled,
And on his course, in triumph, Cortez sped,
With Alvarado, and with Olid there,
The glory of the enterprise to share.
To Xaltocan at length the army came—
A town, and lake, identical in name—
The one within the other's calm embrace,
With causeways stretching o'er the wat'ry space—
A Mexico in miniature that shone

---

* Under the command of Sandoval.
† In the year 1521.

In beauty with a lustre all its own.*
A scene so picturesque, and fair, and bright
But rarely in the valley met the sight.
Along the nearest causeway rushed the troops,
When swiftly, as on prey an eagle swoops,
There swept upon them o'er the rippling lake—
In war canoes that left a foaming wake—
A mighty host of warriors fully armed.
The sudden movement those attacked alarmed,
And faster forward hurried on the van
Till o'er the causeway the invaders ran,
While on each side stones, darts, and arrows flew.
Death—to the allies—freighted each canoe.
Alarm to consternation quickly grew,
When to a chasm in the dike they came.
The Aztec war-cries swelled into acclaim,
And the canoes'-men took defiant aim.
The trumpet gave the signal to retreat
Amid fresh volleys from the countless fleet,
And backward rolled the baffled, living tide,
Which to disaster thus had been decoyed.
Just then to save his life, a traitor cried—
"The army may, in safety, ford the lake,
If only it will follow in my wake!"
'Twas done, though war-canoes their missiles threw,
And hundreds of the swarthy allies slew.
But when the troops the fated city gained
The streets were with revolting carnage stained.
Revenge—how sweet!—was gratified in blood,
And all who could sought refuge on the flood.
Those failing to escape, were foully slain,
And Terror was triumphant in her reign.
Then fell the place to pillage, rude, a prey.

---

* The town was situated on the northern extremity of the lake, which is now called San Christobal.

The victors, with them, bore its wealth away,
And left the flames their havoc to complete.
The Azetcs mourned again their sore defeat.

II.

On to the northward still, the army sped,
And filled the valley, far and wide, with dread;
Three towns—deserted—on their way they sacked,*
And in the fields at night-fall bivouacked,
While on the hill-tops blazed the beacon lights—
The fires that gilded, with their glow, the heights—
And far away, like shadows on the scene,
Dark masses of the Mexicans were seen.
The fairest regions of the Empire lay
Around them, as they journeyed on their way.
Old cities, and quaint villages, were strewn—
How beautiful they looked beneath the moon!—
O'er hill, and valley, set in frames of bloom—
Gay gardens which exhaled a rich perfume,
And in the centre of the valley rose—
As if invulnerable to her foes—
The grand Metropolis of Mexico,
Still mighty, and majestic in her woe,
Her pyramids, and temples soaring high,
As if to catch effulgence from the sky.
In front Tacuba † stood, through which they passed,
When from the fatal dike they hurried fast,
And to the eastward that dark causeway ran—
Uniting shore, and city, in its span,
Across the lake's calm waters, bright, and clear—
The sight of which from Cortez drew a tear.

---

* These were named respectively Tenajoccan, Quauhtitlan, and Azcapozalco.

† The ancient city of Tacuba.

" Behold Tacuba! there an army lies
To guard against invasion, and surprise,
But we must to defeat those arms consign,
And make Tacuba bow before our shrine ! "
Thus to his troops the Spanish leader cried,
To which with acclamation, they replied,
And dashing forward routed all the host—
Tacuba's martial chivalry, and boast—
The cavalry pursuing as they fled,
Until the suburbs with their blood were red.
Yet, undefeated, on the morrow's dawn
They stood again in battle order drawn
Before the city, on the open field.
" Attack," cried Cortez, "and no quarter yield ! "
And cavalry and infantry advanced.
'T was not the plain that shivered, heaved, and
    danced,
But that vast multitude contending there,
Whose clamor floated wildly on the air.
The muskets rattled, and the lances gleamed ;
The rising sun upon the turmoil beamed ;
The feathered arrows from each army flew,
At times obscuring, here and there, the view ;
Stones, darts, and other missiles, too, were flung,
Which from their victims groans, and anguish
    wrung,
And swords once flashing, but now wet with gore,
Through breasts courageous, pitilessly tore,
While " *Adelante !* " sounded o'er the roar,
And " *Christo ! Santiago !* " o'er and o'er.
The Spanish arms triumphant were once more :
The Aztec army in disorder fled,
And Cortez in pursuit his forces led,
Till through Tacuba's streets the flying foe
Escaped with shrill, and dismal cries of woe.
The population, then, in wild affright—

Astounded by the issue of the fight—
Rushed from the city, fearful of their fate.
To pillage, swift, Tacuba fell a prey,
And havoc followed the destroying fray.
Still later, tongues of fire the story told—
While clouds of smoke above them, densely, rolled—
How flames had laid Tacuba's glory waste.
Revenge was sweet to ev'ry victor's taste.*

III.

Behold, Tacuba's ancient palace walls
Gave echo to the loud invader's call,
And round them the invading army lay,
Prepared, and watchful, for a sudden fray.
Days passed,† but not in peace, for ev'ry day,
Tacuba's forces battled for the Right
Against the legions armed alone with Might,
And though beneath the scourge the victors quailed,
Yet they each eve another triumph hailed.
Once by disaster nigh o'erwhelmed were they
When they designed a multitude to slay.
The Aztec army down the causeway fled—
The fatal dike on which so many bled—
And in pursuit the Spanish forces dashed,
When magic-like upon the view there flashed—
For far behind them they had left the shore—
A mighty swarm of boats which downward bore,
Amid a stormy, fierce, and swelling roar,
While the retreating army turned to fight,
And in the rear fresh thousands came in sight.

---

* The Tlascalans were responsible for the conflagration, the Spaniards having done, with partial success, all that they could to stop it.

† The Spanish army remained six days at Tacuba before it began its return màrch to Tezcuco, as originally intended.

In front, and rear, and on each side attacked,
The Spanish leader cried—" I caution lacked
To be thus here decoyed, but let us fly
Back to the shore, and bravely all defy ! "
And so along the causeway they defiled,
While round them raged a tempest loud and wild.
Hard was the battle which they bravely fought—
And with sore havoc to their ranks 't was fraught—
As toward the land they struggled in retreat,
Assailed with pikes, and missiles from the fleet,
And captured Spanish swords, to lances lashed,
Which oft their columns hideously gashed,
While, through the air, stones, darts and arrows
  flew;
And as the fray progressed it hotter grew.
But ere the end the troops regained the land,
And made against their foes a gallant stand,
Where, routing them, they all to camp returned,
And found the needed rest for which they yearned.
" ' T was by a miracle that we were saved,
And wonderful how well the troops behaved,"
Said Cortez to his comrades. Then they knelt,
And uttered thanks, which all devoutly felt,
For that—escape—which Providential seemed,
And so 't was by the Spanish soldiers deemed,
For each believed his mission nigh divine,
And all his foeman's punishment condign.

IV.

Six days had Cortez in Tacuba been,
And vainly sought from war the foe to wean—
For with defiance they his parleys met,
And he beheld the prospect with regret—
When back he to his camp the march began,
His martial figure, leading, in the van.

The Aztecs wrongly judged that this was flight,
And in pursuit they followed, day, and night,
Till by strategic snares, at length, decoyed
They found their forces routed, or destroyed.
The horsemen dashed from out their ambuscade,
And on them made a fierce, and deadly raid,
While swiftly wheeled the infantry around,
And charged with fury that nigh shook the ground.
Thus panic-struck across the plain they fled,
And left behind their wounded, and their dead,
The cavalry in hot pursuit for miles.
"How strange," ·they mourned, "are the invaders'
    wiles!"
At length Tezcuco, and their camp, appeared,
And by their comrades they were loudly cheered.
Since they the march began, two weeks had flown,
And, of their progress, naught the while was
    known
To those who thus in garrison remained—
And health, and strength, by idleness regained;—
So eagerly they, now, the tidings sought,
And heard, with flashing eyes, of battles fought,
And gazed upon the golden spoils they brought.

V.

The tireless Aztecs Chalco, now, assailed, *
And those within its walls their fate bewailed,
And sent to Cortez to implore his aid,
For of the empire they were sore afraid.
So with three hundred Spanish soldiers, brave,
And twenty horsemen, with their trappings, gay—
As glad to fight as they were prone to pray—
Marched Sandoval to save.   He battle gave

---

* Within three days of the return of Cortez to Tezcuco.
Pronounce Tez-suko.

To all the Aztecs round the city massed,
And routed, and defeated, them, at last,
Then climbed the mountains from the plain below,
And laid their strongholds in that region low. *

A fortress rose upon a rocky height.
" A bird alone can reach it in its flight ! "
The native allies, as they faced it, cried,
But Sandoval, as he the summit eyed,
Exclaimed—" I naught impossible believe !
What cannot, here, a son of Spain achieve ? "
And—from his steed dismounting—forward sprang,
While from his lips the cry—" Saint Jago ! " rang.
On up the steep ascent he led the way,
Amid a storm of missiles, dense as spray,
And falling rocks, that leapt from crag to crag—
As bounds when hunted, to its death, the stag—
Nor for a moment did his courage flag ;
And lo ! at length the fortress walls he scaled,
And, with his comrades, those within assailed !
The struggle, then, was short, but desperate—
Each side impelled by fury, and by hate—
And few escaped of all the Aztecs there.
The lion had been bearded in his lair.
Some headlong o'er the battlements were thrown ;
Some leapt the precipice with dying groan,
But by the sword the multitude were slain,
And blood in currents wandered to the plain.

Then to his camp brave Sandoval went back,

---

* These were two towns; one called Huaxtepec—surrounded
by extensive gardens like those of Iztapalapan—lying five
leagues to the south of Chalco, among the mountains; and
Jacapichtla, which, fortress-like, was perched on a rocky emi-
nence, almost inaccessible, about twelve miles to the eastward of the place first mentioned.

Believing Chalco safe from fresh attack,
And by fatigue, and angry wounds oppressed.
He, in Tezcuco, sought again for rest,
But ere he gained the needed boon, behold !
New envoys came, and warlike stories told.
The Emperor of Mexico—the bold—
Had watched the troops of Sandoval retreat,
And then across the lake dispatched a fleet—
Two thousand boats, and twenty thousand men—
With orders Chalco to besiege again.
" Return," cried Cortez, " and your work complete !
Show them—our foes—how bitter is defeat ! "
In silence Sandoval, chagrined, obeyed,
And plans for dire destruction quickly laid ;
Then triumph won, by wading deep in gore,
And to the camp—a victor came once more.
Then Cortez to his comrade—" Welcome ! " cried,
" Thy deeds of valor are the army's pride ;
No braver spirit do I know than thine,
And in our annals 't will be thine to shine !
'T was not in anger that I bade thee go
Again to Chalco, there to face the foe,
Nor in reproof, though so 't was felt by thee,
But to behold thee gain this victory ! "*

VI.

The while the brigantines from pieces grew
To shapely vessels, each one stanch, and true,

---

*Cortez had been displeased in the first instance with
Sandoval's return while, as he then believed, Chalco was in
an unsettled state, and Sandoval felt injured by being sum-
marily ordered back, but when Cortez became familiar with
the facts, he saw that he had done him an injustice, and
freely acknowledged it and warmly greeted him when they
next met.

And thrice the Aztecs to destroy them tried
Ere they were launched upon Tezcuco's tide—
For they in these but evil could discern—
Yet failed each time to capture, or to burn.
From points remote, by mountain, sea, and plain,
Fresh embassies had come to bow to Spain,
And from her sons protecting aid to gain,
Tezcuco's lord advising them to this
As certain to eventuate in bliss.
Three ships, too, into Vera Cruz had steered—
A welcome sight 't was when they there appeared !—
With ammunition, arms, two hundred men,
And much beside, the army sighed for then.
Not least of all were eighty mettled steeds,
That well supplied the straitened army's needs :
And Papal bulls a holy friar brought,
Which those who sought indulgence gladly bought.*
The new recruits in camp were loudly hailed,
And well, with all that Cortez had, regaled.
Thus Fortune smiled upon the Spaniard's arms,
While Ceres lavished at his feet her charms.†

VII.

Again was Chalco threatened by the foe,
And Cortez, now, himself, would strike the blow.
So with three hundred Spanish infantry,
And thirty of his well-tried cavalry,
With hosts of native allies in the rear,

---

* Whether or not these vessels were part of the expedition
sent by Cortez to Hispaniola, for supplies, and recruits, is
unknown.

† Cortez had harvested in the granaries of Tezcuco large
quantities of ripe maize, and other agricultural products,
found growing in the vicinity of Lake Tezcuco.

He marched on Chalco, with an eye severe.*
There through Jeronimo, Marina too—
Both to his cause, through varied fortunes, true—
He with the friendly chiefs held interview,
And told them he would soon require their aid
In giving force to Mexico's blockade.
" Have all your levies ready when I call,
And those now fighting into line may fall ! "
To which they made affirmative reply,
And cried—" For Spain, and Cortez, we will die ! "
While those already in the field obeyed,
And with his own, their legions stood arrayed,
Until a larger host than e'er before
Their arms, beneath the Spanish banner, bore.
Then south, to where the wild Sierra rose,
In majesty he moved to face his foes,
And into its recesses boldly rode,
As if he knew, to great success, the road.
The giant peaks—a fence of bristling arms—
Aspired to guard the lovely valley's charms,
While in the shelter of their wild embrace
Green meadows lay, with bloom upon their face.
As through its gorges, deep, the army passed,
The foe its progress, here and there, harassed.
From lofty heights, where towns seemed perched
   in air,
There thundered down—from rocky stair to stair—
Huge boulders on the heads of those below,
While arrows rained upon them, woe on woe.
At length, by losses stung, cried Cortez—" Halt !
Scale yonder cliff, and carry by assault ! "

---

* The march was begun by Cortez on the 5th of April, 1521,
with the determination to scour the country to the south as
effectually as he had already done that to the west. This
was a second reconnoitring expedition, and Sandoval was
meanwhile left in command of the camp at Tezcuco.

The storming party clambered up the height—
The army resting on its arms, in sight—
But thicker came the arrows, rocks, and stones,
And in the mountain pass were heard their groans.
Of what avail were helmet, or cuirass,
Or panoply of steel, or shield of brass,
Against this torrent from the mountain's brow?
'T were vain to strive, their way to further plough,
When man and Nature thus opposed their course.
Such missiles overwhelmed their feeble force.
Already of their number eight were killed—
Men deeply in the ways of warfare skilled—
And all the rest were wounded. Cortez saw
The task was hopeless, and exclaimed—" With-
    draw ! "
The order to retreat was nigh too late
To save the army from a tragic fate,
For marching fast across the valley came
Another army, hostile in its aim.
The broken files were quickly drawn in line,
And Cortez turned to thwart the foe's design.
Not waiting for the enemy's attack,
He led his forces to the valley back,
And met the Aztecs on the open plain,
Ere they the mountain passes could attain,
Then boldly charged into their masses, dense,
And with the horse and foot made gaps, and rents.
The onset was so furious, and fast,
That they, before it, broke and fled aghast—
Fled—routed—to the wild Sierra's breast,
For refuge in its fastnesses, and rest,
While in pursuit the angry victors flew;
And all who fell within their reach they slew.

VIII.

The march was, through the mountains, then resumed,
And high the pinnacles above them loomed.
Two cliffs, each with a fortress crowned, they passed,
And, as before, with missiles were harassed.
The eminences near each other rose,
And populous were both with well-armed foes.
" The morn's disaster we must now retrieve
By gilding with a victory the eve ! "
Cried Cortez, as he turned a mountain bend.
" Scale then the highest of the cliffs, and rend
All who that airy settlement defend ! "
The order was with promptitude obeyed,
But vainly was the deadly task essayed.
The morn's disaster was repeated here,
When camped the troops, until the morrow, near,
Their baffled leader, mortified, and grave,
Resolved, again, the precipice to brave.
His purpose by the Aztecs was divined,
And so the forces of the cliffs were joined.
Short-sighted strategy, indeed, was this—
To grasp a shadow, and the substance miss—
For at the dawn the height deserted, now,
Was by the army climbed, and from its brow
They fired upon the other till defeat
Drove its defenders swiftly, to retreat.
Then cried they—" We capitulate ! Forgive !
Ascend our mountain height, but let us live ! "
Not on the victors lost was this appeal,
And all were spared who to the Cross would kneel,
Which moved another force ere long to yield *
And wisdom thus in lenity revealed.

---

* Namely, the garrison on the cliff which had been unsuccessfully stormed on the morning of the previous day.

IX.

Two days the army lingered in the pass,
And solemnized each morn, and eve, a Mass,
While all around sequestered beauty beamed,
And in the sun bright birds, and insects gleamed.
Then Cortez, for his forces, led the way
Southwestward, through a region, green, and gray,
With the Sierra's peaks above, around,
And verdure carpeting the rocky ground.
Through mountain mazes, wild, and deep, they
　　went,
And even here inhaled the roses' scent.
Huaxtepec a friendly greeting gave—
It erst had bowed to Sandoval, the brave—
But other towns, deserted, silent lay.
Their people all had fled, in fear, away,
And now upon the army's flank, and rear,
Pursued, and fought, with arrow, sling, and spear.
So they a prey to flames, and pillage, fell,
And lurid lights were shed on peak, and dell.

Now down the Cordillera's sweeping slope—
Borne on by courage, av'rice, zeal, and hope—
The army marched, with hearts that sighed for
　　spoil,
And heeded not, howe'er severe, the toil.
The scoria and slaggy lava told
Of fierce volcanoes, silent now, and cold.*
But vegetation, here and there, was rank,
And water bubbled up from Nature's tank.
Still pressing on, a city came in sight,
Which filled the Spanish troops with keen delight.

---

* Volcanoes now extinct in Mexico were active at the time
of the conquest.

'T was Cuernavaca's pyramids that gleamed—
And this, of old, with opulence had teemed. *
But formidable ravines round it ran
Too wide to leap by either horse or man,
Save where these narrowed on a mountain plain,
Which they, by marching far, alone could gain.
Their ranks were to the Aztecs' fire exposed,
Who screened from harm, and only half disclosed,
Hurled missiles, and defiance, at the foe.
" A passage seek," Hernando cried, " below,
Through which both horse, and man, may safely go."
'T was sought in vain. Two trees howe'er there
    grew
On either side the ravine, and they threw
From leaning trunks—which high above embraced—
Their lengthy boughs that closely interlaced.
By the aërial bridge, thus Nature-formed,
The allies said the city could be stormed,
And o'er it then to pass one Aztec tried,
And climbed in safety to the other side ;
Then others of his race as quickly crossed
But some—by falling—in the cleft were lost ;
Then Spaniards one by one, the feat essayed,
And for the help of saints, and angels prayed,
And all, but three, who ventured crossed the breach.
These—losing hold—passed out of human reach.†

Fast formed the soldiers of the growing arch,
And swiftly on the city made a march,
Unseen by Aztec multitudes, whose eyes

---

* The Aztec name of the city was Quauhuahuac. It was
the ancient capital of the Tlahuicas, and Cortez reached it on
the ninth day of the march from Tezcuco.

† Between twenty and thirty Spaniards, and many Tlascalans
crossed in this manner. Cortez, with the main body of the
army, meanwhile remained higher up the ravine.

When they beheld them, flashed intense surprise.
They came as if they'd fallen from the clouds,
And boldly plunged amid their swaying crowds,
Where they were fighting Cortez and his host,
And utt'ring oft the while, some taunt, or boast.
The Spanish leader saw his little band
Before the Aztec arms thus bravely stand,
And labored to protect them all he could,
And, too, to mend a bridge that spanned the flood.*
This—to the wonder of both armies—done,
Amid the glories of the setting sun,
The troops of Cortez crossed the bridge, and, lo!
Dashed furiously forward on the foe,
And to the rescue of their comrades brave,
Whom naught but timely succor, now could save.
The Aztecs, bravely on resistance bent,
Into their ranks their volleys thickly sent,
Then backward reeled, and—shattered—fled pursued
Into the wild Sierra's solitude.
The victors pillaged wheresoe'er they chose,
And high the flames above the city rose.

X.

No further south, and west, would Cortez go,
But northward turn to follow up the foe,
Recross the mountains, to the valley back,
And ev'rywhere the Aztec hosts attack.
The southern slope he climbed to gain the crest,
And paused 'mid pines, and stunted oak, for rest.
By toil, and thirst, the army grew depressed,
For here with water they were seldom blest,
And hard, and rugged, was their mountain road,
While of his spoils each bore a weighty load.

---

* A torrent of water ran at the bottom of the ravine.

At last, emerging from the forest's gloom,
They faced the valley, beautiful with bloom,
And in its matchless scenery as grand
As phantom scenes of bliss in fairy-land.
'T was but the splendid vale they'd seen before,
Yet all seemed new as here they scanned it o'er,
Just as the point from which they gazed was new,
And so enhanced the pleasure of the view.
The central lake, and Tenochtitlan, lay
Like Paradise, before them, far away,
And, as they in the sunlight brightly shone,
They longed to call that Paradise their own.

Ere long the Field of Flowers * came in sight—
A city rich, and famous for its might—
Whose legions stood prepared the foe to fight,
And bravely they resisted when attacked
Though by the Spanish army rudely racked.
But science, over numbers, still prevailed,
And native hosts, again, defeat bewailed.

Pursued by foes who trampled down their dead,
The routed Aztecs from the city fled,
While Cortez held the gate that to it led,
A few bold soldiers only at his side.
There suddenly, he saw a human tide
Rush o'er the causeway, from the nearest shore,
And charge upon him with exulting roar.
For strong support his comrades seemed too weak,
And vengeance on him now the foe would wreak.
He fell beneath a blow that numbed his brain,
And overwhelmed by numbers. " He is slain ! "
Cried one among the throng, and he was lost—

---

* The name, of the city was Xochimilco, the signification
of which is expressed in the text.

Upon the billows of the battle tossed.
Then forward sprang a native ally, brave,
From sacrifice, the Spanish chief to save—
Sprang like a lion on his leaping prey,
And tore him from his enemies away.
On to the rescue came his comrades near,
And battled boldly, armed with sword, and spear,
While springing to his feet, and on his steed,
He charged them, with his lance, at flying speed.
His troops, returning, joined him in the fray,
And after carnage, dire, regained their sway.

From death the Aztecs Cortez wished to spare
For sacrifice, with native pomp, and care,
Else they'd have slain him while they held him fast,
And by their arms he'd there have breathed his
    last.
Thus, then was saved by Providence his life,
And they beheld him lead, again, the strife,
And gnashed their teeth, in anger, at the thought
That once that tyrant in their toils was caught.
Not yet howe'er the danger had been passed.
From Tenochtitlan * marched an army, vast,
Dispatched the day's disasters to retrieve,
And that beleaguered garrison relieve,
While all the waters of the lake † were dark
With war canoes, each an avenging ark.
The Emperor of Mexico was brave,
And cried—" What, now, can the invaders save?"

Night fell before they came, but, at the dawn,
They stood revealed, in battle order drawn.

---

* The Mexican capital was distant only four leagues from
Xochimilco.
† Lake Tezcuco.

With apprehension Cortez saw their ranks,
And, ere he moved, they charged upon his flanks
With all the fury common to their race,
As if determined to regain the place.
The crossbow, and the musket, answered back;
The cavalry dashed forward to attack;
The infantry, with pikes, like demons rushed,
And in the struggle multitudes were crushed.
The Aztecs in disorder, wild, recoiled
Before the onset, then retreated, foiled,
While the triumphant foe for miles pursued,
For slaughter eager, and in savage mood.
But suddenly the army in retreat,
Which groaned beneath its losses, and defeat,
Met reinforcements marshalled for relief,
And into joy was turned its former grief.
Back swept the tide on the pursuing foe,
To strike for country yet another blow;
And when—with dreadful shock—the armies met,
The field was made with greater bloodshed wet.
The fighting masses in the combat swayed,
Each army forward by its leader urged,
While mingled war-cries through the turmoil rang,
And triumph all uncertain seemed to hang.
But as before, the Christian arms prevailed,
Though by a bold and mighty force assailed.
The battle ended in an Aztec rout—
And from the victors, a triumphant shout—
While slaughter followed fast the flying foe.
All Mexico was startled by the blow!

XI.

The city sacked, and given o'er to fire,
To gratify a stern revengeful ire,
The fierce invaders—laden with their spoil—

Resumed their march, triumphant, o'er the soil,*
And in the burning city's lurid glow,
The fading Empire read of future woe.
The fatal beings, long predicted, lo !
Had come to ravage, and destroy, the land,
And naught against their arms, alas ! could stand.

Two leagues away another city † rose,
Where found the army coveted repose,
For all its people from their homes had fled,
Of their approaching enemy, in dread.
Tacuba lay in sight, not far away,
And, to its gates, hence Cortez led the way,
His line of march by skirmishers beset
Who saw his spoils with anger, and regret,
And charged with fury on his flank, and rear,
And havoc wrought with arrow, sling, and spear.
Tacuba, ravaged, lay in peaceful gloom,
As if resigned, in ashes, to her doom, ‡
But from her highest temple's topmost height
A bright and lovely prospect met the sight,
Embracing Mexico, and all around,
Within the distant, dark Sierra bound,
And thither Cortez took his way, and sighed
O'er all the beauty of the scene he eyed.
"Alas!" said he, "that yonder city, fair,
Which I would, gladly, from destruction spare,
If it but vowed allegiance unto Spain,
Should thus in foul rebellion still remain.
How often I have asked it to return,

---

* Cortez left Xochimilco on the fourth morning after his arrival.

† Cojohuacan, where Cortez remained two days.

‡ Tacuba was distant from the city of Mexico but little more than a league.

And offered the forgiveness it would spurn,
And yet the time has come to crush the foe
By laying Mexico's proud city low!
'T is sad to think what perils we must face
Ere we can conquer this unyielding race,
And call the mighty capital our own.
But we must hurl the monarch from his throne,
And plant the Cross where infidels have reigned,
And God, and all His works, on earth profaned!
We come, as His crusaders, to redeem
The land from darkness, where the truth may beam.
May Jesus help us to accomplish this.
His will be done—our crown eternal bliss!"

Brief, at Tacuba, was the army's stay,
For danger would have followed on delay,
And Cortez longed his camp, again, to greet,
And there survey, with hopeful pride, the fleet.
O'er flooded roads, while torrents fell, he passed,
Till to Tezcuco's gates he came at last,
And, as a brother, Sandoval embraced,
Then cried—"Now on to Mexico we'll haste!"
Three weeks had flown since he the march began,
And toward the bold Sierra led the van.
The while beneath the builders' cunning hand,
The brigantines were fitted, rigged, and manned,
And made all ready for the golden tide,
As for the bridal is the virgin bride.
The circuit of the valley had been made,
And now the time had come for the blockade.

XII.

But little Cortez thought of treason then,
Among his soldiers and brave countrymen,
Yet foul conspiracy, deep-laid and dark,

Which had his life, and others', for its mark—
Beneath the tranquil surface lay concealed.
'T was only by an accident revealed :
A conscience-stricken wretch confessed the plot,
And saw its leader * hung upon the spot.
The rest of these conspirators were spared, †
And in the future battles gladly shared,
Though by their guilt they merited the fate
Which doth on mutineer, and traitor wait ;
But Cortez deemed his Spanish troops too few—
In view of all the work he had to do—
For more to fall by his avenging hand.
He needed all, to devastate the land !
And while his foes in camp his murder planned,
His enemies in Cuba and in Spain
His downfall sought, nor seemed to seek in vain,
But time, and distance, proved a double shield
To one who marched to conquest in the field,
And in the end their machinations failed,
And Cortez as a conqueror was hailed.

XIII.

The morning of the launch was fair and bright,
And all the army hailed it with delight.
To Cortez 't was a solemn, great event—
First of its kind upon the continent—‡
And in its celebration Mass was said,

---

* Antonio Villafana, a common soldier who came over with
Narvaez.   He was hung from the window of his quarters.

† Cortez did not even intimate to them that he was aware
of their complicity in the plot to assassinate himself, and his
officers, but during the rest of the campaign he was provided
with a bodyguard of trusty Castilians.

‡ The first navy worthy of the name ever launched upon
American waters.

While banners to the winds were gayly spread,
And on the air the cannon loudly boomed,
As if to say that Mexico was doomed.
Then, one by one, before rejoicing eyes—
Amid a chorus of exulting cries—
The stately vessels glided toward the lake,
With silver ripples sparkling in their wake.
Down the canal, for half a league, they sped
Ere they were to the lake's broad waters wed. *
Then, with expanded wings, to catch the breeze,
They sailed as proudly as if on the seas,
With music, and with musketry, and cheers
Resounding in a hundred thousand ears.
'T was then that Spanish breasts with rapture
    swelled,
And Cortez conquest, in his fleet, beheld,
And all an anthem sang with one accord—
The grand *Te Deum*—glory to the Lord.

XIV.

Before the camp the forces, now, were massed,
And in review—by Cortez eyed—they passed, †
When he harangued them in a stirring strain:—
" Brave soldiers of the Cross, and sons of Spain,

---

* This event took place on the 28th of April, 1521, the troops being drawn up under arms, and the whole population gathered to witness the ceremony. The canal, half a league in length, twelve feet wide and as many deep, was a work of immense labor, having occupied eight thousand men nearly two months. Its sides were strengthened by palisades of masonry and timber, and it was furnished with dams and locks, and cut through hard rock, at intervals.

† The Spanish portion of the army now numbered eight hundred and eighteen foot, of which a hundred and eighteen were arquebusiers, and crossbowmen, and eighty-seven cavalry—a force larger than had gathered at any time since

I've brought you to the wished-for goal at last,
Through stormy scenes, and perils that are past !
The gates of Mexico we'll soon assail,
Nor to subdue the city can we fail,
For—God-defended—we are strong, and bold.
Our present, and our former state behold !
The Providence that rules in this we see !
Thanks to a watchful, guiding deity !
Less than a year ago we fled pursued,
With broken ranks, in melancholy mood,
And refuge sought from our exultant foes,
To find in Tlascala, at length, repose.
How they contrast—our fortunes then, and now !
Ne'er to the infidel our arms shall bow !
Of future triumphs, past achievements tell.
Who doubts that all, with us, will prosper well?
The battles of the faith we're here to fight,
And spread abroad the holy Gospel's light !
We fight, too, for our honor, and revenge—
We, yet, have much, in duty, to avenge—
For riches, and for glory, and renown,
The Christian Cross, and the Castilian crown !
I've brought you to your foe, now, face to face.
'T is yours to triumph o'er the Aztec race,
And gain, by conquest, all this smiling land.
Go then, and reap ! the harvest lies at hand ! "
There came, in answer, acclamations loud
From all the Spaniards in that warlike crowd,
Who cried—" Hurrah ! for Cortez ! Only lead,
And we will do whate'er may be decreed."

---

the flight from Mexico under the banner of Cortez. The artillery consisted of three large iron fieldpieces, and fifteen lighter guns of brass. Three hundred Spaniards were detailed to man the brigantines, and each brigantine carried a piece of heavy ordnance.

Then Cortez thus his officers addressed,
And, with his daring spirit, all impressed.
" In three divisions, let the army fight. *
While Alvarado will command the right—
His quarters at Tacuba, by the dike,
Where with advantage he, the foe, can strike—
The left will be by Sandoval employed.
From Chalco he his native troops will guide
To Iztapalapan, and there destroy
Whatever in the future might annoy ;
And Olid will the third division lead
To Cojo-hu-a-can, and'there await
The proper moment to co-operate
With Sandoval, and Alvarado, who
With him, in concert, will the fight renew—
While I upon the lake will guide the fleet,
And overwhelm the Aztecs with defeat.
By one day's march the allies will precede
The Spanish troops, for longer rest they need.
The time has come for them to forward go,
And help to lay their ancient tyrants low.
Their eighty thousand arms will not in vain,
For freedom strike, and their adopted Spain."

XV.

The bravest chieftain of the Land of Bread,†
Who first had filled the Spanish troops with dread,
When on the plains of Tlascala he fought,
And in their ranks unlooked-for havoc wrought,
Deep hatred for them, still, in secret, felt,

---

* Alvarado's division included 30 horse, 168 Spanish
infantry and 25,000 Tlascalans; Sandoval's 24 horse, 167
infantry and 30,000 mixed allies, and Olid's 33 horse, 178
infantry, and 20,000 Tlascalans.

† Xicotencatl of Tlascala.

Though he, a convert, 'neath the Cross had knelt.
He loathed the war, though holding a command,
And mourned—how sadly!—o'er his fated land.
'T was he who in the councils of the State
Had warned his elders, ere it seemed too late,
To drive the white invaders from the soil,
Ere they, by them, were doomed to fight, and toil.
But they the young hot-blooded chief reproved,
And all his angry counsel disapproved.
This chieftain from the camp his army led,
And to the breeze his native banner spread,
But when it halted for the night he said—
" Against this warfare I rebel at heart,
And wish no more in such to act a part.
I, with a chosen few, will homeward hie,
But ye can forward march to fight, and die ! "
So saying he departed on his way,
And Cortez learned the tidings with dismay,
And sent some friendly natives to pursue,
And urge him to his army to be true.
But he refused to all they said to list,
And in his purpose vowed that he'd persist.
Then Cortez cried—" I'll take him by surprise ;
A troop of horse shall seize him as he flies ! "
'T was done, and, to the camp he, captive, came,
Where he was told his sentence, and his shame.
A gallows was erected in the square,*
And he was led, and executed, there.
His wealth was confiscated to the Crown,
And ignominy covered his renown.
Thus perished one who'd glorified his State—
A hero who deserved a nobler fate,
Who spurned at heart the fierce, invading horde,

---

* Fronting the camp at Tezcuco. No disturbance followed
the execution.

That carried devastation with the sword,
And loved his country, hating these its foes,
Foreseeing, in their train, its endless woes.
If all had, like him, with prophetic eye,
Seen ruin follow when they ventured nigh,
And felt the courage that imbued his breast,
Not Cortez thus would have their land oppressed,
Nor that proud Aztec empire passed away,
Like morning mist before the beams of day.

PART TENTH.

I.

THE moving army met the monarch's eyes,
And well he watched the martial enterprise—
Watched ev'ry movement with untiring gaze,
And planned its sore defeat in divers ways.
He saw Don Olid Alvarado, meet,
While standing in his eyrie-like retreat,
And then upon Chapultepec advance.
There, to the aqueduct, he turned his glance,
And saw the Spanish troops his own attack,
And drive them, in the battle, further back,
Then cut the pipes that led to Mexico,
Which made the city's fountains cease to flow;
Nor e'er again the sparkling fluid ran
Through these, to satisfy the thirst of man,
While that great monument of art, and skill,
Which crowned Chapultepec's dark cypressed hill,
Was left dismantled at the victor's hands,
And crystal floods escaped among the sands.
He saw the two commanders, lead the way,
And storm the fatal dike, and heard the fray,

But though they battled hard 't was all in vain
The causeway's nearest bridge they strove to gain.
He saw his hosts upon the lake and dike,
With valor, and determination strike,
And then repulse, with slaughter, all their foes,
While deadly were their well-directed blows.
He saw those foes, discomfited, depart
For shelter to their camps, two leagues apart,
And thanked Mexitli for this battle won,
And prayed that thus henceforth the tide would
    run.
The while the troops of Sandoval had gained
The streets of Iztapalapan, and stained
With blood, anew, the city, sacked before,
Ere in revenge, 't was deeply flooded o'er :
And there they paused, awaiting the command
To further ravage the benighted land.

II.

The brigantines now glided o'er the lake,
Each leaving silver bubbles in its wake,
While on the shore the natives gazed with eyes
That eloquently told their great surprise.
Each craft to them was like a thing of life,—
Some white-winged demon on a sea of strife,—
Which called the winds to aid it in its flight,
And bore the white men on its breast to fight.
How wondrous to their vision was the sight !
As this flotilla passed a rocky height,
A cloud of missiles from its summit fell,
While echoed through the chasms yell on yell.
There Cortez landed, climbed the steep ascent—
On punishing his foes, audacious, bent—
And to the sword the garrison consigned,
Then, with his troops, his fleet, in triumph, joined.

The waters of the lake were swarming now
With war-canoes, well manned from stern to bow,
Each paddling toward the brigantines with speed—
The Aztec's never-failing water-steed.
A calm prevailed, but suddenly a breeze,
As welcome as 't was e'er in tropic seas,
Caressed the bosom of the shining lake,
Which seemed from dreamy slumber to awake,
And breathed new life into the listless sails,
While wafting perfume from the hills and dales.
The brigantines, in line of battle, flew
Before this Providential * wind, that blew,
And overturned, by hundreds, the canoes,
And helpless swimmers left their dusky crews.
The brigantines their fatal volleys fired,
And as they fired the fleeing foe expired.
But few escaped of all the Aztec fleet,
For they were intercepted in retreat.
The brigantines borne onward by their wings—
Which to the foe were strange, and wondrous
    things—
Gave chase, like eagles pouncing on their prey,
And easy was the task to crush, and slay.
Defeat so utter greater seemed than aught
That Cortez yet, in Mexico, had wrought,
And ever after, o'er this inland sea,
He ranged in undisputed mastery.

III.

The twilight, with its shades, the prospect veiled
As, when the fight was o'er, the squadron sailed
Along the southern causeway, to the west,

---

* So considered by Cortez, who, like his age, was superstitious.

And found at anchor, nigh to Xoloc, rest.*
There, where the smaller joined the larger dike,
Two stony turrets rose up fortress-like,
And wider grew the causeway.   Cortez cried—
" This suits me well, and I will here abide.
The garrison I'll quickly put to flight,
And pitch my camp within their walls to-night ! "
When on the causeway shone the morrow's sun,
It showed the work of Cortez had been done.
The cannon from the fleet were landed there,
And in position placed, with skill and care.
Of Olid's troops, one half were ordered on,
And messengers to Sandoval had gone
Commanding him to haste, with all his force,
To Olid's camp, and by the straightest course.†
The Aztecs now discovered, but too late,
Here lay the key to Tenochtitlan's gate,
And stormed the camp with fury, night and day,
To drive the hated Spanish troops away.
The lake again was dark with war-canoes,
All filled with yelling, fierce, and fighting crews,
Who, on the side where lay the Spanish fleet,
Kept at a distance, mindful of retreat,
But on the other, with the dike between,
Close ventured, and attacked with savage mien,
And with their missiles wrought such havoc, rude,

---

* Xoloc was that point of the great southern causeway, extending from the city of Mexico to the mainland, where it was joined by a branch causeway from Cojohuacan, and was situated half a league from the capital, and nearly midway in Lake Tezcuco between the city and the shore.   The towers referred to were fortresses surrounded by stone walls, and occupied by an Aztec garrison.

† Olid was stationed at Cojohuacan, near the shore end of the causeway leading to the spot occupied by Cortez, so that the latter through him could obtain supplies from the surrounding country.

That Cortez through the dike a channel hewed,
Through which two brigantines in safety passed,
And so no more the foe the camp harassed.

IV.

The two great highways, now, to Mexico—
Those west, and south—were wrested by her foe.
A third remained, upon the northern side,
The dike of Tep-e-jac-ac, long, and wide.
Thence Alvarado from Tacuba went,
And bravely fought, and scaled each battlement,
Till, on the dike, he, in his camp, reposed,
With all the causeways to the city closed.
Not more complete the blockade could have been,
And Quahtemozin saw it with chagrin ;
But Cortez, not content with this alone,
More quickly sought the monarch to dethrone,
And, to surrender, Tenochtitlan force ;
So to the march again he'd swift recourse.

V.

Once more at dawn the Spanish troops arose,
And, under arms, prepared to meet their foes.
The solemn, stately, and imposing Mass—
No morn without it was allowed to pass—
Was then performed to reverential ears,
And from believing minds it banished fears,
For to their faith the sons of Spain were true,
Yet wickedness they practised, daily, too.
The Spanish chieftain marched before the van,
Along the dike, which to the city ran,
Designing Tenochtitlan to attack
And leave a line of ruin in his track.
Ere long he halted at a bridgeless breach,

Where, on the other side, beyond his reach,
A solid rampart rose to screen his foes,
Who yelled defiance as they struck their blows.
The Spaniards fought, but to dislodge them failed
Till on each side a brigantine assailed.
The Aztecs, then, retreated from the fire,
Though not till racked and rent by carnage, dire,
And from the brigantines the soldiers leapt,
And in pursuit along the causeway swept,
While Cortez, and his comrades swam the space,
And followed, close behind them, in the race,
Till to another open breach they came.
There foes again from ramparts took their aim,
And those pursued, behind them shelter found.
Each swam the gap as swiftly as a hound,
While Aztec arrows thickly flew around.
The brigantines again were brought to bear,
And musketry, and cannon thundered there
Until the place was captured as before
Amid the battle's cries, and angry roar.
Thus breach on breach was carried to the end,
The Aztecs, eager, each one, to defend.
The victors, in their course, the ramparts razed,
And massive stones from out the dike were raised,
With which they filled the chasms in their way,
A source, as they progressed, of much delay;
But in the end the capital was gained,
And Aztec blood again its precincts stained.

VI.

They now were in the same broad avenue
As they, on coming first, paraded through,
When Montezuma welcomed them in peace,
And they from warfare found a brief release.
It crossed the city, running north to south—

'T was known to all as Tenochtitlan's mouth—
And straight, and wide, with buildings lined, it ran.
In triumph, Cortez forward led the van.
With combatants the roofs were covered o'er,
Whose missiles through his ranks in torrents tore,
While in the distance dusky masses thronged
To fight the foe, for whose defeat they longed,
And who, so foully, had their country wronged.
" Destroy the buildings ! " was the stern command,
And to obey each soldier raised his hand.
The allies who had labored on the dike,
And filled the chasms, now were first to strike,
For to Destruction's work they gladly sprang,
And shrill, and loud, their savage war-cries rang.
The Spanish troops advanced ; the foe retired,
But turned at times, and on their foemen fired.
A wide canal, across the street, at length
Gave to the fleeing Aztecs fleeting strength.
They crossed in safety, and the bridge destroyed,
And screened by ramparts, on the other side,
Their missiles showered, and pursuit defied ;
But when the heavy guns were brought to play
They opened for the musketry a way :
The breach grew wider, and they fled the fray,
And those who'd stood for two long hours at bay
Crossed o'er the stream, and followed up the chase
Until they'd reached their former camping-place—
The square where, erst, their palace-barracks lay,
From which they fled to suffer fresh dismay
On that wild night of carnage on the dike.
For that in vengeance they had yet to strike.
On one side Montezuma's palace stood,
And on another rose that scene of blood—
The war-god's mammoth pyramidal fane,
Which though by fire assailed, and filled with slain,
Still reared its mighty figure to the skies—

Like Cheops, which both Time and man defies—
Surrounded by a wall* and lesser fanes,
Or of those sacred places, the remains.

The Spaniards halted as they faced the view.
They felt this second advent they might rue,
But Cortez gave his well-known battle-cry—
" St. Jago !   Comrades, let us at them fly,
Ere they can rally!" and he waved on high
His own true sword, while with the other hand
He grasped his target, leading his command,
And took them boldly through the temple's gate
Where fled the Aztecs to escape their fate,
For they with terror there beheld their foe
Again the scourge of hapless Mexico.
The frantic priests, with cries, and gestures wild,
From terraces upon the temple piled—
Which round it, in their convolutions, coiled—
Urged on their people to the deadly fray,
And chanted in their ears some warlike lay.
A squad of Spaniards by their chieftain led,
Up to the terraced temple's summit sped,
And from the heights the priests, in fury, threw,
And all beside within its cloisters slew.
The holy cross, and symbols, they had placed
Within its walls, could nowhere, now, be traced,
But where they'd once the war-god overthrown,
Another idol occupied a throne,
Rich in barbaric ornament, and bright
With sparkling gems—a strange, fantastic sight.
The Christians laid it low with fierce delight,
And then rejoined their comrades massed below,
As on them sprang the wildly-maddened foe.

---

* The *coatepantli*, or wall of serpents, which enclosed the
great *teocalli*, and its extensive array of religious edifices.

The sacrilegious outrage on their fane—
The spectacle of priests, and teachers slain—
The desecration of their sacred shrine,
Led all as one with fury to combine,
And, with a yell of frantic horror, rush
The panoplied iconoclasts to crush.
These, taken thus by storm, in sad surprise
Awoke the echoes with their battle-cries,
And desperately fought to stem the tide,
But by the torrent they were forced aside,
Or trodden down, and many, fighting, died.
They backward fell, disordered, to the square,
But legions, fresh, gave battle to them there,
And ere they rallied they were put to flight
'Mid Aztec yells of triumph, and delight.
Their cannon they abandoned to the foe,
And reeled as if beneath a crushing blow.
The allies caught the panic as they fled,
And through their ranks confusion quickly spread,
While from the house-tops missiles thickly flew,
And blinded those retreating to the view,
And hard it was to single foe from friend,
While harder still they found it to defend.
'T was all in vain that Cortez cried aloud
To that excited, and retreating crowd.
His voice was in the stormy uproar drowned.
The torrent swept in fury all around,
And all seemed lost indeed when—lo !—he heard
Approaching sounds that all his feelings stirred.
The tramp of horses, swiftly drawing near,
Fell like enchanting music on his ear,
And, with delight, he saw the troop advance,
And deal destruction with the sword, and lance.
They charged where they their foemen thickest
    found,
And trampled them by hundreds on the ground,

While they with terror all the Aztecs filled,
And strewed their path with wounded, and the
   killed ;
For though so few, gigantic they appeared
To those who horse and rider doubly feared.
With superstitious, and o'erwhelming dread,
They from their fierce assailants turned, and
   fled,
And panic through the Aztec legions spread.
Then Cortez rallied his retreating troops,
Formed into battle-line disordered groups,
And joined his horsemen in a swift pursuit.
The Aztecs with a mighty yell, and hoot,
Rushed through the temple gates in wild retreat,
And in confusion down the stately street,
While Cortez, in possession of the square,*
Recaptured all the guns he'd planted there.

The hour of vespers had already come,
And from the trumpet, and resounding drum,
There sounded the loud summons to return.
In this the army safety could discern,
For night would soon o'ertake them, and 't were
   vain
To longer in the battling throng remain.
The Aztecs followed as they marched away,
And left them disappointed of their prey,
And filled the air with cries, and howlings wild,
When toward the dike, in order, they defiled ;
But all their missiles failed to turn the tide,
And Spain again all Mexico defied.
The camp at Xoloc was regained at length,
And wearied Nature sought in slumber strength.

---

* The *tianguez.*

VII.

In Tenochtitlan rage, alarm, and gloom,
This shadow of a dark, impending doom,
Stirred all the city to its inmost core ;
And Quahtemozin's heart, with grief, was sore.
Of what avail had his defences been,
The Valley's Queen,* from fresh assault, to screen ?
Surprise, and disappointment, he expressed,
But patriotic ardor warmed his breast.
He still would battle to defeat the foe,
Nor cease to fight while he could strike a blow.
Deep consternation through the city spread,
While all the country round was filled with dread,
And some who unto him before were true—†
The chiefs of places distant to his view—
Now to his foes, for friendship, sent to sue,
Thus undermining, more, and more, his throne,
And leaving him, the more, to fight alone,
While adding fuel to Invasion's fire,
And heaping up—alas !—disasters dire.

VIII.

Tezcuco's prince ‡ and fifty thousand braves,
Prepared for battle, fearless of their graves,
Now joined the camp of Cortez on the dike.
" Such hosts," he cried, " must conquer when they
    strike ! "
To each division he assigned a third,

---

* Tenochtitlan, or the city of Mexico.

† The territory of Xochimilco, and several tribes of Oto-
mies, dwelling on the western confines of the valley, among
others.

‡ Ixtlilxochitl, who had been placed on the throne of Tezcuco by Cortez.

And to this distribution none demurred.
Then he a fresh assault, with method, planned,
By which he hoped to triumph o'er the land.
The three divisions under his command
Were ordered to advance, before the foe
Had well recovered from the latest blow,
And so along the dikes which spanned the lake
The martial lines were seen their way to take.
The three long causeways Quahtemozin eyed,
And o'er this fresh invasion sadly sighed,
Yet to resist it all his forces massed,
Determined to do battle to the last,
And urged his troops to conquer, or to die,
And ne'er from Spain's invading host to fly.

IX.

'T was with dismay that Cortez saw the foe
Had cleared the breaches of the wreck below,*
And through them left the floods again to flow,
While each one, as before, was fortified,
And held by troops, who bravely his defied.
Once more all o'er the work had to be done,
But breach by breach, the path was slowly won,
The brigantines assisting on each side,
And firing till the foe had fled, or died.
'T was afternoon ere all the gaps were gained,
And all alike with blood were deeply stained.
Then Cortez to the city led the way,
His forces eager to renew the fray,
For they like bloodhounds were for blood athirst,
And deemed their foes, as infidels, accurst:
Yet, step by step, they found their march opposed,

---

*About two-thirds of their number had been thus restored
to their previous state by the Aztecs.

So well the hostile legions were disposed,
And with such resolution they were armed ;
But death the bravest of the brave disarmed.
In anger Cortez reached the open square,
While cries of hate, and triumph filled the air.
The war-god's sacred pyramid rose high,
Beneath the splendor of the beaming sky,
And the low range of palace buildings lay *
As when they held all Mexico at bay.
The ancient palace was the nation's pride,
Within whose walls great Montezuma died,
And to destroy it Cortez, now, desired.
" Apply the torch ! " he cried, and it was fired.
While, from within, the lurid flames escaped,
The city with a pall of smoke was draped,
And while to ashes fell the blazing pile,
The face of Cortez wore a bitter smile.
The burning ruins, crashing, reached the ground,
And Tenochtitlan mourned to hear the sound.
All save the stone-work vanished from the view,
While clouds of dust far o'er the city flew.
The House of Birds,† which, too, adorned the square,
Was quickly made its fiery fate to share;
And all its feathered captives perished there,
Save some that from their burning prisons broke,
And soared through the ascending flame, and
    smoke—
Their plumage gay with yellow, red, and green—

---

* The old palace of Axayacatl, formerly the Spanish barracks.

† It was a light and elegant building, of wood and bamboo,
standing near Montezuma's palace on the side of the square
which was opposite to the barrack-palace just destroyed, and
contrasting with the heavy stone buildings around. It contained specimens of all the richly-plumaged birds found in and
near Mexico.

Then hovered far above the troubled scene,
And, screaming, to their native forests, fled,
Of man, and fresh captivity, in dread.

With horror, and chagrin, the Aztecs gazed
Upon the buildings as they brightly blazed,
And hatred into savage fury swelled
As they, their foes, the Tlascalans, beheld,
The work of desolation urging on ;
And with them fighting, as if both were one,
Their neighbors the Tezcucans, forward led
By one of yore in Tenochtitlan bred.*
"False-hearted traitor ! " from the roofs, they cried,
" Who thus would fight on the invaders' side !
False to thy country, to thy race untrue,
For ever hide thy visage from the view ! "
But taunts like these, though full of wrath and gall,
Seemed lightly on the chieftain's ear to fall,
And he his way with resolution held,
Though kinsmen round him—"Traitor ! traitor ! "
     yelled.
Ambition had his love of country killed,
And, by success, remorse in him was stilled.
His aim was now fresh infamy to earn.
It was, he knew, too late to backward turn.

X.

In vain the havoc Cortez wrought was done :—
No triumph, by the flames, his arms had won.
His foes were lashed to fury by the fire,
And meditated vengeance, deep, and dire,
And hurled their missiles with still deeper hate,
At those who came to burn, and desecrate.

---

* The young prince Ixtlilxochitl.

The Spanish leader, disappointed, sighed
To see how boldly they his arms defied,
And gave the trumpet-signal to retreat,
For dying day was speeding night to meet.
The Aztecs on his army wildly sprang,
And loudly through the air their voices rang,
As toward the causeway the invaders turned,
And madly they for Spain's destruction yearned.
They closely followed the receding rear,
And bravely fought with arrow, sling, and spear,
While, when the horsemen turned to drive them back,
They desperately parried each attack,
And tried to tear the riders from their steeds.
Not more heroic could have been their deeds;
They gave their lives to strike a single blow,
Content to die if they could smite the foe.
They threw themselves beneath the horses' feet,
The better, thus, the horsemen to defeat,
And none that night the camp at Xoloc gained
Whose garments by his wounds had not been stained.

XI.

'T was well that while the conflict here was waged
The Aztecs, at the dikes were, too, engaged,
Where Sandoval, and Alvarado fought—
But, vainly, to advance to Cortez sought—
For, thus divided, Cortez found his foe
Less able to inflict a deadly blow.
Yet Cortez though so savagely assailed—
While to induce surrender he had failed—
Determined to continue his attacks,
Nor for a day his enterprise relax.
The morning saw his troops advance, in force;
The evening saw them backward take their course,
And, under cover of the shades of night,

The Aztecs labored with persistent might
To clear the breaches the invaders filled,
And new defences on their banks to build.*
Thus o'er, and o'er again, the work was done,
And neither seemed a triumph to have won.
The three divisions daily tried to meet,
But all their efforts ended in retreat.
In vain they rest, in storm and darkness, sought:
By night as well as day the Aztecs fought.†
The three divisions were, at once, assailed,
And neither side, in making havoc, failed.
The day and night alike were battle-stained,
And yet no conquest the invaders gained.
The bleak, and rainy, season of the year ‡
Afforded little that the heart could cheer,
As shelterless the troops in camp reposed,
And on their arms their weary eyelids closed;
Prepared to rise to Battle's trumpet call,
And into line, with martial ardor, fall.
Three months of stern privation, toil, and strife, §

---

*Alvarado guarded the breaches in the dike he occupied at night, and so saved this endless labor, but Cortez said that this duty was beyond the strength of men engaged in such arduous service during the day as were those of his own division.

† This was contrary to the previous habits of the Aztecs. Their forces moved at night from different points in concert, at the signal of a beacon-fire, or the war-god's drum.

‡ From July to September.

§ Prescott says that the surface of the causeways, flooded by the storms, and broken up by the constant movement of large bodies of men, was converted into a quagmire, which added inconceivably to the distresses of the army. Diaz, who served in Alvarado's division, remarks:

"Through the long night we kept our dreary watch, neither wind, nor wet, nor cold availing anything. There we stood, smarting from the wounds received in the fight of the pre-

While in their ranks disease, and death were
  rife—
Thus, on the causeways, slowly passed away,
And Mexico still held them all at bay;
But Famine, by degrees, was stealing in,
And, in the end, its victory would win.
Already 't would have devastation wrought
Had not canoes the country's products brought
By stealth, in darkness, from the friendly shore—
A source which, now, would yield, but little more,
For as the country round renounced its sway
This succor, with its sources, passed away:
But though the ancient trunk its branches lost—
Nipped by Invasion's blight, and killing frost—
It still defied the storm that raged around,
And—firmly rooted—bravely held its ground.

Not only on the land the contest raged,
For war upon the water, too, was waged,
Where stratagem supplied the place of force—
In Aztec arms a favorite resource.
Thus, once in ambuscade canoes were laid,
Where reedy thickets hid them in their shade,
While piles were driven in the shallows near;
Then boats decoyed the brigantines, that here
Became entangled in the trap below,
When from the ambush shot the angry foe,
And on the brigantines fell blow on blow.
Nigh all on board were wounded; some were
  slain,
And Cortez heard the tidings, sad, with pain.

---

vious day. In short so unintermitting were our engagements, both by day and by night, during the three months
we lay before the capital, that to recount them all would
make the reader fancy he was perusing the incredible feats of
a knight-errant of romance."

XII.

The cities, which had Spain's protection sought,
Now, to his camp their warlike legions brought, *
Who bravely with their brother allies fought,
And at each dike, like demons, havoc wrought.
Supplies were gathered from the country round,
And in abundance maize, and fruits were found.
The allies oft—if history be true—
Their bodies nourished with the foes they slew,
While in the ancient city Aztecs ate
The immolated victims of their hate ;
And this with holy zeal, and solemn show,
For their religion—woeful !—taught them so. †
Alas ! that stain so foul, on face so fair,
Should e'er have marred the lines of beauty there.

The storm around the city gathered force,
But Quahtemozin swerved not from his course,
And with undaunted courage faced the foe,
Resolved to rise or fall with Mexico.
He saw his vassals to the stranger turn—
The sway of their declining empire spurn ;
He saw his city wasted day by day,
His armies decimated by the fray,
And night illumined by the glaring light
Of burning buildings—an appalling sight ;

---

*To the number, according to Cortez, of a hundred and fifty thousand.

† The Aztecs did not, however, partake of human flesh to gratify a depraved animal appetite, but in obedience to the behests of their religion, and their cannibal repasts were confined to the bodies of those who had perished on the altar of sacrifice at the hands of the priests, who having gashed their prostrate victims' breasts with a sharp razor, inserted their hands and drew forth the quivering hearts, which they held aloft to the Sun.

He Pestilence, and Famine, saw advance,
Each armed, by Death, with a destroying lance,
But all the horrors of the siege grew dim
In his fierce hatred of his foemen, grim.
That hatred served to fire the drooping heart,
To wing the arrow, and to point the dart,
And Quahtemozin, still, for vengeance cried,
And all the legions of his foe defied.

XIII.

Impatience in the Spanish camp prevailed,
While all, the rigors of the siege, bewailed,
And deemed their lot was harder than the foe's.
" Cut short," they cried to Cortez, " these our woes,
And let us in the city deal our blows—
There have our camp, and nightly court repose ;
Our conquest sooner we can there achieve,
And gladly we these roofless dikes will leave."
To please his comrades Cortez gave assent,
And with rejoicing cheers the air was rent.
" Prepare ye then to make a grand attack,
And if ye, to the dikes, are driven back,
Lay not to me, but to yourselves, the fault
Of making what I deem a rash assault.
Advance not where ye cannot well retreat,
For Aztec foemen, as ye know, are fleet ;
Fill all the gaps, and breaches, as ye go,
And stand prepared for ev'ry sudden blow.
The three divisions will together strike,
And each in concert move along its dike,*
All aiming in the market-place to meet,
And resolute the heathen to defeat ! "

---

* Sandoval was, however, ordered to remove most of his
forces from the northern causeway, and join Alvarado.

Thus Cortez spoke, and dawned ere long the day
On which his troops were marshalled for the fray.
The ne'er omitted morning Mass was said
Ere they were forward, to the city, led,
The brigantines advancing at their side,
With native boats which through canals could glide,
All armed, and manned, to pierce that city's heart,
And through its water highways swiftly dart.

The suburbs, which had oft with gore been stained,
In safety by the Spanish chief were gained.
Thence to the market square * three roads appeared,
And, quickly, into these a way was cleared.
Thus one division into three was formed,
While stones, and arrows, on the army stormed.
On either side the widest road there ran
A deep canal, of nigh as great a span,
And through it breaches, here and there, were made,
Through which the troops, advancing, had to wade,
For all the bridges had been torn away,
The movements of the army to delay.
The squadron that along this road defiled †
Grew with success, and carnage, rash and wild,
And, like the wind, pursued the flying foe,
While the canoes to follow were not slow.
They paused not bridgeless breaches to repair,
Nor deemed how soon they'd prove a fatal snare :
They only cared to reach the market square.
Of all their comrades in advance they swept,
And ev'ry gap they found they swam, or leapt.
The goal for which they longed was nearly gained,
And each canal with Aztec blood was stained,

---

* The Square of Tlatelolco, the largest open space in the city, and the market for its supplies.

† This was commanded by Alderete, the royal treasurer, an officer of much distinction.

When Cortez, who another squadron led,
Was by this rapid movement filled with dread.
He, as he went, had all the breaches closed,
But those in whom he'd confidence reposed
Did not, he feared, this weighty duty heed.
Why fled the foe with such uncommon speed,
If not his forces to destruction lead?
Surprise, and stratagem, might havoc work,
And in success, disaster here might lurk.
His troops were halted, while he crossed to view
The dike-like street, so swiftly hurried through.
There—to his consternation—open lay
The breaches, left unclosed to save delay.
A chasm, wide, his further progress stayed,
While by a sudden sound he stood dismayed.
'T was of a distant conflict, loud and fierce,
Which seemed alike the earth and sky to pierce,
And yells, and war-cries, o'er the clamor rose.
The Aztecs—lo!—had turned upon their foes,
And toward the breach the tide of battle rolled.
There Cortez stood, and with him some as bold,
Who strove the breach to fill, but strove in vain
Ere he beheld with growing fear and pain,
A rushing, roaring multitude advance.
He read the dreadful story at a glance.
Just then the blast of Quahtemozin's horn
Awoke the echoes of the tragic morn,
And seemed with savage fury hosts to fire,
Who wreaked on the invaders vengeance, dire.
On came the Spanish troops in headlong haste,
By countless maddened Aztecs hotly chased,
All surging in the battle's deadly throes,
And, mingled in confusion, friends, and foes.
Fresh Atzec legions poured upon the scene,
And none more stormy Cortez e'er had seen;
But bravely, with his comrades, at the breach

He stood a helping hand, across, to reach,
And horror-stricken at the waste of life
Involved in this, to him, disastrous strife.
He saw his soldiers' blows at random fell,
While their assailants made their weapons tell,
And from the house-tops blinding volleys flew,
And many of the flying squadron slew,
Who in their rout each other trampled low,
And, like a torrent, flew before the foe.
Into the chasm * plunged the foremost files—
The victims of the Aztecs' fatal wiles—
And one another trod beneath the flood,
Which soon was crimsoned with their ebbing blood.
Some strove, but vainly, o'er the gulf to swim,
While some reeled backward from the chasm's brim,
Or from its glassy, and deceptive, tide,
And in its troubled waters, mangled, died;
Some over heaps of fallen comrades passed,
And some into the foes' canoes were cast,
And to the fanes, in triumph, borne away
For immolation—yea, Mexitli's prey.
But at the breach still Cortez stood, to save,
And rescued hundreds from a yawning grave,
And many from the captive's awful fate,
While striving hard the panic to abate.†
Yet vainly to the fugitives he called;
They fled, confused, distracted, and appalled.
Darts, stones, and arrows thickly fell around,
But these no entrance in his armor found,
And from his polished helmet glanced aside.

---

* It was ten or twelve paces wide, and filled with water, at least two fathoms deep, by which communication was established between the canals on either side of the dike-like roadway.

† The breach at this spot was, subsequently, named by Cortez the *puente cuidada*, or sorrowful bridge.

At length—"Malinché! See!" the Aztecs cried,
And held two gory Spanish heads in view,
While "Sandoval!" and "Alvarado!" too,
They shouted as their trophies they displayed,
And signs that both had perished thus they made,
Which blanched the cheek of Cortez as he gazed,
Alarmed, defiant, wond'ring and amazed.
Then rushed they on him, like a hungry wolf,
And dragged him down into the fatal gulf,
And strove to place him in a war-canoe.
To succor him—his faithful comrades flew,
And in the struggle, fierce, their weapons drew.
With sword, and lance, they ran assailants through,
But for the contest they were nigh too few.
Lo! o'er his wounded, and his prostrate form,
Those heroes fought amid the deadly storm,
And rescued him, at last, from Death's embrace—
A sign, to them, of sanctifying grace—
Though of their number some there were who fell—
Slain, captured, wounded—where they strove so well.
A steed was brought to Cortez, and he rode
Along the miry and the crowded road,
Pursued, on either side, by war-canoes,
And pelted by the volleys from their crews,
Who captured all that stumbled down the slope,
And these forever bade adieu to hope.
But one, who held the banner of Castile,
Plied with such havoc his destroying steel
As, from their clutches, freedom to regain,
And shun the horrors of the war-god's fane,
While with him he his country's standard bore—
A tattered rag, bespattered with their gore.*
A cry of disappointed rage arose

---

* This was the ensign, Corral, who had slipped down into the canal.

At that glad moment from his baffled foes,
For in the flag they saw, with longing eyes,
A priceless trophy, and a splendid prize.

At length the open city Cortez gained,
And to his warlike purpose true remained.
Behind the loud artillery he stood,
And backward forced the wild, pursuing flood,
And made the roadway red, with Aztec blood.
Then rallied he his broken files, in haste,
And with his horsemen, brave, his foemen faced, *
And gave the trumpet-signal to retreat.
To linger would, he knew, bring worse defeat,
But he would yet the tide of triumph turn,
And from the day's disaster wisdom learn.

XIV.

To Sandoval, and Alvarado—two
As brave commanders as e'er weapons drew—
He sent the dismal tidings of the day,
And bade them to their causeways speed away;
But they already moved in full retreat,
For, like their comrades, they had met defeat.
All with their arms that morn had prospered well
Till Quahtemozin's horn—a startling knell—
Upon their senses from the temple fell.
Then, though their goal—the market square—was
     near,
And though they heard their distant comrades
     cheer,
Their instincts told them they had much to fear,
And ere the signal's echoes died away,
They heard the sound of an appalling fray,

---

* The cavalry had not been previously brought into action.

While, with redoubled fury, on them rose
Their erst retreating multitude of foes.
The struggle lasted till the distant roar
Grew faint as surf upon a stormy shore;
When, sudden as the lightning, legions new
Broke, like a flood, upon their troubled view,
And rushing forward cried "Malinché's dead!"
And on the pavement threw a gory head,
Then sweeping, in a torrent, down the street,
Compelled an instantaneous retreat,
And followed in pursuit, with savage hate,
Like an avenging Nemesis of fate;
Till back upon the dikes their foes retired,
And from intrenchments there their cannon fired,
Which swept the causeways, while the brigantines
Performed the part they played in former scenes.
The Aztecs, from the guns, once more recoiled,
And felt themselves for further havoc foiled.

XV.

The while the troops of Cortez in retreat,
Again the causeway felt beneath their feet,
While the pursuing legions here, at last,
Before the ships, and cannon, stood aghast,
And those who ventured on the dike were slain—
Cut down as, by the sickle, is the grain.
On high, in noonday splendor, shone the sun,
And yet so much, that morning, had been done.

Dejected, Cortez to Marina turned,
For wisdom rare in her he'd oft discerned.
"Alas! Marina," mournfully he spoke,
"To all your truths I have at last awoke.
These Aztecs are unyielding as the grave,
And of our allies none are half so brave.

'T were vain to hope the city, now, to save.
Ere we can conquer, we must raze it low,
And bring to ashes haughty Mexico!
This grieves me much, for I would gladly spare
The structures of a capital so fair.
But, for the present, I must linger here,
And look to thee for solace, help, and cheer.
My wounds oppress me, and demand repose.
'T is well to rest from combat for awhile,
And bask—how fondly!—in thy sunny smile."
Then to the camp there came, with flying speed,
Well mounted on his faithful, foaming steed,
The brave, heroic Sandoval we know,
Who ne'er deserted friend, or shrank from foe.
He came the tidings, sad, to glean, and tell,
And learn if all had gone, with Cortez, well.
The Aztec hosts had cried that he was slain,
And through the army went a thrill of pain.
"Don Sandoval," said Cortez to his friend,
"You to the army, while I rest, attend,
For Alvarado is I fear too brave,
And I would save him from a captive's grave.
These wounds of mine have crippled me so sore,
That I can battle, ere they heal, no more.
Our losses have been heavy, for the foe
Struck, in his fury, a destructive blow,
And sixty-two Castilians, alive,
Now in the temple with their captors hive,
Besides a multitude of allies, bold;
While killed, and maimed, in numbers yet untold,
Fill up the measure of our sore reverse;
Yet though so bad it might have ended worse.*

---

* Two field-pieces and seven horses also fell into the hands
of the Aztecs on this occasion.

'T was through a comrade's rashness all was done.*
We but for this a triumph might have won.
Still all is not by this disaster lost,
Though much in life, and prestige, it has cost.
We, by these dikes, the city still command,
And Conquest, yet, will give us all the land !
So cheer thee up, my brave, heroic friend :
The Lord of Hosts his servants will defend,
For are we not crusaders of the Cross,
Whose death would be the great Jehovah's loss ? "
Then to his camp the rider hurried back,
And, as he went, he braved each scout's attack.
The sun still shone above the western heights,
Recalling days of joy, and past delights,
And o'er the splendid valley poured his beams,
And made the temples gay with golden gleams,
While all the towers glistened in his light.
The city lay calm, beautiful, and bright,
Contrasting with the sable scenes of strife,
Which but that morn, within it, were so rife.
The sun sank lower in the golden west ;
The time drew near for vespers, and for rest,
And far, and wide, a tranquil silence reigned,
As if o'er all Queen Peace had sway regained,
When suddenly was heard that awful sound,
The war-god's drum, which rang the valley round.
The horrors of the past were all recalled,
And nigh the boldest of the bold appalled.†
The startled soldiers to the temple turned,
And winding up its mighty sides discerned

---

* Alderete, the royal treasurer, who commanded the squadron between the canals.

† This was the second time the great drum was heard by the
Spaniards, the only other occasion being that of the *noche
triste.*

A long procession—for the air was clear,
And distant figures seemed like objects near.*
Some solemn act of Aztec faith, they knew
Was now transpiring there, within their view.
They needed not the captives, stripped, and white—
To them a galling, and impressive sight—
To tell them of their comrades' mournful plight,
And of the scene of sacrifice so drear,
The thought of which, from many, drew a tear.
They saw the captives, urged along by blows,
And made to dance in concert with their foes.
They saw them laid on—one by one—the stone,
And, in imagination, heard them groan
As, from their breasts, their bleeding hearts were
    torn.
'T was sad to see those war-worn heroes mourn
As they beheld their fellow-soldiers' fate,
Nor knew when such might e'en themselves, await.
Each reeking heart was on the altar laid,
While round it gory priests, with fervor, prayed
Before their idol, gorgeously arrayed—
The image of the Mars of Mexico—
Mexitli, fatal to both friend, and foe.†
To depths below the mangled forms were thrown,
Where fierce fanatics claimed them for their own,
And made a solemn feast of their remains,
In honor of their deity, and fanes.

The Aztecs near the dikes, united, rose,
With frantic fury, to destroy their foes,
When they the distant spectacle beheld,

---

* Alvarado's camp was hardly a mile from the city.

† It was a part of the religious duty of the Mexicans to sacrifice their own people on certain occasions, as well as their
captured enemies, at the shrine of the war-god.

And wildly charged, while they as madly yelled.
"Death, thus, to all our enemies!" they cried,
And, sweeping on, the Spanish hosts defied,
But these, not unprepared for their attack,
With muskets, guns, and arrows drove them back,
And, while the cannon thundered in the air,
The Mexicans, abandoned to despair,
Retreated—mangled—in their camp to grieve,
And schemes of vengeance, in the future, weave.

PART ELEVENTH.

I.

THERE followed now, five weary, strifeless days.
Save when the Aztecs turned from hymns of praise
To make a sortie on their tranquil foes,
Who sought, in peace, the healing balm repose.
The Mexicans, elated with success,
The while arrayed themselves in gala dress,
And feasted, danced, and sung the time away,
And with rejoicing made the city gay.
But this glad jubilee, to Spanish eyes,
Was like a flame that flickers ere it dies.

II.

Within the war-god's fane, the highest priest
Predicted, as he closed the solemn feast—
To cheer the monarch, and his soldiers, brave—
That naught could, now, the Spanish forces save,
And that Mexitli ere eight days were o'er,
Would lead them captive, there to fight no more—
Prophetic words the Aztecs all believed,

And dreamed of conquest, and of peace achieved,
And thundered the prediction to their foes,
While aiming to destroy them with their blows.
The oracle's prediction, like a knell
Upon the native allies, fighting, fell.
Their arms against their country's gods were raised.
They read in all the beacon-fires that blazed
The prophecy they felt would be fulfilled.
What ground had they on which escape to build,
Save by retreating from this failing cause,
Which outraged all their liberties, and laws?
In secret they resolved on speedy flight,
And, under cover of the shades of night,
They stole, in silence, from their camping-ground,
And o'er the valley journeyed, homeward-bound.
Thus troop by troop, deserting, disappeared
Before the coming wrath—the doom they feared.
Few, now, of all the allied host remained,
And o'er them—blighting courage—Terror reigned.
Tezcuco's chief, and Tlascala's were true,
But from their flags nigh all their troops withdrew.
The breath of superstition, which they felt,
Seemed, all the fabric they had raised, to melt,
Like icicles that glisten in the sun,
And then, invisibly, to water run.
The Spanish soldiers saw, with sore dismay,
The army of their allies pass away—
The dusky troops on whom they'd long relied,
And by whose numbers they'd their foes defied.
The darkest hour, before the dawn, had come,
And some grew sad, and silent as the dumb.
To them the Spanish cause looked hopeless now,
And to the storm they stood prepared to bow,
Like brave men on a sinking ship, resigned—
All at the mercy of the sea, and wind.
Their ammunition, and supplies were low,

And all around them, bristling, stood the foe.
But, on the prospect, Cortez gazed, serene,
And saw beyond the dark and troubled scene.
The prophecy he treated with disdain,
And on the dikes, defiant, would remain,
But those deserting thus he feared would rise
Ere long, against him, and his enterprise,
And so, to urge them to return, and wait--
And boldly share the Spanish army's fate,
Till the predicted time had passed them by
And proved the prophecy a priestly lie—
He sent his trusty scouts, who pleaded hard,
And promised, from disaster, all to guard :
But vainly, now, those legions, they implored,
Who cried—"Alas ! we perish by the sword ! "

III.

The Spanish arms were overcast by gloom,
And many saw, in sacrifice, their doom.
But though by wounds, and ceaseless vigils, tried,
They steadfastly all Mexico defied.
The Aztecs, by success, had daring grown,
And felt their foes, as captives, soon would groan ;
And day by day, in sorties, they essayed,
Through Spanish blood, as victors proud, to wade,
And sprang like tigers to the deadly fray,
But ever by the guns were held at bay.
Night after night the pealing drum awoke
The echoes, and the sleepers, as it spoke
In tones of thunder, o'er the silent lake,
While captives round the temple's walls would take
Their mournful way to sacrifice, a fate,
For them, most horrible to contemplate. *

---

* The Aztecs sacrificed only a few of their captives at a

The light of countless torches on them gleamed,
And through the fiery glare the pageant seemed
A spectacle of horror, born of hell,
Which made each Spanish breast with hatred
    swell,
As from the camps the army eyed the scene
With sad forebodings, and with deep shagreen.

IV.

The Spanish army constant were, and true,
Nor faltered in the work they had to do.
A brave example husbands found in wives
Who in the battle's front exposed their lives—
Brave heroines who with the camp had come,
Prepared to follow—with their lords—the drum,
And who, in time of need, like men would fight,
And find, in martial deeds, a keen delight. *
"We Spanish wives our husbands love," they
    cried.
"In danger, duty calls us to their side,
With them to share it, and with them abide!"
Oft one of these her consort's armor wore—
While he by slumber would his strength restore—
And mounted guard where he had stood before.
Another, like her, armed with sword, and lance,
Once rallied routed squadrons with her glance,
And led them backward great success to gain,
Though in the struggle she—alas!—was slain.

---

time, and thus were enabled to lay fresh victims nightly on the
altar of their war-god. Guzman, the chamberlain of Cortez,
who was one of the last to perish, lingered eighteen days in
captivity.

* These were Castilian women, the wives of soldiers, who
had accompanied the expedition when it sailed from Cuba.

·V.

Though deep were their distresses, and their woes,
The Spanish troops still boldly faced their foes;
Their cannon swept the dikes, and drove them
  back,
With slaughter, to their camp, at each attack;
Still on the lake their brigantines were seen,
Nor more severe the blockade e'er had been ;
And while fallacious hopes the Aztecs buoyed,
They saw gaunt Famine through their army stride,
And, undisputed, in their city reign—
A foe more fatal than the arms of Spain.

VI.

At length, the time predicted passed away,
And still the Christians held their foes at bay.
For these the prospect still more gloomy grew;
How false had proved their oracle, they knew,
Yet they for peace, nor quarter e'er would sue,
But battle bravely to the bloody end,
And to the last their liberties defend.
The chiefs who to the Spanish cause were true, *
Now, to their banners, the deserters drew,
And thousands of the allied host returned
When they the priestly artifice discerned,
To whom forgiveness Cortez freely gave,
Though, as deserters, their offence was grave—
And welcomed them, with gladness, to the lake,
Where lay the fortunes of the war at stake.
"They come," he cried, "as from the silent land,
And here I see an all-protecting hand ! "

---

* The Tezcucan and Tlascalan chiefs.

His army still was weak, but he was bold,
And to his trusty comrades cried, " Behold !
Our distant allies for our aid appeal,
And though so weak, our weakness to conceal,
Two hundred of our bravest we can spare,
To them, the succor which they need, to bear.
The Aztec monarch has his allies there,
Who fain would battle to restore his sway.
These we can sweep like autumn leaves away,
And when the Cross, and Crown, have won the day
Our soldiers can return, with flying speed,
To join the camp where we their valor need.
To Sandoval this duty I assign,
And let his days of absence be but nine." *
The work was, as commanded, bravely done.
The Spanish heroes all their battles won,
Laid waste the hostile regions where they fought,
And to the camp their spoils, and trophies brought.
There on their ears the welcome tidings fell
That with the camp the while all prospered well,
And that a vessel freighted with supplies,
At Vera Cruz had cheered the watchers' eyes.
She erst for blooming Florida had sailed,
But winds and waves against her long prevailed,
And when this port of refuge she had found,
No more was she to Flora's region bound,
For she was seized, and with her all she brought.
No service she for Ponce de Leon wrought,
Though all her freightage with his purse was bought.†

---

* Tapin was associated with Sandoval on this occasion, and with two hundred and eight Spanish troops, including twenty-eight cavalry, about equally distributed between them, they took opposite directions, and accomplished their purpose, returning within ten days.

† The vessel was one of Ponce de Leon's fleet, and contained among her cargo an abundance of powder—what Cortez most wanted.

Romantic knight, he cursed his luckless star,
And all who dared his vessel's course to mar:
But Cortez saw in this a watchful care,
And, with his army, bowed the knee in prayer,
Then, gladly, with rejoicings rent the air,
And thanked the Lord for having sent her there,
(With powder, too, of which he nigh was bare).
" His eye," he cried, " is on us everywhere,
And, 'mid our perils, we His mercies share! "

VII.

'T was now, with strength renewed, that Cortez rose
Again to strike his sore beleaguered foes,
But not as he had struck in days before.
Where he of yore had spared he'd spare no more.
" 'T is with reluctance, comrades," he exclaimed,
As, to the army, he his plans proclaimed,
" That I decree the city, waste be laid,
For all its walls against us are arrayed,
And all its bridges, and canals, are snares,
Where we may be entangled unawares.
The flooded depths with ruins we must fill
And raze the buildings with determined will.
Before advancing we must these destroy,
For thus alone can horse and foot deploy!
And thus alone we can our foes disarm,
And leave them impotent for further harm.
Behold them still defiant, as of old—
Undaunted by disaster, fierce and bold!
Such natures to submission ne'er will bend,
While strength is left them still their foes to rend;
Nor can misfortunes crush them ere they die:
They to the last will sound their battle-cry,
And their young monarch peace and friendship
    spurns,

And only for our capture vainly yearns,
All heedless of his train of future woes,
And only burning to destroy his foes.
Alas! that Tenochtitlan, grand and great,
Should meet with such a melancholy fate,
And that a trophy, rich in wealth, and charms,
Should thus be lost to our triumphant arms!
The stern necessity of war we see:—
Go forth, and execute this hard decree!"

VIII.

The work of devastation then began,
And Cortez labored, bravely, in the van.
To ruins fell the structures in his way,
While raged around a well-contested fray,
For step by step his progress was delayed
By squadrons in hostility arrayed.
Canals, and breaches, turned to solid land,
Beneath his strong, and desolating hand,
And all the glory of the Valley's Queen,
As he advanced, departed from the scene.
The ray of promise, which had shed its light,
And filled the Aztecs with profound delight,
Was now succeeded by the gloom of night.
More hopeless to their eyes the prospect seemed
Because that ray had for a moment gleamed.
But they with Hatred and Despair were armed,
For these not foes, nor Famine, had disarmed,
And with the fury born of passions wild,
They fought, and, fighting, still those foes reviled.

IX.

One effort more still Cortez yet would make,
The resolution of the king to break.

Three captured nobles he, as envoys sent
To beg that he'd to terms of peace consent,
And further waste of life, and wealth, prevent,
Though with reluctance 't was that they obeyed.
Their mission made them of their fate afraid.
" Tell him that he," the Spanish chieftain spoke,
" His evil fortune should no more provoke.
All that he e'er can do, has, now, been done,
And yet behold ! how soon will set his sun.
His troops have bravely for their country fought,
Yet see to what a pass at length they're brought !
What hope for him, and them, can, now, remain ?
To battle longer would be worse than vain.
He stands besieged, deserted, and alone,
With all around him hostile to his throne—
His ancient allies eager for his life.
Can he survive on such a sea of strife ?
His safety only in surrender lies.
Has he no feeling for what meets his eyes—
His dying people, and these crumbling walls ?
Has he no ear for Mercy when she calls ?
Let him allegiance to this flag proclaim,
And I will greet him in my sov'reign's name,
And write Forgiveness over all the past ;
But—mark !—this proffered pardon is my last.
If 't is, as here I tender it, embraced,
The crimes of all the Aztecs are effaced,
Their rights shall be respected as my own,
And Quahtemozin still shall grace his throne ;
But if rejected woe be unto ye !
For from impending doom ye ne'er can flee ! "

The monarch heard the tale, with flashing eye,
And cried—" Than thus surrender, I would die ! "
But still he called a council of the wise,
With whom he had no close, or kindred, ties,

To say what course his country should pursue.
Like him they to their native land were true,
But some to peace, and some to war were prone,
And all the priests said—" Peace is good we own,
But not with these invaders of our soil,
Who come, alone, to vanquish, and despoil.
Let us remember Montezuma's fate,
And how they dragged him from his high estate,
And paved his way with sorrows—captive, chained.
Can we forget how they our shrines profaned,
Or yet with slaughter all our city stained?
They've stripped its treasures from our bleeding
    land,
And, now, surrender, to their arms, demand.
No! better it will be, our gods to trust,
Than to be trampled deeper in the dust;
And better, battling for our country, die,
Than with the wishes of our foes comply,
And live henceforth in bondage and in pain.
No! we may yet our native land regain!"
" Since this is so," then Quahtemozin cried,
" Let us to conquer, or to die, decide,
And ne'er again of base surrender speak,
But on our foes devouring vengeance wreak;
And if we ne'er can this our empire save,
We still can perish as becomes the brave!"

X.

The army on the dikes, in waiting, lay
To hear what Quahtemozin, now, would say,
And paused the while from havoc, and the fray,
Till—on the morning of the second day—
The answer came, but not in peaceful guise:
And Cortez saw it with astonished eyes.
'T was sudden, and intended to surprise,

And Cortez cried—" He still our arms defies ! "
On came the Aztec forces with a roar
That sounded to the lake's remotest shore.
Through all the city's gates the hosts advanced,
And brightly in the sun their weapons glanced.
On poured the mighty, and the swelling tide
Whose course 't was Quahtemozin's lot to guide—
And stormed, with fury, the besieging foe,
Who staggered—as they struck—beneath the blow.
By numbers overwhelmed they seemed at last,
But still withstood the sortie's angry blast ;
And from their loud-mouthed cannon missiles flew,
And, tearing through the masses, hundreds slew,
While by each dike the brigantines were fought,
And, with their guns, rude, deadly havoc wrought.
The musketeers their volleys thickly poured,
And, all around, the raging battle roared,
'Mid clouds of smoke which o'er the waters rolled.
The Spanish fire, upon the Aztecs, told,
And, soon, in wild confusion back they reeled,
And left the Christians masters of the field,
Their fury dying into murmurs low
As they receded into Mexico.

XI.

Again the city's streets were wet with gore,
And devastation progressed, as before.
Day after day the work of ruin sped,
And gloomy desolation wider spread.
The Aztecs' rage was impotent to save
The Valley's Queen, though all her sons were
   brave.
Alas ! that they were born to such a fate—
Men who in courage proved so truly great.
They saw their stately edifices fall,

The honey of existence turned to gall ;
They saw their shrines swept ruthlessly away,
And all they loved, beneath the Spaniards' sway—
The wealth, and beauty of their city fled,
Their ancient fame, like Montezuma, dead.
The great canals they labored long to build
Were with the ruins of their glory filled,
And where the sun had gilded palace heights
Was now a desert with extinguished lights.
Well might the scene to frenzy drive them on—
Thus to behold their cherished glory gone,
And all their treasures laid before them waste.
This, this indeed 't was bitterness to taste.
But they were still defiant to their foes,
And bore up grandly under all their woes.
" Go on," they to the Spanish allies cried,
" And bury in the dust your native pride !
Where ye destroy ye'll have again to build,
And with deep sorrows, and remorse, be filled.
If those ye fight for conquer, woe to ye,
And if we triumph, ye our slaves will be ! "
And, in the end, the prophecy proved true.
Their country's conquest they survived to rue.

PART TWELFTH.

I.

UNTIRING, still, was Devastation's hand,
And ruin gloated o'er the prostrate land.
The Spanish arms no rest, or mercy knew,
And fiercer this unhappy conflict grew.
Day after day Destruction's work was done,
And battles by Invasion's hosts were won,

But, step by step, Resistance curbed their course,
And force was met, defiantly, by force.
Yet while they gained in strength, from day to
    day,
They saw the Aztecs dwindling fast away,
For to their camp fresh native allies came,
But on their foes preyed Famine, like a flame.
Oh ! countless horrors of a siege so dire.
Behold, a nation, in its throes, expire !

II.

Weeks passed away, and Horror rampant, reigned,
But on the foe Invasion slowly gained.
The Spanish forces met as they advanced,
And in their joy they gaily sang, and danced.
The three commanders, now, each other faced,*
And fervently as comrades, old, embraced.
The dead, unburied, thickly round them lay,
As forward the invaders took their way—
A sign the living, by their woes oppressed,
Cared not for those already gone to rest ;
A sign, too, of extremity, and need.
No more the Aztecs to their dead gave heed,
For, famine-stricken, they were weak indeed.
The ground was stripped of herbage, root, and
    weed,
And ev'ry tree was shorn of leaves, and bark—
Till each was like a phantom, strange, and stark—
To feed the famished legions of the brave,
Who tottered on the confines of the grave,
Yet, who would rather suffer here, and die
Than—conquered—to the foe for mercy fly.

---

* Cortez, Sandoval, and Alvarado.

III.

Within their houses when the Spaniards came,
Lay prostrate bodies—dying, dead, or lame—
And mothers who no more their babes could feed,
Who from their woes by Death would soon be
    freed,
The fountains of their nature famine-dry.
But not in peace were these allowed to die.
The Spanish allies razed their dwellings low,
And all within thus perished at a blow.
No age, or sex was spared.   A common fate
Awaited all the victims of their hate.
But even here not one for mercy cried,
For as he lived the Aztec bravely died.

The Aztec women like their lords were brave,
And labored hard their country's cause to save.
With missiles they the soldiers' arms supplied,
And o'er the wounded and the dying sighed.
They felt the glow of patriotic pride,
And courage, and a constancy, sublime,
Like those of Carthage in the olden time,
And Saragossa's maids in modern days.
Heroic Spirits !   Let us sing their praise.

IV.

The spacious market square at length was gained,
And Spanish hands the temple, near, profaned,*
And gave its idols to the roaring flames,
Amid vociferously loud acclaims,

---

* This was a *teocalli* on the north side of the city, inferior
only in size to that of the war-god. It was captured and
burned by Alvarado.

Though long and fierce the battle raged below
Ere it was wrested from the bleeding foe.
All save the pyramid to ashes fell,
But that remained the tragic tale to tell,*
While o'er it waved the banner of Castile,
And at its base flashed bright Toledo steel.
Ascending to its summit Cortez viewed
The region he had made a solitude.
The palaces, and temples, were no more,
And all the scene a look of ruin wore.
The busy marts of industry and trade,
With all their splendors, in the dust were laid.
The groves and gardens, too, had passed away,
And Tenochtitlan in her ashes lay,
Save where some mighty temple rose on high,
As if Invasion's ravage to defy.
Unrazed a narrow section still remained,
Within whose limits Famine rampant reigned.*
The people, yet surviving, gathered there,
While Pestilence was floating in the air,
And by their numbers, for these still were vast,
Increased the horrors even of the past ;
But though enfeebled by their countless woes,
They hurled their missiles still upon their foes,
And 'neath the victor's charge exhausted fell
While battling for the land they loved so well.

---

* Like the war-god's *teocalli*, it was a pyramidal structure, built of sun-dried brick, and only the wood and fancy-work about it was combustible.

* Seven-eighths of the city had been destroyed. The remaining eighth—between the great northern and western causeways, the modern Barrio de San Jago—comprehended the district of Tlatelolco, into which the population, still large, was crowded, although there were not accommodations for a third of their numbers.

As from the *teocallis* in the square,
The raging flames diffused a lurid glare,
The lamentations of their race arose.
"Our gods," they cried, "are victims to our foes !
The tragic drama must be near its close!"

V.

The pent-up Mexicans, in mute despair,
Their fate awaited, willing death to share,
While, daily, greater grew the heaps of dead,
And less and less their scanty stock of bread :
Not bread indeed, but aught that crept, or grew ;
And even babes, their starving mothers slew,
To satisfy the cravings which they felt.
A bitter lot to these had Fortune dealt.
The streets were filled with famished, houseless
    throngs,
Who bore, in silence, all their woes, and wrongs.
In ragged raiment all exposed were they
To rains by night, the burning sun by day,
And one by one they yielded up their breath.
Among the dead they fell asleep in death.
At ev'ry step the dead, in piles, were seen,
And Horror brooded grimly o'er the scene.
The city was a charnel-house, and all
Was covered by Corruption's deadly pall.
The pestilence, the multitude appalled.
To stay it to their deities they called,
But all their oracles, at length, were dumb.
"Whence, now," they asked, "can succor to us
    come?"
They sought relief in superstitious rites,
And fancies wild—imagination's flights—
But no relief from earth—or heaven—came.
In vain they cried aloud the war-god's name.

Yet in the midst of all these scenes behold!
The monarch Quahtemozin still was bold—
Calm, and courageous ever, as of old.
With death, and ruin, round about him, lo!
He yet refused submission to the foe.

VI.

For days the Spanish forces hushed the fray,
And cried—"Surrender! ere we further slay,"
Expecting to submission they would bend,
Wrung by distresses, which the heart might rend,
But none surrendered to that stern demand.
True was each Aztec to his native land.
Then Cortez said—"Prepare for fresh assault;
I'll sow the ground with carnage, and with salt!"
As he advanced, to meet him chiefs appeared,
Who cried aloud as they his presence neared—
"Ye are, we know, the children of the sun!
Behold how swift is he his course to run!
Why, then, so tardy ye? why here delay
To end our griefs, and terminate the fray?
Oh! crush us, all at once, and give us rest
From all the woes by which we stand oppressed?
Our war-god waits us in another clime!
We yearn to meet him.   Hasten, pray, the time."
"I come," said Cortez to the famished chiefs,
Who piteously showed their wounds, and griefs,
"To ask you to submit, and not to kill,
Though ye are at the mercy of my will.
Why does your monarch in the war persist,
When he can see 't is futile to resist?
Confer with him, and bid him meet me here;
His person I will spare, nor need he fear."
That he would come, they brought the tidings back,
But he the while prepared for fresh attack,

Nor meant to meet the Spanish chieftain there.
The promises they brought were false, but fair.
Twice these were pledged, and broken, ere the
     blow
Was struck by Cortez to disarm his foe.

He led his forces forward yet once more.
The battle opened with the cannon's roar;
The musketeers their deadly volleys poured;
The horsemen charged, with lance, and burnished
     sword;
The brigantines shot missiles from the lake,
While thunder o'er the valley seemed to break;
The allies rushed, like hounds, upon their prey,
And clouds of smoke obscured the light of day.
For this assault the Aztecs stood prepared,
And boldly the invading legions dared.
The strongest of their troops were in the front
To face the battle's devastating brunt,
To shield the feeble, and the crippled crowds,
Who threw their weapons from the city's shrouds.
The roofs were covered with excited throngs,
Who scowled upon the authors of their wrongs,
With hatred, and defiance, in their eyes,
And thirst for vengeance in their frantic cries;
While mingled with them women bravely stood,
And babes with lives thus blasted in the bud—
All destined, soon, to welter in their blood.

VII.

The Aztecs' battle-cries rose shrill and clear
As that invading multitude drew near,
And from their shrunken arms their weapons
     flew,
While fierce and wild the bloody conflict grew.

Stones, darts, and arrows, from *azoteas* * rained,
And all around with running blood was stained.
The women and the children missiles threw,
And cried—" We, too, to Mexico are true ! "
But from such feeble hands the volleys came
They missed, too oft, the object of their aim,
And fell with little damage on the foe,
Who swarmed around, and madly surged below.
The Aztecs, hemmed within a narrow space,
Were brought, with fierce destruction, face to face.
The scythe of Death—remorseless—mowed them
    down,
And Cortez cried—" We fight for Cross, and
    Crown ! "
With heaps of slain the ground was covered o'er,
And deep in channels ran, like water, gore,
Till each canal with crimson floods was dyed,
But still the Aztecs all their foes defied.
Confusion thickened, turmoil louder grew ;
Like tigers at each other foemen flew.
Barbaric yells rang hideously shrill,
And seemed, for miles, the valley round to fill ;
While o'er the groans of men in dying throes
Vile Spanish oaths, and execrations, rose.
The wounded in their anguish cried aloud,
Ere they were trampled by the rushing crowd.
The women, and the children, wildly shrieked,
While vengeance, by the sword, was on them
    wreaked.
The victors' heavy blows fell thick and fast.
Men stood before the spectacle aghast.
The rapid roll of musketry was ·heard,
While through the air the missiles hissed, and
    whirred,

---

* The roofs of the houses.

And blazing buildings into ruins fell,
Consigning hundreds to their burning hell.
The dust, in clouds, was mingled with the smoke,
And roaring cannon distant echoes woke.
" The women, and the children, pray ye, spare ! "
Cried Cortez to his allies fighting there,
But all unheeded fell his words on them :
The tide of death he could no longer stem.
The hurricane had passed beyond control.
He saw in man a brute without a soul.
'T was not till forty thousand had been slain
That to its sheath returned the sword of Spain.*

VIII.

The Spanish arms retreated for the night,
And on the dikes awaited morning's light,
Then to renew, if needed, the attack,
And all, now, left of Mexico, to sack.
The hours of darkness were in silence passed,
Where the besieged, unyielding still, were massed.
No sounds save those of agony were heard,
Nor aught, that caught the ears of watchers, stirred.
'T was like the gloom, and silence, of the grave
Where stunned by the terrific blow, but brave,
The Aztecs, speechless, and despairing, lay
Awaiting, like their foes, another day.
Home, kindred, fortune, friends were swept away!
With naught to live for, life had lost its charm,
And death seemed like a shield to screen from harm.
Death had for them no terrors, and no stings :
Through it they soared, to Paradise, on wings.

---

* This is the number given by Cortez himself. Ixtlilxochitl,
the Aztec historian, says that 50,000 were slain and captured
in this terrific onslaught.

But in the Spanish quarters mirth prevailed,
And with their best the forces were regaled,
While sounds of music from the causeways came,
And voices rent the air with their acclaim.
Lights, from the scenes of revel, brightly gleamed,
And blazing fires across the waters beamed,
While all was ready for the morrow made,
And all for conquest on that morrow prayed.

IX.

The morning chased the gloom of night away,
And Cortez led his army to the fray,
To crown the work of the preceding day,
Ere Mexico could rally from the blow :
Now was the time he knew to strike her low,
And end the struggle with his daring foe.*
Across the waste where once the city stood—
A blasted plain of ashes, dyed with blood—
The troops advanced, from calm Tezcuco's flood—
For ever on the dikes they camped at night,
But with the dawn marched forward to the fight.

Before he battled Cortez called a halt.
" I would not now," he cried, " again assault
The feeble remnants of the Aztec race,
Or turn to shambles their abiding-place,
If they would but surrender to the sword,
For I can, mercy, to the weak afford.
Let all embrace—submissively—Castile ! "
By Aztec lips he sent a last appeal,
To Quahtemozin of the lion heart,
Who vowed he'd from his purpose ne'er depart.

---

* It was the 13th of August, 1521, the day of St. Hypolito—
the patron saint of modern Mexico.

He sent to Cortez, briefly, this reply—
" Behold me willing here to fight, and die,
And all the foes of Mexico defy,
And ne'er will I surrender unto them;
I'll to the last defend my diadem.
Let the invaders do whate'er they will,
My fated land shall find me faithful still ! "

" Go," Cortez to the messengers replied,
" And bid your people stem the bloody tide.
Their hour is come, for death awaits them all,
And Mexico for evermore must fall.
Tell Quahtemozin that his reign is o'er,
And what he knew of yore he'll know no more,
For I must end this tragedy, in gore,
And pierce the dying empire to its core ! "

His troops became impatient of delay,
And clamored to be guided to the fray.
Then Cortez gave the order to advance,
And waved, he from a roof, anon, his lance,
The signal to attack the fated foe,
Who stones, and arrows, now, began to throw.
The Aztecs, densely massed, with angry eyes,
Let loose, in hate, their thrilling battle-cries,
And threw their feeble volleys through the air,
With energy that savored of despair.
The heavy guns, in thunder tones, replied,
And forward rushed the devastating tide !
The allies, with a frantic thirst for blood,
Swept all before them like a roaring flood,
And spared not, in their fury, sex, or age,
But vented on their foes devouring rage.
Why tell the tale of horror o'er and o'er?
Worse was the carnage than the day before,
And each canal was bridged across with slain,

While women begged for mercy, but in vain,
And Terror held an undisputed reign.
The earth was wet with blood, as if with rain,
And over all there waved the flag of Spain.
The Christian's hand was on his victim's throat,
And o'er his tortures he was seen to gloat.
He slew the heathen in Jehovah's name,
And Christian clergy sanctified the shame.

Some plunged into the lake to flee their foes,
But even there were pelted by their blows.
Some sought to cross the waters in canoes,
But baffling found the cruising Spanish crews,
Who, from the brigantines, their missiles aimed.
Death, wheresoe'er they turned, its victims claimed.

The combat quickly thickened on the lake,
And thunder o'er its bosom seemed to break.
The brigantines were wrapped in clouds of smoke,
Whose cannon echoes, all around, awoke.
In hot pursuit of swift canoes they sailed,
Nor to o'ertake the flying foemen failed,
But even here the Aztecs bravely fought,
And havoc in return for havoc wrought.
Three war-canoes at length were there espied
Retreating, swiftly, o'er the golden tide.
With wings outspread a brigantine pursued.
They tried, but vainly, to, pursuit, elude,
For like a hawk that gives a sparrow chase,
The brigantine was victor in the race.
The Spanish crews were slowly taking aim,
When " Stay ! oh ! stay !" they heard a voice ex-
    claim,
" The monarch of the Aztecs is on board.
We would not have him perish by the sword,"
And Quahtemozin rose, and stood erect.

" With me," he cried, " do what ye may elect.
For I'm the ruler of this stricken land,
And seek no mercy at the victor's hand!
To Cortez—your commander—lead me, pray,
But spare my wife, nor these—my nobles—slay!" *

The brigantine her captives bore away
To where the ruins of the city lay.
The fallen monarch listened to the fray.
" Poor Mexico," he sighed, " has lost the day!
No longer will my valiant heroes fight,
When they behold me captured in my flight.
Their sun, alas! has set in endless night!"

The tidings of his capture quickly spread,
And then arose a wail as for the dead,
While sounds of battle swiftly died away.
The conflict ended with the monarch's sway.
His people cared not to prolong the fray
When he had fallen to their foes a prey,
And so threw down their weapons in despair,
And beat their breasts, in grief, and tore their hair.
The boats upon the lake surrendered, too,
And followed Quahtemozin, two, and two.

X.

When Cortez of the royal capture heard,
With exultation all his blood was stirred.
He summoned those who wrangled o'er the prize †

---

* Among those with him were Coanaco, the deposed lord
of Tezcuco, and the lord of Tlacopan.

† The brigantine which captured the Aztec emperor was
commanded by Holguin, but as Sandoval had command of
the fleet he demanded that Quahtemozin should be surrendered to him on board his own vessel, which Holguin refused,
and so a hot dispute arose.

To bring him, as he stood, before his eyes,
But on the way to treat him as a king,
Nor add to his captivity a sting.
He spread a crimson cloth, and homely fare,
And bade Marina for a guest prepare.
She—ever lovely, and as true as fair—
Through all the conquest's troubled scenes had
    passed,
And now she gazed on victory at last.

XI.

Escorted by the troops, the monarch came
As proudly as became his royal fame,
And Cortez met him with a greeting grave,
And bowed in honor of the hero brave.
The captive's eye was lustrous, dark, and full,
Which in its depths, revealed him sorrowful,
While passive resignation, in his face,
Concealed the courage that had fired his race.
Fair in complexion, and robust of form
He looked the hero who had braved the storm,
And yet in manner he was calm, and mild,
And gentle, and engaging as a child.
" All that I could I've done," he bravely spoke,
As 'mid his captors he the silence broke.
" I labored to defend my country well,
And struggled harder than the tongue can tell
To crush the fierce invaders of the soil,
But such has proved, alas ! a barren toil,
For I'm at last, a captive where I stand,
And conquered is my hapless native land !
What care I now what happens unto me ?
I would, in death, from all these horrors flee.
Deal unto me, Malinché, what you will,
But on the wife I love, inflict no ill.

Despatch me with the weapon that you wear :—
Why need I longer for this body care ?
The glory of my race has passed away,
Nor Hope upon the future sheds a ray.
Why then, to suffer, should I wish to stay ? "

Marina caught his words, as fast they fell,
And as interpreter she acted well,
And roused in Cortez admiration's glow.
He saw a hero in his captive foe,
Who in misfortune showed a spirit brave,
And, cool with courage, shrank not from the grave.

" Fear not," said Cortez, " I will spare your life,
And treat with care, and tenderness, your wife.
With valor you have fought, and nobly done,
And though the Spanish arms success have won,
I laurel courage even in a foe,
And own you've lustre shed on Mexico ! "

Then Quahtemozin's bride was forward led,
Who to her lord when first enthroned was wed.
Thus through her brief and blissless wedded life
Her lot was cast 'mid thrilling scenes of strife.
Yet she was scarce a woman in her years,
But for herself had, like her lord, no fears,
Though for her country grief, her husband tears.
She was her father's—Montezuma's—pride,
And deeply she had mourned him when he died,
But now her cup of sorrow overflowed.*
Her face the anguish of her feelings showed.
Her beauty by the tempest had been swept,
And, with unrest, her heart within her leapt,

---

* She—Tecuichpo by name—was the youngest daughter of
the unfortunate Montezuma, and had married her cousin, Quah-
:emozin, on his accession to the throne.

But still her charms enraptured those who gazed ;
And all her grace, and lovely features, praised.

XII.

The hour for vespers had already passed,
And all the sky with clouds was overcast.
To Sandoval the captives were assigned,
And to their fate they—sadly—seemed resigned.
" To Co-jo-hu-a-can convey them all,
And I will follow ere the night doth fall ! "
Cried Cortez to his comrade, bold, and true,
And Quahtemozin from his side withdrew,
While with him went the empress of his heart.
" Such loving souls 't would be a sin to part.
The woman's beauty enmity disarms ! "
Exclaimed the chieftain of the Spanish arms,
Won by the magic of her peerless charms.
The Spanish forces to the dikes returned *
To seek the rest for which their spirits yearned,
For, where they'd battled, thickly lay the dead,
And by the carnage pestilence was bred.
The rain descended as they marched away,
And darkness gathered o'er the dying day.
Ere long a tropic storm, in fury, broke,
And God, in thunder, from the heavens spoke,
While lightning through the valley, grandly flashed.
Peal after peal among the mountains crashed,
And o'er the ruined city, rumbling, rolled,
Which struck with awe the boldest of the bold,
And shook the crazy ruins, as they stood,
And echoed o'er the hills, and foaming flood.
The Aztecs heard their gods amid the blast
And at their shrieks, and moanings, felt aghast.

---

* Under the command of Alvarado, and Olid.

They heard them fly affrighted, howling on,
And when the storm was hushed they deemed them
   gone—
For ever from their ravaged valley fled—
To join the spirits of their people, dead.

XIII.

The fallen monarch on the morrow cried—
"Who for the living remnant will provide?
Mexitli! o'er the dikes my people guide,
And let the wants that wring them be supplied,
For 'mid those ruins they are life denied,
And little longer they can there abide,
Where Famine stalks, and all with blood is dyed,"
While as he spoke he o'er their fortunes sighed,
And murmured—"Would that I, ere this, had died!"
Though still unbroken was his native pride.
The wish was quickly gratified, and, lo!
Along the dikes defiled the ranks of woe—
The legions, who survived their empire's doom,
And in the future saw but pain, and gloom.
That tens of thousands still were left to mourn,
When hosts so vast had reached their final bourne,
Awoke among the conquerors surprise,
Who on them gazed, with wonder in their eyes.*
The straggling files moved slowly to the shore,
And three days passed ere all had journeyed o'er.
They formed a melancholy, dismal train
That spoke of famine, pestilence, and pain.
The sick and wounded on each other leaned,

---

* The number who survived the siege is variously estimated
at from thirty to seventy thousand souls, including women,
and children, Herrara, and Torquemada agreeing upon the
lowest estimate, and Orieda swelling the number to the highest.

With ghastly gashes from the sight unscreened,
And feebly tottered, dying on the way,
Nor cared they longer in the world to stay.
Men, women, children,—wasted, and in woe,
Turned, as they went, to look on Mexico—
To cast a long, and loving glance behind—
And on the city's site a blank to find,
Where lay the bodies of their kindred, slain—
Men who had fought like heroes, but in vain.
There on unburied heaps the vultures preyed,
While weeping widows for the fallen prayed,
And maidens in their anguish cried aloud,
And to the earth were down, with sorrow, bowed.
Ah! who can tell how many of the brave
Found in that awful siege a bloody grave? *

XIV.

The victors burned, and buried, now, the dead,
And here and there a spoil their av'rice fed,
Though scanty was the treasure that they found.†
But wealth lay hidden in the lake, and ground,
Where it would glisten ne'er upon their view;
How, thus, to foil their foes the vanquished knew.
But coarser booty to the allies fell,
With which they deemed themselves rewarded well.
No more were they by Cortez needed here,

---

* The estimates of the number of the Aztecs who were killed during the siege, which lasted about three months, varies from one hundred and twenty thousand to two hundred and forty thousand, the highest estimate being given by Ixtlilxochitl. This is quite possible, considering that the capital in addition to its own population was filled with recruits from the surrounding country. The losses of the allies during this time were also heavy, the Aztec historian asserting that of the Tezcucans some thirty thousand perished.

† About a hundred and thirty thousand castellanos of gold.

And so their chiefs he summoned to appear,
And then dismissed them with a brief address,
In which he praised their valor, and success.
So to their homes in triumph they returned.
How brief that triumph they ere long discerned!
The Spanish soldiers, too, were glad, and gay,
And gave themselves to revels for a day,
But, on the next, they met, in grand array,
To celebrate the conquest they had won,
And crown, with prayer, the valiant work they'd
  done.
Above them waved their banners in the sun—
The soiled, and tattered flags by battle stained—
The emblems of the glory they had gained.
These, which so oft through scenes of strife had
  passed,
Their shadows, now, on peaceful heroes cast,
Who, piously, their litany rehearsed,
And in devotion were, like priests, immersed,
While they, aloft, the Virgin's image raised,
And this, their sign of man's redemption, praised;
Then bowed the knee in sacramental prayer,
While strains of music floated on the air,
And asked their God, who'd led them to success,
Their triumph o'er the infidel to bless.

XV.

Thus after all the siege the city fell—
Nine months of strife, each army fighting well.
With courage, and with constancy sublime
The Aztecs battled through that awful time,
Preferring there to shed their blood, and die,
Than to their foemen—" We surrender ! "—cry.
Three hundred years, and more, had passed away
Since in the valley first they made their stay—

A wand'ring tribe from far northwestern plains,
Who conquered as they came, and built their fanes,
And cried—" Thus much our oracle ordains :
That we should roam no more, but here abide,
And raise a city that shall be our pride,
Whose name shall Tenochtitlan ever be,
And all our foes before our arms shall flee ! "
Their conquests, by degrees, the valley swept,
And then across their mountain-wall they leapt,
And, o'er the broad extent of tableland,
Descended with destruction in each hand,
And onward rolled to where the ocean lay,
Till they were held by distant tribes at bay.
The while their city with their progress grew,
And rose a splendid object on the view,
Where art, and science, trade, and busy life,
'Mid rude barbaric rites, were strangely rife,
Till, in the end, unrivalled was its fame,
And feared, if not revered, its mighty name.
Then o'er the sea, from lands unknown, there came—
As by their ancient oracles foretold—
The pale and fierce invaders, strong, and bold,
Who laid their empire, and their city, low,
And filled the land with carnage, and with woe.
They in the zenith of their glory fell,
Though they resisted the invaders well,
And from the roll of nations passed away,
Like those who, for themselves, of yore made way.
But not by foreign foes alone they died :
Internal hate, they saw, their hosts divide,
And this Invasion, as a weapon, used,
And rancor, wheresoe'er it could, diffused.
The weakness of the nation bare was laid :
Against itself its forces were arrayed ;
And so it yielded, where it could not stand,
And fell, a conquest, at the victor's hand.

It served to point a moral in its fall,
Which 't is not wholly idle to recall—
That nations, and that rulers, lose their sway—
And to their rivals fall an easy prey—
Who rule not by the sceptre, but the sword :
These, in the end, must perish like the gourd.

EPILOGUE.

THE story of the Conquest, now, is told,
And little more the poem can unfold.
The city from its wreck began to rise
Beneath the spur of Spanish enterprise,
And legions of the vanquished toiled to build
For those who'd all their land with mourning filled.
The victors discontented with their spoils—
Too small a prize for their excessive toils—
For Quahtemozin's torture loudly cried,
And Cortez, basely, with their wish complied,
But firm, through all, his fortitude remained.
No treasure-tidings from his lips they gained.
Not here his griefs were ended for, alas !
His days in bondage he was forced to pass.
For years he saw the seasons come and go,
But naught they brought his race, save woe on woe.
Yet Mexico again adorned the view—
Upon the ancient site, a city new,
Which he had watched as day by day it grew
Beneath the busy hands of mighty throngs,
Who sang, but not with joy, their native songs.
Yes, Mexico again was grand, and great. *

---

* In less than four years from the destruction of the city
Mexico was rebuilt. The new city was less extensive than the

She rose as if superior to Fate,
And native hosts who'd with the Spaniards fought
Now day by day with those re-building, wrought,
So proving the prediction uttered, true,
That victors thus their victory would rue:
And while the hapless natives of the soil
Were sore oppressed by never-ceasing toil
The flag of Spain waved o'er the hapless land,—
From the Atlantic to Pacific's strand,—
For Cortez spread his empire far and wide,
And onward swept, resistless as the tide. *
Few were the foes who e'er his sword defied.
Yet while he labored for the cause of Spain,
And for her sought fresh conquests to attain,
Velasquez, and Fonseca crushed him down, †
But to his succor came at last the Crown,
And he received his well-deserved renown. ‡
Velasquez broken-hearted, ruined, died,
While to the earth was bent his lofty pride,
And soon Fonseca, like him, passed away,
Chagrined to find he held no longer sway.§

---

old, but its superior in strength, and magnificence, and it
occupied exactly the same site, and was constructed on the
same general plan.

* Within three years after the conquest Cortez had brought
under Spanish dominion a region more than four hundred
leagues in length on the Atlantic coast, and five hundred
leagues in length on the Pacific.

† Velasquez, governor of Cuba, and Bishop Fonseca, the
Spanish Colonial Secretary, both of whom were his inveter-
ate foes, the former for reasons already explained, the latter
because he espoused the cause of Velasquez.

‡ His acts were confirmed, and he was made Governor,
Captain-General and Chief Justice of New Spain by Charles
the Fifth by a commission dated Oct. 15, 1522.

§ He died in 1523, the year after the acts of Cortez were
confirmed against his protest.

For thirty years a living blight was he,
On those who won their glory o'er the sea.
He checked Columbus in his enterprise,
And long on Cortez cast his evil eyes.

Ere this had Cortez, still on conquest bent,
Brave Alvarado, with an army, sent
To sweep the Cordillera's southern slope—
An enterprise from which he'd much to hope—
And not in vain he prayed for great success,
And asked the Lord his gallant troops to bless,
For Alvarado Guatemala gained,
Though not, alas! till blood its valleys stained.
To far Honduras other squadrons sailed,
Who, too, with speedy conquest were regaled,
While o'er the victors Olid held command.
But traitor-like he claimed the conquered land,
And vowed no more he'd leader recognize,
"For this," said he, "I claim my own emprise."
"Not thus will I be cheated of my prize,"
Cried Cortez, with revengeful, flashing eyes,
"I'll go myself, and this my foe chastise!"
And so he to Honduras led the way,
There to extend his conquests, and his sway,
And with the army marched the throneless King—
The eagle that no more its way could wing—
Whose heart with anguish he was prone to wring,
For as a captive he a burden proved,
And Cortez wished him from his sight removed,
Yet feared to set so great a hero free.
Who knew what Quahtemozin yet might be?
He still in him could strength, and danger see,
And watched him with a timid, jealous eye,
As if he felt a potent foeman nigh.
Ere long vague whispers of a plot he heard,
And this within him cruel passions stirred

" The monarch, he is guilty ! " he averred,
" And I, from justice, ne'er will be deterred ! "
With treason he poor Quahtemozin charged,
And on its great enormity enlarged.

This capped the climax of his countless woes,
And brought his sad existence to a close,
For Cortez cried—" The traitor I will hang ! "
And to the work his soldiers, gladly, sprang.
These to a ceiba-tree the victim led—
A tree whose limbs in majesty were spread.
There, with intrepid spirit, he exclaimed—
" Naught have I done of which I feel ashamed,
Yet I, though guiltless, thus am foully blamed,
And sentenced to be murdered where I stand
By those who robbed me of my native land.
But I foresaw the fate for me in store
When I was captured, to be free no more.
I knew Malinché's words would prove untrue,
And that I'd live my trust in him to rue.
Oh ! that I'd perished when my empire fell.
The story of my life is sad to tell."
Then, as he to his nobles said good-by,
The face of Cortez met his sparkling eye,
And he was heard reproachfully to cry—
" Why so unjustly do you take my life,
And wring with anguish my devoted wife,
When you protection promised ?—Base indeed
Must be your heart to do so foul a deed,
And God will scourge you, Cortez, for the crime !
Remember this ! I leave the rest to time ? "
And with him perished on that ceiba-tree
Tacuba's lord, and other nobles, three.*

---

* His execution took place at the beginning of Lent, 1525,
after a captivity of more than four years.

As bravely as he'd lived the monarch died,
And o'er his fate his scattered subjects sighed.
While he survived, their eyes were turned to him,
Whose lustrous deeds not even time could dim,
But when, at length, from life he passed away
They seemed no more to wish on earth to stay,
And to the yoke of their oppressors bowed,
With bitter lamentations, deep, and loud.
Without a struggle thus, resigned, they sank,
And to the dregs Submission's potion drank.
His bride survived to mourn his hapless fate,
And, in her sorrow, was disconsolate,
But soon a Spanish knight the empress wooed,
And not in vain he for her favor sued,
For Spanish nobles traced descent, with pride,
In after ages, from the Aztec bride.*
Marina still with Cortez—at his side—
Was seen upon the toilsome march to ride,
And she was still the gallant army's pride ;
But near the time approached when she no more
Would be what she had been so long before.
She saw, with gladsome eyes, one smiling morn
The once familiar spot where she was born.†
"This is," she cried, " the fairest place on earth,
And, oh ! my mother—she who gave me birth—
I love her though she sold me as a slave !
Is she alive, or sleeps she in her grave ? "
She lived, and Cortez bade her, then, appear,
And to the camp she came with doubt, and fear.
Marina ran to meet her, and the two,
Across the gulf of Time, each other knew,
And there the mother, and the child embraced,

---

* The Princess Tecuichpo married successively three Castilians of noble descent.

† In the province of Coatzacualco.

While all the past from mem'ry was effaced,
And, when from other lips reproaches fell,
'T was filial love that made her bosom swell,
And she replied—" My mother I forgive,
And may she long in peace, unbroken, live.
She knew not what she did with me, of old,
When to the traders I, for life, was sold.
But all is good that leads to good, I feel,
And I am now a daughter of Castile,
While as a Christian I am rich in grace,
And far above my poor, benighted race,
Who worship gods that can no help afford.
My trust is in the Christian's cross, and sword ! "
Then, as if back her mother's love to win,
A ring she gave her, and a golden pin,
And other jewels, rare, of those she wore,
For she of trinkets had a goodly store.
" This reconciliation seemeth sweet,
And it hath gladdened me to see you meet,"
Said Cortez to the mother, and the child,
And as he spoke the rugged soldier smiled.
Then turning to Marina, speaking low,
While from his heart his language seemed to flow,
He added—" You have loved, and labored well,
Through all the fortunes which my lot befel,
And I am moved to gratitude, and fain
Would see you reap a rich reward from Spain,
For you have nobly served both Cross, and Crown,
And who deserves, if 't is not you, renown ?
If you would here abide I'll give you lands,
And, with a Spanish knight's, will join your hands.
In marriage you, with him, will little rue,
For his regard, like mine, for you is true.
The son you bore me I will watch with pride, *

---

* Cortez had one child by Marina—Don Martin Cortez—

And he shall reap his honors at my side.
Would I could do for you, Marina, more,
But I have told the story oft before! "
The proferred land, and proferred hand she took, *
Though with a trace of sadness in her look.
She felt at heart a widow, though a bride,
And o'er the loss of him, so loved, she sighed.
He loved her too, but his ambition soared.
To wed Marina he could ne'er afford,
If he would reap the harvest of his sword.
But there, in happiness, she passed her days,
And, to the last, Castilians sang her praise.
To royal heights he cast aspiring eyes,
Now that he stood absolved from nuptial ties.
The wife he married in his manhood's morn
Was, like himself, of humble parents born,
And when—his conquest won—she sought him here,
But little in his home she found to cheer.
For her no more had Cortez love and smiles,
And, sickened by the journey from the isles,
She died ere three short months had passed away,
And dying sighed—" Farewell ! I would not stay." †

When Cortez reached the region of his quest,
And in Honduras forests courted rest,
He found the traitor Olid lived no more.
An envoy he had sent had shed his gore,
And Olid died, beheaded where he'd reigned,

---

who rose to a high position, and was made *comendador* of the
Order of St. Jago; but in 1568 he was accused of treasonable
designs against the government, in the city of Mexico, and
put to the torture.

* She was lawfully married to Don Juan Xamarillo, a Castilian knight.

† Her death occurred in Mexico in 1524, three months after
her arrival from Cuba.

While true to Cortez still his troops remained.
Here Nicaragua's conquest next he planned,
For he had heard of treasures in the land,
But tidings came which moved him to return,
For danger he, in tumult, could discern,
And Mexico proclaimed that he was dead.
So o'er the sea, by brigantine, he sped,
But thrice was backward swept by wind, and wave,
And nigh beneath the billows found his grave.
At last on Cuba's shore his bark was cast,
And two long years of pain had o'er him passed—
Since he from Mexico had turned his face—
Ere he returned to his accustomed place.
Then like a pilgrim from the grave he came,
His rights as chief of Mexico to claim.
This fanned the flame of his expiring fame ;
And men with bated breath pronounced his name.
'T was like a resurrection from the dead,
And wonder, through the land, his coming spread.*
The shadow of his former self he seemed,
And ardor in his eye no longer beamed,
For he was sick in body, and in mind,
And deemed that Fortune was no longer kind,
While former friends, of foes had played the part ;
But his reception warmed his drooping heart.
In triumph o'er his enemies he rode,
And, bright with hope, again the future glowed.
Not long howe'er this triumph he enjoyed.
His joy with sorrow soon became alloyed,
For Spain humiliation dealt him now,
And to another he was forced to bow.†

---

* He returned to Mexico, in June, 1526.

† Louis Ponce de Leon arrived in Mexico in July, 1526, to
supersede Cortez temporarily in the government, and investi-
gate charges made against him to the Court of Madrid. He
died within a few weeks, but delegated his authority.

O'er his success his foes had bitter grown,
And calumny, with tongues of hatred, sown.
" Aspersed, accused, I will not linger here,
But go to Spain, and prove my record clear,"
Said Cortez proudly, and he boldly sailed
To meet whoe'er his character assailed.
The comrades he had trusted long, and most—
Whose deeds of glory were their country's boast—
Went with him on his voyage o'er the main,
And, with rejoicing, saw the shores of Spain.
The port of Palos burst upon their view,
And there they first heard tidings of Peru,
For Cortez by Pizarro then was told
Of that far country of romance, and gold,*
From which he came for needed aid to sue,
To rally round him, too, a warlike crew.
But, newly found, it still unconquered lay—
A western wonder, and a rich Cathay—
Already doomed to fall an easy prey
To ruthless hands whose mission was to slay.
" A noble conquest you have bravely won ;
And I my work begin when yours is done !"
Exclaimed the future hero of Peru.
" Be to yourself, your Cross, and country true,
And as I've done you, too, perchance may do,"
Said Cortez, in reply :—" Behold we meet
Where great Columbus landed from his fleet
When first he from the New World came to tell
The story of the work he did so well.
But five, and thirty years since then have passed,
Yet what events are crowded in the Past !
The New World woos the Old World's enterprise,
And vast achievement in its future lies."

---

* Cortez reached Palos in May, 1528, and there met Pizarro
who had just arrived from the Pacific to solicit aid and authority, for his conquest of Peru, which he had just discovered.

At Palos Death took Sandoval away,
While Cortez knelt beside his bed to pray.
He sadly mourned his comrade, true and brave,
And wept, in tender sorrow, o'er his grave.*
Then onward to Toledo he repaired,
And like a monarch on his journey fared,
For Aztec chieftains swelled his pomp, and train,
And Spanish nobles welcomed him to Spain.
The people thronged the conqueror to view,
And gazed in wonder on his retinue.
Since first Columbus from the New World came
No son of Spain had earned such splendid fame,
And—Charles—the haughty monarch of Castile—
A greeting gave which filled his heart with weal.
The man the monarch had been told to fear,
As one who to the throne would ne'er give ear,
But make himself of Mexico the king,
And at his native land defiance fling,
Had come a loyal vassal to the throne,
Not claiming aught he'd conquered as his own.
The Marquess of the Valley he became,†
And royal honors clustered round his name,

---

* Gonzalo de Sandoval died at the age of thirty-one.

† The Emperor Charles V. conferred the title of Marquess of the Valley upon Cortez on July 6. 1529, together with vast estates in Mexico. He also gave him the rank of Captain-General of New Spain and the South Sea coasts, but would not restore him to the Governorship, a Viceroy of Mexico with concurrent military authority being subsequently appointed, in the person .of Don Antonio de Mendoza. It was the policy of the Crown to encourage him, and explorers generally, as discoverers, but not as rulers of the countries they had conquered. We saw a conspicuous instance of this in the case of Columbus. Cortez was thereupon presented with a charter giving him the right to explore and conquer, at his own expense wherever he pleased in the Southern ocean, his compensation to be one twelfth of all his discoveries.

While wealth in lands with these the Monarch gave
As just rewards for enterprise so brave.

Thus basking in the favor of the Crown,
And in the full enjoyment of renown,
With traces still of youth, and comely looks,
A mind not wholly uninformed by books,
And manners that were courtly, and refined,
Which brilliance with gentleness combined—
Bland, winning, always elegant, and kind—
The hero of the conquest wooed his bride
And led her captive with exulting pride,
For she was lovely in her form, and face,
Her youth, and beauty, glorified by grace—
A noble creature of a noble race.*
With her—the joy of these his halcyon days—
Existence seemed a dream of love, and praise,
And both, ere long, together crossed the deep,
His riches in the conquered land to reap.
There, on his laurels, he reposed awhile,
And made the cultured earth, in harvests, smile,
While with abundance Ceres blessed his toil,
And brought him riches from the teeming soil.
At length he wearied of his calm pursuits,
And, in adventure, sought for other fruits.
He yearned to find, and conquer, regions new,
And of the future glowing pictures drew.
Both north, and west, his squadrons ranged the main,
But little glory brought to him, or Spain,*

---

*This the second wife of Cortez was Juana, daughter of Count de Aguilar, and niece of the Duke de Bejar.

† Cortez fitted out two squadrons in 1532, and 1533, for discovery to the northwest, on the Pacific, and another in July, 1539, which resulted in important contributions to geographical discovery along the Pacific coast, but in the loss of three hundred thousand castellanos of gold to Cortez, whereby he was much embarrassed during the rest of his life.

Though they had ranged the ocean far, and wide,
From Rio Colorado's blushing tide
To Panama's bright island-studded bay,
And to the isle of Cedros, far away,
Where, rich in treasure, California lay.
Of these adventures Cortez met the cost.
"Three hundred thousand *castellanos* lost,
And not a ducat gained,"—he murmured low,
"Is all I have for all I've done to show!
Though rich before I, now, am poor in purse,
And I have borrowed gold, and, worse, oh! worse,
I've pawned the very jewels of my wife,
And made myself a slave to Debt for life!"
But he the Sea of Cortez had explored,*
And Science gained a triumph o'er the Sword.
While thus, an errant knight, he roved the sea
His bride had sighed—"He'll ne'er come back to
   me!"
For she within her palace walls was left
Of much for which she yearned too long bereft,
And shipwreck oft was pictured to her mind
As in the night she listened to the wind.
Alone, and but a stranger in the land,
She felt the absence of a guiding hand,
And when the tidings came that he had come,
She wept in gladness, and with joy was dumb.

Though baffled, still for conquest Cortez yearned,
And to the north his eager eyes were turned.
Another expedition he designed
Another land like Mexico to find,
But here Mendoza † foiled him in his plan,
And placed the enterprise beneath his ban,

---

* The Gulf of California.
† The Spanish Viceroy.

And curbed him here, and there, in divers ways.
" Not thus," said Cortez, " I will spend my days,
To see my rights so filched from me away.
Before the Crown my wrongs I'll quickly lay,
And go in person to the Spanish court,
Mendoza's interference to report."
To those he loved he fondly said adieu,
And toward the Old World vanished from the New.
His son, and heir, a boy of tender age, *
Alone was sharer in this pilgrimage.
The Monarch, then, was absent from his realm,
And Spain was like a ship without a helm,
But to the Royal Council he complained,
And hoped—how vainly !—he his suit had gained.
Long, long he lingered, suing for his rights,
Through weary days of pain, and sleepless nights.
All barren proved where wealth he hoped to find,
For justice here was slow as well as blind.
At length Castile's proud Emperor returned,
And from his lips the wrongs he suffered learned.
But Cortez was no more the shining star
Which once had beamed so grandly from afar.
Pizarro's star had flashed upon the view,
And fixed the eyes of Europe on Peru,
While Cortez stood eclipsed by heroes new.
The Monarch heeded little his appeal,
And cold he felt the heart of Old Castile,
But still he waited, suing for his due,
And years elapsed ere he despairing grew.
Then he began for Mexico to yearn,
And pictured bliss in store on his return,
For there his bride, a lordless lady, sighed,

---

* Don Martin, eight years of age. The voyage was made
in 1540, ten years after the return of Cortez to Mexico with
his second wife, the Marchioness.

And back she longed to see him at her side,
And consolation sought in solitude,
And o'er her desolation loved to brood.
But ere he left his native land behind,
And while for home, and kin, he sadly pined,
He sickened, slowly sank, and calmly died, *
And o'er his corse his son, in sorrow, cried.
Spain's greatest nobles bore him to the grave,
And Seville mourned the loss of one so brave. †
Thus passed the hero from the world away,
Aspiring to a realm of endless day,
Nor shrinking from his journey to its shore
Across the gulf that all at last explore.

---

* Cortez was taken sick at Seville on his way to embark for
Mexico, and on the 2d of December, 1547—more than seven
years after his last return from Mexico—he died at the
neighboring village of Castilleja de la Cuesta, in the sixty-
third year of his age. His son, then fifteen years of age, was
with him when he expired, and he left besides three daughters by his second wife, then residing in Mexico, all of whom
made brilliant marriages.

† Cortez was buried with pomp in the Monastery of San
Isidro in Seville, but in 1562 his remains were removed to
Mexico by order of his son, Don Martin, and placed in the
Monastery of St. Francis in Tezcuco. In 1629 the remains
were again removed, and on the decease of Don Pedro, the
fourth Marquess of the Valley, they were transferred by the
government to the Church of St. Francis, in the city of Mexico, and re-interred with great ceremony. In 1794 they were
removed to the Hospital of Jesus of Nazareth. The male
line of the Marquesses of the Valley became extinct in the
fourth generation, when the title and estates descended to a
female branch.

BOOK THE THIRD.

THE
CONQUEST OF PERU.

PREFATORY.

THE PROGRESS OF DISCOVERY.

[Period from 1520 to 1530.]

THE sea was Europe's field of enterprise,
And to it nations looked with wistful eyes.
A western passage to the glowing East
Alike engrossed the merchant and the priest,
And to a science navigation grew.
O'er the Atlantic white-sailed coursers flew.
Thus, steering south, Magellan found the Straits,
That to the Southern Ocean proved the gates,
And, sailing through, the vast Pacific found,
And made his name forevermore renowned. *
For Asiatic shores he steered his bark,
But Death soon chose the hero for its mark—
Let fly an arrow from its mighty bow—
And laid Magellan, ere he reached them, low. †

---

* Magellan entered the famous Straits named after him on November 7, 1520, and on the 28th of the same month sailed into the great Southern Ocean, which he called the Pacific.

† Ferdinand Magellan died on the outward voyage to India. He was a Portuguese, in the service of Spain.

His ship, returning, passed by islands new—
The Phillipines, all wondrous fair to view,—
And speeding by where Table Mountain rose,—*
Crowned with its fleecy coronet of snows—
Sailed back, in triumph, to the coast of Spain.
She round the world was first to plough the main—
To circumnavigate this earthly sphere—
And make the way, for those who followed, clear.
Ere long Bermudez, roving o'er the sea,
Discovered islands, rising on his lee,
That in their name immortalized his own. †
Then Verrazzani on the ocean shone—
His flag the *Fleur-de-lis* of France,—
Whose ship was named befittingly—" Advance,"
His mission north, the mainland to explore.
Eight hundred leagues of our Atlantic shore,
From Florida to Massachusetts Bay—
He journeyed past upon his wat'ry way ;
Then onward, with exploring ardor, steered,
And soon bleak, rocky Nova Scotia neared,
But perished, in the end, a castaway,
Though when or how no mortal e'er could say.
Italians were famous on the deep,
Yet, though they found, they ever failed to keep,
And in the New World ne'er a rood of soil
Rewarded them for all their zeal and toil.
They strove for others, who the glory won,
And reaped rewards for deeds that *they* had
    done.
Columbus gave the western world to Spain,
And Cabot crossed the main for Britain's gain—

---

* The Table Mountain, near the entrance to Table Bay,
Cape of Good Hope, so called by John the Second, after being
named by Diaz the Stormy Cape.

† The Bermudas were discovered in 1522 by Juan Bermudez.

Though, too, he sailed for Spain, in later days, *
To search for Ophir's, and Cipango's bays,
And gaze on Tharsis—great in ancient lore—
And riches draw from its abundant store.
But though toward oriental goals he toiled,
Disasters, one by one, his purpose foiled;
Yet where Brazil blooms under blushing skies
He well displayed his hardy enterprise.
Through virgin forests, where La Plata flowed,
He, on its azure tide, far inland, rowed;
And saw the Uruguay, with smiling face,
The waters of San Salvador embrace;
And ploughed the Paraguay two hundred leagues,
While braving countless perils and fatigues.
Mendoza followed where he'd paved the way,
And Buenos Ayres rose beneath his sway.†
To Florida, the land of endless bloom—
Where many went for wealth, but found a tomb—
Spain looked as to a region of delight,
Where all was bright, and lovely to the sight,
And Luke Velasquez, eager to explore,
Sailed once again to cruise along its shore;‡
But he, ere long, deplored, he e'er embarked,

---

* Cabot, not finding public patronage in England, sought employment from Spain, and in 1526 sailed from Seville with five vessels, but owing to shipwreck, mutiny and the want of provisions, he was unable to pass through the Straits of Magellan. He therefore landed on the east coast of South America, and explored the rivers La Plata and Uraquay, and then remained two years on the Paraguay, after which he returned to Spain.

† Pedro de Mendoza, with twelve ships and two thousand men, reached the river La Plata in 1535, and made settlements there, and on the Paraguay.

‡ He sailed with three ships in 1524, four years after his first expedition, when he kidnapped a number of natives for the slave market. One of his ships was wrecked, and two hundred of his men were cut off by the natives.

For by misfortunes all his course was marked.
Then Narvaez sailed to claim it for the Crown,*
And make a conquest pregnant with renown,
His laurels, lost in Mexico, regain,
And from his reputation wash the stain,
But warlike natives drove him from the land,
And, still in sight of its alluring strand,
His ship was swallowed by the raging sea,
Which swept him, too, into eternity.
Then Gomez from Corunna ploughed his way †
To find an eastern passage to Cathay,
And searched among the seas where summer smiles,
For storied regions—the Molucca isles.
He found them ne'er, but Cuban waters wooed,
And continental shores, with wonder viewed.
Of natives of Castile 't was long his boast
That he was first to skirt this northern coast.

Adventure spread its sails from Britain's shore,
The western world, with ardor, to explore,
And, through it, seek a passage to the East,
And on its splendors and its riches feast.‡

---

* Pamphilo de Narvaez having received a commission from Charles V. to conquer and govern Florida, sailed in March, 1528, with five. ships and four hundred men, but after disastrous encounters with the natives, he was lost off the coast in November the same year, and the enterprise failed.

† Stephen Gomez was sent by Charles V., Emperor of Spain, in 1525 on this mission, and he was the first Spaniard who sailed along the northern coast of America, he having on his return voyage, after sighting Florida, gone as far north as Cape Razo in the 46th degree of north latitude.

‡ In 1526 Thomas Tison, an Englishman, was resident in the West Indies ; and in 1527 two ships equipped by Henry VIII. sailed to search for a northwest passage to India. One of these was wrecked on the shores of Newfoundland, but the other returned to England. William Hawkins of Plymouth, also, voyaged to Brazil about this time.

Thus Hawkins to Brazil his way pursued,
And gorgeous scenes of tropic beauty viewed,*
While France again adventured on the sea,
And Cartier sailed—his ship—the "*Fleur-de-lis*"—
And to the broad St. Lawrence found his way,
But saw no passage leading to Cathay—
The geographic phantom of the day.†
Another voyage made the gallant Gaul,
And gave its royal name to Montreal
Ere Champlain, De la Roche, and Roberval
Had journeyed from the New World to the Old,
And glory won as navigators bold.
Champlain of these was blazoned most by Fame,
And in the noble Lake which bears his name
He lives a deathless hero of renown.
Not thus Columbus has been handed down
On this great New World continent of ours,
But none the less on high Columbus towers.
Americus ‡ America has named,
But in Columbia is Columbus famed,
And laurels evermore will round him twine.
Too oft caprice and accident combine
To dim the deeds that best deserve to shine.

---

* William Hawkins of Plymouth returned to England from his voyage to Brazil in 1530, a native chief accompanying him.

† Cartier, with a squadron of three ships, sailed from France on May 19, 1535, and arrived off Newfoundland on August 10, 1535, which being the day of St. Lawrence the name of that martyr was given to the gulf opening before the expedition. In September of the same year the vessels ascended the river and anchored at the island since known as Orleans. From this Cartier proceeded in a boat to the principal Indian settlement on the island of Hochelaga, where the city of Montreal now stands, at the foot of a hill which Cartier called Mont-Real (Royal Mountain.)

‡ Americus Vespucius.

PART I.

PREPARING FOR THE CONQUEST OF PERU.

[Period from 1525 to 1533.]

THE Aztec conquest stirred the wond'ring world,
And bold explorers' sails anew unfurled
To seek some undiscovered Mexico
From which both fame and boundless wealth would
    flow,
And, magnet-like, Peru attracted these—
By Indian signs, the marvel of the Seas.

Ere Vasco Nuñez de Balboa died
In view of the Pacific's waters, wide,
That martyred hero—deathless be his fame—
Heard stories of a land—Peru by name,*
And planned adventure to its distant shore,
Paved, he was told, with gems and golden ore,
But death cut short his truly grand career,
And Justice o'er his murder shed a tear.
Pedrarias, his slayer, little knew
In losing him, perchance, he lost Peru,
For years went by, and still unfound it lay,
And ere its conquest he had passed away.†
Yet on the sea not idle had been Spain.
From Panama her ships had ranged the main
In quest of that chimera of the age—
Which led Columbus to his pilgrimage—

---

* Vasco Nuñez De Balboa was beheaded by order of
Pedrarias, the governor of Darien, in 1517, and the conquest
of Peru did not take place till 1533—1534, while Pedrarias
was superseded in the governorship in 1527.

† Peru under the Incas was called *Tavantinsuyu*, signifying
" the four quarters of the World."

A strait that linked the oceans by its span,
And led from Europe through to Hindostan.
Thus to the north the coast had been explored,
And conquered by the all-unsparing sword.
The Spanish flag o'er Costa Rica waved;
The Spanish troops had Nicaragua braved;
Veragwa * was a conquest at their hands,
And far they plunged into Honduras lands,
Where—ruling o'er the dusky native race—
They met the troops of Cortez face to face.
'Twas not till dazzled by the enterprise
Which Mexico presented to their eyes
That, one and all, they felt an impulse, new,
To seek and conquer beautiful Peru.
Then from their ranks Pizarro forward stood,
Prepared for deeds of blood on field or flood.

II.

Pizarro was no longer young, but brave,
And felt no fear of danger, or the grave,
For he had in the New World long explored,
And carved his way to glory with the sword. †
Yet Fortune ne'er had blessed his lot with gold,
Though, in the future, wealth he saw, untold,
If he could but discover that Peru,
Which almost seemed to lie within his view,

---

* Veragua.

† Francisco Pizarro was born in Truxillo, in Estramadura, Spain, about 1471, and was therefore about fifty years old at the time of the conquest of Mexico in 1521. It is uncertain when he emigrated to the New World, but history first makes mention of him at Hispaniola in 1510. He was afterwards one of the followers of Balboa, in Darien, and was with him at the time of the discovery of the Pacific. Subsequently he settled at Panama, with Pedrarias, and took part in the expeditions to the north.

For he had heard vague rumors of the land
Since first he reached the vast Pacific's strand.
But one with ducats, and with enterprise,—
Who'd ever looked on him with kindly eyes—
He found in Luque—a vicar of the church—*
Who gave his purse to aid him in the search;
And one with courage equal to his own,
Who with himself to local fame had grown,
In Diego de Almagro he perceived.
With favor he Pizarro's plans received,
And in a common cause embarked the three,
To gather wealth, and laurels from the sea.
A vessel these equipped, and quickly manned—
Her hundred headed crew, a reckless band—
Of which Pizarro took supreme command,
And to the south, in Andagoya's track, †
He sailed to find, to conquer, and to sack;—
And Panama receded to a speck
As he surveyed his kingdom from the deck,
And gazed upon the islet-studded bay
With eyes that saw bright visions of Cathay.
November's storms were coursing o'er the main,
And weeping skies shed floods of tropic rain,

---

* Hernando de Luque was a Spanish ecclesiastic, and Vicar at Panama, who had control of funds, and in this transaction acted as the agent of Gaspar de Espinosa of Panama, while Almagro was a soldier of fortune, over fifty years old, and they became with Pizarro equal partners in the expedition to the South. This was in 1524.

† Andagoya had made a voyage from Panama to the south in 1522, and proceeded as far as a headland which he called Puerto de Pinas, when he returned bringing more glowing accounts of the people and countries beyond than had been previously received. Pizarro sailed from Panama with about a hundred men in the middle of November, 1524, and Almagro was to follow in another and smaller vessel as soon as it could be equipped, Pedrarias, the governor, having consented to the expedition in consideration of a share of the profits.

But bravely on his way Pizarro held,
While high along the coast the Andes swelled—
Far-stretching, and magnificent to view,
O'er which the condor, sailing slowly, flew.
He anchored in the river of Birú,
But finding naught to cheer him where he lay
He to the south again pursued his way,
Once more to land where tangled thickets rose—
Man's progress through the forest to oppose—
And then o'er ocean steer again his course.
Ere long rude tempests with appalling force—
Their mighty thunder, pealing loud, and hoarse—
Broke o'er, and nigh engulphed, his crazy craft,
Which seemed as unprotected as a raft,
As on the mountain waves it rose, and fell,
And reeled, and shivered on the bounding swell,
While backward it was beaten by the gale—
A helpless thing, with neither spar, nor sail.
Unceasing toil, and famine, told their tale
In wasted bodies and in wolfish eyes,
In looks of anguish, and despairing sighs,
But to the joy of all on board, at last
The vessel found a refuge from the blast.
Yet on the shore they succor sought in vain,
And almost longed to sail again the main,
And cursed their lot, and clamored to return,
For there no wealth, or laurels they could earn :
But in Pizarro they a leader saw,
Whose stubborn will was to himself a law.
He faced privation with determined front,
And like a hero bore misfortune's brunt.
" To fail will be my ruin ! " he exclaimed,
" And I shall be by enemies defamed.
Though all I see around me now is drear,
Protected by the Cross I'll linger here,
While on, my bark shall, to the islands, speed,

To gather fruits my gallant troops to feed,
Ere I with them the way to glory lead!"
His crippled ship receded from the view,
And vanished on the distant waters, blue;
But long he waited for that ship's return,
And vainly strove its coming to discern,
Till six sad, weary weeks had passed away,
And twenty soldiers fell to death a prey.
Then far at sea the welcome sail was seen,
And like a thing of life it graced the scene.
The famished throng, ashore, the prospect hailed,
And with abundance all were, soon, regaled,
While ghastly features brightened into smiles
Before the banquet from the pearly isles.
Upon their wasted forms, and hollow eyes
Their comrades gazed in pity and surprise,
And gladly all the Port of Famine fled,
And left a cross to show where lay their dead.
Still to the south his ship Pizarro steered,
But from the shore to wander far he feared,
And so its windings slowly he pursued,
And with an anxious eye the prospect viewed.
He searched for *El Dorado* day by day,
While cheered by Hope upon his weary way.
Anon he landed, and a battle fought,
And havoc, rude, among the Indians wrought,
Who, seeking vengeance, then, invaders slew,
While from their bows their feathered arrows flew. *
Discomfited, Pizarro sailed away
Toward Panama's bright azure-tinted bay,
And landed at Chicamá on its shore, †
For he no more could sail the ocean o'er

---

* This was at a headland called Pueta Quemada, where five
Spaniards were killed, and many wounded.
† A short distance west of Panama.

Until his shattered ship was rigged anew,
And fresh recruits had reinforced his crew.
Here he, awaiting her return, remained,
While, with the golden trophies he had gained,
She for the city sailed, the tale to tell
Of cruel fortunes that her lot befell :
And while he waited with a chosen few
A caravel, one morning, near him drew.
It bore Almagro, and a warlike band,
And shouts of gladness rose from sea, and land.
The two old comrades then each other faced,
And with a more than Spanish warmth embraced. *
Almagro told Pizarro how he'd sailed,
And been by strange, and warlike, tribes assailed,
But to discover countries, new, had failed ;
How by a weapon he had lost an eye,
And been compelled from hostile lands to fly ;
And how he for his comrade searched the main,
And coasts, and the horizon scanned in vain,
Till fearing he, and all his soldiers, brave,
Had in the restless ocean found their grave—
And finding that his craft was leaking fast,
While stormy winds had sprung her only mast—
He homeward turned her weather-beaten prow,
And much rejoiced to find his comrade now. †
More than Pizarro's, was Almagro's spoil—
The fruit of daring and incessant toil—
And as they viewed the mass of golden ore,
With avaricious eyes they longed for more.

---

*Almagro with the assistance of Luque had fitted out a small caravel, and sailed from Panama, with between sixty and seventy men, to join Pizarro, but not till long after the departure of the latter.

† He had called at the Pearl Islands, and ascertained where Pizarro was to be found.

III.

Almagro back to Panama repaired,
But to return, not yet Pizarro cared.
His comrade to Pedrarias appealed,
And begged for aid to plough this fallow field,
And reap the rich rewards that it would yield ;
But he condemned the enterprise as vain,
And spoke of bold Pizarro with disdain,
Yet, to that hero, Father Luque was true,
And placed his voyage in a fairer view,
By which his friend Pedrarias was won,
Though to Pizarro justice scant was done.
He made Almagro equal in command,
With equal rights in each discovered land,
And this Pizarro learned with wounded pride.
" How cruel is Pedrarias ! " he sighed,
While of Almagro, now, he jealous grew,
And murmured—" He to me has proved untrue."
But when the comrades met, Almagro vowed
To wrong Pizarro he was far too proud.
Yet by distrust Pizarro was oppressed,
And deep its seeds were planted in his breast,
Though on the surface not a ripple stirred,
And from his lips escaped no angry word.

IV.

To Panama Pizarro took his way,
For he had grown impatient of delay,
And in returning, he had naught to fear,
For Luque had made his path, and record clear.
These, with Almagro, signed their compact there,
Which gave to each of spoils an equal share,
While, for a paltry sum in virgin gold,

Pedrarias surrendered wealth untold.
They then invoked a blessing from on high—
With eyes uplifted toward the beaming sky—
On their ambitious, and unholy cause,
Which violated Heaven's primal laws,
And said—"The Prince of Peace will sanctify
What, in his sacred name, we ratify,"
Forgetting that to plunder, and to kill
Were both forbidden by His holy will:
But, guided by the spirit of their age
They saw no wrong in such a pilgrimage.
All infidels they deemed their proper prey,
And called on God to arm them for the fray.

V.

An expedition, new, to journey south
Became the theme that passed from mouth to mouth.
With two staunch vessels, larger than the last—
Though each had but a solitary mast,
And eighty restless spirits for its crew—
Almagro, and Pizarro, for Peru
Left Panama, and vanished from the view.
The river of San Juan soon was reached;
The Gospel to the heathen there was preached,
And from their bodies ornaments of gold—
Which seemed unbounded riches to unfold—
Were filched beneath the banner of the Cross,
And gold was mingled thus with earthly dross.

---

* Pedrarias relinquished his share of the fruits of future conquest for a thousand *pesos de oro* which was paid to him, leaving the enterprise entirely in the hands of Pizarro, Luque, and Almagro, who on the 10th of March, 1526, executed, with much ceremony, a contract by which they partitioned equally among themselves the countries they might conquer, Luque having contributed twenty thousand *pesos de oro* to entitle him to an equal share with his associates, who in the event of failure were to be held responsible for the repayment of this amount.

There where the river wandered to the sea,
Where grew the cypress, and the ceiba tree,
Pizarro cried—" I'll linger here a while,
And court capricious Fortune's cheering smile,
While back Almagro sails for fresh recruits,
And with him bears away our golden fruits,
To tempt the daring to our enterprise.
All Panama will see them with surprise,
And toward us turn with avaricious eyes.
Then while Almagro guides his bonnie bark,
We'll shed our light on regions that are dark,
And send our second vessel to explore
Still further south this treasure-pregnant shore ! "

The ships receded slowly from the view,
Where sky was blended with the ocean's blue,
While from the strand Pizarro waved adieu,
And for their safe return devoutly prayed,
Then for himself besought Almighty aid.
Time passed, and hard he labored to explore
The deep recesses of that wooded shore,
But at each step the forest denser grew,
And more, and more, umbrageous in its hue.
The Andes towered in the distance, high,
Each snow-clad peak aspiring to the sky,
While far below the terraced hills were spread,
And to the giant mountains grandly led.
Ravines of vast and shady depth were seen,
Where flowers lighted up the forest's green,
And lent a tropic beauty to the scene.
There birds by Nature painted to adorn,
With vocal sounds gave welcome to the morn,
With plumage splendid as the rose's bloom,
Contrasting gayly with the sylvan gloom,
While monkeys leapt, and chattered in the trees,
And blossoms gave their incense to the breeze :

But there huge serpents lay in massive coils—
And woe to those who fell within their toils—
And alligators hungered for their prey.
With darkness the Sultana of the Night
Shed over all her placid, silver light,
And to and fro, before his dreamy eyes,
In countless numbers danced the fiery flies.
Thick were the dangers of his tangled way,
For native hosts attacked him day by day,
And he beheld his forces melt away.
Subsisting on the forest's scanty fare—
The cocoa-nut, batata, prickly pear,
The fruit of mangroves, and the yellow maize—
They yet to God for these gave fervent praise,
But by degrees they famine-stricken grew,
And oft they bent the knee, for help to sue.
At length there hove a welcome sail in sight,*
And famished figures trembled with delight.
The pilot Ruiz soon his story told,
And to Pizarro gave both gems, and gold,
For he had found a country rich, and new,
And heard great tidings of the land Peru,
And seen the raft-like bolsa sailing near
With feelings both of wonder, and of fear;
And where it then on ocean wooed the breeze,
Its form the wand'rer still, in gazing, sees.
Ere long another vessel was discerned,
And cries arose—" Almagro has returned !"
With fresh recruits—full eighty men—he came
To gather wealth, and win his way to fame,
And he was greeted by his comrades there
With ringing shouts of joy that rent the air.

---

* This was several weeks after the departure of Ruiz, who had sailed as far as Punta de Pasado, about half a degree south.

Then southward both the barks together steered,
And here and there the coast for shelter neared,
For high the winds, and waves, at times would rise,
And threaten with defeat their enterprise.
The Isle of Gallo, and St. Matthew's Bay,
Broke on their view like visions of Cathay.
The hand of Culture beautified the scene,
And man, unlike the savage, here was seen.
Balsamic trees their fragrant odors shed,
And luscious fruits hung thickly overhead,
While the cācāō in plantations grew,
And in and out of ceibas parrots flew.
Along the coast of Quito there were towns
Embosomed in the palm-trees' spreading crowns;
And picturesque, and lovely to the eye,
The country seemed beneath its azure sky,
But native hosts assembled on the strand,
And warned the strange invaders from the land.
Pizarro, and Almagro then returned—
Though for the riches of the clime they yearned—
To gather fresh recruits to swell their train,
And fight the battles of crusading Spain.
Almagro sailed to Panama again,
And left behind Pizarro, and his men
To mourn their lot on Gallo's island shore
Till he came back, and succor to them bore;
For they were sore oppressed by woes, and want—
A famished crew, with features wan and gaunt,
And, save their leaders, all would fain have fled
Back to those homes from which their course had
    led.
Pizarro saw with pain their discontent,
And back to Panama his vessel sent,
With those on board who clamored most to leave,
Or who were prone malicious plots to weave.
Thus from the world he cast himself aloof,

And chose the vault above him for his roof.
There, with his crew, upon that desert isle—
Where Fortune on his lot ne'er shed a smile—
He passed long weary weeks of anxious pain,
And day by day he heard them oft complain,
And watched the while for succor from the main,
Subsisting on the products of the soil,
Gleaned from the forest by unceasing toil.

VI.

In Panama Almagro told his tale,
And asked for fresh recruits with him to sail,
But deep distress was pictured in his crew,
And few there were but now distrustful grew.
Don Pedro * had condemned the enterprise,
Which seemed a wild adventure to his eyes,
And sent two ships Pizarro's troops to save,
But to return Pizarro was too brave.
With sword in hand he traced a sandy line,
And said—" The southern side of this is mine,
For riches, pleasure, and Peru are there,
While on the north see hunger, and despair!
Shun Panama, and poverty, like me,
And trust your fortunes, comrades, to the sea!"
He stepped across the line that he had drawn,
As if he saw already Conquest's dawn,
And thirteen heroes followed where he trod,
Exclaiming—" Hail! Pizarro! Trust in God!"
The rest in peace to Panama returned,
The fame and fortune they had sought, unearned,
While on that lonely isle Pizarro's band
Dreamed, like knight-errants, of the promised
    land.
There—while before them lay the ocean wide—

---

* Pedro de los Rios, the successor of Pedrarias.

With morning prayers, and hymns at eventide,
They passed their weary days in hope, and fear,
And o'er their fortunes shed, at times, a tear.
Without a ship, with arms and raiment scant,
And want revealed in bodies weak, and gaunt,
They looked as helpless as a shipwrecked crew,
And not the future heroes of Peru,
Whose names would be embalmed in Spanish lore.
Ere long they built a raft, and left the shore,
And to Gorgona's wooded island steered,
Where Nature less unkind to man appeared,
And there from Panama awaited aid,
And daily for the needed succor prayed,
For to Almagro, and the faithful Luque
They never ceased for help, and cheer to look.
But nigh eight long, and dreary, months had passed
Ere pencilled on the deep there rose a mast,
And with exulting hearts they cried—"A sail!
A friendly sail from Panama! all hail!"
Though no recruits it—to Pizarro—bore,
But came to rescue those upon the shore,
It fanned the flame of hope within his breast,
And gave to dreams of Conquest greater zest.
He saw the means to sail along the shore,
And to the south its wonders, new, explore.
He gladly left the island out of view,
And fair winds blew his vessel toward Peru.
For twenty days she ploughed her lonely way,
Nor anchored till she reached a splendid bay,
Which we, in modern phrase, call Guayaquil,
Where fluttered first the banner of Castile.
The Cordilleras, sweeping from the strand,
Rose to stupendous heights, sublimely grand,
Capped far away by Chimborazo's crown,
Which, from the heavens, looked, in splendor, down—
A mighty dome wreathed with eternal snows,

The image of a giant in repose ;
While Cotopaxi's white and dazzling cone
Flashed in the lustrous sun that on it shone.
Within the bay a city—Tumbez—lay,
And there Pizarro halted on his way,
And by the hand of Plenty was supplied,
For naught he found—to him, and his—denied.
The choicest fruits that grew in all the land
Were brought in rich profusion to his hand—
Bananas, plantains, cocoa-nuts, and pines,
And luscious berries clustered on their vines—
With tempting yucca, and the golden maize,
While lovely maidens, winning in their ways,
Brought lamas, and vicunas to his side,
Which—" little camels "—he with pleasure eyed.
Their fawn-like forms, and peerless fleeces, fine,
Which with a living lustre seemed to shine—
Their arching necks, and almost speaking eyes
Filled him with admiration, and surprise,
And he conveyed them gladly to his ship,
No more in mountain solitudes to skip.

VII.

Still to the south Pizarro held his way,
Cheered by the sights he saw from day to day.
On Payta, and Truxillo* then he gazed,
And by their splendors owned himself amazed,
But when the port of Santa he had passed—
Where all he saw his fondest dreams surpassed—
He turned his vessel's prow, and backward sped,
While Hope its glow of promise o'er him shed. †

---

* Pronounce—*Tro-heil-yo.*

† He had penetrated to about the ninth degree of south latitude or nine degrees further than Diaz, or any former navigator, when he headed his ship again toward Panama.

His scanty crew forbade achievement here,
Though conquest to his heart was ever dear,
But he would to these fruitful shores return,
And glory for his arms, and country earn
By winning them, a trophy, for the Crown.
He thirsted for that honor, and renown.
He tarried here and there along the coast,
Which of no common loveliness could boast,
And at each town beheld a swarthy host,
Who came with friendly greetings to the shore,
And gave him presents that he homeward bore;
While men, and maids, to merry music danced,
And eye to eye in happy fervor glanced.

VIII.

The warble of the mocking-bird was heard
Through fragrant woods by balmy zephyrs stirred,
And piping, whirring cardinals were seen,
With flaming plumage, through the leafy green.
Flamingoes, bright, and scarlet in their hue,
Flashed quickly on, then vanished from, the view,
While gorgeous parrots chattered as they flew,
And monkeys gambolled in the nutty boughs
Like festive spirits on a long carouse.
A wilderness of palms allured the eye,
And spread their fronds beneath the beaming sky,
While almonds, and palmettoes threw their shade
Where vegetation never seemed to fade,
New life so quickly followed on decay,
Renewing ever what had passed away.
Its mighty shells the calabash displayed,
And in their bloom great aloes were arrayed,
While to the cedar passion-flowers clung,
And from the cypress honey-suckles hung.
The cherimoya held its luscious load;

The pomegranate, too, its riches showed ;
The fig and date their fruit, and blossoms, wore ;
The red banana tempting clusters bore,
And the cācāō bent, with burdens, o'er,
While cotton, and tabaka, side by side,
Were sprinkled o'er the valleys far and wide.

IX.

'T was now three daring scions of Peru,
With willing minds, were added to his crew,
While of his sailors here some begged to stay
To pass in idle bliss their lives away,
And they were left beneath the Inca's sway.
When Panama in sight at last appeared
Pizarro by the multitude was cheered.
Since he departed eighteen months had flown,
And little of his doings had been known,
But now he came as from another world,
And tattered sails, in conscious triumph, furled.
Discovered, but not conquered, was Peru,
Yet that event was pictured to his view.
Where he had been derided he was praised,
And in his honor torches brightly blazed.
His comrades warmly welcomed his return,
And, in their future, glory could discern ;
But even now they vainly asked for aid :
Against them those who governed were arrayed,
And it was then decided to appeal
Directly to the monarch of Castile.
With this intent Pizarro crossed the main,
To tell his story to the Court of Spain. *

---

* The funds of Almagro, Luque, and Pizarro had fallen so
low that it was with difficulty fifteen hundred ducats were
raised to enable Pizarro to undertake his voyage.   He left
Panama in the spring of 1528, accompanied by Pedro de Can-

A solitude of waters, vast, and blue,
For weary weeks lay spread before his view,
As on the broad Atlantic's mighty swell
His creaking vessel, trembling, rose and fell,
Ere Seville gave him welcome from the sea,
But left him for awhile no longer free.
He owed a debt he vainly strove to pay,
And to a dungeon he was borne away,
Exclaiming—"Debt, O tyrant, see thy slave!
'T is hard to be a debtor, and be brave."*
But Seville waxed indignant when she knew
A prison held the hero from Peru,
And Spain's proud monarch ordered his release,
And bade him to Toledo go in peace.
There, 'mid the pomp and glitter of the Court,
Pizarro made his marvellous report,
And Charles the Fifth applauded his career
As to the tale he gave attentive ear,
And o'er his vassal's sorrows shed a tear
As he beheld him on his lonely isle,
While Fortune on his lot refused to smile.
Deserted, and forsaken, he had toiled,
Nor in the end, though thwarted oft, been foiled.
The Emperor approved his enterprise,
And saw that in Peru there lay a prize,
Which might—who knew?—soon rival Mexico,
And from whose shores new streams of wealth
 would flow !

---

dia, and taking with him some of the natives of Peru, as also several lamas, and the gold ornaments presented to him along the coast. He reached Seville early in the summer of the same year.

*The Bachelor Enciso then in Seville, who had taken part in the colonization of Tierra Firme, had a claim against its early colonists, of whom Pizarro was one, and hence the imprisonment of the latter for debt.

But Charles was then absorbed with mighty schemes :
Success was crowning his ambitious dreams,
And he his native kingdom had to leave
In Rome a crown—as victor—to receive.
His Gallic rival he had captive made,
Who at his feet his sword—defeated—laid ;
And in the flush of triumph bravely won—
For danger he was never known to shun—
He rose, a hero, to the German throne,
And sceptre after sceptre called his own.
But ere the monarch took his way from Spain,
In this the heyday of his splendid reign,
He asked his Queen Pizarro's cause to aid,
And she his prayer before her Council laid,
And gave him, as rewards for all he'd braved,
The rank and splendid honors that he craved.*
But ere 't was done a year had passed away,
And he'd begun to sicken of delay,

---

*The Queen executed the *Capitulation* defining the powers
and privileges of Pizarro on the 26th of July, 1529. It secured
to him the right of discovery and conquest in New Castile, as
Peru was then called, just as Mexico was originally called
New Spain for two hundred leagues south of Santiago. He
was created Governor and Captain-General of the Province,
as well as Adelantado and Alguacil Mayor for life, with a
salary of seven hundred and twenty-five thousand maravedis.
Almagro was declared entitled to the rank of an hidalgo, and
made Commander of the fortress of Tumbez, and Father
Luque was rewarded with the Bishopric of Tumbez and the
protectorate of the Indians, while Ruiz was appointed Grand-
Pilot of the Southern Ocean. The remaining twelve companions of Pizarro on the desolate island were made hidalgos and
cavalleros. The salaries of all embraced in the instrument
were to be paid out of the revenues of the conquered country,
and Pizarro was required to raise a well equipped force of two
hundred and fifty men at his own expense within six months,
and to be prepared to leave Panama six months after his return
there for Peru, so that the Crown had no pecuniary risk in
the expedition.

For in his purse the ducats fewer grew,
And none to fill it o'er again he knew.
Yet none the less he gloried in success,
And prayed the Lord his enterprise to bless,
While to the Queen in rev'rence deep he knelt,
And told, in words, the gratitude he felt.

X.

Pizarro to Truxillo took his way,
Where as a child he grew—a castaway—
And sought adherents for his enterprise,
Among the masses who, with wistful eyes,
Gazed on the hero from the distant land,
Who promised wealth to all who joined his band ;
And those who knew him in his youthful days,
When he was given o'er to heedless ways,
Were loudest now in speaking in his praise,
And kinsmen he had never known before,
Glad welcome gave him to his native shore.*
From nothing he had raised himself on high,
And still a brighter future could descry.
Thus to return to this familiar scene
Afforded him a pleasure truly keen,
For here his palmy fortunes he displayed,
Where he had been a supplicant for aid.
A self-made man he gloried in his fame,
And vowed to make illustrious his name.
But though he labored with determined will
His ranks, within the stated time, to fill,
He found himself unequal to the task,
And for assistance—humbly—had to ask.

---

* Among these were four brothers, three of them like himself, illegitimate, Gonzalo, Juan and Francisco Martin—and
the other—Hernando—legitimate.

'T was then that Cortez proved a friend indeed,
And filled his purse in this his hour of need,
For he for one so like himself could feel,
And dear he held the honor of Castile.

XI.

At length from San Lucar Pizarro sped,
While wintry skies no sunlight o'er him shed.
'T was half in stealth he sailed, for still his crew
Would, by the Crown, have been adjudged too few,
And more he could not get, which well he knew.*
Three vessels formed the squadron he had manned,
And o'er which, now, he held supreme command.
These called at the Canaries on their way,
Then, steering westward, kissed again the spray,
And, with rejoicing, reached the destined shore,
And welcome tidings to the New World bore.
Pizarro found his comrades waiting there,
Where skies were bright, and balmy was the air.
From Panama, with speed, Almagro came,
And greeted those who met him with acclaim,
While he embraced Pizarro with delight,
And hailed him victor in a noble fight.
But when he heard at length Pizarro's tale,
Against him he began to loudly rail.
" This perfidy of yours I cannot bear ;
With me all honors you were pledged to share,"

---

* The six months allowed by the terms of the capitulation having expired, Pizarro left St. Lucar in one of his three vessels in January, 1530, for the Isthmus of Darien *via* Gomera—one of the Canaries—where his brother Hernando was to meet him with the remaining vessels. He had not recruited quite the stipulated number of men, and having heard that the government officers were about to visit his fleet, he left in haste, and, false representations being made as to the number on Pizarro's vessel, the other two were suffered to depart.

Exclaimed Almagro, " but behold the deed !
You for yourself, with self-debasing greed,
Have sought rewards that equally were mine,
And in yourself tried guerdons to combine.
Yet when you sailed, to plead our cause in Spain,
You vowed you'd strive no selfish end to gain,
But here you come, supreme in your command,
While I am left dishonored in the land,
Though with you I, an equal sharer, toiled.
Think not Pizarro thus that I'll be foiled ! "
Pizarro made excuses to his friend,
And strove his reputation to defend,
But anger lingered in Almagro's breast,
And he was filled with yearnings and unrest.
Ere long from San Domingo Luque returned
And of the quarrel of his comrades learned,
When quickly he espoused the peaceful side,
And to the right Pizarro sought to guide,
Who yielded to his counsels, and exclaimed—
" To wrong Almagro I would feel ashamed :
My equal still that hero I will hold,
Both in his rank, and in his share of gold,
And I will to the Monarch of Castile,
For confirmation, make a prompt appeal.*
But, be it known, his cause I made my own
When suing for assistance from the throne,
And if on *me* rewards too thickly fell,
'T was not because I failed to serve him well.
I humbly took whate'er the Crown bestowed,
Yet told how much I to Almagro owed,

---

* Pizarro promised to relinquish the dignity of Adelantado
in favor of Almagro, and to petition the Emperor to confirm
the act and further to solicit a distinct government for him
after the conquest of the new country. He also confirmed the
contract with his associates for an equal division of the spoils
among them.

And asked for Luque the bishopric he gained.
Ingratitude has not my honor stained!"
Thus wrath by words of kindness was appeased,
And Luque with this solution well was pleased,
Though still there lurked in proud Almagro's breast,
That keen distrust, which robbed him of his rest,
And which in time proclaimed itself in deeds,
For here were sown of tragedy the seeds:
But now the comrades joined their willing hands
To seek and conquer the discovered lands.

XII.

But few save those Pizarro brought from Spain
Would with him now adventure o'er the main,
For all well knew the story of the past,
And feared the next would but repeat the last;
But he was bold, and—plus his scanty crew*—
Sailed, with three ships, to conquer all Peru.
They bore away a consecrated host
To spread the gospel on a distant coast.
In solemn Mass each one had bowed the knee,
And vowed he would a brave crusader be,
And wet his lips with sacramental wine
Ere he began a work he deemed divine,
For infidels he claimed as lawful spoil,
And plunder the reward of all his toil.
At Panama Almagro lingered still,
Another ship with fresh recruits to fill,

---

* This, Pizarro's third and last expedition, sailed in January,
1531, from Panama, and numbered a hundred and eighty men,
and twenty-seven horses, but it was much better provided with
arms, ammunition, and equipment than any previous one
fitted out by the associates. This was far below what had
been stipulated for between Pizarro and the Crown, but
Almagro remained at Panama to await fresh recruits.

Ere he set forward in Pizarro's track
With him the fated empire to attack.

When to St. Matthew's Bay Pizarro came
He landed in pursuance of his aim,
And with his forces marched along the shore,
And from the natives filched their golden ore,
And where they failed to yield he shed their gore.
Thus quickly he amassed a shining hoard,
While terror reigned where'er was drawn the sword.
Thence to the ships the treasure was conveyed,
Nor long upon the coast they then delayed,
But voyaged back to Panama with speed
To fan in other breasts the flame of greed.

Ere long there came a vessel with supplies,
And Spanish dons to watch the enterprise—*
To see that justice to the Crown was done,
And claim its share of all the prizes won.
Then fresh recruits from Panama appeared,
And by Pizarro's troops were loudly cheered. †
The forward march soon led to Guayaquil,
Where he unfurled the banner of Castile,
And to the isle of Puna, near, repaired,
And Nature's bounty with the natives shared. ‡

---

* The vessel came from the isthmus and brought the royal treasurer, the comptroller and other high officers appointed by the Crown to attend the expedition. These were to have accompanied Pizarro from Spain, but owing to his abrupt departure they were obliged to follow him.

† This reinforcement was small, consisting of about thirty men under an officer named Belalcazar, who afterwards attained distinction in Peru.

‡ The island lies at the mouth of the river of Guayaquil, and is about eight leagues in length by four in breadth.

There the cācāō in plantations bloomed,
And flowers, gay, the balmy air perfumed,
While luscious fruits were pendent on the trees,
And man reposed in indolence and ease.
There grew the date, the cedar, and the pine,
The palm, the chestnut, and the flow'ring vine,
The sycamore, the ceiba, and the oak,
From which the song of birds—how gladsome!—
     broke.
But there Pizarro's presence proved a blight,
And Peace from all the region took her flight,
For whispers of conspiracy were heard,
And foully were its people massacred.
The steel-clad horsemen charged with flying speed,
And like a demon seemed each armored steed,
While countless numbers yielded to the few,
Who with relentless fury hundreds slew. *
The strife was hardly o'er when lo! in view
There rose two specks above the ocean's blue.
Two vessels came with fresh recruits on board,
Each well equipped with armor, and a sword,
And at their head De Soto, proud and brave,
Who found, in later days, a famous grave.†

---

* Only three or four Spaniards were killed in this affray, but many were wounded, among them Hernando Pizarro, who led the cavalry. The origin of the fight may be thus described : —The people of Tumbez, adjacent to Puna, on the mainland, were the detested rivals of the inhabitants of the island, and ten or twelve of the latter of the rank of Chieftains whom Pizarro had made prisoners, on the strength of reports that they were conspiring against him, were abandoned to the mercy of their enemies of Tumbez, who immediately massacred them. This aroused the people of Puna, who sprang upon the Spanish invaders, but were repulsed with great slaughter.

† This reinforcement consisted of a hundred men, besides horses for the cavalry, commanded by Hernando de Soto, the future discoverer of " The Father of Waters."

They seemed like priceless blessings from on high
To those glad eyes that watched them sailing nigh.

Pizarro hailed their coming, with a smile,
And sailed to Tumbez from the troubled isle.
Aud pondered o'er his enterprise the while.
There he from native tongues heard tidings, new—
That civil war distracted all Peru.
Two rival brothers struggled for the throne,
Which had of yore, devolved on one alone.
But when their sire, the Inca, passed away *
He left them heirs to a divided sway,
To each assigning half the realm he ruled.
For such a change they were but little schooled,
And though for years in peace the brothers reigned,
They warred at last, and blood their country
  stained.
At-ah-u-all-pa, and Hu-as-car fought,
And havoc on the soil of Quito wrought
Till in the end Huascar, overthrown
Was captive led, the crown no more his own. †
Atahuallpa ‡ then usurped command,
And claimed the sovereignty of all the land—
The sceptre of the Children of the Sun,
Which he had thus ingloriously won.

---

* The Inca Huayna Capac died, it is supposed, toward the end of the year 1525, nearly seven years before Pizarro reached the island of Punca. Contrary to previous custom, he assigned while on his death-bed the ancient kingdom of Quito to his son Atahuallpa, and the rest of the empire to his son Huascar, the latter being the heir apparent to the throne, while the former was his favorite.

† This occurred early in 1532, a few months before the landing of Pizarro.

‡ According to Oviedo, the correct name of the Inca was *Atabaliva*, but Garcilasso, his kinsman, wrote it *Atahuallpa* as in the text, and this spelling has been adopted by Prescott.

'T was at this crisis that Pizarro came,
At Tumbez landing with aggressive aim. *
And there he heard the tidings of the strife,
And of the evil passions that were rife.
He saw in these distractions of Peru
A welcome prospect open to his view,
For in its weakness he his strength perceived,
And in his brain his plans of conquest weaved.
He knew that Cortez on dissensions throve,
And to repeat his grand achievements strove.

XIII.

Pizarro found the city lying waste—
With all its ancient splendor nigh effaced,
And all its people from its precincts fled—
Deserted like a city of the dead.
He showed his disappointment in his eye,
And o'er the ruined region heaved a sigh;
Nor long he tarried on the ravaged scene,
But led the way, the country's spoils to glean,
And gather whatsoe'er would serve to guide,
And future deeds of enterprise decide.
He led his troops across the table-land,
And sent De Soto with a trusty band
To skirt the vast Sierras, capped with snows;
That high above them, in the distance rose. †
In wonder gazed the Children of the Sun
On those who'd thus their country overrun,
And gave them welcome to their wild domain,

---

* Some of his men on landing from the bolsas were attacked by the natives, and three of their number were massacred, while the city of Tumbez itself was found deserted and laid waste, the inhabitants having fled to the interior.

† Pizarro began his march into the interior from Tumbez early in May, 1532.

And in submission bowed to haughty Spain,
Though little knew they what allegiance meant,
Or to what thralldom 't was they gave consent.
When in a valley—watered by a stream—
Whose beauty made their eyes with rapture gleam
They camped amid a grove of spreading trees,
Which rustled softly in the gentle breeze,
And thither those at Tumbez left repaired, *
While all for future needs a town prepared.
The valley—Tangarala—soon became
A city, and San Miguel by name—
The first the Spanish founded in Peru,
And which to note beneath their sceptre grew,
Though now it moulders, ruined, and decayed,
And sleeps in sunlight and the palm-trees' shade.

Here, now, Pizarro to his soldiers turned:
"These golden spoils," said he, "ye well have
    earned
But I would have ye yield them all to me
That thus the world our great success may see,
For back our barks to Panama shall sail,
And of our wealth, and prowess tell the tale.
From future spoils ye all shall be repaid,
So to surrender these ne'er feel afraid,
For fresh recruits will follow in our wake
When they behold the gold our ships will take!"
The troops responded to their chief's appeal
With willing hearts, and self-denying zeal,
And soon the ships receded from their view,
To show how rich in treasure was Peru.

---

* The garrison left at Tumbez sailed with the ships for the
new settlement, and were moored in the river which watered
it. The site of the city was, however, afterwards changed—
owing to the unhealthiness of the spot—to the banks of the
Piura, where it still bears the name of San Miguel de Piura.

XIV.

Pizarro's troops ere long the march resumed *
Across a land that like a garden bloomed
To seek the Inca's camp that westward lay
Among the hills, unnumbered leagues away. †
The region wore a smile upon its face,
And mild submission marked the native race.
Gigantic trees in stately forests grew,
Which drank no rain, but nightly sipped the dew, ‡
While crystal rills from mountain channels flowed,
And babbled to the breeze their dulcet ode.
The Cordilleras high above were seen—
A mighty background to the splendid scene—
And birds of gaudy plumage thickly flew,
And from the fragrant blossoms nectar drew.
Bright verdure threw a mantle o'er the ground,
And added to the charm of all around,
While blushing fruits the teeming earth bestowed,
And, in the sun, their tints with beauty glowed.
Wide, undulating fields of yellow maize,
With lustre shone in its pellucid rays,
And lamas, and vicunas grazed in peace—
Grace in their form, and treasure in their fleece.
Towns, hamlets, and canals lay here and there,
And life seemed blissful in that summer air,
Where Plenty shed her blessings from the soil,

---

* Pizarro left San Miguel on the 24th of September, 1532, five months after landing at Tumbez, on his march to the camp of the Inca.

† Ten or twelve days march.

‡ Rains may be said to be unknown in Peru, although phenomenal showers are believed to have occurred, but the night dews are sufficiently heavy to supply the needs of vegetation.

And for her harvests claimed but little toil.
A paradise Pizarro's troops beheld,
Whose callous breasts with thoughts of Conquest
  swelled,
But, to achieve the object of their aim,
They vowed 't was all in friendship that they came,
And so the hapless Children of the Sun,
To share their bounty with their foes, were won.
Their spacious halls gave shelter, and repose *
When each day drew serenely to a close,
And thus Invasion's path was smoothly paved,
While over bloodless scenes its banner waved.

XV.

Pizarro halted on his onward course
To rest and to review his scanty force : †
Then turning to his troops he said—" Behold !
We march to conquest in a land of gold,
And wealth, and glory on each hero wait ;
But know ye, comrades, that 't is not too late
For those who doubt success—if such there be—
To backward turn.   To do so all are free.
Let those alone who go with all their heart
Take in this enterprise a stirring part.
The rest can to the valley town return,·
Nor shall they lose their share of all we earn.

---

* As in Mexico so in Peru, a fortress or caravansary intended for the use of the Inca on his journeys, was met with at every town, and most of the hamlets, and in these buildings the Spaniards camped nightly.

† The halt took place on the fifth day of the march from San Miguel in a beautiful valley. The troops in all numbered one hundred and seventy-seven, sixty-seven of these being cavalry, three arquebusiers, and not more than twenty cross-bowmen.

But I will this adventure still pursue,
Though I have for my comrades left but few,
Nor pause till I have conquered all Peru!"

Of all that little band there were but nine,
Who to desert their fellows made the sign,
And with their loss Pizarro stronger grew,
For well he knew them to his cause untrue.
The rest with acclamations rent the air,
And vowed his fortunes they would gladly share.

The march was then resumed, with willing feet—
And hearts courageous, that with ardor beat—
And led to Zaran in a mountain vale—
A town within a happy, fruitful dale—
Where tidings of the Inca's camp were gleaned.
It lay at Caxamalca,* mountain-screened,
And there Atahuallpa held his court,
And of Pizarro's advent heard report.
That chief without delay De Soto sent,
The Inca of Peru to compliment.
And tell him how, attracted by his fame,
To do him honor, they, as strangers, came,
And while he journeyed with a chosen few,
Impatient those he left behind him grew,
For full a week elapsed ere he returned
To tell the tale for which Pizarro yearned.
Then back to Zaran he, rejoicing, rode,
Where all their gladness, at his coming, showed.
An envoy from the Inca's camp he brought,
Who for his monarch Spanish friendship sought,

---

* Now called *Caxamarca.* It was on the other side of the
Cordillera from that on which Pizarro lay encamped and De
Soto before reaching it had to pass through two other towns,
namely Caxas, and Guancabamba.

Inviting them to visit his abode,
While in profusion presents he bestowed.
Pizarro gave him welcome, as a friend,
And hung him o'er with ornaments of glass,
And crowned him with a cap, with bells of brass,
Then promised to the camp his way to wend,
And from his foes the Inca to defend—
Two native youths interpreting the speech,
Which fell, in order, from the lips of each. *

XVI.

Again the Spanish forces forward sped,
With, as before, Pizarro at their head,
And reached the mighty Cordillera's base,
Then climbed, with slow ascent, its rugged face—
Rock piled on rock, with forests dark below,
And high above the sun-illumined snow,
With garden glimpses here and there between
In frames of deep and sombre evergreen,
And peasant homes that perched on lonely heights
Amid a grouping of enchanting sights.
Across this rampart, rising to the skies,
The troops defiled with dauntless enterprise—
Through labyrinths of passes, strange and new—
Wild, beautiful, magnificent to view.
Pizarro cheered his men upon their way,
And paused at times to raise his eyes and pray.
" Let all," he cried, " go forward, brave at heart,
Resolved to nobly act the hero's part,
And buoyant with the Christian's fervent hope,
Nor fearing that your numbers ne'er can cope

---

* Pizarro's language to the envoy, and *vice versa* was inter-
preted by two Peruvian youths who had accompanied Pizarro
home on his previous voyage, and who were taught Castilian
during their stay in Spain.

With those who gather on the mountain slope,
For God doth ever battle for his own,
And oft to us he hath his goodness shown !
The swarthy heathen he will humble low,
And they the true and holy faith shall know !
We go to preach the gospel of the Cross,
Regarding all beside, as earthy dross,
But we shall be rewarded, too, with gold,
And rank in glory with the knights of old !
The Lord our banners will to Conquest guide,
And Spain will sing our praises, far and wide ! "
" Lead on ! " the soldiers shouted in reply ;
" We'll follow, though it only be to die,
For to the cause of Jesus, and of Spain,
We 'll ever true and dutiful remain ! "
All felt themselves the heroes that they were :—
The spirit of Knight-Errantry was there.

Up craggy steeps, by precipices deep—
Where the vicuña sportively would leap,
With vast abysses yawning far below,
Through which was heard the gurgling torrent's
    flow—
The army of Pizarro bravely toiled,
Nor by the mighty Andes were they foiled. *
Through narrow gorges by convulsions rent,
Where gloomy pines diffused their pitchy scent ;—
By beetling rocks that oft opposed their way,
And stood between them, and the beams of day ;—
By—now and then—a fortress frowning down
From some defiant cliff's commanding crown—
Which kindled apprehensions of their foes,
Though all deserted, on the view they rose ;—

---

* Pizarro led the advance with forty horse, and sixty foot, while his brother Hernando commanded the troops in the rear.

Through icy regions on the mountain crests,
Where loathsome condors built their airy nests,
They journeyed on with courage in their breasts.
The eastern slope lay open to their gaze,
While peak on peak flashed in Apollo's rays.
The rear, and the advance together came,
And hearts grew light in Hope's refulgent flame.
'T was then, with tidings, glad, that scouts returned,
And envoys in the distance were discerned.
These by the Inca had been sent to greet
Those who were thus invading his retreat,
And with them they, as presents, lamas brought,
And textures, rich, and beautifully wrought.
To Caxamalca these would show the way,
Where lo ! the army of their empire lay,
And their proud Inca—mighty in his sway—
Held court in all his brilliant array.

Through rocky passes the descent began,
And strangely winding was the course they ran,
While far below the splendid valley lay,
The mountains round it, grand, and wild, and gray,
Their sombre forms contrasting with the green
Which in that vale of beauty decked the scene.
The busy hand of Culture there was seen,
And growing crops diversified the land,
While Caxamalca's city, white, and grand,
Shone like a virgin diamond in the sun,
And countless tents beyond it were revealed,
Where camped the Inca's army in the field.
Before the sight a few in secret quailed,
Though all in outward show the prospect hailed,
For well they knew that they must forward go,
Nor show a timid step before the foe.
Pizarro ne'er would order a retreat,
Save in the dire event of wild defeat,

And all were eager to amass the spoil
Which promised to reward them for their toil.
So on they marched with ardor in their eyes,
Resolved to strike for, and to win, the prize,
And down the slope they passed—a gleaming line—
While Hope their courage fortified, like wine.

XVII.

The Inca gazed upon the cavalcade
As this advanced, in pageantry arrayed,
With streaming banners, and with glist'ning steel—
The vanguard of the legions of Castile—
And down the vast Sierra's sweeping side
Came on as though it all Peru defied—
With feelings both of wonder, and alarm.
Yet why should strangers mean to work him harm?
Or why should he be fearful of so few,
When they for him had vowed their friendship, too?
He marvelled whence these wand'rers came, and
    why,
While thirst for knowledge kindled in his eye.
What world was that from which their ships were
    blown?
To him 't was all as wondrous as unknown.
Not now would he their near approach oppose,
But hail them friends until he found them foes.

XVIII.

The Spaniards into three divisions formed,
As though they would have Caxamalca stormed,
And thus, in battle-order, onward sped
Till Caxamalca echoed to their tread.
Its streets deserted by its people lay,
And from their dwellings all had gone away.

The last were built of stone, and sun-burnt clay,
Some roofed with wood, and others thatched with
    cane,
And all the seats of luxury, and ease,
Not more designed to shelter than to please.
A mammoth square, by spacious buildings girt,
Lay on the charming city's southern skirt,
And on its outer side a fortress frowned.
A hill beyond was with another crowned,
But from their massive walls, of solid stone,
No sound escaped, nor was a missile thrown.
Within a shady grove a temple, high,
Looked up, with spiral walls, to court the sky—
The shrine devoted to the shining Sun,
To whom the honors of a God were done,
And Virgins of the Sun—devout, and young—
His praises had, for ages, sweetly sung,
For Phœbus was Almighty to their eyes,
And ruled the earth, and kingdoms in the skies.

PART II.

The Overthrow of the Empire of Peru and the Execution of the Inca in 1533.

Already day was drawing to a close,
And wearied troops looked forward to repose, *
But in delay Pizarro danger saw.
He wished to fill the Inca's mind with awe,
So he dispatched De Soto to his camp,
And thither went his troops with bounding tramp,
His brother, too—Hernando—in the rear—

---

*It was late in the afternoon on the 15th of November,
1532, when the Spaniards made their entry into Caxamalca.

All mailed, and armed with burnished sword and
    spear.*
They swept along with blast of trumpet, shrill,
Which, with its echoes, seemed the vale to fill,
And ere their mettled steeds a league had sped
They found the Inca's camp before them spread,
And up the slope extending far away.
The troops, astonished, gazed on their array,
But, if they felt, they showed not their dismay.
Some, under arms, were formed in battle line,
Though they were calm, and peaceful in design,
While at their ease, stood, idly, all the rest,
Yet moved by wonder that their looks expressed.
The Inca's quarters near De Soto lay,
To which a vassal quickly led the way—
A terraced house, surrounded by a court—
Which seemed to serve for pleasure, or a fort—
And in the court—the centre of a throng—
All faithful nobles who had served him long—
The monarch of the Children of the Sun,
Whose race was now—alas!—so nearly run.
There sat he with a cushion for his throne,
The crimson *borla* o'er his forehead thrown,
And fringe-like hanging nearly to the eyes,
Whose diamond flashes uttered his surprise.
But, saving these, his face was in repose,
And apathy seemed only to disclose.

II.

De Soto and Hernando † slowly rode—
With three behind—in front of the abode,

---

   * Hernando De Soto took with him fifteen horse, and Hernando Pizarro—the brother of the conqueror, twenty more.
   † Hernando Pizarro.

And there, still mounted, to the monarch bowed.
Hernando spoke in accents clear and loud :—
" I come as an ambassador, O King,
And hither tidings from my brother, bring,
Who, hearing, far away, of your renown,
Resolved to render honor to your crown.
Already he has camped within the town,
And prays you'll on the morrow meet him there
When he his friendly mission will declare.
He brings a sword, that at your service lies,
And bears the Cross, his faith to symbolize.
To that all Christians humbly bow the knee,
And we will preach the Gospel unto thee,
And out of darkness bring refulgent light,
And turn to Christian day barbaric night.
We come, O Prince ! to glorify thy reign,
And our success will be Jehovah's gain !" *
To this the Inca uttered no reply,
Nor from the ground uplifted he his eye,
On which Hernando silence broke again.
The monarch made him answer briefly then
That all he heard was far beyond his ken,
But that upon the morrow he would seek
Those who had come so far with him to speak.
With the approaching dawn his fast would end,
And he would greet Pizarro as a friend.
That night his men could camp around the square,
And, with his chieftains, he would meet him there.
The Inca eyed De Soto's fiery steed—
Alike renowned for beauty and for speed,
Which champed the curbing bit, and pawed the
  ground
As if impatient far away to bound—

---

* The Peruvian Felipillo was the Spanish interpreter upon
this occasion.

But he concealed his wonder, nor betrayed
How much he of the future felt afraid.
De Soto gave his willing charger rein,
When fast and far he dashed across the plain,
Then wheeling round and round, with grace and
  skill,
He showed the horse responsive to his will,
And when he backward rode at flying pace,
As if for life he ran a reckless race,
He checked the noble brute in full career,
And flecked with foam the Inca seated near,
Who moved no muscle in surprise or fear,
But marble-like composure still preserved.
Refreshments to the strangers then were served
By dark-eyed beauties with surpassing grace,
Each with a glow of pleasure on her face.
From golden bowls the sparkling chicha flowed,
For which the Spanish knights a fondness showed.
The native wine—the product of the maize—
Fermented in the sun's absorbing rays,
For peer and peasant had an equal charm,
And in the cup there lurked but little harm.

III.

The Inca bade the cavaliers adieu,
And soon the horsemen vanished from the view,
And reached Pizarro's side the tale to tell,
How at the camp they were received so well,
But with forebodings gloomily oppressed.
Could they from such a king his sceptre wrest,
And crush the army that obeyed his nod?
If so their strength could only come from God.

Night threw her heavy mantle o'er the scene,
And far along the mountain sides were seen

The watch-fires of the army of Peru.
All save Pizarro shuddered at the view,
For well their danger the invaders knew,
But he was calm, and resolute, and brave,
And for his soul no terrors had the grave.
His eye was quick despondent hearts to spy ;
His ear was quick to catch the sullen sigh,
And with regret he saw the courage wane
Of those who had the victory to gain—
A fatal sign if once allowed to spread,
For fear by such despondency was fed.
To cheer their drooping spirits was his aim,
And he began to paint their future fame
If they were to the Crown and Cross but true.
Then courage kindled in their breasts anew.
Religious zeal would fire their hearts, he knew—
And all exclaimed—" We will our duty do ! "
" Remember," said Pizarro, " we are strong,
And armed with Right against barbaric Wrong,
And numbers are as nothing to our foes
When in Jehovah we our trust repose !
In God we have a buckler, and a shield
Far stronger than our arms upon the field,
While wealth and glory wait us here below.
The infidel—remember !—is our foe."

Then he a council called, and plans disclosed
That startled all to whom he these proposed.
To seize the Inca in an ambuscade,
And rout his army with a cavalcade,
Was, in a word, Pizarro's bold design.
" Consider well," said he, " this plan of mine.
It seems a project wild and rash indeed,
But Providence I feel has such decreed,
And if 't is done, it should be done with speed.

What from inaction have we here to gain?
Our duty is to end the Inca's reign,
Or we, perchance, may at his call be slain,
For now for us—behold !—there's no retreat,
And we must brave the danger of defeat.
The Inca may appear to-day a friend,
And yet to-morrow may his friendship end.
To-night our troops the city will defend,
And with the morn we'll each and all prepare
The monarch at his coming to ensnare.
To lead him captive we must boldly try,
But failing this—remember !—he must die,
For woe to us if he should from us fly
When once the thrilling struggle has begun.
Our race, not his, would then, alas ! be run,
But with his capture we should win a prize
That with success would crown our enterprise.
As Cortez Montezuma led away,
So we can seize the Inca as our prey,
And bend him, and his country, to our sway,
Then reap the riches that around us lie.
The time for action, comrades, now is nigh ! "

IV.

The sun upon the morrow brightly rose,
And grandly gilded the Sierra's snows,
Revealing to the eye a thousand charms,
While in the camp the trumpet called to arms.*
His troops Pizarro briefly, then reviewed,
And told them of the course to be pursued,
And stationed them in buildings round the square,
And bade them for the signal-gun prepare,
Then, with their war-cries ringing in the air,

---

* This was on Saturday, the sixteenth of November, 1532.

And hearts undaunted, boldly forward rush,
The Inca capture, and his army crush!
He saw their arms were ready for the fray,
And that each steed with tinkling bells was gay
To add, by clangor, to the foe's dismay.
This done, he, with his soldiers, bent the knee,
In solemn Mass, before the Deity,
And prayed the God of battles those to shield
Who for the Cross were soon to take the field;
And with religious ardor all were filled,
While thus was courage in their breasts instilled.

V.

'T was nigh to noon before there came in view
The escort of the monarch of Peru—
A long procession stretching far away,
Advancing in magnificent array—
A warlike host that battles oft had won,
With arms, and banners gleaming in the sun.
Then to Pizarro's camp an envoy came
In his—Atahuallpa's—royal name
To say that he was then upon the way—
With all the troops, in arms, beneath his sway—
His promised visit, bent on peace, to pay,
To which Pizarro promptly made reply
That howsoe'er he came he wished him nigh,
And as a friend and brother, he would greet
The sov'reign he had come so far to meet.
High o'er the vast procession he was seen
On stalwart shoulders, in a palanquin,
With nobles marching thickly at his side
In raiment that with gorgeous tints was dyed,
And decked with gems, and ornaments of gold—
A scene both grand, and thrilling to behold.
Far as the eye could reach their banners flew,

Led by the royal standard of Peru,
And fifty thousand men advanced in line,
With martial bearing, and equipments fine.
How rash appeared Pizarro's bold design!

VI.

When half a mile from Caxamalca's gate
The army halted, and with signs of state
The Inca touched again the solid ground,
And troops began to pitch their tents around.
Pizarro's breast with strange emotions swelled
As he this unexpected halt beheld,
While from the monarch came a page to say
That he no more would march that sultry day,
But with the morn his journey would renew,
And then Pizarro welcome to Peru.
Pizarro felt herein that danger lay,
And urged him to continue on his way,
For he had preparations, costly, made,
And for his speedy coming therefore prayed.
He knew suspense was wearing to the heart
When each was burning to perform his part,
And that suspense, prolonged, would eat away
The courage of his soldiers for the fray.
His fate, and fortunes, hung upon the day!

VII.

Pizarro's message changed the Inca's plan,
For he the forward march again began,
But, now, with but a chosen retinue.
He left behind the army of Peru,
As he in Caxamalca meant to stay
Till dawned upon the world another day,
And then rejoin his army where it lay.

These tidings thrilled Pizarro with delight,
For he was eager for the coming fight,
And longed to make his capture ere the night.
The Inca seemed to rush into his snare,
In which he saw a providential care,
For he was both fanatical, and blind,
Believing God this change of plan designed,
The Infidel, accurst, to overthrow,
And raise the Cross where he was trampled low.

VIII.

Distrust was distant from the monarch's mind,
And naught of coming evil he divined.
No danger in the strangers he could see.
Could they, so few, aught to be dreaded be?
How helpless seemed these waifs from o'er the sea !
He felt himself so absolute, and great—
Surrounded by such signs of highest state—
That he was to suspicion little prone.
He looked upon Peru as all his own,
And sacred to his people was his throne.
He never dreamed his guests would strike a blow,
Or in Pizarro he would find a foe.
He felt so strong, self-confident, secure,
That, like a child, he yielded to the lure.
Alas ! that he his foes so little knew.
The Spanish hawk beguiled the dove Peru.

IX.

'T was sunset ere the grand procession's van
To pass through Caxamalca's gates began.
First came a train of vassals, singing songs,
And beating shells as resonant as gongs;
Then others, who were higher in degree,

And others still, who nobles seemed to be,
For they in azure garments were arrayed,
And wore as emblems of their lofty grade
Bright rings of gold, depending from their ears,
And carried in their hands emblazoned spears.
Still more in white, and white and red, were clad,
Whose chant was low but musical and glad.
These bore their silver maces in their hands,
And round their wrists a few had copper bands.
High over all, and in his palanquin,
The Inca, on a golden throne, was seen.
The royal car with lustrous plumes was lined,
And plates of burnished gold, with skill designed ;
And all the glowing rainbow's splendid dyes
Within its narrow compass met the eyes.
There sat the monarch calm, and dignified,
And with a look of majesty, and pride,
The royal *borla*—emblem of the crown—
Above his brows, in tassels, hanging down,
While, o'er this chaplet, in his raven hair,
Were golden trinkets of devices rare.

At length the grand procession reached the square,
And marching to its centre, halted there.
Six thousand of the Inca's retinue
Had gathered round him in Pizarro's view,
But nowhere was the Spanish chieftain seen,
While all his troops were hidden from the scene.
" What meaneth this ?—the strangers, where are
    they ? "
Atahuallpa then was heard to say,
And as he spoke a priest approached his side—
Pizarro's friend, and spiritual guide—
Valverde, with a Bible in his hand.*

---

* Fray Vicente de Valverde, a Dominican friar, Pizarro's
chaplain, and subsequently Bishop of Cuzco.

"I come," said he, "according to command,
To dissipate the darkness in your soul,
Aud lead you to a bright, eternal goal—
To teach the true—the Christian—faith Divine,
And cause you all your idols to resign.
In Father, Son, and Holy Ghost believe,
And as a convert baptism receive ;
Declare submission to the crown of Spain,
And deem the change your own, and country's gain ;
Give welcome to Pizarro as a friend,
And to his will obediently bend ;
Do this, and he will you, and yours defend ;
Refuse, and then your empire he will rend.
Behold in him a soldier of the Cross
Who in your splendor sees barbaric dross,
And who, by potentate and Pontiff armed,
Is not to be by infidels disarmed.
He comes to conquer and convert Peru,
And boldly he his Master's work will do,
And reap a crown of glory in the skies,
For great and holy is our enterprise.
Join with him then, in heart, and soul, and hand,
And glorify your race, and native land,
So shall your portion be eternal bliss !
Can you resist—O Savage Ruler !—this?
Christ and St. Peter wait for your reply !
Abjure your errors,—to salvation fly ! "

The Inca's eyes were seen to flash with fire,
While dark became his brow with sudden ire
As Felipillo, in his native tongue,
These words repeated of impending wrong.
"I will," he cried, "be subject unto none !
One monarch here shall rule, and only one,
And earth can boast no greater prince than I,
While, in the sun, my God behold on high.

There he for evermore, in light, will live !
Your brainless Pope my land to you may give,
As I might give the universe to him,
But ne'er would I give wing to such a whim.
Demented men may talk of things as vain,
But I had looked for other things from Spain.
As for my faith, 't is changeless as the sun,
Which through all seasons doth his journey run.
Your God, you say, was crucified, but mine
Upon his children doth for ever shine.
But why so strangely speak you unto me,
And for what purpose came ye o'er the sea ? "
The friar to his Bible pointed then,
But books were far beyond the Inca's ken.
He took it in his hand, and turned it o'er—
While all his face a look of trouble wore—
Then threw it—with vehemence—rudely down,
And followed this with an indignant frown,
Exclaiming, with the action,—" It is base
To strive to thus subvert another race !
Go tell your comrades that I'll tarry here
Till they before me—one and all—appear,
And give the satisfaction I demand
For all the wrongs they've heaped upon my land ! "

The friar raised the volume from the ground,
And felt his angry passions all unbound.
Then rushing to Pizarro thus he cried—
" We waste our breath on dog so full of pride,
Who scorns to take the Gospel for his guide !
See how with troops the fields are filling fast !
The time for action, swift, has come at last.
Set on at once, you stand absolved by me !
Before the Cross the Infidel must flee ! "
Pizarro said—" The hour, indeed has come ! "
And waved the signal scarf, and tapped the drum.

The fortress quickly fired the fatal gun,
And there and then the contest was begun.

Pizarro, springing forward to the square,
Rent with his battle-cry the drowsy air—
" *Christo y Santiago !* "—thrilling sound—
Which many voices echoed all around,
For ev'ry Spaniard answered it aloud,
And of that ancient war-cry all were proud.
" St. Jago—at them ! " fell from ev'ry man
As on they charged,—Pizarro in the van,
And " *Jesu Christo !   Adelante !* " rang
From ear to ear amid the awful clang.
Both horse and foot into the *plaza* poured,
While, in their tones of thunder, cannon roared,
And smoke in volumes rolled across the view.
The troops, like furies, on their victims flew,
Who panic-stricken knew not what to do.
Surprised, and blinded, stunned, and in dismay,
They vainly strove to tear themselves away—
To fly for refuge from the sudden fray.
The native host—embracing high, and low—
In dense confusion reeled beneath the blow—
Surged wildly like a tempest-driven sea—
Plunged like a steed impatient to be free,
And then were trampled down by iron feet—
By cavalry both terrible, and fleet,
While, right and left, the horsemen fiercely slew,
And fast the dreadful carnage thicker grew.
Unsparing, cruel, merciless, and bold,
Their deeds were such as made the blood run
    cold.
Their swords, and lances flashing through the
    gloom
Told the survivors of their coming doom,
And horse and rider filled them with affright.

Could they, unarmed, such awful monsters fight?
They shuddered unresisting—at the sight.

The way was closed to all escape by flight.
With dead was filled the entrance to the square:
And what a scene of horror there was there—
What agony, and bloodshed, and despair—
What writhings of the wounded ere they died!
Description by such anguish was defied!

At length the wildly rushing multitude,
By the relentless cavalry pursued,
Broke through the wall of stone, and sun-dried
    clay
That held them in, and madly tore away,
The horsemen in pursuit, like demons, still—
Resolved where'er they could to maim, or kill—
And striking them in all directions, down,
Believing they would thus achieve renown,
And serve alike the cause of Cross and Crown.

The while around the Inca raged the fight—
To him an awful, and appalling sight—
Whose capture was the object of the fray.
His vassals round him—helpless—stood at bay,
And threw themselves in his assailants' way,
And with their breasts his body strove to shield,
While 'mid the slaughter to and fro they reeled.
To force the horsemen back they vainly tried,
And clinging to their horses, bleeding, died.
But others took their places as they fell—
What words can of their deep devotion tell?—
And others strove their riders to dismount—
How sad it is the story to recount!—
With loyalty as touching as 't was true.
What more could mortals for their monarch do?

The Inca stunned, bewildered, and dismayed,
Glanced vainly round for refuge or for aid.
He saw his faithful vassals falling fast,
And looked the picture of a king aghast,
Scarce comprehending all his eyes surveyed.
His palanquin was by the tumult swayed—
Rocked to and fro upon the heaving crowd,
While, all around, the battle raged aloud.
He on the overwhelming ruin gazed
A helpless being, by the tempest dazed—
A mariner upon a sinking ship,
Forlorn, and with a prayer upon his lip,
With thunder, and with lightning in the air,
And at his heart pulsations of despair.
He could not, though he tried, avert his fate.
The hounds of hell upon him seemed to wait.

At length of savage slaughter weary grown—
While on their work the sun no longer shone—
The soldiers sought to take the Inca's life,
And terminate at once the bloody strife,
Afraid that he, as twilight died in night,
Might still elude them by disguise, or flight.
'T was then Pizarro like a Stentor cried—
" Let none his weapon toward the Inca guide!
Who strikes him down shall like his victim die! "
And as he spoke he saw an arrow fly,
Aimed at the palanquin that now was nigh,
When stretching out his arm to ward the blow
It struck him, and the blood began to flow—
The first and only blood a Spaniard shed,
Though thickly round him lay the Indian dead.
Still fiercer grew the struggle for the prize,
Still wilder grew the battle's frantic cries,
And more, and more the royal litter reeled
Till those who bore it fell, and o'er it heeled.

To save it, then, from crashing to the ground
Pizarro reached it at a single bound,
And caught the falling monarch in his arms,
While in his face was mirrored war's alarms.
A soldier snatched the *borla* from his head, *
And captive to the buildings he was led,
No more the monarch he had been before,
His native glory with his capture o'er.

All efforts at resistance ended now,
And to its fate the country seemed to bow.
The Inca's seizure spread with lightning speed,
And grave disaster each in this could read.
It fell upon them like a broken charm.
All saw that it foreboded further harm,
And all took flight in sorrow, and alarm.
The troops, in the adjacent fields encamped,
Like startled deer, in self-defence, decamped,
While in pursuit the horsemen madly rode,
Nor in the heat of triumph mercy showed,
But down with savage fury thousands mowed.
Night's mantle fell, at length, upon the scene—
While shed the placid moon her silver sheen
As if to calm the storm that raged below—
When in dark Caxamalca's bloody square
The soldiers rallied at the trumpet's blare.

X.

A frugal banquet in the hall was spread
And there the Inca broke Pizarro's bread.
The Captor, and the Captive, side by side,
Each other oft with looks of wonder eyed,
And when, through Felipillo, who was nigh,

---

* The soldier's name was Estete.

Pizarro spoke, the Inca made reply,
And either felt unconscious of his fate,
Or showed a fortitude sublimely great.
"'T is but a freak of war," he calmly said,
"But I deplore, as well I may, the dead.
Of all your deeds since landing I have known,
But I ne'er dreamed of danger to my throne,
For all Peru—remember!—is my own!
Your numbers seemed for mischief strangely few,
For what, I asked, could such invaders do?
Across the mountains, hence, I let you come,
And, though I could have spoken, I was dumb.
I ne'er believed that Caxamalca's plain
So soon would reek with my defenders, slain,
Or that the few the many would assail,
And o'er them with such suddenness prevail.
But it is done, and I am here with you!
Be merciful, I pray you, to Peru!"

XI.

The Inca's age was thirty years, or less,
And there was grace, and fitness in his dress.
Robust of frame, and comely in his build,
And in the duties of his station skilled,
With lustrous eyes, and somewhat massive head,
He looked like one to wield a sceptre bred.
In manner grave, yet affable withal—
With mirth, or sternness, ready at his call—
And in his speech deliberate, and slow—
His language gliding with an easy flow—
He claimed attention even from his foe.
Pizarro sought to mitigate his gloom,
For he was sad though he could joy assume,
And equanimity was prone to feign.
"Regrets," said he, "my noble friend are vain!

Though you no more may o'er your country reign,
Save as a vassal in the name of Spain,
Your fate is but the lot of all her foes,
For o'er her its protection Heaven throws.
We came to preach the Gospel, and the Cross.
You treated both as if they were but dross,
And on Valverde cast an evil eye ;
And so your pride was humbled from on high.
But courage, you may still confide in me,
And wear the crown of immortality.
Renounce your idols, and the faith embrace,
And Christ will lead you to the throne of Grace ! "

XII.

That night Pizarro all his troops addressed.
" The Lord of Hosts," said he, "our arms has
    blessed ;
A miracle has saved us from defeat!
Let all give thanks at the Redeemer's feet !
No drop of blood the Infidel has shed,
But we can count around us thousands dead !
Our lives for things still greater have been spared,
But we must stand by night and day, prepared,
For we are here encompassed by our foes.
Then let us watch !—watch even in repose,
For vigilance security will guard,
While fortune oft by negligence is marred."

XIII.

The morrow dawned upon the scene of blood,
And bathed it in the sun's refulgent flood.
A host of captives gathered in the square,
Where Carnage breathed its odors on the air.
" Let these," Pizarro cried, " inter the dead

Ere pestilence within the walls is bred."
Then horsemen to the Inca's quarters sped
To seize the spoil, and scatter those around,
Ere noon returning with the booty found—
Gold, silver, jewels, and devices rare,
Which made each soldier long to clutch his share—
And troops of captives to their fate resigned,
But eager their imprisoned chief to find,
The Inca's wives and nobles in the train,
And all alike in mourning for the slain—
A sad, and touching spectacle of woe,
But, still unheeded by their cruel foe.
So great they were in numbers, some exclaimed—
"Let these be slain, or at the least be maimed.
They ne'er with amputated hands can harm,
Or prove a source of danger, or alarm,
While terror through the land will thus be spread,
And all Peru will hold us more in dread!"
But this Pizarro scouted as a wrong
Which might resistance foster, or prolong,
And bade the captives homeward wend their way,
Save those he ordered in the camp to stay,
To labor for the conquerors, and wait.
Each soldier lived, with servitors, in state,
While flocks of llamas furnished dainty fare,
And stores of fabrics garments, rich, to wear—
Choice textures made of cotton, and of wool,
Of which the Inca's magazines were full.
Pizarro on to Cuzco would have pressed,
Nor longer in the valley paused for rest,
But distant, far—six hundred miles—it lay,
And rugged, strange, and toilsome was the way.
His forces, too, were scanty for the feat,
And he for this was loth to risk defeat,
Though gladly he'd the capital have sought,
And, as he journeyed, deeds of valor wrought:

But Prudence warned him in his camp to stay,
Nor venture from the Inca far to stray.
He to St. Michael couriers bade repair,
And spread the tidings of his conquest there,
And hurry reinforcements to the scene,
Where all who came could gold, and glory, glean.
Then built he Caxamalca's walls anew,
And banished signs of ruin from the view,
And there a Christian temple quickly grew,
Though of the heart's religion naught he knew.
He in religious forms would bend the knee,
But watered ne'er, of piety, the tree.
While Church, and State, as one defended he,
The zeal of Cortez ne'er Pizarro felt,
And as a soldier, not a saint, he knelt.

XIV.

Atahuallpa from his captive's cell
Heard morn and eve the temple's speaking bell—
Rung by the hand, and o'er the mountains brought.
That sound he deemed to him with evil fraught,
For in Religion's name the Spaniards fought.
'T was meant to cover all the crimes they wrought,
And who could tell how soon his life they'd claim,
And with that bell salvation, then, proclaim.
He pondered much, and cried, at length—''T is
    gold
That makes these white invaders here so bold.
Religion, and ambition—each of these—
Perchance impelled them hither o'er the seas,
But love of gain has swayed them more than all,
And I, by gold, may liberty recall.
At least I'll try how potent is its charm
To shield my trembling throne from further harm,
And save from deeper woe my hapless land,

And stay the fierce invader's gory hand :
Nor will I long to test my fate delay.
Huascar whom I've conquered in the fray,
And who at Andamarca captive lies,
May bribe his guards, and bid the country rise,
And, while I'm helpless here, may wear my crown,
And rob me of my merited renown."
So to Pizarro's av'rice he appealed,
And, by his words, his wealth in gold revealed.
" If you," said he, " will only set me free
This floor ere long by gold concealed you'll see."
Pizarro deigned no answer but a smile,
And felt of this incredulous the while.
The Inca read his feelings in his look,
And ill his incredulity could brook.
" Nor this alone," said he, " I'll do but more.
Your room I'll fill twice o'er with silver ore,
And this, thus high, I'll pile with shining gold—
Cups, plates, and vessels of artistic mould." *
And—standing—as he spoke, his hand he raised.
Each Spaniard on his comrades gazed amazed,
Yet deemed his splendid promise but a boast,
Though of his wealth they'd heard along the coast.
Pizarro shared his cavaliers' surprise,
And lust of treasure kindled in his eyes.—
" What if the Inca thus," he spoke, " can do,
And all he says should prove—how welcome!—
    true ?
No harm can come if I acceptance yield,
So let the contract by our lips be sealed."
A line, in red, along the wall he drew,
Full in the pensive, gazing Inca's view,

---

* The apartment to be filled with gold, was, according to the
Secretary Xerez, (Cong-del Peru) about seventeen feet broad by
twenty-two feet long, and the line drawn by the Inca on the
wall was nine feet from the floor.

And said—" So high the metal piled must be
Ere sixty days have sought eternity,
And I declare the captive Monarch free."

XV.

To Cuzco royal messengers repaired,
Nor temples there, nor palaces they spared,
But stripped them of their treasures one by one,
And these to Caxamalca hurried on,
While others on to other cities sped,
And called for gold, like hungry men for bread.
A guarded life the while the Inca led,
His wives, and nobles, round him at his will,
And all responsive to his wishes still,
Yet all beyond his prison walls denied.
Thus, though unshackled, he for freedom sighed,
While spouse, and vassal, mourned his hapless fate,
And strove his crushing sorrow to abate,
And in submission, slavish, bent around,
And touched, in reverential awe, the ground.
This deep devotion to a fallen chief,
And eagerness to mitigate his grief,
And yield obedience to his ev'ry word,
The Spaniards to distrust, and wonder, stirred.
They from his ancient faith to turn him tried,
And said—" Embrace the Gospel as your guide.
Your God has left you all forsaken here :
Renounce him, and your course to Glory's clear."
But to the ardent Sun he still was true.
The old he loved, and trusted not the new.

XVI.

When of his rival's fate Huascar knew
He more than e'er for freedom eager grew,

And offered greater ransom e'er than he, *
Aspiring on the Inca's throne to be.
Atahuallpa heard of this with pain,
And feared his brother o'er him yet might reign,
And deeper still his jealousy became
When from Pizarro's lips he heard his name.
The Spaniard said—" Huascar here I'll bring,
And learn, by trial, who's the rightful King,
And, with my sword, to either turn the scale,
Nor through it in my scheme of conquest fail.
Against the other I the one will play,
And thus the surer make my righteous sway."
Kings so had done—and oft in days before,
Though naught he knew of such historic lore.
Atahuallpa said—" Huascar slay!"
The order sped to where the captive lay,
Who, ere the Spaniards reached him, passed away.
Submerged in Andamarca's flowing tide
The rightful heir—his brother's victim—died.
Yet when the tidings reached the Inca's ears
He feigned surprise, and sorrow e'en to tears,
And told Pizarro the unwelcome tale,
With seeming indignation turning pale.
Of deep remorse he felt, perchance, the sting,
And grieved to think he'd done so foul a thing.

XVII.

Great heaps of shining treasure, strangely wrought,
Were day by day to Caxamalca brought
By toilers more than willing for the task—

---

* Huascar secretly sent a message to Pizarro to that effect
in the hope that the latter might release him, and declare him
to be the rightful monarch. The treasure he intended to draw
like his brother Atahuallpa, chiefly from Cuzco, before the
Inca had time to despoil the city.

Their Inca's freedom all they cared to ask,
Each on his shoulders bearing high his load,
And singing plaintive songs along the road.
With gloating eyes the Spaniards gazed on this,
And in the hope of riches found their bliss :
But gold, and silver, only fed their greed.
The more they had the more they seemed to need.
They saw at last their fondest dreams surpassed,
Yet but reproaches at the captive cast,
For, by impatience urged, they vented spleen,
And cried—" Make haste.   Too tardily you glean."
Suspicions of uprisings, too, had they,
And fears that, soon, their wealth might steal away,
For miser-like—their treasures brought them care—
The heavy load their av'rice made them bear.
" I meditate," the Inca said, "no ill,
And all Peru's obedient to my will,
But far away imperial Cuzco lies,
And though the city naught to me denies
Its wealth, I know, is slow in reaching here,
Yet rest secure, and deem me—friend—sincere.
To prove my truth, I thither pray you send,
And those who go, my pass-word shall defend."
Pizarro ordered troops to there explore,
And speed the work of gleaning golden ore,
And more with Don Hernando * in command
To search for warlike hosts throughout the land,
But peace prevailed where'er they wandered there,
And scent of flowers floated on the air.
Vast flocks of llamas browsed on mountain heights,
And shepherds lived 'mid pastoral delights,
While condors o'er them soared in splendid flights.
Gray towns, and hamlets, met the roving eye,
And fields of maize, some ripe with golden ears,

---

* Hernando Pizarro, a brother of Francisco's.

And some with green, and tender, sprouting spears,
While far below the Cordilleras' crests
Flew gorgeous birds with crimson on their breasts,
And valleys teemed with colors bright and gay,
Which Flora labored grandly to display,
And blooming orchards bore their luscious load,
And Nature far and wide her bounty showed.
The natives gave them welcome oft, in throngs,
And danced before them singing plaintive songs,
And hospitably gave them of their cheer,
Though feeling awe not wholly free from fear.
Hernando to a temple came at length—*
A building like a fortress in its strength—
And overthrew the idol there enshrined,
And to its place a giant cross assigned,
Then preached the gospel to the heathen round,
And rifled buried treasures from the groun l,
And added riches thus to fresh renown.
At last he heard that near a mountain town †
An army lay, toward which he took his way—
Across the Andes toiling day by day—
And with his scanty comrades faced the host,
For martial courage was his proudest boast,
And numbers failed to make him feel afraid,
Though he so few could summon to his aid.
The monarch's greatest captain ‡ held the field,
And stood in all his majesty revealed
With five and thirty thousand at his call,
Yet powerless he seemed among them all.
He let no words of hostile meaning fall,
Nor struck a blow, but yielded to the foe,
Who bade him thence to Caxamalca go,
And mitigate his hapless sovereign's woe,

---

* The temple of the tutelary deity in the city of Pachacamac.
† Xauxa. ‡ Challcuchima.

And thither with the Spaniards he repaired,
Nor—in his awe—to fight, or question, dared.
Then, when his steeds were shod with silver ore—
For worn away were shoes that erst they wore—
Hernando journeyed backward with his prize,
And brightened with his tale Pizarro's eyes.
The Indian captain sought his monarch's side,
And laid aside his dignity, and pride.
He—used to homage—then, a burden bore,
And bared his feet, and signs of sorrow wore.
" Would," he exclaimed, as he the Inca neared,
"That I'd been here when first the foe appeared;
Not thus would thou a captive have been made
While I, through blood, to rescue thee could wade; "
And weeping, then, he kissed the Inca's hands,
And said—"O master, utter thy commands : "
Yet unresponsive, he—the Inca—gazed,
And heard himself without emotion praised,
His noblest vassal lowly to his view,
And all the rev'rence rendered but his due,
For, still, Peru—though captive—held him king,
And all his people loved his praise to sing.
Around his person pomp was still maintained
As in the days when he in freedom reigned,
His houris, and his nobles, at his beck,
The *Wautu*—turban—worn his head to deck,
The crisom *borla* hanging to his eyes,
And all his garments bright with pleasing dyes—
Some of vicuña wool—the finest made ;
And oft was he in robes of state arrayed—
While waited on with reverential care—
And what he'd worn another ne'er could wear,
But found its way to consecrated flames. *

---

* No utensil or garment used by the Inca could ever be
used by another, and whatever was laid aside by him was consigned to a receptacle kept for the purpose, to be afterwards

The Spaniards showed respect, and taught him
  games—
To marshal men on mimic fields in chess,
And play with dice—yet watched him none the less.

XVIII.

From the imperial city, known to fame,
To Caxamalca, back the Spaniards came,
And told of Cuzco's splendors and extent,
And how in hammocks they had journeyed there,
With gold, and comforts, meeting ev'rywhere.
Each crowded town gave welcome as they passed,
And Cuzco proved as wealthy as 't was vast,
And feasted them in palaces of gold.
Pizarro marvelled at the tales they told,
The glitt'ring piles of treasure they displayed, *
And all the honors to the Spaniards paid,
Nor heeded he the outrage they had done—
The sacrilege in temples of the Sun—
Their insolence, their viciousness, and greed,
Nor all the hate their violence served to breed.

XIX.

Ere this Almagro joined Pizarro's band
With forces, fresh, from New Granada's strand. †
Three ships had borne them to St. Michael's bay—
Two hundred men equipped in war's array,

---

burned, for it would have been regarded as sacrilegious to
make common use of anything that had been touched by him.

  * They brought with them two hundred *cargas* of gold—each
carga borne by four Indians—besides silver.

  † Almagro reached Caxamalca about the middle of February, 1533, after landing at San Miguel in December, 1532.

With fifty steeds impatient for the fray—
And of their comrades' fortunes learning there
They sent them tidings, claiming, then, their share.
Pizarro hailed their coming with delight,
And saw in growing numbers greater might.
He met his friend Almagro, and was glad;
But o'er their meeting Indian hearts were sad.
Before this fresh invasion—fatal sign—
The captive Inca felt his hopes decline,
And with a load of sorrow, hard to bear,
He yielded slowly—drooping—to despair.

XX.

The soldiers clamored for their share of spoil—
The fruit of daring, and intrepid toil—
And all the Inca's ransom paid in gold—
Barbaric but artistic in its mould—
Passed into molten metal, as of yore
Ere it was fashioned from the virgin ore.
Vase, salver, ewer, goblet, urn, and plate,
And things of beauty, met a common fate,
And into bars, and ingots, found their way.
The hands that erst had made them now unmade,
And works of art as simple gold assayed,
While native craftsmen mourned their wasted skill,
And labored to destroy against their will.
Of these a few, alone, escaped the wreck
Spain's monarch, and her palaces to deck.
The splendid booty was divided then,
Pizarro dealing shares to all his men,
The royal fifth reserving for the crown,
And for himself an emblem of renown—
A chair of fretted gold—the Inca's throne. *

---

* This was of solid gold, worth twenty-five thousand *pesos.*

Such precious spoils had ne'er before been known,
Nor e'er have gladdened since explorer's eyes.
A golden triumph crowned the enterprise.
The English, French, and Portuguese, in vain
Had sailed the seas for such prodigious gain.

XXI.

The eager Spaniards—" On to Cuzco ! " cried,
Expecting there to treasures, new, divide,
And on to grander conquests swiftly stride.
The captive Inca said—" My freedom's due,
For to my promise I have proven true."
Pizarro owned his ransom had been paid,
And yet to set him free he felt afraid.
' T was but a coward's fear of future ill
That made him dread the Inca's evil will,
And brood in silence o'er concealed designs.
" The Inca's star," he thought, " too brightly shines,
And, blindly, all who hear his word obey.
If freed he'll yearn for all his ancient sway,
And to resistance rouse, perchance, Peru.
What else can I than slay the captive do ?
And yet I would not seem to thus decree

---

de oro, or castellanos, each being equivalent to about three dollars and seven cents of United States coin. The total amount of the booty in gold was one million, three hundred and twenty-six thousand, five hundred and thirty-nine *pesos de oro,* the commercial value of which at that time Senor Clemencin of Madrid, in his Memoirs of the Academy, and Prescott, agree in estimating at about three millions and a half of pounds sterling, or nearly fifteen millions and a half of dollars. The silver was valued at fifty-one thousand, six hundred and ten marks. The Inca's ransom, however, had not been fully paid, although Pizarro through the notary attached to the expedition, acquitted the Inca of all further obligation relating to it, and this was publicly proclaimed to the camp.

But leave to others what I fain would see.
I'll rouse distrust.　The camp for blood will cry.
Atahuallpa then, methinks, will die,
And of the deed, though dark, the blame I'll shun.
There's danger here while this remains undone."
Ere long 't was rumored Indian hosts would rise,
And claim the captive monarch as their prize,
And wrest the ransom he had paid his foes,
And rain on Spanish armor crushing blows.
From lip to lip the startling story flew,
At each recital gaining something new.
Huascar's friends pronounced the fiction true,
And on the Inca all the onus threw,
While Felipillo—traitor to his race—　　.
Strove hard to bring his monarch to disgrace.
The Spanish troops were quick to take alarm,
And deemed the sovereign meditated harm.
Pizarro, frowning, sought him where he dwelt,
And in the rumors feigned belief unfelt.
"What treason's this you meditate?" said he.
"Is this the gratitude you feel for me
Who've, as a brother, always served you well.
Your purpose I would learn, and bid you tell."
"You jest," replied the Inca in surprise:
"For me 't would be to thus conspire unwise,
Nor should I e'er, to war, my sons advise.
Against the Spaniards vain 't would be to rise,
So strong, and valiant, and so swift are they.
No thought have I, or mine, of such a fray.
Oh, Captain, jest with me no more, I pray!"
And as he spoke his face composure showed,
For simulation there had no abode,
And on his handsome features played a smile
As if to say—" In this I'm free from guile."
'T was consciousness of innocence that beamed,
But this to Spanish eyes deceptious seemed.

"A captive," said the "Inca, here I lie—
A helpless pris'ner in your hands am I.
How, then, could I the thing imputed plan
When I'd be first to fall beneath the ban?
Against my will my warriors ne'er would fight,
And well they know your overwhelming might;"
But he to win the Spaniard's favor failed,
And naught he said to drown distrust availed.
His limbs were chained where they before were free,
In which a sign portentous he could see.
A stronger guard, and closer watch were kept,
And o'er the change his wives, and nobles wept.
Still through the camp the baseless rumor flew,
And as it travelled more alarming grew.
The soldiers feared in force the foe would come,
And stood prepared to hear the signal drum,
Expectant hour by hour of fresh alarms,
And sank to slumber only on their arms,
While bridled steeds were saddled night, and day.
Thus, racked by dread, Pizarro's army lay,
And from the camp was banished all repose,
While toward the monarch murmurs loud arose.
Almagro's troops declared themselves his foes.
"His death," they cried, "our safety will secure,
But nothing less can make our footing sure."
Pizarro heard, but seemed on this to frown,
And brave De Soto scowled the menace down.
To him Pizarro said—"Go search the land,
And see if insurrection shows its hand.
Go where the rumors say the forces wait.
On you, perchance, may rest the Inca's fate."

XXII.

When from the camp De Soto took his way
The troops' alarm increased from day to day,

And on Pizarro calls were loudly made,
Which he—as if compelled to yield—obeyed.
"Let him at least," the Spaniard said, " be tried,
And by the verdict at the camp abide."
Twelve charges, then, against him he preferred,
And these with wild, and wond'ring looks he
    heard,
For all but one to ancient ways referred—
To customs handed down from olden times—
And lawful acts were stigmatized as crimes.
He looked to find a friend, but looked in vain,
Among the bronzed, and bearded, sons of Spain.
Hernando, * once his friend, was on the main,
And toward Castile, with gold, pursued his way,
And from the camp De Soto long might stay.
The case Pizarro, and Almagro, tried—
No other judge was seated at their side—
And Felipillo, as directed, lied,
Nor long it took the judges to decide.
They found the Inca GUILTY, as designed,
And on the spot the fatal warrant signed,
Which to the stake his body, soon, consigned.
" The culprit burn alive," the sentence read,
" And this be done before the day hath fled."
The priest Valverde said—" A righteous doom !
He merits not interment in a tomb : "
But some there were among that martial throng
Who now began to feel the deed a wrong,
And, thus to do, Pizarro's power denied,
And said—" In Spain the Inca should be, tried."
Yet overwhelming numbers silenced these,
And cried—" We stand by all our chief's decrees.

---

   * Hernando Pizarro, who had sailed for Spain, with the
royal fifth of the treasure, and to give an account of the
achievements of the conquerors to the Emperor Charles V.

To all of us the Inca's guilt is clear,
And why should we to execute him fear?
Let those who will against Pizarro fight,
But this we know,—our leader's in the right,
And if a few—disloyal to his sway—
Should to disorder wish the camp a prey,
Then shall their names hereafter bear a stain,
And on the record ill appear in Spain."
High words to open rupture nearly led,
And bitter things on either side were said,
But by the strong the weak were swiftly crushed,
And Opposition's manly voice was hushed.
The mass refused the Inca's life to spare,
Yet Justice left her protest written there.

XXIII.

The tidings quickly reached the Inca's ear,
And for a moment filled his mind with fear.
His worst forebodings scarce for this prepared,
And, where before he'd wavered, he despaired.
He felt the blow a thunderbolt of fate,
And wept in sorrow o'er his hapless state.
"Naught," turning to Pizarro, he exclaimed,
"Have I e'er done of which to feel ashamed.
Why then should I to suffer thus be made,
And why should you my person so degrade—
You who but friendship have from me received?
Alas, for me, so bitterly deceived!
Have I in vain my treasures rendered you?
Oh, tell me why man thus to man should do?
I give my gold but hold existence dear.
Oh, spare me this, and take whate'er I've here.
Twice o'er will I my ransom gladly pay,
And o'er my country give you boundless sway,
And by a pledge each Spaniard's life secure—

And rest assured—O Chief—my motive's pure—
If you'll but shield me, now, from Death's embrace,
And let me live to mourn my fallen race."
Pizarro turned, with troubled look, away,
But not a word to comfort he'd to say.
The Inca's sad entreaty touched his heart,
But none the less he'd play his cruel part,
And to his soldiers' clamors seem, to yield.
The monarch felt his fate already sealed,
And all his pleadings with Pizarro vain,
And, feeling thus, found courage in despair,
And fortitude calamity to bear.
Like morning mists before the shining sun
His fears dissolved. "The worst," said he, "be
    done."

XXIV.

The trumpet's sound through Caxamalca's square
Awoke its echoes on the evening air,
Proclaiming unto all the Inca's doom.
O'er all the vale there hung a pall of gloom,
For in the west the sun had sunk from view,
And Night her mantle o'er the prospect threw—
Night just emerging from the twilight's arms
Before the moon had shed abroad her charms.
Out in the square the torches shed their glare,
And all the Spanish troops had gathered there.*
Chained hand and foot the Inca forth was led,
And at his side Valverde bowed his head,
And said—" Your superstition fling away
And at the throne of Grace for mercy pray.
The Saviour's blood will wash your sins away,"
For though the priest to death consigned the chief,

---

* This was two hours after sunset on the 29th of August,
1533.

And ne'er with pity viewed the captive's grief,
He for his soul's salvation strove with zeal
To serve the Cross, and glorify Castile,
But to the Sun the Inca still was true.
Valverde fierce with indignation grew.

XXV.

The Spaniards to the stake their victim bound,
And piled his pyre with fagots all around.
Once more the Cross Valverde raised on high,
And cried—" Embrace you this before you die,—
And be baptised, if you to bliss aspire.
If so you do, not thus you'll here expire,
But, strangled, perish unconsumed by fire."
" If this indeed," the monarch spoke, " is true,
I'll as you wish in these last moments do."
Pizarro said—" The promise I endorse.
Unscathed by flames—if so—shall be thy corse."
Valverde then, baptised him where he stood, *
Exclaiming—" Now you're numbered with the
  good."
The Inca toward Pizarro turned his eyes—
Eyes full of thought that seemed to agonize,
And said—" In Quito let my dust repose,
For there a cedar o'er my mother grows.
There I was born, and passed my sweetest days,
And uttered first to Phœbus tuneful praise :
And for my children, oh ! compassion show.
Such bitterness as this they ne'er should know.
Around them throw Protection's kindly shield,
And may their wounds by time at length be healed.

---

* He was baptised in the name of Juan de Atahuallpa—
the name of Juan having been given owing to its being the
day of St. John the Baptist.

All those I love I leave in charge to you,
And to the world I bid a long adieu."
His handsome features, which were stern before,
A touch of tender melancholy wore,
And all the muscles of his stately frame
Relaxed from rigid tension, now, became,
While Resignation seemed to lift him up,
And stoic-like he drank the bitter cup.
Then calmly he submitted to his fate,
Nor long for execution he'd to wait.
The fatal noose about his neck was wound;
The tight'ning stick was twisted sharply round,
And he—garroted—in a moment died,
While Spaniards murmured *credos* at his side
From God's avenging wrath to save his soul,
And lead him to the Blest's eternal goal.
Thus, with their victim's plunder rich, they prayed,
And friendship with a murder, foul, repaid.

XXVI.

Through all the hours of that eventful night,
And till the sun renewed its welcome light,
The Inca's body, bound and strangled, lay—
A ghastly sight to meet the opening day:
But then the Spaniards bore the corse away,
And, in the church they'd fashioned by the square,*
They o'er it with their dirges filled the air,
Aud there Valverde said—" A crown he's won.
A new and brighter life he's now begun."
His obsequies with solemn pomp were done,
And mourning garb the leading Spaniards wore,
And feigned to feel with timely sorrow sore—

---

*The Spaniards had altered a native building into a place
of worship which they called the church of San Francisco.

A solemn farce which mourning mocked—a show
That travestied and counterfeited woe.
The air without was full of wailing cries
Which to the throne of Grace appeared to rise,
And drowned the Spaniards' voices heard within
As if rebuking, in their anguish, sin.
A rush, and lo ! the doors were opened wide,
And women hurried to the Inca's side—
His wives and sisters, moaning as they went—
And gave to frantic grief the freest vent,
And cried—" To us the Inca's rites belong.
We'll celebrate them here with prayers, and song,
And where he rests our lifeless forms shall lie ;
Our duty, and our pleasure, is to die,
And, with him, to the land of spirits fly—
The bright, and splendid, mansions of the Sun.
Our work is done : our race on earth is run."
The Spaniards said—" Begone ! why come ye
   here ?
Ye desecrate the Christian Inca's bier,"
And drove them—howling—from the sacred place—
Each with despair depicted in her face.
Some slew themselves in secret ere the night,
And to the world of spirits took their flight—
To join the Inca in the realms of light—
And mourning filled the land—a woeful sight.

Beside the church the Inca's dust was laid,
And Spaniards ne'er to Quito this conveyed,
But, when from Caxamalca journeyed they,
His kindred bore the prized remains away,
Nor knew the Spaniards—later—where they lay.*

---

*Tradition says the body was carried to Quito, but the
Spaniards long afterward—thinking that treasure had been
buried with it—searched there for the remains in vain.

XXVII.

Scarce o'er the Inca's form had closed the grave,
When coming troops the cry of greeting gave,
And forward rode De Soto to the square,
While plaudits from his comrades filled the air.
" No foe," he cried, " no hostile force I found.
The country's peaceful here and all around."
He learnt the Inca's fate with keen surprise,
And indignation kindled in his eyes.
He sought Pizarro with an angry look,
And uttered words that savored of rebuke.
" Too rash, alas ! " said he, " too rash you've been :
No rising wheresoe'er we went was seen,
Nor aught I met but friendship on my way.
How came you one so guiltless thus to slay ?
Why not have sent him to be tried in Spain ?
And from his murder what can Spaniards gain ? "
Pizarro, wearing mourning garb, replied—
" I acted rashly, true : Requelmé * lied ;
Valverde, too, was wanting as a guide,
And these, and more, deceived me day by day,
And cried—' Beware ! the Inca plots a fray : ' "
But each accused, the charges made denied,
And wore an aspect of offended pride,
Upbraiding him—Pizarro—for the deed.
Thus in the camp was sown Dissension's seed,
And words between the leaders mounted high,
And rising anger flashed from eye to eye,
While each upon the other threw the blame.
Their own contention proved their act a shame,
And showed their victim guiltless—wrongly slain.
His murder, now, the Spaniards felt a stain.

---

*The Royal Treasurer, who had come with Almagro from San Miguel.

No darker deed Pizarro e'er had done—
Than this—against the Children of the Sun,
Though greater carnage, far, he'd wrought, and
   rude,
And though in blood he'd oft his hands imbrued.
"T' was broken faith, and cruelty refined—
"T' was wickedness and treachery combined—
To take the life he promised to preserve,
And like a foe a friend so basely serve,
And time will ne'er a blot so foul efface.
The heartless slaughter of a helpless race
Ere this had stamped Pizarro deeply base,
But doubly base a crime so wanton seemed,
And naught its vile atrociousness redeemed.
Could Retribution fail to mark the man,
And hold him ever after 'neath the ban ?
Or, like his victim doom that he should die ?
Who can avenging Providence deny,
Or from his own accusing conscience fly ?
Long after this Pizarro passed away—
Red-handed, foul Assassination's prey.*

XXVIII.

The Inca's death spread universal gloom,
And all Peru in this beheld its doom.
The Children of the Sun were sore aghast,
And saw their ancient glory o'er at last.
To other hands the Inca's sceptre passed,
And those who'd lived beneath the monarch's sway,
And learned to love, to honor, and obey,
Like steeds without their riders now were left—

---

*Pizarro was assassinated by Spanish conspirators at Lima
on the 26th of June, 1541 ; nearly eight years after the execution of Atahuallpa.

Of all that erst had guided them bereft.
From order to disorder passed the realm,
When he—their ruler—left the nation's helm,
And old restraints that held in check before
Gave way to wild excess unknown of yore.
Corrupted by the Spaniard's thirst for gold
The natives, who had prized it ne'er of old,
With lustful eyes surveyed the glitt'ring ore,
And as they gleaned it thirsted still for more,
And hid it in the forest, and in caves,
And buried it in deep, secluded graves—
To guard it from the spoliator's hand
Till he no more was ruler in the land.
Their chiefs commanding regions far away
Asserted, now, an independent sway,
And rife was revolution through Peru.
The old was superseded by the new.

XXIX.

Pizarro camped at Caxamalca still,
And sought a chief the Inca's throne to fill—
One who would prove obedient to his will,
And play his part—subordinate—with skill,
Through such esteeming he'd the easier rule.
He in Toparca found a pliant tool—
A brother of Atahuallpa slain—
Who humbly vowed subservience to Spain.
That Manco was the rightful heir he knew—
Huascar's brother whom his kinsman slew—
But, to the Spaniards, felt he'd prove untrue,
So he with pomp the young Toparca crowned
Amid the cannon's and the trumpet's sound,
And on his brows the crimson *borla* hung,
And at his feet imperial garlands flung,
While Indian vassals, round him, homage paid,

And Christian priests before him knelt and prayed.
Toparca was the reigning Inca now,
And all Peru was told to him to bow.

XXX.

The troops to Cuzco turned their eager eyes,
For all in this beheld a dazzling prize—
Its palaces, and temples, bright with gold,
Ere long to yield their numbers wealth untold.
From Caxamalca's square they marched away
With banners streaming, and with music gay.
Five hundred strong, or less, in all were they,
Of whom a third were mounted for the fray.
Toparca with the army took his way
Borne in Atahuallpa's palanquin—
A lustrous mass of crimson, gold, and green—
With all the outward signs of high estate
As if he were indeed a monarch great,
And not the royal puppet of an hour
Who held not though he seemed possessed of power,
While Challcuchima,* in a litter too,
Was chief of his imposing retinue,
Which moved in dense and picturesque array.
Their course along the Inca's highway lay,
That to Peru's imperial city led
Across the Cordillera's rugged bed,
And naught the march impeded day by day
Until they reached the vale of Xauxa.†
Then native warriors gathered by the stream,
Which in the sunlight there was seen to gleam,
And tore away the bridge that spanned it o'er,

---

* Atahuallpa's foremost military commander, who accompanied Hernando Pizarro to Caxamalca from the place where his army was camped near Xauxa.

† Pronounce *Zau-ex-á.*

And stood prepared for action on the shore.
The Spaniards all undaunted swam the breach,
And landed safely on the sandy beach,
When in dismay the Indian army fled,
And in pursuit the angry Spaniards sped,
And slaughtered all who failed their wrath to flee,
Then cried aloud—" We've won the victory ! "
And desecrated each barbaric shrine,
And placed the emblems of their faith divine—
The Child and Virgin—where they'd idols found,
And consecrated, all around, the ground,
Valverde's voice in prayer ascending high.
" 'Tis now," said he, " we feel to Jesus nigh.
To Him, and not ourselves, be all the praise."
There, in the vale, Pizarro camped for days,
And bade, the while, De Soto forward go
With sixty horse to face again the foe,
The osier bridges torn away restore,
And far along the royal road explore.
Where e'er he went he saw aggressive signs
Suggestive of the enemy's designs—
Burnt villages, and barricades of trees,
And torrents, that had erst been crossed with ease,
Now deep, unbridged, impediments to speed.
'T was hard he found at Bilcas to proceed,
For through the air a flight of missiles flew,
And here and there a fighting Spaniard slew,
But through the wild Sierra on he pressed,
Nor paused to give his weary soldiers rest.
Then, when entangled in the mountain chain,
Fresh missiles on their ranks began to rain,
While from the rocky passes thousands sprang,
And through the air their cries—resounding—rang.
Down like a torrent poured the Indian throng—
A multitude whose numbers made them strong—
And overthrew the rider and his steed,

And carried consternation in their speed.
Those foremost, climbing up the steep ascent,
Were backward in disorder—reeling—sent
On those—their comrades—toiling close behind,
Whose battered steeds careered, confused and
    blind,
Amid the storm of arrows, darts, and stones,
Which drew from wounded riders plaintive groans.
De Soto saw destruction near at hand,
And strove to kindle courage in his band,
And cheer them with his ringing battle-cry,
That through the mountains made the echoes fly.
" *Christo y Santiago !* " was the sound
That e'en the dreadful din of battle drowned.
Beyond the gorge a level plain was seen—
With rocks around it—carpeted with green,
And madly tried the Spaniards this to gain,
Nor heeded—as they went—their comrades slain,
Aware that all their dismal fate would share
If they much longer lingered battling there.
At length they gained the broad and level ground
Where horse and rider scope for action found.
Once more De Soto made the rocks resound
With ringing cries that warmed the warrior's heart,
And spurred him on to play a hero's part.
Once more was felt the battle's shock severe,
And hundreds fell beneath the sword and spear,
But firm remained the legions of Peru.
Ere long, o'er all, the night its mantle threw,
And hid the hosts contending from the view.
The Indians felt of vict'ry now secure.
De Soto said—" The foe's defeat is sure,
For Christ will ne'er desert us in our need.
The Christian's triumph—mark me !—is decreed.
But trust in God, and all will yet be well.
We'll long survive of this the tale to tell.

I've tidings sent Pizarro ere to day,
And warned him of a fierce impending fray,
And begged for forces, fresh, without delay.
Our comrades, now, perchance, are on the way,
And, may be, soon we'll hear their trumpets bray.
Repose till dawn, and we'll the fight renew,
And to the Cross and Crown be staunch and true."

That night Almagro by Pizarro sent—
The air with trumpets in their hearing rent,
To which their bugles quickly made reply,
And echoes all around were heard to fly.
'Twas welcome music to De Soto's ears,
And banished in a moment all his fears.
Almagro joined him ere the night had flown—
While neither moon nor star above them shone—
And told how on he'd urged his weary steeds,
When tidings reached him of De Soto's needs,
In fear that ere he brought his comrade aid
He'd in the dust, with all his band, be laid.

The morrow dawned magnificently fair,
And cool, and breezy, was the mountain air,
While with dismay the Indian host surveyed
A larger force against their arms arrayed
Than on the eve preceding, when the fight
Had only ceased as fell the shades of night.
"'T is vain," said they, "to strive with such as these,
Whose numbers swell whene'er their leaders please,"
And ere a blow was struck they fled the scene,
Nor where they'd fought before again were seen.
The passes now were free to all their foes,
Who cried aloud—"In God we trust repose!"
And onward pressed with hope within renewed,
And left the wild Sierra's solitude—
O'er which they saw the condor slowly sail—

To camp beyond it in a verdant vale,
And wait Pizarro's coming, and ere long
He joined his comrades in a martial song.
Then Mass was said, and prayers arose on high—
A solemn scene beneath that azure sky—
And each invader felt crusading zeal,
And vowed to fight for Jesus, and Castile.

Thus spoke Pizarro when they'd ceased to pray—
" I left my treasure—comrades—on the way *
With forty men to guard it night and day,
And make the native multitude obey,
And there the young Toparco, sad to say,
To death, remorseless, fell an easy prey.
Methinks that Challcuchima, moved by hate,
In secret planned the Inca's hapless fate,
And urged to arms the hosts ye fought so well.
In him I see an instrument of hell.
Yet still he lives though manacled and chained,
Nor with his blood my hands shall e'er be stained
Until his guilt to all is rendered clear.
A captive thus I've brought him—Spaniards !—here."
The captive chief was tried, and guilty found,
And to the stake ere night his form was bound,
The priest Valverde kneeling at his side
Exclaiming—" Take you Jesus for your guide ! "
But, unconverted, in the flames he died,
And to his god ere dying bravely cried—
He who had been Atahuallpa's pride.

XXXI.

The fagots scarce had burned themselves away—
While where the chief had stood his ashes lay—

---

* At Xauxa.

When toward the camp there came with great
  display
A native noble friendly in design,
Who said " By right divine the throne is mine ! "
'T was Manco, to the crown the rightful heir—
Huascar's brother, with a royal air—
Who deeming, to the foe, resistance vain,
Now sought protection from the sons of Spain.
Unheeding those who prayed he'd strike a blow
And lay the fierce invading Christians low.
Pizarro gave the prince a welcome kind,
And said " In me a friend you'll—Manco—find.
I journeyed here to serve Huascar's cause,
And punish those who'd trampled on the laws."
He saw in him an instrument of power
To serve the mighty purpose of the hour—
A puppet who a royal part could play,
And give him o'er Peru a monarch's sway,
And said, " To Cuzco onward come with me,
And to Castile and Jesus bow the knee ! "
On through the wild Sierra sped the band,
And soon again were battling hand to hand,
But with defeat they overwhelmed their foes,
And won, beyond the narrow pass, repose.
At length that day, ere sank the sun from view,
They near to Cuzco's savage splendors drew,
And saw the city gilded by its rays,
And showed their admiration in their gaze.
Long lines of solid buildings, white and low,
Decked out the distance in a golden glow,
And gave a look of grandeur to the vale,
While mountains round it bared their rugged breasts,
And reared on high their sharp volcanic crests.
Pizarro lay beyond the gates till morn *

---

* The morning of the fifteenth of November, 1533.

When through the camp was heard the rousing
  horn—
A signal ev'ry Spaniard round him knew.
The leader cried—" The march we'll now renew,
And Jesus guard each one to Country true ! "
The suburbs with a countless throng were filled,
Whose tongues were by their own amazement stilled.
To them the spectacle indeed was grand—
A pageant foreign to their native land—
A startling but magnificent display.
In solemn awe they viewed the bright array—
The glitt'ring arms, the riders and their steeds,
The fierce Pizarro famous for his deeds,
The armor that was worn by each and all ;
And all they saw but tended to appall.
Their bearded faces and complexions fair,
The fineness and the color of their hair,
Their lofty port, their martial mien, and tread,
But wonder through the native legions spread.
Were these indeed the Children of the Sun
Who'd thus their native land so soon o'errun ?
And as they heard their trumpet notes resound,
And seemed to feel the horsemen shake the ground,
They felt themselves but pigmies by their side,
And o'er their country's falling fortunes sighed.

On toward the square through narrow streets and
  long—
And paved with pebbles—marched the Spanish
  throng,
While through each street a limpid brooklet flowed,
And buzzards here and there their plumage showed.
Of brick, or stone, but lightly thatched with straw,
Each dwelling seemed, the stern invaders saw,
And habitations thickly lined the way,
Whose outer walls were oft with colors gay.

The city's square was vast indeed to view,
And overlooked by mountains green and blue.
On ev'ry side extended buildings low
As white—save for artistic forms—as snow—
The palaces of Incas now no more,
Bedecked within with shining golden ore.
O'er one of these a graceful turret rose,
Which, wisely, for himself Pizarro chose,
While camped his soldiers in the square below
Alert to meet—whene'er assailed—the foe,
But Cuzco struck no self-defending blow.
Though on a rock a fortress crowned the scene—
The strongest that Pizarro e'er had seen—
And troops in dusky multitudes were there,
No missile from its ramparts ploughed the air,
But silently it yielded to the strong—
Another linklet in the chain of wrong.
Down from its stony walls Pizarro gazed,
And gazing, far and wide, the prospect praised—
The mountains so magnificent and wild,
And rocks on rocks in rugged masses piled,
And waterfalls that sparkled in the sun,
While Cuzco's vale extended far below—
Where ceaseless verdure wore a golden glow—
The city rising grandly on its face,
Combining with its splendor fitting grace,
And over all the sky's pellucid blue
Enhanced the fascination of the view—
A sky but seldom sullied by a cloud.
The city's heart a sparkling river ploughed—
By bridges spanned at ev'ry thoroughfare—
Whose stony banks displayed artistic care.
Thus smoothly flagged—from quarries deep and
    gray—
For twenty leagues, or more, extended they.
Four lengthy streets—right angled—left the square—

Fine pebble-paved, and white as china-ware—
And lost themselves in far extending roads
Diversified by picturesque abodes,
While Cuzco's temple to the Sun inscribed—
Which alien language yet has ne'er described—
Revealed its golden splendors to the sight
In his—the glorious Sun's—refulgent light.

The Spaniards gazed around with gloating eyes,
And in each fane and palace saw a prize,
Then stripped them all for booty, and were glad,
While Cuzco o'er the sacrilege was sad.
The plates of gold upon the temple's walls
And those that beautified the palace halls,
By rude despoiling hands were torn away,
And sepulchres, where royal mummies lay,
Were rifled of the jewels of the dead,
And plunder only Spanish av'rice fed.
Rapacity was rampant, and the spoil
Too well rewarded the invader's toil,*
Till—o'er abundant—gold less prized became,
And those who'd won it chanced it on a game—
For gambling to the Spaniards was delight—
And fortunes vanished in a single night.
Thus riches swiftly winged themselves away,
While one ere sunrise played the Sun away,†
And then to desperation fell a prey.
Some with their wealth sailed—gladly back to
    Spain,

---

* Sancho, the royal notary, estimated the amount at only 580,200 *pesos de oro*, and 215,000 marks of silver, but other authorities said it exceeded Atahuallpa's ransom.

† One soldier as his share of the booty received an image of the sun in gold, and this he lost by gambling in a single night, whence arose the Spanish proverb *Juega el Sol antes que amanezca*—play away the sun before sunrise.

But more were eager greater wealth to gain,
And in Peru resolved to still remain,
As proud usurpers o'er the land to reign—
The hapless country now become their prey.
Peru lay crushed beneath the Spaniards' sway.

FINALE.

Ere long by lust of conquest fired anew
De Soto—who'd exploited in Peru,
And voyaged back to Spain for forces new—
By tales alluring to his banner drew
Six hundred men, well armed, with many mailed—
The bloom of Spanish chivalry—and sailed
To find and sack some new Peru, but failed,
Yet found instead the world's most mighty stream,
Whose waters like a mirror seemed to beam.
But soon, while on achievement bent, he died
Beside the Mississippi's splendid tide,
That flows three thousand miles with swelling
    pride—
The noble river he had first descried,
And o'er it left the flag of Spain to wave—
And in it found an undenoted grave,*

---

* De Soto, who had become famous as one of the companions of Pizarro in Peru, sailed with six hundred followers, from a Spanish port in 1538 to conquer Florida, a project favored by Charles V. After touching at Cuba they reached the port of Spiritu Santoa nd disembarked. Most of the ships were then sent back to Cuba, and the adventurers, many on horseback, but the majority on foot, commenced their long and weary march. On April 25, 1541, they came to the Mississippi river, which De Soto himself was the first European to behold, probably at the lowest Chickasaw bluff near the thirty-fifth parallel of latitude. After wintering on the

Yet immortality, a courted prize—
For love of fame had spurred his enterprise,
And prowess he for gold and glory gave.
Whate'er his faults we can but deem him brave.
De Soto's fate a warning proved to Spain,
Who in these regions saw no hope of gain ;
So for a span of six long score of years
No Spaniard followed these bold pioneers,
And undisturbed the Mississippi flowed,
And sang alone to savage ears its ode.

But now, behold! how vastly changed the scene.
What marvels fill the gulf that lies between!
Columbia, of our Western World the queen,
Gives greeting to Columbus from her throne—
To him who voyaged to the great unknown
And found this New World, now so great and
   grand
Which proved to him indeed the Promised Land.
Four hundred years since then have passed away,
And mark its wonders, far and wide, to-day!
Columbia stands a monument to him,
And through the ages naught his fame can dim.
All eyes can see the splendor of his prize,
All tongues unite to praise his great emprise,
And celebrate his matchless deed of yore,
When first the New World wooed him to its shore—
The grandest venture that the Sea has known.

---

banks of the river Washita, and meeting with constant dis-
couragement, they determined to follow the Mississippi
toward the sea, but when in the vicinity of Natchez and on
May 21, 1542, De Soto died, and the body of the discoverer
was wrapped in a mantle and sunk in the middle of the great
river. Those who had been his followers then built boats
and escaped down the Mississippi, but it was not until September 10, 1543, that they reached the river Panuco—their
numbers reduced to 311.

The New World sings his praise from zone to zone,
And with it all the Old World nations vie.
Columbus, like Columbia, ne'er can die.
He lives immortal, and with laurel crowned—
This mighty hero who the New World found.

Fain would I still pursue my splendid theme,
For in my brain a thousand fancies teem,
And in my breast impulsive feelings swell,
Which prompt me more than e'er I've told to tell,
And paint the Western World's superb career
To this the Great Republic's latest year,
But life is short, my poem waxes long,
And some, mayhap, will weary of the song.
So to my readers, one and all, adieu,
With hopes, anon, acquaintance to renew.
'T is sad to part, and, parting, say farewell—
A word whose sound is solemn as a knell—
But here below we only meet to part,
And sorrow waits on joy in ev'ry heart.
Yet I would fain still sing Columbia's praise,
Who now Columbus crowns with fadeless bays,
And all her glory and her grandeur paint—
Though well I know 't would be in colors faint ;—
For words too oft our feelings fail to tell
When most divine our thoughts within us swell,
And, most sublime, on Fancy's wings we soar.
Yes, I could sing her praises o'er and o'er
With tireless zest—Columbia, gracious queen,
The fairest, grandest that the world has seen.
In her Columbus finds his greatest fame—
A splendid recognition of his name ;
And as she greets him from her mighty throne—
Her realm as great as e'er the world has known—
She grasps his hand across four hundred years,
And utters plaudits that, perchance, he hears,

While o'er her waves the emblem of the free
That tells of glory great on land and sea.
May that proud banner wave eternally.
Columbus and Columbia hail to ye!
And ever may Columbia greater grow—
And from her fountain endless blessings flow—
Till all the New World rests beneath her sway.
All hail the prospect of that halcyon day!
And let the New World celebrate each year
Columbus Day, * and hold his mem'ry dear—
All—North and South—America as one,
With Peace-winged Progress ever speeding on.

---

* Discovery Day, 1492—namely, October 12, old calendar; or October 21, new calendar.

EXPLANATORY NOTE.

In this metrical narrative of maritime and military exploration, invasion, and adventure—this panorama of discovery, conquest, and colonization—is embraced the history of the New World for the first fifty years after it was made known to civilized man by Columbus, by the end of which time Mexico and Peru had been conquered. In this recital is embraced every voyage undertaken from the Old World to the New, and every event of importance that transpired in the New World, during that eventful time; while the careers of Balboa, Cortez, and Pizarro, as well as those of Alonzo de Ojeda and Ponce de Leon, and their principal companions, have been traced in detail. This detail may, indeed, be considered as superabundant as the traditional old woman found the Atlantic, when, on the occasion of an unusually high tide, she tried to sweep it back with a broom from the vicinity of her doorstep. But the die is cast.

When I made historical accuracy an indispensable condition of my task, I, of course, knew that fact and fancy would often prove as antagonistic as oil and water. But it is something to be able to say, that not a single event of importance in the history of the New World, within the period named, has been omitted from the narrative; although verse needs to be something more than a budget of facts, and I hope I have not lost sight of that one very important fact. To the works of Robertson, Prescott, Washington Irving, and others, bearing on my theme, I have made constant reference for the facts, as well as to many of the original sources of information 'from which they necessarily drew their materials, and these I have collated with as much care as if I had been writing a prose history.

It was my original intention to bring this metrical history of America down to the present time, in the same chronological order thus far observed, and this purpose I may still carry out; although, in dealing with events subsequent to the Conquest of Peru, far greater brevity may be expected than marks my descriptions of those that went before it. The history of the United States of America is a grand, magnificent and suggestive theme, and if I fail to prove myself equal to sketching its outlines, and filling in the picture, in fitting verse, it will not be for want of glowing ardor in my task. But I remember that a certain piece of advice, once given to those about to marry, was " DON'T," and perhaps I ought to apply the same advice in the case of my historic muse, and say *"Don't"* in soliloquy.

" An epic poem, having for its fabric all that pertains to the inspir‧
ing subject, "The Song of America and Columbus," presents to the
extent of nearly three hundred pages, a judicious selection from
this vast wealth of all that is most picturesque and at the same
time, historically most important. The material, possessing in itself
the elements of adventure, scenic beauty and patriotism, here loses
nothing by being rendered into verse. The poetry is very good, and
its value is enhanced, by historical accuracy."—*The Chautauquan
for January*, 1893.

" It is doubly welcome—First, because it is an extremely interest‧
ing story, written with all a true poet's ardor and zeal, and clothed
in language at once beautiful and [graphic. Secondly, it gives us a
complete narrative, in a pleasing form, of the life and adventures of
Columbus. Mr. Cornwallis' Song should be read by all who love a
charming poem, with an inspiring and interesting subject, set forth
in the sublime and impassioned language which a true poet, in love
with his subject, alone knows."—*Boston Republic.*

"It has in it some very good lines, showing that the author has
some rare gifts in the poetic line. The book is worth owning and
reading."—*New York Journal of Commerce.*

"A very full and quite accurate history of Columbus' life and
achievements in verse. It is quite an agreeable instance of an editor
of a financial gazette having the capacity and the leisure and the
happy taste and turn for working up so many detailed historical
incidents into a no mean epic, and we could earnestly desire that
the gifted author might spend a full energy and patience, as well as
his undoubted genius upon a poem that should come to stay. All
the more one so wishes since he writes with such an evident spontan‧
ity and joy in his work as to make his readers personally like him.
It is quite marvelous what a good general idea one gets from it of
the great discoverer's life and work."—*New York Christian Intel‧
ligencer.*

" Rapidly turning the pages we find our poet in the full tide of
inspired description. The volume closes with this eloquent apostrophe
to the great Admiral."—*New Orleans Times-Democrat.*

" It is the story of the New World told in verse of much merit. It
is worthy of a place in literature. This may be appreciated from
this extract containing a description of the Hudson River."—
Brooklyn Citizen.

" An ambitious work, which is virtually the history of America in
the age of discovery. That this poetical narrative of the four voy‧
ages of Columbus was composed out of pure love of the inspiring
theme is shown in the spontaneous flow of verse and the genuine
enthusiasm which marks the entire production. The writer's use of
the heroic couplet has resulted in many sublime passages."—*Phila‧
delphia North American.*

" Of course it could not be expected in a poem of this length, and
embracing such a variety of subjects, that there should not be some
inequalities; but there is no doubt that whatever else the author
may or may not be, as a novelist or financial writer, he is unques‧
tionably a poet. The divine afflatus may not inspire him to the same
extent as a Homer, a Milton, or a Longfellow, but it is there, if in a
lesser degree, and the brain that can weave line upon line in the

manner and to the extent we have here is not of the common order. The book is very handsomely gotten up, and will be valuable as a souvenir of a memorable event."—*San Francisco Daily Report.*

"Mr. Cornwallis is a fluent and ready writer, with obviously thorough knowledge of the story to be told. His versification is smooth and rhythmic, and his verbal fertility remarkable. It can be said for it that it is graceful, fluent and intelligent, and furnishes a story of America attractive and readable, as well as approximately correct. It is decidedly respectable from a historic point of view."—*Chicago Times.*

"Mr. Cornwallis has shown a laudable ambition, and he possesses considerable power of graphic description in verse. There is a great deal in the narrative which is interesting and well told."—*Boston Congregationalist.*

"As an epic poem the book is worthy of praise, and the lines scan well."—*Mobile Daily Register.*

"His verse is spirited throughout, and he sometimes coins a phrase of striking beauty and originality. The Song is full of high patriotism, and a gloriously optimistic view of the nation and the race."—*Detroit Tribune.*

"Among the numerous Columbus volumes, this poem, which is indeed an epic, is entitled to special mention."—*Boston Traveller.*

"The descriptive portions are vividly drawn. The Song will no doubt be read with admiration and instruction."—*Harrisburg Star-Independent.*

"The 'Song of America and Columbus' is sung in a sturdy volume of verse."—*Chicago Evening Post.*

"The first part of the book presents in a spirited style 'The Song of America in 1802.' The verse runs in entire smoothness, and bears the impress of sincerity and enthusiasm. The work is a fitting tribute to Columbus and to the great Republic."—*Chicago Herald.*

"We know more than one financial man who is a poet. The purpose of the author is commendable, and we have read poems with far less merit or *raison d'etre.*"—*New York Observer.*

"The lines give evidence of the writer's facility in versification, and are marked by much picturesque description."—*Boston Golden Rule.*

"The verse runs with entire smoothness, and bears the impress of sincerity and enthusiasm. The work is a fitting tribute to Columbus and the Great Republic."—*Boston Home Journal.*

"Mr. Cornwallis' description of the tropical luxuriance which greeted the eyes of Columbus, and his portrayal of the simple life of the natives is evidently inspired by a thorough sympathy with his subject and with the beauties of nature. His work will doubtless receive all the attention which he hoped for it, and its trifling defects of rhyme and rhythm will escape notice in the midst of so much that is good."—*Philadelphia Evening Item.*

"We may concede him, beside historical accuracy, a very smooth and on the whole ryhthmical versification. Where the historical method is not too closely followed it rises to quite a poetic height. Many will read his verses with pleasure, and find in them many beauties."—*New Orleans Picayune.*

"It has power and fire and vigor."—*Boston Watchman.*

"The scope of the composition is vast, for this volume embraces descriptive accounts of the four voyages of Columbus, and of the precursors of his great discovery, and the sequel of our national history. This is a great deal to be compressed within the limits of a narrative poem, but the writer's enthusiasm is both hearty and sincere. He carries his readers smoothly over the centuries. The distinction of " The Song " is that it accords unique importance to the industrial grandeur of the United States."—*Philadelphia Ledger.*

"It is full of enthusiasm, and has some striking descriptive poetry."—*Philadelphia Presbyterian Journal.*

"There are many good lines in our poet historian's work. He is a good-natured singer, and certainly does not lack enthusiasm, while the encyclopedic range of his heroic poem demands a wide view of the history of navigation, of the annals of scientific and political progress, and especially of the America that was, that is, and is to be. The volume [certainly takes the reader out of the beaten track of literature, and it may act as an antidote to an unhealthy tendency of the day to go crazy over short stories, dwarfed essays and sketchy work in general."—*Portland* (Me.) *Daily Eastern Argus.*

"It is safe to say that this laudable purpose—historical accuracy—has been achieved. The verse is mellifluous. It contains more of geographical and ethnological information than most text-books in those departments of knowledge. Anybody reading the catalogue of aboriginal tribes is instantly reminded of the enumeration of ships in the Iliad, and in the matter of cataloging, Mr. Cornwallis need not take off his cap to Homer or any other bard. The book as a whole is a very interesting contribution to Columbian literature."—*Buffalo Courier.*

"Mr. Cornwallis is a versatile writer and with a rich vocabulary, and he writes rhythmic verse."—*Kansas City Times.*

"It is a wonderfully fertile and fluent body of rhyme. Though in conception it is merely a greeting to Columbus and Columbia in one breath, as it were, it expands into a descriptive narrative of the voyages and career of Columbus, not neglecting his precursors even, and describes, finally, the sequel as seen in the United States."—*Brooklyn Daily Eagle.*

"It moves along in a spirited way. Very few, if any, of the salient points of our great country have escaped being apostrophised by this poet before he sweeps into a more heroic strain."—*St. Paul Globe.*

"It deals with a noble theme in a dignified and serious style."—*Buffalo News.*

"It is written with much smoothness and careful attention in the main to rhyme and rhythm. The volume will be found to be of considerable interest."—*Chicago Mail.*

"He certainly rhymes with all the spirit and fervor of an old-fashioned patriot."—*Philadelphia Evening Bulletin.*

"A very clever poem. It is the story of the New World very readably put, and should be in all households."—*Pittsburg Press.*

"It reads smoothly and easily. The writer has kept close to the story, and is at no loss for choice language. The book is likely to find favor in the eyes of the reading public."—*Pittsburg Commercial Gazette.*

"There is much in the book to entertain, and the sentiment will commend it to the patriotic."—*Burlington Hawk Eye.*

"It is true to historical facts, and at times is really poetical."—*Utica Morning Herald.*

"It would seem like the work of a lifetime. The whole is at least an earnest, laudable and enthusiastic effort at patriotism."—*New Haven News.*

"Incompatible though they may appear, finance and poetry sometimes go hand in hand. Such was the case of the banker-poet, Samuel Rogers, and such is the case of Mr. Stedman. A third illustration may be found in Kinahan Cornwallis, editor of the DAILY INVESTIGATOR."—*Boston Courier,*

"There is a good deal of information and study in this volume, and one stands aghast at the labor it implies."—*Hartford Courant.*

"The narrative is given in attractive style. We look forward with pleasurable anticipations to the continuation."—*Albany Times-Union.*

"The volume is well worth reading."—*Cincinnati Enquirer.*

"We present the following sample of its general merits, interest in which is enhanced by the fact that few of us know how many tribes of redmen the coming of Columbus started on the road to extinction."—*Troy Times.*

"Mr. Cornwallis has produced a poem which deserves something better than a passing mention. We think the public will demand so many copies of this bright, cheery and instructive poem that the author will find his labor of love a good investment."—*N. Y. Sunday Times.*

"An exceedingly ambitious work. Besides an invocation to Columbus it gives in easy verse, chiefly iambic couplets, the entire history of Columbus and the discovery. The alternate theme is naturally the World's Fair at Chicago, and the book is timely and interesting."—*N. Y. Mail and Express.*

"He, in his preface, is more severe on himself than most critics will be on his work. It has the merit of heroic endeavor and historical accuracy. To this we might add a freedom from any effort to make the verse a sacrifice to facts. It is easy reading, and will no doubt please many. We give the following extracts."—*Cincinnati Christian Standard.*

"This is a successful attempt to put into verse the story of Columbus and his predecessors. There are really fine stanzas in these pages, some of which we wish we had space to quote."—*Boston Zion's Herald.*

"The 'picturesqueness and beauty of our native Indian names has often been pointed out, but it was reserved for Mr. Cornwallis fully to subdue them to the uses of poetry. He says: '—*Chicago Evening Journal.*

"The author justly claims for this work—a poetic narrative of the history of America—the merit of historical accuracy. In this volume however, we get only one dose of it, and it is not an unpleasant one. We give a few specimens."—*Boston Morning Star.*

"It forms an instructive and entertaining volume."—"*Buffalo Enquirer.*

"A few lines will give some indication of the vivacity and felicity of Mr. Cornwallis's manner. Even more spirit and invention is displayed where he enumerates the aboriginal tribes. Homer's Catalogue of Ships is nothing to this astounding *tour de force.*"—*Boston Beacon.*

"There are some glowing pictorial passages."—*Godey's Magazine.*

"The many who take pleasure in reading Columbus literature, and who enjoy poetry, will relish this story of the great navigator in heroic verse."—*The Springfield* (Mass.) *Daily News.*

"The narrative itself is written with evident care for historical accuracy; the diction is unaffected and respectable."—*Boston Literary World.*

"It contains many evidences of poetic skill."—*Hartford Post.*

"Mr. Kinahan Cornwallis, who has long been well known as an able and enterprising journalist, and is also the author of novels that have had a fair popularity, has come out in a new *rôle*, that of poet. The theme is a grand one."—*Montreal Gazette.*

"When we have read the book through, we are ready to burst forth in the same spirit and sing, 'O Kinahan Cornwallis, not even the Great Corliss ever got up so much steam as you on the Columbian theme.'"—*The Atlantic Monthly.*

"Other praiseworthy and instructive books of the quarter have been   *   *   and 'The Song of America and Columbus, or the Story of the New World,' by Kinahan Cornwallis."—*Current History, Detroit.*

"The rhyming is accurate, the lines are fluent, the history is orthodox, and the whole is probably as readable as any poem of 278 pages could hope to be."—*New York Evening Telegram.*

Of "A Marvellous Coincidence"—A strange story of Adventure, by the same author, the Philadelphia *Item* says—"The story is agreeably and pleasantly told and diversified with plenty of action and dialogue. Despite the fact that the marvellous occupies a large part in the plot the probabilities are all along fairly well maintained. The plot has certain faults which however do not in any degree mar the reader's interest in the work. The verdict of those who read it will be that it is a tale with an ingenious plot, worked out on natural and simple lines of sensational and romantic interest." Mailed free on receipt of 50 cents by the DAILY INVESTIGATOR. Office 52 Broadway New York.

WORKS BY KINAHAN CORNWALLIS.

The Song of America and Columbus;

OR,

The Story of the New World.

" One of the most interesting contributions to the great mass of Columbian literature is a poem, epic in length as well as in some of its
aims. If one will dip into the poem he will find something to repay.
He will find, to begin with, that Mr. Cornwallis is fully conversant
with his theme, and that one of the great merits of the composition
is historical accuracy. It is often difficult to be historically accurate
and poetic at one and the same time, but this stumblin-gblock has
been very cleverly escaped by the author, although he persists in
bringing out the facts. The verse is for the most part iambic penta-
meter, and it flows as smoothly as any that Pope ever wrote. The
diction is of the best, and the thought is often striking. Notice these
lines in an apostrophe to Columbia. Wherever there is an opportunity for the manifestation of true poetic sentiment, it is generally
employed to good advantage. The work is enthusiastic, apprecia-
tive and patriotic, and is well worth reading."—*The Evening Dispatch*, Columbus, Ohio, Feb. 18, 1893.

" He has gone out of the beaten track and treated his subject in an
original poetically descriptive manner. The work is large and com-
prehensive, but scarcely deserves the author's own description of being elephantine. Coming at an appropriate time when America is
celebrating the quadro-centenary, this effort should do much towards
quickening the undoubted enthusiasm which this exhibition is provok-
ing, while amongst the many mementoes that will be sought after, the
fact of a national poem having been specially published should leave
little difficulty as to the form this memento should take. There are
some fine descriptive passages, especially in the narrative of the voyages. The book concludes with a stately ode anent the Chicago
event."—*The Brighton Gazette*, England, Feb. 18, 1893.

" As an American National and Patriotic poem it has no peer, and
the talented author can well feel proud of his brilliant effort."—*The
Harrisburg* (Pa.) *Telegram.*

" Mr. Cornwallis has been inspired by a great and stirring theme :
yet has not only realized its full requirements, but has endeavored to
rise to their height with creditable success."—*The Leicester Post*,
England, Feb. 8, 1893.

" Mr. Kinahan Cornwallis has accomplished a gigantic task in writing a poetical narrative of the history of America. This is an attractive way of reading history. That he has made it interesting is
undoubted, and the graphic descriptions of the beauties of the various countries are very vivid."—*Sala's Journal*, London, Feb. 4, 1893.

" A fine production. We love to read it. Many people will be fascinated with it; and we feel safe in saying that it is one of the finest
productions the great event has brought out."—*Cincinnati Western
Christian Advocate*, Feb. 15, 1893.

"If ever a stupendous poetical task was attempted it was when Mr. Cornwallis began his poetical narrative of the history of America in celebration of the Discovery. There is much that is praiseworthy in it. There is a certain metrical aptness in the verse, and the story is told concisely as well as rythmically. One admires Mr. Cornwallis's enthusiasm."—*The Portland, (Me.,) Transcript.*

"With a theme so vast and attractive, the whole cannot fail to be interesting. This first volume promises well. To undertake such a work required a boldness not far removed in kind from that which led the great discoverer to embark upon his perilous mission, and one would naturally expect equal boldness of treatment, nor are these expectations unrealized. All through the book there is evidence of considerable dramatic power. Such a work, made melodious by a versifier so skilful, forms pleasant and instructive reading."—*The Ardrossan Herald*, Scotland, Feb. 24, 1893.

Adrift with a Vengeance.

A Tale of Love and Adventure.

The Chicago *Tribune* of Jan. 16. 1871, says: "In the weak, wishy-washy, everlasting flood of novels it is refreshing to get a really good story now and then, and such is 'Adrift with a Vengeance,' by Mr. Kinahan Cornwallis. The novel is in reality a story of adventure, and the scene therefore constantly shifts, and the hero is led through an amazing variety of adventures, so that an opportunity is afforded the writer for his descriptive powers, and these he applies with no ordinary ability to natural scenery, social life, and manners and customs in almost every part of the known world. The pages of this novel are literally crowded with pleasant incidents, told in a very graphic way, which has the unusual merit of not being sensational."

The Albany *Evening Journal* of Nov. 25, 1870, says of "Adrift with a Vengeance:" "Although this is, we suppose, a novel, it could with almost equal propriety be called a book of travels or of adventure, for it takes the reader all over the world by sea and by land, and introduces him to such odd places and to such droll characters, and everything is presented so vividly and so graphically that it seems more like a true story than a work of fiction. But it is a novel, and one of the very best. There is nothing sophomoric about it, for its author was a mature thinker long before he took up his pen to write 'Adrift.'"

The New York *Evening Post.* of Nov. 5, 1870, says: "CARLETON'S last success is a novel entitled 'Adrift with a Vengeance.' by Mr. Kinahan Cornwallis, well known as the editor of the New York *Albion.* The scene of the story constantly shifts from land to sea, and by turn lies in all the continents and Oceanica. and the hero passes through an almost infinite variety of adventures to find himself at last in the House of Lords. The work abounds in vivid descriptions of natural scenery and of social life. at one time horrifying us with a bull-fight at Lima. and at another delighting us with a wedding breakfast at Delmonico's. From beginning to end there is not a dull page; the incidents, though crowded, are not out of the range of probability, and the reader's excitement in the story is always genuine and never morbid."

The New York *Commercial Advertiser*, of Nov. 11, 1870, says: " The story is well told; the style is easy and natural, and the reader is interested throughout. The writer has a vivid imagination and a graceful pen."

The New York *Evening Express*, of Nov. 12, 1870, says of " Adrift with a Vengeance: " " This tale of Love and Adventure will be devoured by lovers of fiction, for its marvellous incidents and its thrilling scenes, which although given in a style that approaches the realistic and the natural, have all the vivid effects produced in novels of the strictly sensational school. We cannot analyze the story, which combines all the striking incidents of travel and adventure, stereotyped in similar productions, but reproduced by the author with admirable skill and ingenuity, in comparatively new forms which absorb the reader's attention until the close of the volume. To lovers of the marvellous and the exciting we can safely recommend the work as one that will satisfy their most expectant desires."

The New York *Times*, of Nov. 25, 1870, says of " Adrift with a Vengeance: " " Those fond of scenes of thrilling adventure will find in this romance ample matter for the most intense interest. The book is fraught with wonderful escapes and records of peculiar enterprise, and displays a remarkable knowledge of the varied hunting episodes of strange climes. Parallel with the romance of travel and the chase, there runs the narrative of the course of true love, so that those to whom the 'sports of field and flood' fail of interest, will find the congenial record of the phases of the tender passion amply repay the perusal of the volume. Altogether, the book is an excellent type of the popular fiction of the period."

The New York *World*, of Nov. 25, 1870, says of " Adrift with a Vengeance: " " Mr. Cornwallis has undertaken in this volume the task of writing a sensational novel with a moderate undercurrent of sentiment, in which the adventures are numerous and exciting, and the love incident of the most approved character. The plot is fairly sustained, and would, perhaps, have been stronger had it been told in the third person; but in the narration of adventures this is amply compensated for by the vivacity which the personal relation always insures. Although strictly to be classed under the sensational school, and possessing some of its excellent features ' Adrift with a Vengeance' is nevertheless free from the worst characteristics of that style."

Frank Leslie's Illustrated Newspaper, of Dec. 10, 1870, says of " Adrift with a Vengeance: " " Lively in style, graphic in description, with a plot somewhat involved but well worked out, indicating the practised hand of an accomplished man of the world. Mr. Cornwallis is a master of the ways of society, and his characters are obviously typical."

The New York *Herald*, of Dec. 25, 1870, says: " One of the best satires on the sensational novel of the day which we have read is ' Adrift with a Vengeance,' written by Kinahan Cornwallis. The book is decidedly rich, and ought to be widely read. It is the best thing of the kind published."

The New York *Evening Telegram*, of Dec. 27, 1870, says: " 'Adrift with a Vengeance ' is as exciting a story as one could wish to read. * * Mr. Cornwallis has written a very readable story. He writes in an agreeable style."

The New York *Citizen and Round Table*, of Nov. 26, 1870, says of "Adrift with a Vengeance:" "Mr. Cornwallis is favorably known as the editor of the *Albion*, and the author of a number of entertaining books. 'Adrift with a Vengeance' is his latest work. It is a novel which was published as a serial story in the *Albion*, and was received with sufficient favor to justify its republication in book form. It is full of adventure of the most exciting variety, and the hero, after passing through experiences sufficiently varied to supply a dozen lives with interest and excitement, finally becomes an English Earl. Mr. Cornwallis writes fluently and with much vivacity, and his latest story will be sure of a large circle of interested readers."

The New York *Evening Free Press*, of Nov. 28, 1870, says of "Adrift with a Vengeance:" "Kinahan Cornwallis is a familiar name in journalism, and promises to become as familiar in literature. 'Adrift with a Vengeance' is, in fact, a novel of the English standard for cleverness. The author has adopted that autobiographical *naivete* of narration, which made 'David Copperfield' and 'Alton Locke' so famous in their day, but which has since been worn threadbare with reiteration. In its use—that is, in writing in the first person —an author produces a book either intensely stupid and egotistic, or intensely interesting; and Mr. Cornwallis has succeeded in giving his new novel the quality of intensity in the latter direction. Mr. Cornwallis must be complimented, therefore, for having done successfully that which can be done only by a master. The general *ensemble* of the story is 'David Copperfield' over again. The author of 'Adrift' has in him the elements of a master novelist, and has only to develop them—to express himself. There is need enough, *mehercule*, of a great master of fiction in this country. 'Adrift with a Vengeance' is exceedingly graphic in description and bold in invention—is, in a word, finely imaginative in passages, and abounds in the picturesque, graceful and *insouciant* ease of the true literary artist. The volume is the hit of the season."

The *Scottish American*, of Dec. 1, 1870, says of "Adrift with a Vengeance:" "This is a tale that we have but to commence reading to make sure that we will get to the end of it."

The New York *Scientific American*, of Dec. 3, 1870, says: "Kinahan Cornwallis, the accomplished editor of the *Albion*, has given us in this volume a very graphic and entertaining story, which combines incidents of social life, travel and adventure in a most thrilling and interested manner. We can cordially commend this book as one well suited to enliven the family circle on the dull Winter evenings."

The New York *Star*, of Nov. 7, 1870, says of "Adrift with a Vengeance:" "The versatile author of this admirably-conceived and very entertaining story is well known as a journalist of many years' standing. 'Adrift with a Vengeance' is the story of a youngster, Washington Edmonds, told in the first person much in the style of 'David Copperfield.' He passes through about as many trials and tribulations as that eminent worthy. The interest is maintained to the end, the dialogue is easy and natural, and the whole book shows itself to be the work of a highly imaginative mind, and an easy, graceful writer."

The New York *Home Journal*, of Oct. 12, 1870, says of "Adrift with a Vengeance:" "From a hasty look at the advance sheets of the work, we find them rich, not only in promise, but in performance, that should give Mr. Cornwallis assurance, as they undoubtedly will his readers, that he has not mistaken his vocation. Its pages are crowded with incident and adventure and 'hairbreadth 'scapes' in South Africa, Australia, and upon the treacherous deep, enough to furnish forth many such volumes."

The Philadelphia *North America*, of Dec. 8, 1870, says of "Adrift with a Vengeance:" " He (the author) here tells a vivid story of English and American life in an agreeable manner that will be read with interest. * * There is genuine and unflagging interest from first to last."

The New Orleans *Picayune*, of Dec. 3, 1870, says: " ' Adrift with a Vengeance ' is a fiction of varied interest, abounding with adventure and striking descriptions of scenery, character and social life. It is crowded with incident."

The Chicago *Times* says: " The author has given us in this book an average of one thrilling episode for every three pages. This will constitute the story an invaluable work of reference for all compilers of attenuated serials in the weekly family papers, as they can find enough material in ' Adrift with a Vengeance ' to set them up in business for the next dozen years. The author is a veteran writer, and all of his works have been characterized by the same oddity of title and spirit of contents that characterizes ' Adrift with a Vengeance.' "

The Detroit *Free Press* says of " Adrift with a Vengeance:" " The story, though leaning somewhat toward the ' Robinson Crusoe ' and ' Masterman Ready ' style of literature, is a lively and entertaining one, filled from title to *finis* with the most varied of adventures."

The Philadelphia *Telegraph* says: " ' Adrift with a Vengeance.' by Kinahan Cornwallis, from the press of Carleton, is a story of adventure which contains many exciting incidents and some highly graphic descriptions of scenery and life in all parts of the world. Mr. Cornwallis, who is well known as the editor of the New York *Albion*, is an able writer, and in ' Adrift with a Vengeance ' he has produced a very interesting story that is full of life and animation from first to last."

The Boston *Evening Transcript* says: "Mr. Kinahan Cornwallis has, in ' Adrift with a Vengeance,' given us an animated adventurous tale, full of exciting scenes on land and sea, shifting from mid-ocean to Delmonico's, and from Lima to the House of Lords. Extraordinary but not impossible, eventful but not hyperbolical, the interest of the tale never flags, and it is full of graphic force and personal zest."

The Brooklyn *Eagle* says of " Adrift with a Vengeance:" " There is abundance of lively incident—fights with wild beasts and wild men, shipwrecks, bull-fights, perilous journeys, narrow escapes, much hardship of all sorts—and the characters of the romance are as diversified as the events described."

The Philadelphia *Press*, of Nov. 26, 1870, says: "Mr. Cornwallis has produced in ' Adrift with a Vengeance ' a story full of action and variety, with many changes of scene and many phases of society."

The Cincinnati *Times* says of "Adrift with a Vengeance:" "The work abounds in vivid descriptions of natural scenery and domestic life, and the incidents are sufficiently startling to enchain the reader's attention to the close."

The Cincinnati *Chronicle*, of Dec. 9, 1870, says of "Adrift with a Vengeance:" "Crowded with incidents, and as full of exciting adventure as the most exacting reader could demand. This story by turns amuses, horrifies and interests us. The life of the hero is a checkered one, and his experience is sufficiently varied to keep up a constant interest in his descriptions of the phases of social life through which he passes. There are few dull pages in this volume."

The Troy *Times* says: "The style is graphic, and the plot, which is natural, evinces considerable ingenuity. Those who enjoy fiction will be likely to read this book through if they begin its perusal."

"Mr. Cornwallis has given the public in this work a novel of more than ordinary interest. The plot is fresh and vigorous, and with love or adventure, or both, delightfully commingled, every page is made attractive. It takes in, and most entrancingly too, everything from a bull-fight at Lima to a wedding breakfast at Delmonico's. The novel will make a hit."—*The St. Louis Democrat.*

"Those who are fond of dare-devil adventures, hair-breadth escapes, and a touching description of man's constancy and devotion and woman's love and fidelity, will read this volume with emotions of unmixed pleasure. There is nothing dull or uninteresting from the first to the last page. There are many passages descriptive of scenery and places which rise into the regions of both the grand and the beautiful."—*San Francisco Pioneer.*

"The book contains many glowing descriptions of life and manners in the countries visited by the hero, and will gratify the most insatiate appetite for adventure."—*New York Tribune.*

"Mr. Cornwallis is fertile in imagination, and the multitude of incidents in his story sustains the reader's excitement and interest from the commencement to the happy conclusion."—*The Providence* (R. I.) *Telegraph.*

Pilgrims of Fashion.

Cloth, $1. Published by Harper & Bros.

"His Bull Run battle-piece is well executed. The whole work is good, and cannot fail to please numerous readers."—*Boston Evening Traveller.*

"This is a well-written novel."—*Cincinnati Enquirer.*

"It is a continued series of healthy observations upon the recklessness and needless extravagance of society. The plot is well arranged and handsomely carried out, and the reader can while away an hour in the perusal of the book with profit."—*Portland Advertiser.*

"It is animatedly written."—*Boston Evening Gazette.*

"'Pilgrims of Fashion' contains many well-directed blows at the worshippers at Fashion's shrine. The plot is excellent, and is well carried out to the end."—*New York Express.*

"The work is powerfully and graphically written."—*Philadelphia Press.*

"A work of an uncommon order, and remarkable for its originality and freshness."—*Salem Register.*

"Unless we are greatly mistaken this work is destined to create a sensation in the literary world. It is artistically constructed; the style is pure and scholarly; the moral is healthful. It abounds in vivid descriptions of nature and life, and the interest never flags from the opening to the closing chapter."—*The Albany,* (N. Y.) *Evening Journal,* January 31, 1862.

"The characters of his story are artistically delineated, and the descriptions are remarkably fine. The style of the work is pure and refined, and the language is classically English. We congratulate Mr. Cornwallis on his first American novel, and hope to hear from him again in the same field."—*Frank Leslies' Illustrated Newspaper,* Feb. 15, 1862.

"Pilgrims of Fashion is a very well told and intensely interesting story of both hemispheres dedicated to the author's friend Charles Reade, who brought out the London edition of the work for him through his own publishers, Trubner & Co., just as Mr. Cornwallis brought out for Mr. Reade the first American edition of "The Cloister and the Hearth," through Rudd & Carleton of New York, from advance sheets mailed to him. It is full of graphic and picturesque descriptions and dramatic scenes."—*The New York Herald.*

Royalty in the New World;

OR,

The Prince of Wales in America.

With Steel Engraved Portrait of the Prince.

Being a Summer Tour through the British Provinces and the United States, in 1860. 1 vol., 75 cents.

From the *New York Herald.*

"QUEEN VICTORIA AND ROYALTY IN THE NEW WORLD—Among the pleasant souvenirs of the visit of the Prince of Wales to this country we may include the following letter from Queen Victoria, through her Secretary, Sir Charles Phipps, C. B., Keeper of her Majesty's Privy Purse, to Mr. Kinahan Cornwallis, who,as correspondent of this journal traveled with the royal party throughout their tour on this continent. In accepting and thanking him so gracefully for the copy of his book relating to her son's travels, the Queen has paid no common compliment, for it is well known that it is contrary to the usual custom for her to receive gifts of any kind, either from her own subjects or foreign citizens. The exception to the rule in this case shows that an impartial narrative and reliable history, coming from an American source, of the events of the Prince's progress through this country, has been properly appreciated by those most intimately interested. We need only say, in comment, that 'Royalty in the New World' is worthy to fill the niche so willingly assigned it in the royal library."

"WINDSOR CASTLE, Jan. 19, 1861.

"SIR: It was only yesterday that I received your letter of the 30th of November, accompanying a copy of your work, entitled 'Royalty in the New World, or, The Prince of Wales in America' destined for her Majesty the Queen. I lost no time in presenting your work to

the Queen, and it was very graciously accepted by her Majesty. I have received the Queen's commands to thank you in her name for your attention. I have the honor to be, Sir, your most obedient, humble servant.   C. B. PHIPPS.
" KINAHAN CORNWALLIS, ESQ."

" The following letter from Maj. General Bruce, the governor of the Prince of Wales, conveys a merited tribute to the accuracy of the book."

"MADINGLEY HALL, CAMBRIDGE, Jan. 20, 1861.
" DEAR SIR: I only received two days ago your letter of the 30th of November last, together with two copies of your work entitled ' Royalty in the New World ' and am directed to convey to you the Prince of Wales's thanks for the one which you forward for his Royal Highness's acceptance. I am extremely obliged to you for the other, which you kindly present to me. You have evidently striven to give a faithful narrative of his Royal Highness's progress, and of the gratifying reception which he met with, both in the British Provinces and in the United States of America. I am, dear Sir, your obedient servant,   R. BRUCE.
" KINAHAN CORNWALLIS, Esq."

From the Duke of Newcastle, The Cabinet Minister in charge of the Prince:—

" LONDON, Feb'y 8, 1861.
" DEAR SIR: Pray accept my thanks for a beautifully bound copy of your new book ' Royalty in the New World.' My very pressing engagements since I received it have hitherto prevented my reading it, but I hope to do so before long. Let me assure you. and those with whom you are associated, how anxiously we all desire in this country to see a happy termination to the troubles which are now afflicting the United States. The accounts from thence are watched with an intensity of interest scarcely less than that which three years ago attached to every mail from India. I am, dear Sir, yours very truly
" NEWCASTLE."

"Mr. Cornwallis has embodied a complete history of the royal visit in an exceedingly interesting book of travel, which the public, we are sure, will peruse with much pleasure and profit. As an eyewitness of the events which he records, his descriptions. which, for graphic simplicity and vigor could not be surpassed, have a peculiar value, and there is a consequent freshness imparted to his writings, which otherwise would be hardly attainable. We have here, in the handsome volume before us, not only a panorama of the tour, but pictorial glimpses of the history and present state of the country through which he passed. We here meet with much that is new, and much that is both instructive and amusing. and, in turning over the pages, we have been hurried from grave to gay, from lively to severe, with a rapidity worthy of the best of novels; yet, we have noticed throughout, the strictest adherence to the facts, and the most well-weighed words in everything upon which an opinion is pronounced. Every page might be quoted with advantage to the author. But we have said enough to induce our readers to get the work, and judge for themselves."—*New York Herald*, Dec. 9, 1860.

" Last week, the *Critic*, our leading literary paper, gave a long, discriminating. analytical criticism of the ' Tour of the Prince of Wales in America,' by Mr. Kinahan Cornwallis, and gave it very high praise as a most graphic, sensible narrative."—Extract from the London Correspondence of the *New York Herald*, April 3, 1861.

A Panorama of the New World.

Being Travels in Australia and South and North America.

In Two Volumes.

" Mr. Cornwallis is a pleasant traveller, enthusiastic, persevering, and overflowing with good spirits. His former works have already taught us to appreciate his perfect fitness for the particular walk of literature which he has adopted; nor will the present work diminish his popularity. A quick and discriminating eye, rapid powers of combination, a true feeling for nature, and a wholesome large-hearted sympathy with his fellow-men, are his leading characteristics; and before we have read through fifty pages of his book, we claim him as a friend, and wander on with perfect confidence in our guide, wherever he may see fit to lead us. The Panorama is the result of three years of travel, and the variety of scenes which it depicts, is consequently very great; nor do we think we can do Mr. Cornwallis better justice, than by transferring two or three of these to our own columns. We are indebted to Mr. Cornwallis for many agreeable hours. We have met with few descriptions more graphic than our lively author's picture of a first night at Melbourne. But we are exceeding our limits, and reluctantly take leave of Mr. Cornwallis, with a couple of anecdotes illustrative of Yankee delicacy."—*Literary Gazette*, London, July 23, 1859.

" A book that will be read; for it is fresh and sparkling, lively, true, and original."—*Morning Herald*, London, June 7, 1859.

" Nothing can be more spirited, graphic, and full of interest, nothing more pictorial, or brilliant in its execution. It is all life and animation; full of humor and amusement. The poet combines with the wit and judgment of the cosmopolitan to produce a perfect and in every way attractive picture."—*The Globe*, London.

" None, perhaps, have succeeded in making their descriptions so graphic and amusing."—*The Morning Chronicle*, London.

" His account of the Spanish settlements of Valparaiso, Pisco, Lima, and Panama, are the most entertaining, because the freshest, portions of this ' Panorama of the New World,' and shows how readily an author may amuse and instruct us, when he adds to the stock of knowledge."—*The Atlas*, London, June 4, 1859.

" We can give a ready welcome to Mr. Cornwallis's books. There is honesty of good humor about the proprietor of this new Panorama, while there is in his boisterous talk really much useful information. Many travellers have visited and written about Australia, but Peru and Panama, through which Mr. Cornwallis returned leisurely to England, afforded somewhat newer ground. This part of the Panorama, therefore, is particularly full of interesting sketches. Of a bull-fight, far exceeding in cruelty the cruelest of Spain, these volumes contain a long and animated description."—*The Examiner*, London, June 4, 1859.

" The work is replete with interest, and contains information on every subject connected with the countries of which it treats. . . . The volumes before us demand a detailed critique, for the author has evidently bestowed the greatest amount of attention upon them; and the result is the production of one of the most amusing books of travels ever written, equal, in many respects, to ' Eöthen ' and ' The

Crescent and the Cross.' Having ourselves travelled through the United States and Canada, we can vouch for the accuracy of the description of those countries, their scenery, inhabitants, and manners. . . . In taking leave of Mr. Cornwallis, we can only express our hope that, ere long, we shall be called upon to notice other productions from his talented pen. Few authors combine so much amusement and instruction. We can honestly recommend the '.Panorama of the New World' to all. classes of readers."—*The Review*, London, June 7, 1859.

" He is a lively, rattling writer. His descriptions are never dull. The sketches of Peruvian life and manners are fresh, racy, and vigorous. The volumes abound with amusing anecdotes and conversations."—*The Weekly Mail*, London, June 12, 1859.

" Mr. Cornwallis seems resolved that the public, who have received his former productions with favor, should not forget him. He now publishes the narrative of the events connected with nearly three years' travels in the West; his first volume being dedicated to Australia, his second to Valparaiso, Callao, Lima, Panama, Toboga, Jamaica, New York, Cincinnati, Detroit, Buffalo, the Falls of Niagara, Albany, Philadelphia, Washington, Baltimore, by New York to Boston, and from thence to the banks of the St. Lawrence, Montreal, and Quebec—a goodly line of travel; and of most of those places we have accounts, more or less diffuse, written in Mr. Cornwallis's lively and amusing style, with occasional glimpses of places on the route. . . . He (the author) has produced works, from which the public derive both information and amusement. We ought to be glad of the chance which has procured us such a mental pabulum, and wish for a renewal of the pleasure which the graphic description of strange scenes, strange people, and strange events must always give rise to. We could make many more amusing extracts; our limits will only allow us to select the following passage, and we assure our readers they will not regret it, if the specimens we give should induce them to procure this work."—*Naval and Military Gazette*, London, June 18, 1859.

" Mr. Kinahan Cornwallis is already known as the author of some amusing books of travels, and his ' Panorama of the New World ' is behind none of its predecessors in sketching picturesqueness and graphic interest. In the first volume, decidedly the most attractive part is that in which the peculiarities of colonial life are hit off with life-like reality. Life and the mode of trade in Melbourne, the mysteries of ' old-chummism ' and ' new-chummism' life at the diggings, bush-ranging, hunting kangaroos, and all the other features of Australian life, are hit off with a life-like reality. Perhaps the ' diggings' themselves were never better described, than in the pages which Mr. Cornwallis devotes to them at Bendigo. Here is the daily routine of a digger's life dashed off in a few strokes." —*The Critic*, London, June 18, 1859.

" Readers will be pleased with his lively, careless style, and amused with his anecdotes illustrative of society in Australia. . . . The description of the bull-fight at Lima is especially good—perhaps one of the best we have ever seen—but, unfortunately, far too long to extract."—*The Press*, London.

" He has the faculty of describing, in a very agreeable and readable way, the scenes and people he mingled with or passed through. There are episodes of colonial adventure, which are narrated with a picturesque simplicity and vigor not surpassed by Charles Reade.

He is a shrewd observer, and communicates his observations with freshness and perspicuity."—*The Tablet*, London, August 6, 1859.

" The author of these volumes is already favorably known as one of those ' wandering Englishmen,' who has the faculty of describing agreeably what he sees and hears in his journeyings over the world. The travels of Mr. Cornwallis have been decidedly extended, and have been previously recorded in works of great merit. His present contribution to the literature of movement, comprises visits to Australia and South America, and his adventures, if not startling, form quite a sufficient basis for the story he has to tell, which he tells easily, frankly, and pleasantly. The book will repay perusal, and has an air of freshness about it."—*The London Illustrated News*, July 15, 1859.

" As a traveller, the author is well known to the reading public. . . . . Viewed either as a book of amusement, or a work of information, it will be an acceptable addition to the *utile et dulce* class of literature, which gives in a free and easy style, bold sketches of the striking things incidental to extensive travel. ' *Hic et ubique*,' ought to be the motto of the accomplished writer of ' The Panorama of the New World,' which we have great pleasure in recommending to our readers."—*The Sunday Times*, London, July 3, 1859.

" Mr. Cornwallis has been a great traveller, and dashes off impressions of the countries he has visited in a gay rattling manner. He is a gay observer of manners, with a quick eye for the picturesque and the odd, and with a strong proclivity for the funny. Any one may agreeably spend an hour or two over the gay, rapid chapters. The record of his wanderings to and fro upon the face of the earth is amusing, and we award it the possession of interest."—*The Eclectic Magazine*, London, August, 1859.

Howard Plunkett; or, Adrift in Life.

A Novel in Two Volumes, Price, 21s.

" It is a bold, clever book. There is a vigor and exuberance throughout, and in some of the scenes a graphic power and reality. The author has talent and vigor, and the power of writing an amusing story."—*The Athenæum*, London.

" A tale so full of incident, developing so much of character, can hardly fail to be interesting: but that interest is greatly enhanced when, as in the present case, the narrative is well sustained, and the portraits of the various personages are drawn with vigor, and no ordinary ability."—*The Observer*, London.

" The author of this work has certainly great skill in constructing a story, and arranging its component parts. The characters are numerous, most interesting, and aptly sketched. Striking are the scenes, vigorous the descriptions. Some of the events relating to the young outcast's life, who walks the wilderness of the world alone, are exceedingly well described. We have life in its varying phases pictured before us in many a diverse land. The story commences and concludes at home: but in its course it wanders far and wide, from the bright and rolling waters of the gorgeous Mississippi to the lofty banks of the Yarra Yarra."—*The Sun*, London.

" The author of this novel has evidently seen much of life, and, moreover, possesses the ability to give vivid reflections of what he has seen. There is, consequently, much to admire in the course of the story; and whether in the old world or the new, at home or at the antipodes, he keeps alive the reader's attention, and affords pleasant entertainment. Considerable talent is displayed in the production of the varied scenes, and the manners of society are hit off effectively therein."—*The News of the World*, London.

"Worked out with great ability, and no ordinary power."—*John Bull*, London.

" Far superior to the ordinary volumes of the circulating library. Mr. Cornwallis has evidently travelled much and seen much of the world, and some of the best parts of his story are, probably, scenes which he has himself witnessed. We have spoken well of Mr. Cornwallis's poem ' Yarra Yarra,' and recognize in him the art of writing well."—*The Literary Gazette*, London.

" It possesses the merit of boldness, vigor, and ease of style. The style is of a free and dashing order, and there is a large amount of very clever writing in the novel. That there is some vivid pictorial matter is evident enough from the following extract."—*The Dispatch*, London.

" ' Howard Plunkett' is a unique work. This peculiarity is not owing to descriptions of manners and scenery, or to facetiousness. The native coloring is something much more deeply dyed than that. There are no bulls in the tale; but the writer's mind seems one huge reservoir of bulls held in solution. There is an audacious impossibility about the book, a genial incoherency, and a bubbling gaiety, which render the whole quite unparalleled. But exactly because this novel is so real, it is indescribable. The tale must be read to be understood. . . . The elopement and the incidents that followed are described at great length; but we cannot enter on its details, further than to remark that no part of the book shows more conspicuously one of the author's greatest excellences. He makes his *dramatis personæ* talk as people really talk. Thus, for instance, only one sentence of the bride's conversation after her marriage is recorded, but then it is just what a real Angelina would have said. She repeated over and over again, ' *I really do wonder what Aunt Foster will say.*' "—*Saturday Review*, November 7, 1857.

" He can exhibit characteristically, if not dramatically."—*The Spectator.*

Two Journeys to Japan.

Second Edition, Two Volumes, 21s. Illustrated by Colored Plates, from Original Drawings by the Author.

" It is full of amusement—lively, graphic, and full of interest. He possesses the art of letting in light upon all the topics which he undertakes to discuss. A real talent for description is a somewhat rare gift, and this traveller really possesses it. Through his pages we, for the first time, obtain a true notion of that part of Japan which he visited. The country, under his pencil comes out fresh, dewy, and picturesque before the eye, with its cedars, its camphor-laurels, its tapering volcanoes, its winding valleys, its long sweeps of undulating plains. He certainly possesses a talent for description, and places a series of very striking pictures before the minds of his readers. But he is not exclusively picturesque; he likewise makes the most of other interesting subjects, as eating, drinking, dressing, bathing, and worshipping idols."—*Chamber's Journal*, Edinburg, Feb. 12, 1859.

" Mr. Kinahan Cornwallis is well known to the British public as an amusing and spirited writer. His books teem with life and activity. When he wanders in a meadow, he brings with him the odor of the grass and the wild flowers; when he mixes with the aborigines, he carries ;from amongst them, fresh and distinct in his memory, the wildness of their gestures and attire, the strangeness of their appearance, and their customs; in fact, whenever he travels, and writes about what he has heard and seen, we feel as if we also had participated in the scenes which he depicts. In concluding, we thank Mr. Cornwallis for his entertaining and lively volumes. He is an amusing, sprightly, and observant traveller."—*Daily Telegraph*, London, March 31, 1859.

"His two journeys, as his title-page indicates, were made in 1856 and 1857. Each time he enjoyed most miraculous good fortune; for he seemed to carry a spell with him which dissipated Japanese suspicion, and procured him all sorts of privileges. It is a paradise of flowered silks, lacquer, yellow, vermillion. ivory. velvet-lined saloons, and fantastic elegancies; and Mr. Cornwallis, living the life of Telemachus or Æneas in this world of luxury, continually bursts upon some scene even more Eden-like and primitive . . . . . The poet Spencer, in his Allegro visions, never saw more freely the hundreds of unarrayed damsels dancing, lily-white, in fairy-land, than this traveller sees the mellow bevies of Japan wading in baths of Boccaccian simplicity; plunging, like Phrynes, into the seafoam; or standing statuesquely as Greek slaves. Mr. Cornwallis pursues his pilgrimage, admires the latticed and matted houses, more like Swiss in their toy-like symmetry, and then breaks upon a succession of Paradisaical scenes, which he describes with a characteristic unction. The mystery of Japan melts away as we follow Mr. Cornwallis through happy valleys, palaces of sublime magnificence, villages of abstract cleanliness, and throngs of dignitaries in whose presence the world of Japan grows pale. All this goes to make up an amusing book. His knowledge of Japan is considerable."—*The Athenœum*, London, Feb. 12, 1859.

" Mr. Cornwallis has produced a very agreeable and interesting book; qualities which are much enhanced by a number of illustrations of Japanese scenery, customs, and costumes, well executed. in chromo-lithography, from his own drawings.—*Birmingham Journal*, England.

" The book has great value in depicting the manners and customs of a hitherto strange people. It is an amusing book."—*The World*, London.

" For brilliancy of execution we can compare it only with *Eöthen:* for descriptive power and graphic portraiture, we have rarely read its equal. The author has had opportunities which no other Englishman has had of studying the manners and customs of the Japanese."—*The Globe*, London.

" The book is an amusing book, pleasantly written, and evidencing generous feelings."—*The Literary Gazette*, London.

" We meet Mr. Kinahan Cornwallis on the same easy terms of life in El Dorado, sophisticated London, unsophisticated Nookoora, exclusive Japan—shining as novelist, historian, scientific observer, conversationalist, explorer, and moralist, with unmitigated fluency and startling rapidity."—*The Saturday Review*, London, April 30, 1859.

" Mr. Cornwallis recently gave us a very good book on the new El Dorado, British Columbia. To that he now adds a very good one on Japan and its people. They who love travel and adventure, and wish to inform themselves about Japan and the Japanese, will like Mr. Cornwallis's work, wherein they will find animated descriptions of natural scenery, and of almost everything appertaining to the customs, manners, and pursuits of the people of all degrees."—*Sunday Times*, London, Feb. 26, 1859.

" He saw a good deal of the Japanese and of the country, and gives pretty minute descriptions of all the towns he visited. The account of Nagasaki, and of Mr. Cornwallis's friends, Noskotoska and Tazolee, is very interesting; but for that, and the summary of the history of Japan, and its religion, we must refer to the volumes, which are illustrated by colored lithographs from drawings by Mr. Cornwallis, and will well repay perusal."—*Naval and Military Gazette*, London, Feb. 26, 1859.

" There has not been so interesting a book of travels since Warburton's ' Crescent and the Cross.' "—*Scottish Press*.

" The author has given us two interesting volumes. It (the work) furnishes many charming glimpses of Japanese life. We have risen from its perusal with great pleasure and profit."—*The Constitutional Press*, London, Feb. 26, 1859.

" What Mr. Cornwallis has here presented will engage the public attention, for it is given in a readable and attractive style: and the scenery, habits and manners, are made to pass in succession before us like a collection of photographic pictures. The author describes all that passed under his notice, during his two visits to Japan, with so much liveliness and ease as to afford much satisfaction, whether the work be taken up for information, or merely the entertainment of a leisure hour; and there is every likelihood of his literary labors being rewarded by the favorable opinion of the public.—*The News of the World*, London, March 6, 1859.

" Mr. Kinahan Cornwallis is well known in the literary world as the writer of ' El Dorado,' and other popular productions; and in the work before us we find no falling off whatever. It is beautifully illustrated, is replete with interest, and contains information on every subject connected with the country on which he treats. Not only have we an excellent historical and geological sketch of the country, but a thorough insight into the habits and manners of the Japanese." —*The Review*, London.

" These volumes contain a vast amount of information about Japan and her people, clever and amusing."—*The Leader*, London.

" Mr. Cornwallis describes, in very agreeable language, what he saw, did, and heard, during two visits to that marvellous country, Japan. We can earnestly recommend Mr. Cornwallis's book to our readers."—*Morning Herald*, April 2, 1859.

" The author exhibits much knowledge of Japanese life. He has written a very amusing book."—*The New Quarterly Review*, London, April, 1859.

"Few can take up Mr. Cornwallis's interesting work without wishing it may be their lot some day to visit the islands of Japan."—*The China Telegraph*, London.

" Among the guests at the ball given by Gen. Cass on Friday evening last, in honor of the Japanese Embassy, was Mr. Kinahan Cornwallis, a gentleman well known in literary circles in England, and of considerable repute, both as an author and traveller. In the course of his travels he five years ago visited Japan, of which country he afterwards published in England a very spirited description. Two of the present Embassy, who had seen him at Simoda, on meeting him the other day at Washington, at once recognized him. Mr. Cornwallis has only recently arrived in this country, but it is not his first visit, as in the fall of 1855 he travelled through the Union, and subsequently embodied his opinions of American men and women in one of his books, entitled ' A Panorama of the New World,' which speaks very flatteringly of ourselves, and shows its writer to be a man of wide sympathies, liberal sentiments, and, what is better, few prejudices."—*The New York Herald*, May 26, 1860.

New El Dorado; or, British Columbia.

Dedicated, by permission, to the Right Hon. Sir Edward Bulwer-Lytton, Bart.

Second Edition, price, 10s. 6d., cloth. With a Map and Illustrations by the Author.

" So little is known of British Columbia, a territory that promises to open up an immense field of enterprise to the mother-country, that Mr. Cornwallis may fairly congratulate himself upon being, if not the only, at least the most modern, historian of the colony. Mr. Cornwallis tells us, in pleasant language, how he wandered from California to New Columbia, what he saw there, and what, in his opinion, are the prospects of emigrants, whether as diggers or agriculturists. As a handbook to British Columbia, this volume, which is dedicated, by permission, to the Colonial Secretary, may be recommended as authentic, useful, and well timed."—*The Morning Post*, London.

" Mr. Kinahan Cornwallis, a gentleman who has had considerable experience of the gold fields of Australia, and who graphically described what he saw and learnt in his work call ' Yarra Yarra,' has lately returned from British Columbia, and having been present almost from the first at the golden district bordering on the Fraser River, has just published a very interesting account of his sojourn there. The work is exceedingly opportune. It is very spiritedly written, and will amuse as well as instruct, and necessarily obtain an immense circulation."—*The Observer*, London.

" The book is full of information as to the best modes existing or expected of reaching these enviable regions, and of many matters of commerce, trade, and production. The book is therefore not merely interesting, but instructive, and we are glad to find so useful a collection of facts on a movement pregnant with events of which we can as yet only dimly appreciate the full consequences."—*The Morning Chronicle*, London.

" The book gives all the information it is possible to obtain respecting the new colony. It is altogether of a most interesting and instructive character."—*The Star*, London.

" Historical and descriptive of British.Columbia. It will be found both entertaining and useful."—*The Sunday Times*, London.

" There is information in the volume to render it acceptable."—*The Athenæum*, London.

" A highly useful work. The chapters on the ascent of the Fraser, and the bivouac beyond the Forks, will be found particularly interesting."—*News of the World*, London.

" A book on emigration from the pen of one who *knows* what he is writing is in the highest degree acceptable, because we find in it more of practice and less of theory. The book is interspersed with much that is animated and interesting, while the geographical position, climate, and peculiarities of the colony are thoroughly elucidated. As a handbook to British Columbia, nothing could be more useful, instructive, or valuable; and as such, to that class we particularly commend it."—*Weekly Mail*, London.

" No wonder that this book has gone through a first edition, when we consider the importance of the subject and the admirable manner in which it is handled. Truthful delineation of the state and resources of this newly-discovered treasure-land is its great characteristic. As a useful and almost necessary appendage to the emigrant, this work is entitled to the highest praise; while to those who ' live at home at ease,' we can cordially recommend it, as containing the most animated and interesting descriptions of a country which may ere long vie with, if not eclipse, the golden regions of Australia and California. We lately noticed, in most eulogistic terms, the well-known poem by the same author, entitled ' Yarra, Yarra,' and happy are we to find that in Mr. Cornwallis's case it is not *poetas et prœterea nihil*. The ' New El Dorado ' will outlive all ephemeral productions of the hour, and become a book of reference in the standard library of travels."—*Sporting Magazine*, London.

" We can recommend it to those who are curious as to the general features which such a region presents, and looking for amusement." —*Press*, London.

" With all the graphic advantages of a personal narrative, he has gathered a considerable amount of information respecting the country, its inhabitants, natural productions, and resources, which will doubtless be found useful to future adventurers, who will thus go there furnished with all it is possible to convey through the medium of a work intended to be amusing as well as useful. The Appendix comprehends a large amount of local and statistical matter, valuable because it is authentic; and a colored Map of that region and Vancouver places before the reader a complete plan and guide to the most important localities named in the text."—*The Dispatch*, London.

" It is a very interesting and valuable work. Extracts from it are beginning to plentifully abound in our papers."—*Toronto Globe*.

" All testimonies, from the very pleasant and interesting book of Mr. Cornwallis to the last correspondence received, agree in attributing great capabilities of producing wealth, both agricultural and mineral, to the district of Columbia."—Extract from a leader in the *London Standard*.

"Mr. Cornwallis's book will repay perusal. It contains twenty-three chapters on the new gold movement, its dazzling prospects, the physical geography and natural resources of this land of the magic spell, discusses the question of railway communication, and gives us animated pictures of the gold hunters' life. There are some glimpses also afforded us into the manners and beliefs of the Indians."—*The Westminster Review*, London.

"Mr. Cornwallis is a shrewd man of the world, and has given us a very clear account of the auriferous districts of the country, and of their prospects. His remarks may suggest many a new thought to the emigrant, and his information is precise and well adapted for giving us the knowledge of a *terra incognita*, and a new colony. Many a man will thank him as his pioneer. In the early stages of colonial life we seldom meet with a work so applicable to the real state of affairs."—*The World*, London, January 23, 1859.

"To give some idea of the state of things as they have been till within recent times, we will make a condensed abstract of a gold-searching expedition made by a very intelligent and adventurous gentleman—Mr. Kinahan Cornwallis—who has recorded his experiences in a lively volume, entitled 'The New El Dorado, or British Columbia.'"—*Colburn's New Monthly Magazine*, London, article "British Columbia," February, 1859.

See also the *Edinburgh Review*, January, 1859, article "Hudson's Bay Territory."

"Mr. Cornwallis revels in the primeval wilderness; he glories in pushing up unknown rivers, in penetrating thick jungles, in roaming over horizon-bound prairies, and then returning to the haunts of civilized men to depict, in animated colors, and with his poetic fancies, the scenes that he has witnessed when far removed from the influence and attraction of modern society. The general reader will find much that is of an entertaining character to beguile a leisure hour."—*China Express*.

The Wandering Aborigine.

A Poetical Narrative in Thirteen Books. Fifth and cheap Edition.

Price, 2s.

"We have already spoken well of Mr. Cornwallis' poem, and are glad to find, by this new edition, that the public agree with us."—*The Literary Gazette*, London.

"It is a book that will be read—yes, and relished—by many. Its very wildness has a charm for such of our feelings as are unsophisticated; and the boldness with which it breaks through all conventional restraint is refreshing in these days of civilization-worship. It is misty: but gleams of brilliant light traverse the haze, and strains of Nature's sweetest music blend with the confusion. Mr. Cornwallis is a bold and honest writer; and his work displays some very high imaginative qualities, with vast and varied experience of men and countries."—*The Illustrated News of the World*, London.

"This poetical narrative is bold, picturesque, and full of ardent feelings. What the author had to do, he has done well. It has arrived at the honor of a fifth edition, which speaks considerably in favor of the poem."—*The Dispatch*, London.

" The Australian ' Hiawatha.' "—*The Guardian*, London.

" This clever poem, which on its first appearance attracted some attention, has reached its fifth edition, a circumstance which goes far to confirm the verdict passed by the public upon its merit. It loses none of its interest by re-perusal. The verse is smooth and flowing, and the interest of the subject retains its original freshness."
—*The Weekly Times*, London.

" The plan and execution of this volume, which has already gone through five editions, are entitled to the highest commendation. The subject, Australia, in itself so interesting, and so fitted for poetical expansion and illustration, is treated with no less judgment than skill, and the author fully succeeds in awakening the most delicate feelings of our nature. The story of his love for Quillah Quah is very naturally introduced, and her melancholy fate pathetically described; man's natural affection for the land of his birth occupies a few interesting pages. The fondness with which we recur to pleasures long past, and to friends separated by death, the requiem to the fallen brave, are touched upon with uncommon felicity. The author's address to Nature, ' Oft have I stood and viewed fair Phœbus rise,' is animated and poetical; and in a strain equally flowing, sweet, and affecting, Mr. Cornwallis soliloquizes over the waters of the Arno. The observations on Australia will be read with great satisfaction, as they prove that the writer's prose is as animated, just, and instructive, as his poetry is spirited and characteristically appropriate."—*Sporting Magazine*, London.

" There is strength and beauty in this poem. Love is the grand theme of the author."—*The Court Circular*, London.

See also Dickens' " Household Words," London, July, 1858; article on " The Savage Muse."

My Life and Adventures.

A TALE.

Two vols.　London, 1859.　Dedicated, by permission, to Sir Edward Bulwer-Lytton, Bart.

" The author's power of language in thus depicting most imminent and perilous situations is perfectly irresistible, and has the effect of conveying the whole scene with fearful distinctness home to the imagination of the reader. ' My Life and Adventures,' for the vigor of its descriptions, carrying along with them an equal amount of instruction and amusement, is deserving of unqualified praise."—*The Leader*, London, April 7, 1860.

" It is both amusing and instructive."—*The Observer*, London.

" His descriptions display power, and the style has the merit of carrying us quickly over its pages."—*The Literary Gazette*, London, April 21, 1860.

Wreck and Ruin. *A Novel.* 3 Vols. London, 1860.

The Crossticks. *A Novelette.* 1 Vol. London, 1858.

A Strange Story of Adventure.

A MARVELLOUS COINCIDENCE; OR A CHAIN OF MIS-ADVENTURES AND MYSTERIES.

By KINAHAN CORNWALLIS.

Paper, 50 Cents. For Sale Everywhere, and mailed free on receipt of price. THE DAILY INVESTIGATOR OFFICE, 66 Broadway, New York.